THE FIRST OLYMPIANS

Reviews help other people find this book.
If you enjoy it, please leave a review on Amazon!

Amazon: amazon.com/dp/B0BLN9DT1W
Goodreads: goodreads.com/book/show/63883506

Stay up to date on social media:

Twitter: twitter.com/The1stOlympians
Facebook: facebook.com/TheFirstOlympians
Instagram: instagram.com/thefirstolympians/
Email: thefirstolympians@gmail.com
Join the e-mail list: https://tinyurl.com/2p9pj93d

Copyright 2022

Chapter One: Gordon

They were supposed to leave for the ceremony together, but he couldn't wait any longer. Gordon hurried down the street, alone, and distracted himself with the familiar topics of schematics, power modules, and the order in which wires must be cut and buttons must be pressed. His mom would be there. She had to be.

Only a few more hours, Gordon told himself. After that, he'd have an honest, hard-working job and a new life, and he'd laugh when remembering the "before-times." Premium rations, new clothes, and more origami papers than he'd have time to fold were hopefully coming his way. His mom just had to stay out of trouble until he got the apprenticeship.

His handheld buzzed and Gordon's heart jumped. He took it out of his pocket slowly, part of him dreading the message, then flipped it over fast. Not his mom. Rather, it was his friend, Corrina.

Hurry! You're going to be late.

Gordon jogged past the cramped, thin, two-story buildings made of clay, mud, and rock extracted from the mines. People called them holes, a term leftover from the first settlers who lived deep underground in caves created by ancient lava flows. Their old-district neighborhood was subject to electricity preservation efforts, and Gordon couldn't wait to move them somewhere better. His mom deserved that.

The residential level was closest to the surface, above both the ancient cave systems and the mines. The farm domes stood on one end, on a hill overlooking everything, their pointed tips almost touching the ceiling. Below, people were crushed in a mix of holes, ration distribution centers, and security checkpoints. Medical centers, cafes, and schools made up the remainder of the buildings. They all gave way to the spacious gardens and auditorium of the Mission Control Center, a giant stone and compressed dirt structure beside the mine elevators. That's where the career award ceremony was.

Gordon turned onto Torres Street, the main pedestrian walkway, and a flow of miners in hard hats, farmers in overalls and lab coats, and nurses in blue-gray scrubs walked past.

They were good citizens of the outpost doing their part to help the cause and were on their way home to see their families, or to a well-earned stop at a bar. His dad had been one of them, and they inspired a sense of purpose in Gordon. If they all worked together, they could achieve great things.

The streets grew wider as he walked deeper into the heart of the outpost. It was brighter, and not just because there were more functional overhead lights, but also because of the light seeping out from the bars, cafes, and workshops. The red dirt streets had deep grooves, proof of how well-trodden they were.

"Fresh skewers here! High-quality protein!" one weasel-faced man hollered.

The faintly sweet smell of gutter oil frying filled Gordon's nose. Men in the street were selling food, and an overhead siren told him it was shift change. Prime time.

"C'mon, son, you're a growing boy! You need to put some muscle on those bones," he said, blocking Gordon's path.

Gordon tried to step around the meat-hawker, keeping his head down.

"Hey, you're the Onyango boy, yeah?" the man wiped sweat and oil from his forehead, his voice softening.

"Yeah," Gordon said, shuffling awkwardly around the man.

"Have a skewer, kid. It's fresh!"

"I already ate," he said politely.

"Say hi to your mom!" the man said, turning back to the crowd.

Gordon bit his lip. He hoped he could talk to her soon.

The street food was likely stolen from a farm dome's protein vats, or, worst-case, made from the rodents that lingered around the dumpsters. His dad never ate the stuff, and Gordon did the same. His mom, on the other hand, had no shame. She would take protein wherever she could get it, and always tried to make sure Gordon was as strong as possible too. He hoped he'd no longer have to question the source of his food after today. If he received an explosives apprenticeship, Gordon was headed toward premium rations for the rest of his life.

The career award ceremony was being held outside the Mission Control Center, known as the MCC, in the auditorium that boasted a massive screen and seating for four hundred people. Expansive shrub and flower beds ran along both sides. Real gardens, with live plants in open air, the only of their kind at the outpost. It always astonished Gordon to walk through them and smell the array of different scents, but it made his mom angry. She said it was a shame for plants to take up so much space while people lived on top of each other. She wasn't wrong, just a grump.

Gordon approached the entrance to one of the gardens from the street when a woman's voice erupted from the speakers that dotted the side of every building.

"Earth needs our help! Together, we're reviving the blue planet to its former glory. It takes each and every one of us to achieve this goal. Thank you, brave workers of Olympus Outpost, for doing your part!"

Gordon smiled and hustled through the garden to the ceremony. His mom often said that Olympus Outpost was better in the old days, when she was a kid, and even better before then. She could be right, but to Gordon, it'd always been the same. Maybe she was just yearning for her youth like old people always did. He desperately hoped she'd be there to see him win an apprenticeship. It would show his mom that it was possible for things to get better.

Olympus Outpost, or just "the outpost," was humanity's last chance, and had been ever since Earth's mass-extinction event, known as X-Day. Generations had passed, and living conditions were still tough. Everyone dreamed of sunshine. Humans hadn't evolved to live underground, and even with population controls, they were crammed together like rats on a skewer.

It wasn't perfect, but things were working out for Gordon, and life was certainly better than on Earth. Together, they made it work, and strived toward a better future. His ancestors lived and died with the sole purpose of extracting raw materials to rebuild the blue planet back into the crown jewel of humanity.

Gordon was proud to do his part.

He spotted his friend, Corrina, in one of the back rows. She waved, and Gordon made his way up the stands of the auditorium. People were packed into the seats, spilling into the aisles. Everyone's parents, grandparents, and extended family were there to support their loved ones. And of course, they wanted to see how the career awards would improve their family's income and standing in the community.

Gordon estimated there were eight hundred people stuffed into a space meant for half that. The outpost was claustrophobic on a good day, but the annual career award ceremony was unlike anything else. He was lucky Corrina had saved him and his mom a seat. She was an orphan and had no one cheering her on.

Although, neither did Gordon.

"You're late!" Corrina hissed.

"Woah! So weird to see you with a shaved head! Can I touch it?" Gordon reached out his hand and Corrina playfully swatted it away. Her signature shoulder-length curls were not permitted for the ceremony.

"It's not like you to be late. Did you get detained for being too good of a citizen? Were you too polite to a bot or something?"

"Give me a break! I'm right on time," Gordon said, gesturing to the stage. "And no, no badge of honour for me today. There was a ruckus outside my hole." Gordon gritted his teeth, trying to be quiet as he stood for the pledge of allegiance. It was half-true. There'd been a shoving match outside his hole in the morning.

Corrina gasped. "Your mom?"

Gordon cringed. His aunt died last year, and as hard as it'd been on him, it'd been harder on his mom. She slunk into depression, and then became Faithless, a term for those who no longer contributed to the collective. On the good weeks, she got work from gang members. On the bad weeks, she dumpster dove to put food on their table.

It frustrated him because he knew she could get back on the right track if she just got out of her own way. She was gritty and resourceful, yet sometimes refused to see the simple solutions in front of her. He tried not to let it lead to disdain or embarrassment, but other students loved to poke fun of her unsavory lifestyle. Corrina was one of the few that understood. That's why she was his best friend.

"I, uh. No, it wasn't about her. She'll be here," Gordon said, trying to convince himself.

Corrina put her hand flat on Gordon's back, but he shrugged away.

"She'll be fine," he said. "Everything's going to be great. We're both going to get jobs, and we'll have a big party tonight. And when I get my first pay, I'm going to buy you a wig, so I don't have to look at your shaved head anymore."

"Maybe I'll keep it bald, just because you like it so much."

Someone shushed them, and they turned their attention to the front of the auditorium. Their explosives teacher, Mr. White, a robot with a head full of spinning sensors, sat on the stage in front of the building. The bot was roughly humanoid—it had wheels instead of legs, and an ugly assortment of cameras, radar, lidar and more where a person's head would be. Its midsection was a hard plastic rectangle housing its battery.

"I commit to a life of loyalty to Olympus Outpost," it recited. "I will be faithful to the Foreman who has given us hope and will lead humanity to a new glory. I pledge allegiance to him and excellence when performinnnnn—"

Mr. White glitched and abruptly stopped reciting the pledge. It stuttered back and forth on its wheels and emitted a low drone.

The audience watched, unamused, wondering if it was going to reboot and make them start the pledge from the beginning again. Some covered their ears. The outpost's fleet of robots were aging, and technical issues were common.

Robots were all over the outpost. They worked in the mines, the classrooms, the farm domes, and most importantly, they served as human safety and security. Every second that Mr. White was teaching class, and not glitching, it fed data to the Foreman, the AI network that controlled every aspect of life at the outpost. He decided and enforced all the rules.

And he assigned people jobs. If they deserved one.

There were human teachers in the classroom, too. Gordon had grown particularly close to one master explosives technician, master Tracey, who would be assigned a dozen or so apprentices to take under his wing. Despite Gordon being from a Faithless family, they bonded over a shared love of geology.

He spied the older man at the side of the stage and wasn't sure if his infectious smile or bald head was shining brighter. If he got an apprenticeship, he'd have master Tracey to thank. Getting assigned to him would be the icing on the cake.

The lights above Mr. White's cameras dimmed and its chin tilted down, indicating it was off.

"Electricity rations?" Corrina asked. There was sarcasm in her voice. If there was electricity rationing, the bots would be spared.

Mr. White's head spun three hundred and sixty degrees and re-set. It started to get on with the ceremony, and the crowd sighed in relief that they wouldn't be stuck in a pledge of allegiance loop today.

"Hello, class. I am so proud of you all. We are gathered to celebrate the accomplishments of this year's graduating class. We are also here to assign your lifelong careers. Although I have great confidence that all of you will contribute to Earth's restoration in your own way, these assignments are for those ready for the next step."

Mr. White rolled to the side of the stage. Behind him was a massive screen on the MCC's wall. The Foreman appeared wearing what he always wore, an orange safety vest and a white hard hat. He portrayed himself as a stout man with a gray mustache and soft wrinkles. Gordon thought of him as the outpost's grandfather that never died.

"Ms. Phoebe Baros," the Foreman said. "Awarded a clerk position in the farm domes." He spoke with a twang. Gordon's mom said he used to have a low, bellowing voice, but the AI trained itself to be more approachable and trustworthy. Gordon thought it made him sound out of place. No-one spoke like that.

One by one, he announced the successful students and their name flashed on the screen. They walked up, their faces glowing and their families cheering, and accepted Mr. White's best approximation of a handshake.

Gordon could hear his heart pounding. He'd either become the blaster he knew he could or be relegated to a life of back-breaking labor, rotten food rations, and communal living. He exchanged a nervous glance with Corrina. It was surreal. They were finally graduating.

He pulled out a sheet of folding paper from his breast pocket. Origami was something his dad had taught him, and he used it to calm his nerves and train his fingers for explosive disarmament. If Gordon did win a blasting job, he would have his dad and his origami skills to thank. He folded the thin paper one way, then another. He closed his eyes and kept folding.

Maybe it was a good thing his mom wasn't there. She would have only made him more anxious by talking through the whole thing.

Gordon's mom always walked the fine line between scoundrel and criminal. The first time he realized how close she got to that line was during a food shortage. After receiving a few morsels, she cut her hair, changed her clothes, and re-entered a ration line, determined to get more protein. Gordon wondered how she got past the fingerprint scanners, and years later learned that his mom had a thumbprint implant.

Punishment for that escapade could have been devastating. The Foreman wasn't afraid to target family members, and Gordon would've been without protein rations for weeks, or even months. His mom could've ended up in a forced labor camp, or worse, solitary confinement in a prison hole. He begged her to stop doing things like that, but if anything, her brazenness only increased. The risk was always worth it to her. Gordon was still skinny, but it wasn't for his mom's lack of trying.

His mom blamed the Foreman for his dad's disappearance and his Aunt Tess's death.

Tess wasn't actually his aunt. Not by blood. Only certain citizens of the outpost were allowed to have more than one child, and neither of his parents had siblings. But Tess and her big, brown eyes had been there for Gordon after his dad disappeared. She was the one that took him to play soccer and basketball in the dust fields. She bought him textbooks when his mom didn't have the energy to get out of bed. She helped them both through tough times, until one day robots came and swept her away to a prison hole, and she never came out.

"Mr. Arno Mahlangu," the Foreman said. "Awarded an apprenticeship on the Robot-Human Mediation Council."

"Damn dustlickers," Corrina said with scowl.

"Please, Arno is a genius. He truly, truly deserves this prestigious placement," Gordon said, tongue-in-cheek.

Corrina howled with laughter and a red-headed woman sitting in front of them turned and shot them a dirty look.

Gordon looked away and hid his snickering.

Arno was not the brightest student in their class, but his family had a long history of egregious sucking up to the Foreman. Dustlickers would do anything, including licking the dust off a robot, if it gave them preferential treatment. Many weren't shy about it. Currying favor with the Foreman was the only sure-fire way to success.

For normal people, like Gordon and Corrina, the job award ceremony was a crapshoot. Even though they had good grades, their families' lack of grovelling was a mark against them. Master Tracey said he put in a good word, but it was hard to know the extent to which the Foreman would consider his input.

His mom thought master Tracey was an insufferable dustlicker. She wasn't wrong, but Gordon nonetheless developed a strong friendship with the man. He was kind, hardworking, and incredibly knowledgeable. Any sucking up to the Foreman he did was just what he had to do. There was no shame in it. Master Tracey was certainly way more respectable than the leeches on the Robot-Human Mediation Council.

"Mr. Frederick Neumann," the Foreman said. "Awarded an apprenticeship in mining repair operations. Assigned to master Faisal."

On and on the he went, reading names of Gordon's classmates fortunate enough to be selected. Gordon kept his eyes closed and focused his fingers on his folding. Still, he couldn't stop himself from worrying about his mom.

His mom hadn't been sad after Aunt Tess died, like she was when Gordon's dad disappeared. She was angry. Gordon overhead whispered conversations in their kitchen about overthrowing the Foreman and installing a human-run government.

Delusional fantasies.

Once, his mom told him she thought the entire justification of the outpost, to mine materials to re-build Earth, was a sham. Gordon hushed her. You couldn't let anyone hear those kinds of crazy conspiracies. And besides, anger was pointless. The Foreman was indestructible, and the only way to get ahead was to play by the rules and get a good job. Gordon wished his mom would do exactly that. She was smart, and she'd succeed if she tried, but either her trauma was too much, or she enjoyed Faithless life. He tried not to resent her for it. Despite being put in a tough position, she was doing her version of the "best" she could do.

He loved her more than anything. She was the reason he worked so hard. And he desperately hoped she wasn't hurt or in trouble. His mom was often late. Maybe she just got tied up.

She will be fine.

She always stayed on the right side of the Foreman's fine line. He could only hope the line hadn't moved.

Gordon opened his eyes, the seat beside him still empty. In his hands was a lotus flower, folded to perfection. He placed the origami in Corrina's lap, and she picked it up with a smile.

"Thank you. But that's a pretty crappy consolation prize if we don't get blasting jobs."

"If I make more, you can wear them as a hat until your hair grows back." Gordon pulled out another sheet of folding paper.

Corrina rolled her eyes.

The Foreman read the successful names excruciatingly slowly. He and the robots were one and the same, or near enough. The bots fed all their sensor data to him and received directions back. How much discretion they had in fulfilling his wishes was up for debate, but it seemed like there was some. Gordon could only hope he'd impressed the Foreman with his work ethic. And that his mom hadn't colored his impression of Gordon too negatively.

"Mr. Gordon Onyango," the Foreman said.

His heart skipped a beat.

"Awarded an apprenticeship in explosives. Assigned to Master Tracey."

Corrina screamed in surprise.

Gordon sprang from his seat and hugged her.

The screen panned to a close-up of him and Corrina to polite applause. He collected his breath and walked down to the stage. It was weird and nerve-racking to have so many people looking at him. Gordon was never one for public speaking or being the center of attention.

By the time he got to the stage, he no longer cared. He had done it. He was going to make something of himself. He floated across the floor and collected his apprenticeship offer from Mr. White. He smiled wildly the entire time, not caring if he looked like a maniac. He pumped his fist in the direction of master Tracey who returned two thumbs up.

He walked back to his seat no longer feeling like a boy. He was a man now.

"Your mom is going to be so proud of you," Corrina said when Gordon arrived back at their seats.

"And you too, shortly."

The assignments weren't done yet. Gordon was confident Corrina would be blasting through the rocky Martian crust by his side.

Gordon couldn't wait to share the news with his mom! He'd move them to a nicer neighborhood with no crime. She'd never have to beg for food or wear clothes that were falling apart ever again. She'd never have to worry about anything.

He took his handheld out of his pocket, but there was already a message. She'd finally responded.

"Meet me at home. Now!"

Gordon's fears came rushing back. Was she okay? He wanted to see her, to tell her that he'd got the job, and that everything was going to be great.

"Corrina, I, uh." The words got stuck in his throat. Trying to say it out loud made his face flush with anxiety. He held up his handheld for Corrina to read.

"Oh, Gordon." Corrina put her hand on his shoulder. "I'd go with you but," she held up her hands and gestured to the stage.

"It's okay. You stay. I know your name will be called soon."

His handheld beeped again.

"Dodge the bots. Run!"

They stared at the message, slack jawed.

"Dodge the bots. What?" Gordon said.

"Are you messing with me?" A half smile crept onto Corrina's face.

"No, I swear it!"

The red-headed woman tossed them another dirty look.

"Those?" Corrina whispered.

She didn't have to explain herself. Two peacekeeper bots stood at the bottom of the stands and looked up. The security division of the Foreman, peacekeepers looked a lot like Mr. White, except taller, thicker, and with larger wheels. Their robotic arms featured an array of attachments that differed by the day. Usually batons, other times tear gas, syringes full of sedatives, or tasers. On the rare occasion there was an emergency lockdown test, like a fire drill, they sported menacing spinning blades.

Today they had the blades.

Gordon swallowed hard and slinked down his seat. Something had gone terribly wrong. His mom was in trouble. But were the bots really after him? That seemed unlikely. He had just received a prestigious career award!

He took a peep and saw the peacekeepers rolling up the ramp of an adjacent aisle. His mom was in trouble, and he wouldn't be able to help her if went with the bots. He had to make a quick decision, and he wanted nothing to do with the arsenal of weaponry coming toward him. But still, he was a good student. He never disobeyed the Foreman.

"What do I do?" Time slowed. Gordon's heart raced.

Corrina gripped his arm. "Firstly, we need to stay calm."

"Are you kidding me? I'm gonna crap my pants!"

"Okay. Well, uh, don't do that." A bead of sweat dropped from Corrina's brow onto her lotus flower. "Listen. Your mom is, well, *your mom*. But she's still your mom. Does that make any sense?" She scrunched up her face.

"No!"

Gordon had slid so far down in his seat that he couldn't see the bots approaching. He could only assume they'd arrive any second.

"What I'm trying to say is, run to her! The bots aren't going anywhere. You can always talk to them later." Corrina shrugged, like it was an obvious choice.

Gordon bit his lip and nodded.

He crept across a row of people, making his way to a clear aisle. He glanced back at Corrina, who now looked like she was going to be the one to crap their pants.

She gave him a shooing motion, telling him to go.

Gordon held his breath and moved fast, scooting down the stairs. He was at the bottom, about to slip into the gardens, when an alarm went off. He looked up at the big screen and saw a picture of his mom.

SUSPECT, FAMILY, AND ALL ASSOCIATES
WANTED IMMEDIATELY FOR QUESTIONING

Gordon felt like he'd been pushed off a cliff. No! Why? Why now? Why couldn't his mom have just taken it easy for one day? Why couldn't she just be normal?

He took a quick look up to see Corrina talking to the peacekeepers. Oh no! Was she in trouble now too? He didn't know if he could handle the guilt if she got screwed over because of him. He grimaced before dashing into the gardens.

His mind raced, and it went to the worst places. People that went in for questioning were sometimes not seen or heard from again for a long time. The anxiety of waiting for his name to be called was nothing compared to this.

Gordon ran along a row of lilac shrubs, their sickly sweetness overwhelming him. Everything had been going so well, and now his mom had to go and screw it up. He'd gone from the Foreman's good books to being wanted for questioning so fast it gave him whiplash.

But having a legitimate mining job might give him some power, or at least some leverage. Blasting was a highly skilled apprenticeship program that only admitted the best of the best. The Foreman was protective of mineral production above all else, and if Gordon could convince him of his value in that regard, maybe he could gain some leniency for his mom. He'd have to get master Tracey's help. He was the only person Gordon knew that had any semblance of political power.

But first, he had to find his mom.

Chapter Two: Dalrene

Sitting on a hard, plastic stool at a corner table in the Pickaxe Café, Dalrene sipped her tea to find it was cold and probably had been for some time.

She scanned the crowd again, looking for Janet. There were teenagers speaking gibberish and laughing like idiots, miners numbly throwing energy drinks down their throats in-between shifts, and young mothers exchanging stories while their kids ran around. Dalrene didn't fit into any of those groups, and she worried that would become more obvious the longer she waited. There were no new messages on her computer.

Dalrene's leg tapped impatiently against the underside of the table, its rattling drawing a distasteful look from one of the moms.

She didn't stop. Her granddaughter, Ellie, was around the same age as the woman's child. But Ellie didn't have a mom. Since her daughter died, there was nothing she cared about more than making her granddaughter's world better. Right now, Janet was putting that in jeopardy.

Sixteen processing nodes directing the bots, one brain node coordinating the processors, and four back-up data sites. That's what lay between her and salvation. The first step was to gain access to the back-up servers and install a deletion program that could be executed at the appropriate time. Once she took her big shot, she couldn't miss, and she couldn't risk the Foreman restoring itself and targeting her family with reprisals.

Two inspector robots entered the café and Dalrene stuffed her computer in her bag, crammed it under her chair, and kept her eyes on her cold tea. Not all her gear was legal. Her next instinct was to sneak out the back, but there was no need to risk making a scene. It was mostly likely a random check, a reminder of who was in charge. There was no reason to suspect they were looking for her.

In her earlier days, there'd been no way she'd submit to any search or request by the AI. But now, she needed to pick her battles. Part of her even relished the opportunity to feed the Foreman false information. It was only as smart as the information it gathered and disrupting that in any way was an act of civil disobedience that warmed her heart.

The robots that wheeled up to a nearby table were largely vision based. Their off-white, hard-plastic bodies matched the paint on the walls of the café. Or at least they had, when Dalrene had been young. The Foreman and all of the robots under its command were showing their age. Now, the bots wore dirty, yellow splotches, weathered by years of service.

The cracks in the Foreman had an outsized impact on the most vulnerable citizens. Decreased food production meant families without connections to workers in the farm domes suffered malnutrition. Energy production was down, and people living in the poorest neighborhoods bore the brunt of the rolling blackouts. But that wasn't the worst of it. Dalrene had heard of a child who kept drinking water because a medical robot improperly detected dehydration. Water intoxication caused the child's brain cells to swell, leading to interrupted blood flow, seizures, and eventually death.

Bizarre stories like that were only becoming more frequent.

Deterioration was a tragedy, but also an opportunity. A chance to win support among the public for resistance and to fight back against tyranny. Overthrowing the Foreman was the only way that Dalrene could avenge her daughter's death and ensure her granddaughter grew up in a better world than she did.

When one of the inspector robots stopped at her table, she held up her hand. People of her age were allowed to request a fingerprint ID, as was standard during their childhood. Dalrene's fake prints were the best around, or at least they used to be. It'd been a while since they'd been tested. After a moment, the robot popped out a pad where it expected Dalrene to press her thumb.

She waited for the thumbprint to register and looked in the mirror behind the café bar. Her skin, as black as the mirror's obsidian frame, was more ashen and wrinkled than the last time she checked. Her dreadlocks were short, with only a hint of color left among the gray.

Shit, she really looked like a grandma now. Dalrene shook her head in disbelief at how much her appearance differed from her self-image. Living in the caves was hard on the body. The good news was that she didn't look like a threat to society. Hopefully the Foreman felt the same way.

The inspector bot made a descending, negative sound, and asked Dalrene to give her thumbprint again.

Dalrene's heart rate ticked up. She had a lot of important things to do and did not need a random check to draw attention to her today. She submitted her thumb again and held her breath. The inspector must've been close to calling in back-up, or worse, insisting that she take a trip to a security office.

It stood motionless. Dalrene squeezed her tea mug.

After what seemed like an eternity, the robot made an agreeable sound, and wheeled onto the next guest in the café.

Dalrene exhaled, and the sounds of water boiling and dishes banging re-emerged. The sweet, yeasty aroma of bread coming out of the oven wafted warmly over her. She cleared her throat and sipped some more of her cold tea.

That was too close.

"Need a new thumb?" came a rugged voice from the table beside her.

"What the fuck did you say to me?" Dalrene said. Where she got her biometrics were nobody's business.

The man tilted his head and put his hands up, refusing to repeat his question. He was bald with a well-shaped beard, and a beer gut that probably weighed more than Dalrene. Not many people at the outpost had excess weight on them like that, and it told her that he was either a high-ranking Foreman sycophant or organized crime member.

Dalrene couldn't afford any trouble today, but she also couldn't let anyone snipe at her. Someone scoring a point on you was a quick path to getting beaten up or targeted for a scam. If you showed weakness, you died, game over.

"I don't need a new thumb. But you might, after you go shove yours," Dalrene said.

"Relax," the man laughed. "I'm your fourteen hundred hours appointment... . Mickey sent me," he added, in a hushed voice.

"Oh, right," Dalrene said, annoyed she'd forgotten.

"Why don't you tell me why we're meeting in a busy café?" the man asked. His thick arms were folded across his body.

"You're supposed to sit at my table, for starters."

The man grunted once in reluctant agreement, stood, and sat opposite her.

Titus, that was his name. Dalrene remembered Mickey, her husband, telling her about him. Big Titus was his unoriginal nickname, and he lived up to it. She guessed he was almost seven feet tall. Dalrene was five foot eight, last time she checked. She didn't want to think about how much she'd shrunk since.

"Second," Dalrene said, her voice drawing down to a whisper. "Out in the open is the safest place to be. We're just two old friends catching up. So, why don't you tell me if you've got what I'm looking for."

Titus took a final look over his shoulder and leaned in. Dalrene wanted to smack him across the face for being such a tactless idiot.

"Three-D-printed ballistic weapons, he said, launching into his pitch. "I'm talking semi-automatic firearms, lightweight and true to aim. They can be built and taken apart in less than ten minutes, so it's easy to avoid bot detection. I've got four, but they'll cost you."

Dalrene curled her lip. She could get crappy homemade firearms from any of the other dozen small-time dealers she knew. Titus was going to make her ask for what she really wanted. That was fine. She'd humor him.

"I don't suppose you have ammunition, too?" Criminals rarely used guns because they were too expensive, and ammo was hard to procure. The Foreman didn't use them either.

For Dalrene's money, that was because it had more inhumane methods of violence at its disposal.

"I've got enough to do whatever job you need to do, assuming you're not trying to start a gang war. But I can always make more." He grinned.

"Listen," Dalrene said, "I need equipment I can use. Spray-paint, knives, scissors, metal crowbars. Boots that aren't falling apart. Clothes with metallic fibres and neck coverings that will stop bots from injecting sedatives. Bullet-proof vests. Y'know, practical stuff. And I need what we came here to talk about, so stop fucking around." She jabbed the tips of her fingers on the table as she spoke as if each word was a note played on a keyboard.

Although the outpost was a melting pot, a few distinct ethnic groups remained. Titus belonged to one of them, the Greeks, and he raised his giveaway bushy eyebrows and leaned back, arms crossed. The chair legs threatened to give out.

"What does a grandmother need with explosives?"

Dalrene bit her lip. Mickey should've done this. Titus was his contact anyway. But she was the leader, and he couldn't handle coming to the residential level. His scars ran too deep, and the sight of robots still set him off. It had to be her.

"Stop wasting my time," Dalrene said, pulling her shawl around her arms. "Do you have them or not?"

Titus nodded slowly. "Plastic explosives. Fifty thousand credits per pound," he said.

Dalrene couldn't hold her laugh in. Titus hadn't gotten fat by charging fair prices. To be fair, the penalty for illegal possession of explosives was simply death. There were no labor camps or solitary confinement—you just got hacked to death by a horde of angry bots. Sometimes you got a trial, but those were rigged. Titus was the only one in the whole outpost with what she wanted, and he could charge whatever price he wanted. That didn't mean she was going to pay it.

"I'll buy fifty pounds and you'll give me a deal. Twenty thousand credits each," Dalrene said.

"I've only got twenty-five pounds and the best I can do is forty thousand credits per."

Dalrene scrunched up her face. She wasn't going to pay forty thousand credits per pound. Hell, she wasn't going to pay twenty thousand. But she had to make it seem like a tough decision, and make Titus feel like he'd won. "Thirty thousand," she said.

"I already told you my lowest price. Do you want them or not?"

"I ... Okay," Dalrene said, selling a look of disgust.

"Tonight then," Titus said, uncrossing his arms and clasping his hands together. "I'll send you the details now." He typed something into his handheld, a thin touchscreen. A man like him probably had multiple devices, some connected to the outpost's comms network, and some not. So did Dalrene.

Big Titus heaved himself up and Dalrene was alone again with her cold tea. She pushed it aside and plopped her computer on the table. In a few keystrokes, she sent the meeting time and location to Londi, her first lieutenant. Londi wasn't the best negotiator or political mind, but he was strong and loyal. One way or another, he would make sure they got the bombs.

Her mind went back to Janet, who was now incredibly late, even when considering that covert missions rarely went according to plan or schedule. Janet had been her daughter's friend. Dalrene originally thought of her as a reckless member of the outpost's Faithless population, the group of people that slipped through the cracks and survived on petty crime, or not at all. But they'd grown closer since her daughter's death, and the younger woman's street smarts and enthusiasm had won Dalrene's affection.

They had to install the deletion programs today. The servers were air-gapped, meaning they weren't connected to the network or to each other, except on certain occasions when an escort of bots and dustlickers ferried them to the Mission Control Center. Dalrene didn't know what the Foreman did with the back-ups there, except guess that it was training its AI capabilities. But she did know that it was the one time the servers were vulnerable. It was an exercise that only happened once a year, and she'd paid off the right people to know that it was happening today.

There were four back-up data centers. Londi, Rodriguez, Ionne, and Janet, her four lieutenants, were each assigned one. Janet planned a commotion on the route her target would take. Some of the participants were members of Dalrene's group, some weren't but were paid off, and others were normal citizens caught up in the moment.

The idea was for the disturbance to escalate into a brawl, forcing the bots protecting the back-ups to step in and arrest people. Then, Janet and her team would neutralize the human element of the escort and gain access to the server's ports. How exactly she did that, whether through violence, distraction, or pre-arranged coercion, Dalrene left up to Janet. Tactical, on-the-ground operations weren't Dalrene's strength, and she trusted her lieutenants to get their jobs done. They only needed a few seconds to insert a device that would install Dalrene's deletion programs, as well as provide network capabilities so she could execute them. The Foreman and its bots would be none the wiser.

Londi, Rodrigues, and Ionne had rendezvoused at the café hours ago. Dalrene's gut told her that Janet was already in a prison hole, getting acquainted with the sharp end of a peacekeeper's saw-arm attachment, and that she should pack up her things and move on. The longer she moped over her cold tea, rattling her leg, the more likely she'd end up in the room next to her.

Dalrene was convincing herself to leave when Janet finally burst through the doors of the café, eyes wide, her pupils giant saucers. She looked like she'd popped all her amphetamines at once. Janet pulled the hood of her maroon sweater tight over her frizzy hair. Her hands fidgeted up and down her arms and legs. It wasn't like her to be so unaware and reckless. Something must've totally unnerved her.

"I think I lost them," Janet said. Breathing heavily, she ducked into the seat where Big Titus had sat.

"You're being followed? And you brought them here? To me!" Dalrene fought hard to avoid raising her voice.

"Look, I did the job. Everything is in place," Janet said, raising her palms. "They don't know nothing." Her neck was wet with sweat. She looked desperate, as if she was worried Dalrene wouldn't believe her.

Dalrene stood and leaned into Janet's ear. "We've got to get back deep. To the grotto. Now. Follow me."

Spilling into the street, they left the scent of sweet baking behind and were struck by the outpost's dank, hot air. A hard day's work mixed with an array of metallic and chemical odors. Bright lights and flashing signs danced above them. They kept their heads down and Dalrene weaved them through the crowd of miners, Faithless, and robots.

Her base of operations was underneath the residential level of the outpost, in the cave network they called the deep. It was where the first migrants had settled, and it was a brutal environment lacking the necessities of life, let alone creature comforts. But it was safe. And it was Dalrene's home.

The Foreman didn't dare send its bots to the caves. Outside the reach of its surveillance and communications systems, and far from major sources of electricity, its strength was limited. Dalrene's army took immense security and secrecy measures, so they'd been able to train in peace. Apart from the forty-six permanent residents in her home grotto, there were another eight hundred and ten soldiers dispersed throughout the cave network. Some of those platoon members were permanent, but many were part-time, only heading to the caves to train and prepare.

They all awaited her call to action.

Janet was one of the wiliest Faithless Dalrene had ever met. Her street smarts were honed by years of hard living and duping the Foreman and others into giving her whatever she could get. She had an uncanny knack for knowing what to say to inspector and peacekeeper bots, and she could always sense where and when they would patrol. It'd be an incredible feat if she threw the Foreman off her trail, but if anyone could do it, it would be her. Dalrene didn't want to stick around to find out.

"Hey, miss!" a boy's voice yelled from behind them.

A chill went down her spine.

"Hey, miss!"

She didn't know the yell was directed at them, but it had to be. Dalrene didn't turn around. Instead, she yanked Janet through a crowd of people. They fought their way through the sea of pointy elbows and unforgiving shoulders only to see Janet's face on a screen. Her eyes were covered, but her wide nose, full lips, and round chin were clearly visible. The image replaced every sign, announcement, and menu on every storefront. Text below the picture read:

SUSPECT, FAMILY, AND ALL ASSOCIATES
WANTED IMMEDIATELY FOR QUESTIONING

Dalrene could still hear the boy yelling behind her, but the rest of the crowd hadn't clued in yet. They darted down a less busy street, trying not to draw attention to themselves. Janet pulled her sweater off and Dalrene stuffed it in her backpack. It could still be useful. Thankfully, you couldn't make out Janet's features in the picture. With any luck, they could hide out until the heat died down and then make a break down to the caves. To the deep.

"In here," Dalrene said, opening the saloon-style doors to a dive bar.

The screens above the counter were busted. The room was dimly lit, and not on purpose. A scattered group of men drinking from tall, dark glasses eyed them while they made their way to a booth in the back, but they didn't seem to recognize Janet. Pungent mold and fungus smells attacked Dalrene's nose, and she held her breath to stop herself from retching. She'd grown accustomed to sterility in the deep.

Dalrene exhaled, swore under her breath, and plunked her computer on the table. She couldn't let her revolution end before it even started. She didn't know what she was looking for. There was nothing useful in her comms. A bunch of question marks in a message from Londi. He must've seen Janet's picture.

Dalrene's hacking skills had earned her backdoor access to the Foreman's "Operations Module." She could lock or unlock certain doors. She could turn off specific air recyclers or cause water pipes to back up and burst. She could turn off cameras, like she did in the Pickaxe Café. But she couldn't hack into anything security related or control the bots. She was powerless to stop the Foreman's pursuit of Janet.

Janet fiddled with the whiskey menu. Dalrene caught something about a novel offering of whiskey made from a genetically engineered yeast. She worried about the younger generation. Their best and brightest minds were being wasted on drivel like creating new types of whiskey, or worse, toiling away in the mines. It was up to her to educate them about the history of the outpost and inspire them to rebel effectively.

"I'm going to need new fingerprints, irises, everything," Janet said, chewing on her lip.

She could tell the younger woman's mind was racing a mile a minute. The gravity of the situation was finally catching up to her. Her old life was gone.

"Don't get ahead of yourself. First we need to get you safe."

A siren pierced the air and an inspector bot escorted by three peacekeepers entered. The doors shut and locked with a clinking sound behind them. The men groaned. They'd come to the bar to forget their troubles but found themselves facing a new one.

"Prepare to submit identification," the inspector bot chirped. The bright light it used for facial recognition shone into an unlucky patron's face.

Dalrene's hair stood on end. In a matter of minutes, the bots would be at their table. They couldn't run out the front door. A swarm would tackle them before they made it to the end of the street. And they couldn't hide in the restroom. The bots had no doubt mapped the number of people in the room. She had to sneak Janet out, somehow. It was time to put the access she'd hacked to the test.

She thought of her sweet, sweet granddaughter. Only two *MSY* (Martian Standard Years) old, Ellie still had a chance at a better future. She deserved to grow up playing soccer and having tea-parties with her grandmother. But Ellie wouldn't get those opportunities if she spent her childhood as an enemy of the Foreman because of her.

"What do we do?" Janet chewed on her lip.

"We get you out of here," Dalrene said, pulling up the security information for the building on her computer. "Make toward the restroom then duck into the kitchen. You can't miss the backdoor to the street."

"It'll be locked."

"I'll open it for a minute. And for fuck's sake, act casual."

"And then what?"

"Take this," Dalrene said, taking her shawl off. Make your way to the nearest cave entrance. Go deep, directly to the grotto. Do not stop for anything or anyone. Do you understand?"

"I can't disappear from my son's life," Janet said, wrapping herself in Dalrene's shawl.

"Don't do anything stupid. The Foreman may not have your full identity yet. Don't put him in danger." Dalrene looked past her to the inspector bot making its way through the room and pulled Janet's sweater over her head.

A miner too drunk to keep still for facial recognition was making a scene. "I thought you were looking for a woman? Do I look like a woman to you?" he sprayed spit and beer while he spoke.

"Now, go." Dalrene's voice was quiet yet forceful.

Janet stood with her head wrapped in Dalrene's floral-patterned shawl and walked decisively to the end of the room. She faked a move into the restroom just as Dalrene told her to.

Dalrene opened the door with a keystroke and let out a long sigh. She'd done all she could. Janet was street savvy and knew how to get to the caves faster than almost anyone.

It was out of her hands now.

Dalrene shoved her computer in her bag, her bag under her seat, and pretended to be preoccupied with the menu.

A grin crept onto her face as the bots approached her, the lone woman with a burgundy-colored hood over her head. After not being identified by a bot in years, she was about to submit her thumbprint twice in the same day. Maybe that was a sign her plans were coming to fruition. The revolution had begun.

The robots squeaked closer and closer to Dalrene. Her heart pounded and she hunched over the table with her hood over her head. She didn't want to give the Foreman an inch. Any one mistake could foil everything.

The peacekeepers arrived at Dalrene's booth. Dalrene could see their wheels on the floor, but she didn't lift her head. She waited for what seemed like minutes for them to say something. Instead, a mechanical arm grabbed her by the neck and pinned her against the back of the booth bench.

"What the hell?" Dalrene gasped. No-one else in the bar was handled like this. Did the Foreman know what she was up to? She flailed her arms and hit the bot on its head full of sensors, but it was to no effect. Its grip grew tighter, and her airway got smaller. The cameras stared uncaringly, the AI behind it calculating exactly how close she was to dying.

Did her daughter's dream of overthrowing the Foreman die with her in the back of a run-down bar? Was it over before it started?

"Negative match," the inspector bot chirped beside her, and the peacekeeper slowly loosened its grip.

Dalrene slid back down in her chair, coughing and catching her breath. She spit blood onto the table and tried to regain her composure.

"Yeah, it's not me, you maniacs!" she hollered at the bots. "Go on, get out of here. Go harass someone else."

The bots wheeled to a stop beside the restroom. They'd be waiting a long time if they thought Janet was going to emerge.

She exited through the front door with a smile she was unable to wipe off her face. The Foreman was smart and strong. It learned from its mistakes and had hundreds of robots at its disposal. But it wasn't invincible. It was deteriorating, and Dalrene knew its weaknesses better than anyone else.

Big Titus had joked that she wanted to start a gang war, but she wanted something much bigger and better. She wanted a revolutionary war. And she was going to get one.

Chapter Three: Gordon

Gordon smelled the smoke before he opened the door.

"There you are!" His mom wrapped her arms around him.

"What's going on? And what's on fire?" Gordon moved into the kitchen and saw flames rising from a waste basket in the sink.

"I need to go away for a bit. But I'll be back, I promise!"

"Mom!"

"It will burn itself out, don't worry. How was the job ceremony? Did you get it?"

"Stop with this craziness!" Gordon said, dousing the flames with tap water. "Look, I got the apprenticeship. Everything's going to change. Things are going to be better from now on, but I need you to relax and tell me what happened."

"I knew you'd get it!" his mom said from her room.

Drawers opened and shut, and furniture scraped across the floor. Gordon moved to the bedroom door.

A metal crowbar hit the ground with a thud. Computer equipment and a wig followed it.

She was spooking him even more. Everything his mom threw on the floor made it clear whatever she was planning was going to make things worse.

"Mom," Gordon said, grabbing her by the shoulders. "Talk to me!"

They locked eyes for a few seconds, and Gordon saw something he'd never seen in her before. Fear. His mom's lip quivered, her smile cracked, and her body shook in Gordon's arms.

"I messed up, Gordon," she said, holding her face in her hands.

Gordon's heart dropped into his stomach. "Whatever happened, we'll get through it. We always do. I got the apprenticeship. We'll get a nicer hole and premium rations. You'll never have to work street jobs again." He wanted nothing more than for her to calm down, and for whatever this was to be over.

It was supposed to be a good day!

"Have you heard of the Dead Earth Hypothesis?"

Now she was blabbering about conspiracy theories. His mom had been excited for months about his potential apprenticeship, but now that was all out the window.

Her eyes darted around the room.

Did someone slip her some pills? Maybe she was a witness to a drug deal, and that's why the Foreman wanted to talk to them. Maybe this would all get cleared up when she explained things.

"Mom, take a seat. I'm going to help. I'm going to talk to master Tracey. Whatever you think of him, the Foreman respects him, and he can help it see our perspective. I'm on the good side now, Mom. But I need to know what happened."

"It's true. It's all true. Earth is dead," she said, her eyes wide, her hands gripping his shoulders tightly just as he had done to her.

"Earth isn't dead, it's recovering. We send them minerals every day," Gordon said. "Sit down, I'll get you a drink of water."

A heavy knock on the door stopped Gordon dead in his tracks.

"Ms. Onyango, you're under arrest. Open the door," came an uncanny voice that sounded human yet would never be mistaken for it.

"Crap! I wasn't fast enough!" She teared up but quickly wiped her eyes.

"Open the door and talk to them. You always get yourself off the hook," Gordon insisted. If his mom had one superpower it was getting herself out of tight situations. She was the one with the street smarts who could misdirect a bot and slip away from anything. He was powerless to help.

"This isn't like those other times," his mom said, embracing Gordon again. "This is it for me. I love you, Gordon."

The robots pounded on the door again. It wasn't going to stay standing much longer.

"Go to the cave entrance by the farm domes. Follow this symbol as deep as you can," she said, shoving a chunk of metal into Gordon's palm. "They're good people. You can trust them."

Gordon looked in his hand. There was a fibrous necklace, probably made of hemp, attached to a large pendant engraved with a red number one.

"What? No! I don't get it!" Gordon pleaded with his mom.

"Find the First Olympians!"

"The settlers?" It didn't make sense. The First Olympians were the original pioneers of Olympus Mons. Everyone who lived at the outpost was a direct descendent of them. There couldn't be any First Olympians still alive.

"Shhh!" his mom said, tears streaming down her face. She pushed him into a closet in the bedroom and closed the door.

There was a thud and the front door crashed open. Gordon's heart jumped and he closed his eyes. Someone had drugged his mom, but he still trusted her. Staying quiet was the best thing he could do. His only hope of helping was to get to master Tracey, who would not want to see his newest apprentice go through any legal difficulties.

"You got the wrong person! It wasn't me—I was just a bystander! I don't know what started it!" His mom was talking a mile a minute.

"You made payment to the provocateurs. You can explain in custody." It was the unmistakable tinny voice of a peacekeeper bot.

Part of Gordon wanted to go out there and help explain the misunderstanding. But if they weren't listening to his mom, they wouldn't listen to him. He gripped the metal pendant. Her pleading became increasingly desperate.

"You have the wrong person! I don't know what you want! Let me explain. Please, let me explain!"

"Administering sedative."

"Wait! No!"

There was a clanking metal-on-metal sound. His mom grunted. Gordon didn't know what was happening. He didn't think his mom could win a fight against multiple bots. Could she?

Another thud. His mom's scream shook the hole.

Gordon bit his lip until it bled and his tears mixed with the blood. He couldn't believe this was happening. After all he worked for. After he finally thought he made it into the Foreman's good books.

There was the sound of robots running their hard wheels over the tile floor. Occasionally, they made a chiming sound.

Then, nothing. Silence.

Just the air recyclers humming as always.

And Gordon was more scared than he'd ever been in his entire life.

\#

Every pair of prying black eyes was following Gordon and reporting his location to the Foreman. Or at least it felt like it. As a family member, he was committing a crime by not reporting for questioning. He'd be forced to attend his mom's trial, for whatever she was accused of, and maybe even testify against her.

Unless master Tracey could help. The kind older man had pulled off some of the most legendary and risky blasts in the history of the outpost. He was personally responsible for expanding the potential mineral yield of multiple mine shafts. The Foreman respected him as much as he did any human. Gordon just hoped that was enough to make a difference.

Once, master Tracey petitioned Mr. White to give a student extra time to study after an illness. Another time, he persuaded the Foreman to delay a training exercise in an area of the mine that was dangerously unstable. What Gordon was going to ask of him was admittedly a much taller task than these accomplishments, but it was his only chance.

He stopped for a moment to catch his breath and leaned against a crumbling, abandoned clay building. On the other side of the street, ever-flickering streetlights flashed intermittent shadows across hungry people waiting for ration handouts. They were mostly Faithless, too poor to spend credits in fancy cafes or even buy their own rations.

Their faces were sullen and ashen, and no one made eye contact with him. He'd spent too much time in similar lines and being there struck him with a deep sense of dread. A baby cried, piercing the silence, and his heart jumped.

Gordon shouldn't have to deal with those horrors anymore. He was getting ahead in life. He'd played by the rules. He did everything by the book and got an apprenticeship without anyone's help. He could only hope his mom hadn't screwed it all up.

His handheld buzzed. It was Corrina.

I'm in for questioning. Are you with your mom?

A sharp pain struck Gordon's chest. He wrote a quick response.

I'm trying to get help. Tell me how it goes. Tell me you're okay.

He ducked into an alley and continued his steady climb up the hill, to where all the high-ranking and respected people lived, near the farm domes. He'd only visited master Tracey at his home once, but he remembered it was a much different neighborhood. The holes were larger, with more space between them, and less loitering. And they never got rolling blackouts. One day, he'd buy his mom a hole there.

She'd been so distressed when the bots picked her up. He hoped whatever sedatives they gave her helped straighten her out. It had been difficult to see her so panicked.

Why had she been talking about the caves? Entrances to the elaborate cave network formed by ancient lava flows were all over the outpost. As a kid, every adult told him to stay out. They were forbidden territory. It was surreal that his mom told him to go in. Had she been in them recently? Should he mention her ramblings to master Tracey?

Generations of settlers had lived in the underground caves. But that was centuries ago, and their air recyclers would be busted by now. Besides the thin air, the labyrinth-like maze of tunnels meant that without a good map you could get lost and die of dehydration, even a few hundred meters from the entrance. Last year, a bunch of kids got drunk in the caves and never made it out. Gordon had never been the partying type.

There was only one wide, packed dirt road leading up to the three farm domes. Gordon looked out from a narrow alley, and a convoy of peacekeepers emerged from the middle dome's double iron doors and proceeded downhill, escorting three pallets of rations. Such high security was unusual, and it made his path harder. He stayed in the darkness along the outpost's wall and scurried up the hill, scraping his hands on clay and rock.

Master Tracey's hole was only a few blocks away, but Gordon paused to take in the view from the top of the hill. From this high vantage point, everything looked more romantic. There was a certain nostalgia to the smoke rising from the street-vendor grills and the parade of hard hats marching under the flickering street lights. Above the commotion, the outpost was eerily quiet, even peaceful. This was the last bastion of humanity. There were upwards of six thousand people working together to extract raw materials, build infrastructure, feed each other, and even help Earth.

Despite its problems, he was proud of it. It was home.

At the corner of master Tracey's street was a premium ration distribution center. Gordon looked through the window at the stocked shelves of full-fat cooking oils and fresh produce. It would be a faux pas to come to his master's home without a gift.

In the school bag slung over his shoulder he had a water bottle, some oat ration bars, his mining headlamp, and his precious origami papers. It was hardly an appropriate offering under normal circumstances, but this situation was highly unusual. Master Tracey would understand.

Gordon caught a glimpse of the screen above the checkout and all his anxieties came rushing back. This time, it was his face. The picture was easily recognizable as him, from a scan a few weeks earlier.

PERSON OF INTEREST & ASSOCIATES
WANTED IMMEDIATELY FOR QUESTIONING

Gordon rushed around the corner. He had to get to master Tracey fast!

But the sound of his master's voice stopped him dead, and he backtracked. Outside his hole at the end of the block, the older man was being dragged away by a pair of peacekeepers.

"Please! I don't know what you want! I'll answer any questions you have, honest! But there's no need to treat me like this!"

Gordon watched from behind the ration center, horrified, as they dragged the man he'd been friends with away. Lights flicked on in neighboring holes, and people watched from their windows.

Gordon's legs threatened to give out and he held himself up against the alley wall. He had nothing. No-one. He was all alone. He couldn't help his mom.

If he turned himself in, he would just be food for slaughter. What was she involved in that was so big that the Foreman would grab him and everyone he knew for questioning? He was terrified to find out.

Whatever it was, he couldn't fix it. He slipped down the wall. His dream was over.

Dead. He'd been an explosives apprentice for a few hours, but no more. No-one recovered from something like this. Even if his mom was innocent, he was looking at years of hard labor. The Foreman never admitted mistakes. Not for Faithless.

Worse, he had gotten other people caught up in his problems. Corrina hadn't responded to his message yet. Both she and master Tracey didn't deserve any hardship that came their way because of his actions. He couldn't handle the guilt if anything bad happened to them, although turning himself in didn't mean they would get a better deal. The Foreman didn't work like that.

Was he really going to go into the caves? It was a crazy, terrifying idea. But he trusted his mom more than the Foreman. Despite her antics, she was still his mom, just like Corrina had said.

His dad and Aunt Tess never returned from being scooped up by bots. One day they were there, and the next they were gone. Even if a tenth of his mom's theories about the horrible things that happened in prison holes were true, they were brutal, evil places. When it came down to it, he was more scared of the Foreman than the caves.

Was master Tracey's wife still in their hole? He hadn't met her, but maybe she could help.

He poked his head around the corner and his stomach churned. Two more peacekeepers emerged from master Tracey's hole. Their saw-arm attachments could cut through bone in seconds.

"We told you, we don't know where they are!" A shrill voice yelled from inside.

Gordon pulled back and took fast breaths. Master Tracey's wife wouldn't help him. If anything, she'd turn him over to the Foreman to help clear her husband's name.

The bots' wheels drummed over the dirt road. Were they getting closer? It was hard to tell by the sound.

He wiped sweat off his brow and looked up to see one of the dome roofs. He was close to where his mom had told him to come. He had to go into the caves. He had no choice.

Gordon steadied himself and took another peek down the street. Crap! It was crawling with bots. He could do this. He could. But he had to act fast, before they got any closer. He focused and counted to three.

He darted out of the alley and away from master Tracey's hole.

Thankfully, no-one was out on the streets. He ran to the nearest farm dome. Beside it, and four meters up on the outpost's wall, he spotted a red number one. Gordon fished in his pocket for his mom's pendant.

It was the same symbol.

He stood still for a moment and listened. None of the bots had followed him. For now.

Gordon inched around the back side of one of the three farm domes, in the small space between the outpost's wall and the structure. The domes were tall, their peaks stretching nearly to the cave's ceiling. Made of reinforced steel and glass, they were the best constructed buildings in the entire outpost and had stood for over a hundred years. Their supposedly transparent roofs hadn't been cleaned in almost as long and were covered in so much dust that you couldn't see through them.

A metal plaque was drilled into the wall at the tunnel entrance, and Gordon brushed it clean. Its inscription warned not to enter without sufficient water supplies, navigation systems, and experience. Gordon swallowed hard. He didn't have any of those things.

He took a deep breath. He couldn't believe he was doing it.

The roof of the cave was six feet high, and Gordon ducked as he entered. Everyone born in the low gravity environment of Mars grew taller than their Earth-born ancestors ever had. He weaved around the pillars of dried lava, eyes adjusting slowly to the dim light. It smelled of iron, sulfur, and dirt. It was like the mines without the human scents of explosives, sweat, and clouds of bitter amphetamine smoke.

As Gordon turned the first corner, the light from the tunnel entrance disappeared and his new reality sunk in. The path forked and he didn't know which way to go.

He was all alone.

His mom was in a prison hole.

Master Tracey had been taken into custody.

Corrina hadn't responded, and now she couldn't because his handheld didn't work in the caves.

Terrifying bots were searching for him.

The award ceremony from that morning felt like a lifetime away. His apprenticeship in the mines seemed like a fantasy. He was going to die in this cave, alone and a failure, unable to protect his mom. He held his chest, willing his heart to slow down. It didn't.

He turned on his mining headlamp, and a red glint on the cave wall caught his eye. Scattered among the decades of graffiti was a symbol. A red number one, and below it, an arrow pointing deeper into the caves.

He took a deep breath. He was in the right place. He could navigate forks in the path by following that symbol. At least he'd die doing what his mom wanted.

Gordon trudged deeper and deeper underground, following the arrows underneath the red number ones. The caves were silent, except for the unsteady vibrations of the ancient air recyclers clinging to the ceiling every hundred or so meters. Someone had kept their maintenance relatively up to date.

Strange. He hadn't expected that.

The air was cool and clammy, but Gordon wasn't cold as long as he kept moving. The sides of the cave were largely circular and smooth, almost glossy. School taught him it was due to the way they were formed, by lava tubes. Slow-moving surface lava developed a hard crust, forming a roof above the flow. When a tube emptied, it left a tunnel-like formation, almost like it had been bored by a machine. Millenia had buried them deep underground, but they were unchanged since Mars lost its tectonics so long ago.

Gordon was occasionally overwhelmed by the inertness. It was a dead place, and humans weren't meant to live there. He didn't know how anything could. He supposed that was true of the rest of the outpost too, but there, humans had bent the environment to their will.

The hours passed, and he grew weary. He couldn't tell if it was because the air was getting thinner, or because it'd been a long day. He wished Corrina was on this adventure with him. Her jokes would've been able to keep his mind from going to dark places.

He checked his handheld, hoping that it somehow could've received a message from Corrina, but there was nothing. The only thing it was good for now was telling time. He promised himself he wouldn't look at the clock too often. He started counting his steps. If he didn't find what his mom wanted him to find, he'd check the time again after five thousand steps.

The path of red number ones led him deeper underground. At the start, there had been forks in the cave every fifteen minutes. Now, they were only every hour or so. The graffiti, like the air recyclers, was appearing less frequently. There was even some Spanish sprawled on the walls that must've been super old. No one spoke that language anymore. If it weren't for those changes and the keen sense that he was descending, he could've sworn he was being led in circles.

His dry throat rubbed raw over his Adam's apple, and he rationed a small drink of water. It didn't help much. He wished he brought more. He slapped himself in the face to stay awake. He knew he wouldn't start again if he stopped. The thinning air was going to kill him.

Gordon thought about his dad and his Aunt Tess. His memories of them had faded with the years. He did what he could to honor them, like practicing the origami his dad had taught him, and reading the history books Aunt Tess gave him. But it wasn't enough. The more time passed, the more their faces became an impressionistic outline in his mind.

He shuddered to think that if his mom was sent to a labor camp or kept in a prison hole long enough, he might forget things about her too.

Gordon hummed one of her favorite songs. She had a gravely voice, but it could be warm and sweet too, and she sang while she cooked, cleaned, or did anything really. He promised himself he'd never forget how those sounds made him feel at home.

What had his mom been talking about? School taught them about the First Olympians, the hardy pioneers who arrived in search of good jobs and a better life, only to watch helplessly as X-Day wiped out most of Earth's population. But that was history. How could it possibly be relevant now? And what did it have to do with the Dead Earth Hypothesis, the strange theory some Faithless whispered on the streets but could never fully explain? Normally people argued about what X-Day was, and what caused it. No one agreed. If that's what the Dead Earth Hypothesis was about, Gordon didn't care. The cause of the events all those years ago didn't concern him in the slightest. It was pointless to argue about something that wouldn't change anything.

The hours blended together, and Gordon's legs felt like gelatin. The sweat in his hair had evaporated, and his water bottle was empty. The First Olympians had survived by drinking water that dripped from lava pillars and even formed ponds and small lakes. He'd need to find one of those if he was going to survive.

Except for the occasional bout of tears, he walked like one of the zombies in the books his dad used to read him, straight ahead with short strides. The sameness of his surroundings grated on him, and he felt like a zombie mentally, too. The longer he walked, the slower he got. The thin air had given him a headache. He didn't remember when he stopped counting his steps.

The clock on his handheld said he'd been in the caves for twelve hours. Had he taken a wrong turn? He gnawed on his lip, worried he was screwed. He was unprepared for an expedition this long, and he couldn't imagine having the strength to find his way back to the residential area if he wanted to.

It all went back to when his aunt died. Why couldn't his mom have just reacted normally, like he had? He was the kid. He was supposed to be the one that needed help. Instead, he was left to raise himself. There was no need for things to go this way, to whatever hell this was.

A wash of guilt swept over him. Was that not fair to his mom? She was human too, and everyone had their breaking point. He could never know exactly how all the loss and trauma had impacted her. But his dad always taught him to buckle down in the face of adversity. Why couldn't she do the same? Gordon's thoughts ran in circles just like his feet seemed to.

He realized he was in trouble when he didn't remember seeing the last red number one. There had been numerous branching passages and the caves felt more like a spiderweb than one continuous tunnel. He leaned against the wall with one arm, willing his body to move forward. He hoped he was close to what his mom wanted him to find. Whatever was so important she had never told him about. Whatever caused her to be whisked away by the Foreman and dash Gordon's dreams.

His chest spasmed, and he couldn't control his sobbing once it started. Gordon tried holding his eyes closed with his hands to stop the crying, but it didn't help. He held his hands in front of his face and realized they were dry. His body was too dehydrated to produce tears.

He slouched to the ground. All he could imagine was a robot throwing his mom over its shoulder like a ragdoll while he hid in the closet. His ears still rang from her piercing screams. That might be his last memory of her for years, or maybe forever.

If he did see her again, she might be changed, indoctrinated by a re-education program. And for what reason! It made no sense. All he wanted was to be an explosives apprentice, contribute to the cause, and provide for his mom. Why couldn't the Foreman let him do that? Why couldn't his mom let him do that?

Gordon gripped his knees and tried to choke back his tearless crying. Life at the outpost was never fair, but this was something else. This was senseless and random. Cruelty without explanation.

A new hole pierced his heart. Life would never be the same, like when his aunt or his dad died. But where there had been youthful helplessness and bewildered acceptance in those situations, there was now frustration, and it was building.

In the past, anger had been useless. Now, he needed answers.

Chapter Four: Dalrene

The note from Londi was still on her screen. In two minutes, it would be an hour since she first read it, and the message would auto-delete. But Dalrene was still on the bathroom floor, her face crumpled into her knees. She immediately knew its implication. There was no question, no way out. She couldn't rationalize any other course of action. And yet, she spent the last fifty-eight minutes trying to accept it.

The screen blinked and the message disappeared, but it was burned into Dalrene's mind:

They got her.

Rescuing Janet would be tough, maybe impossible.

Mickey was the only person ever freed from a prison hole. She broke her husband out a year ago, and it'd been rather simple. She'd caused havoc by locking doors, turning on fire sprinklers, and opening a window for him to jump out of.

Dalrene feared that was a one-time trick. The Foreman likely learned from that escapade and packed its buildings full of bots and increased surveillance measures. Indeed, the prison holes Dalrene knew of had their windows filled in.

If she couldn't free her, Janet was going to die, and the only question left would be how. The Foreman's torture and interrogation capabilities were vast, and it would extract everything Janet knew about Dalrene's operations. That's why her lieutenants carried a lethal opioid dose. They called it a "blue-Earth death," and using it was "going to Earth," on account of the drug's sky-blue package. Failing rescue, that blissful, peaceful, worry-free death was Janet's best-case scenario.

Worst-case, she'd be tortured with everything from waterboarding to mind-bending virtual reality loops of her loved ones verbally abusing her. When she was diminished to a hollow husk of a woman, she'd be publicly executed. And the crowd would cheer, desperate to show their allegiance to the Foreman.

Dalrene shuddered and pushed that thought out of her mind, but the one that replaced it was even worse. She couldn't afford to let the Foreman learn her secrets, and she couldn't bear to see her friend suffer that kind of savage treatment. If she couldn't break Janet out, she'd have to put and end to it some other way.

She closed her computer and put it in the cabinet under the sink. The one saving grace was that Janet, and her other lieutenants, had successfully uploaded the deletion code. At anytime, Dalrene could now destroy the Foreman's back-ups. She didn't expect to have that option forever. Either Janet would give up the info, or the Foreman would investigate the circumstances surrounding her arrest and find the code.

Dalrene stood and splashed her face with water. Bloodshot eyes reminded her that, unlike her enemy, she needed sleep. Creases biting into the top of her forehead questioned whether she was too old and tired for the job. This was the war she wanted. This was the commanding role she wanted. Whatever emotions bubbled up, she had to stuff down until the Foreman was dead and buried.

After a few deep inhales, Dalrene left the bathroom and leaned on the railing as she walked down the stairs. Pictures drawn by her granddaughter, Ellie, hung beside pictures drawn by her daughter, Tess, and more practical items such as a nurse uniform and a school schedule. The walls and furniture were all painted white, to reflect as much light as possible. It almost helped make it less dreary.

She was at her son-in-law's, Javier's, hole. Besides the benefit of seeing Ellie, there was the relief of a full, working bathroom, kitchen, and a real bed. She couldn't go back down to the deep until the loose ends were tied up.

Garlic rations were low, so dinner was going to be bland. Dalrene chopped the potatoes and onions as she'd done many times before but realized the cooking oil was empty. Instead, she added a splash of water to the pan.

Life at the outpost only got worse, and never better. That was the immutable law of Dalrene's hard-lived decades. Every day, the Foreman squeezed harder, and people gave more and more, until they broke. It was why Ellie didn't have any textbooks to learn from. It was why she was skinnier than Dalrene had ever been. It was why she was growing up without a mother.

On a normal day, all of that would bother Dalrene to no end. But she couldn't get Janet off her mind. Right now, the Foreman was going through its footage. She had turned off the Pickaxe Café's cameras, but dozens of other cameras could have tracked them through the streets. Could it link Janet to the café, and then to her? Had she put Ellie in danger by coming to their hole?

She told herself she hadn't. It would be fine.

The onions had just become fragrant when Ellie burst through the front door and ran to her grandmother.

"I missed you too!" Dalrene said, hugging her back.

"Grandma, we're going on a field trip to the mines tomorrow," she exclaimed. She had a mop of an afro on her head so big that it reminded her of Tess. Almost too much sometimes.

"That's so exciting," Dalrene said.

In a way, it was good that Ellie didn't know a better life. Having nothing to compare to kept her curiosity and enthusiasm intact and reminded Dalrene why she fought.

Javier came through the door behind them. He was still in his scrubs.

"Hey." He plopped a package down on the counter. "Found some protein. Soy." His hairline had receded since Dalrene last saw him. Stress and age were coming for him too.

"Perfect timing. I'll add it in," Dalrene said, taking the cutting board out of the sink.

"You look horrible," Javier said, crossing his arms.

Ellie ran upstairs, distracted by whatever new game she was playing.

"Could say the same about you."

"How's Mickey?" Javier furrowed his brow.

"I'm fine. Mickey's fine. If there was any real trouble, I wouldn't bring it here. To Ellie," Dalrene said. "Now set the table, would you?"

Javier made a low growling sound, but got the plates out of the cabinet, accepting her answers for now.

"I'll be out of your hair in no time," Dalrene said.

When the warm smell of dinner filled the small lower level, the three of them sat at the square kitchen table, Ellie pushing the potatoes around her plate. They were a bit soft on account of the water.

"Come on, eat-up," Javier said, cutting some of Ellie's potatoes into smaller pieces.

"It tastes better when Lorraine makes it," Ellie said, pushing her plate away.

"Who's Lorraine? Is that your friend?" Dalrene asked.

"No, it's Daddy's friend."

A chunk of soy got caught in Dalrene's throat and she coughed violently to dislodge it. "Oh?" she asked.

Javier's eyes were cast down at his plate.

"I, uh, was going to tell you," he muttered.

"It's okay." Dalrene swallowed hard. "You deserve to be happy. Tess would want that for you."

"Yeah. You'd like her," Javier said, lifting his gaze to hers and nodding. "I'll introduce you. Next time. I promise. Just let me know when you're coming instead of randomly popping in."

"Okay," she said, crossing her arms.

Dalrene's appetite was replaced with a pit of regret. She wondered if Ellie would forget her mother. It would be hard for her not to with another woman in the house. Dalrene loved her granddaughter, but saving Mickey, investigating Tess's murder, and organizing a revolution had swallowed her time and energy. She hadn't helped enough since Tess died.

She took one last mushy bite before putting her fork down. The next time she saw Ellie was going to be under very different circumstances.

They were going to be free.

#

The couch should've felt more comfortable given she hadn't slept on anything other than the ground in months. But Dalrene barely got any shuteye. It was hard to relax knowing that Janet was on the other side of the outpost in much more uncomfortable lodging.

Thinking about Javier's new girlfriend didn't help either. She wanted her granddaughter to have a maternal influence, but it was painful to know someone other than her daughter filled that role. After a few hours of tossing and turning, she got up quietly, careful not to wake anyone.

Her computer on her lap, she opened the latest message from Londi. He'd found the location of the prison hole where they were keeping Janet.

Dalrene could guess how he'd done that, but the specifics didn't matter. What mattered was finding out what was happening inside that building and ending it. She switched to a residential map of the outpost and plotted a path with the least amount of surveillance. The prison holes had fortified their network connections since Mickey's rescue, and if she wanted to access its cameras, she was going to have to splice into the building's cables.

While she was putting on her boots, Javier came down the stairs with a yawn. Seeing Dalrene stopped him in his tracks. "Where are you going?" he asked, crossing his arms.

"Someone needs my help," Dalrene said, trying to keep her tone light. "What about you?"

"Same. Short-staffed, so I got called in." Javier's eyes stayed on Dalrene, questioning her.

"Listen," Dalrene said. "Things are escalating. Shit is going to hit the fan. You should come down to the caves now, before it does. It'll be safer for you both."

Javier stepped closer and put his hand on her shoulder. "I miss Tess. We both do. I know she was on to something, and I believe you, but we're moving on. It's too dangerous, and I have to be here for Ellie. Whatever you've got planned isn't worth it."

"I'm serious," Dalrene said, pulling away. "I'll be back for you two. Be ready."

Her pills, stolen from mining ops, came in plain packaging simply labelled "amphetamines". Bitterness lingered in her throat as she stepped out of Javier's hole and onto the street. She didn't wash them down. Instead, she let the taste sit there. It was a reminder that everything had a price, and the price of alertness was a bad taste and the crash that would follow.

Dalrene slunk along the side of a dark street. Her computer was her main weapon and she held it snugly under her arm, her bag full of technical equipment on her back. The drugs started to kick in, and her mind focused. She worked her way methodically across the outpost, dodging in and out of streets and avoiding the bot patrols.

Third shift was the quietest time of the day, but that wasn't saying much. The low drone of air recyclers and robot wheels still hung over everything. Children slept, so there was no before-school complaining or after-school chattering, but the rest of the outpost carried on. Miners were down in the mines. The propaganda screens were still bright and numerous. Faithless roamed, begging for credits or trying to find unregulated work. Storekeepers stocked shelves, getting ready for the rush between shifts.

Turning onto the street where Janet was being held, Dalrene spotted four peacekeepers checking someone's identification. She dipped into a narrow space between two holes and tried to be quiet. She didn't think they saw her, but the fact that bots were out harassing people on residential streets was a bad sign. The Foreman had increased its patrol numbers.

Slowly, she climbed over the chain link fences that separated buildings and made her way closer to Janet's prison hole. She really was getting too old and was thankful she had her amphetamine pills. She stopped and huddled underneath a metal exterior staircase, pinching her nose between two smelly garbage bins. The bot patrol went by, their wheels whizzing over the ground, and Dalrene checked her breast pocket. Her own blue-Earth death was there if she needed it.

Dalrene made her way up the staircase, careful to minimize her noise. Four holes down was a brown, mud-and-clay structure that looked like all the others. Apart from being windowless, it could be identified because it was the recipient of a cable that ran over the neighborhood. Only the important buildings relied on hardwire network connections. The other difference was that instead of having between one and three families living in each of its three stories, this had none. It was a prison hole with separate rooms for interrogation, torture, and solitary confinement. And Janet was in there.

Lying flat on the roof, Dalrene worked to splice the cable. She'd been good with computers her whole life, having honed the skills she learned from her father by working at the propaganda building. Weaponizing the Foreman's own tools against it satisfied her like nothing else. To her army, it seemed like magic. To her, it was second nature and the most important tool in her toolbox. It also gave her legitimacy. No-one liked a leader that was just a pretty face, and she wasn't a fighter.

Dalrene worked and thought about Mickey. Her husband rarely spoke of his time imprisoned. From what she could gather, he spent most of it in solitary confinement after he gave up information about their daughter. It crushed his will to live. He said solitary was even more inhumane than the torture room that showed Tess's execution on repeat.

At least there he could see her face.

The worst was a combination of a psychedelic, nightmare-inducing drug and a virtual-reality machine meant to simulate drowning. If the Foreman got bored of that, it might pin you down and pour water into your lungs, actually drowning you. Not knowing whether the drowning was real or simulated was half the struggle.

The Foreman had all sorts of threats, promises, tortures, and even specially designed drugs it could use to extract information from people. It would get what it wanted from Janet. No matter how hard she tried, sooner or later, she'd spill the beans. She'd tell the Foreman about the army they were building, the names of all their top members, and their primary and secondary targets.

Dalrene couldn't let that happen. She owed it to herself, to Tess, to Mickey. And to Ellie.

When she connected her computer to the network and hacked into the surveillance feed, Dalrene's heart sunk. Her worst fears were confirmed. There were a dozen bots in the building and all sorts of cameras and motion sensors. There were no windows and no fire sprinklers, so her previous tricks wouldn't work. She wracked her mind. She could access the building's doors and air recyclers. That didn't give her a lot of options.

She flipped through the camera feeds until she found Janet, sitting in a room with nothing but a table and a single chair. A torture bot stood by the door. Her eyes were dark and wet. She was restrained, her hands tied to the table, preventing her from wiping away her tears. Dalrene welled up too. Janet was a fireball of confidence who never let anyone get one over on her. To see her reduced to this state after less than a day of captivity was a punch to the gut, and a reminder of the Foreman's power.

She wanted her army to attack the prison hole and kick off the war. They could overrun the bots and break her free.

But acting on emotional grounds was a good way to make a bad decision. If she directed an attack on the prison, their real targets, the nodes, would be fortified and secured before they had could even sniff them. The smartest move was to kill Janet now, before the Foreman could get a grip on her mind and she exposed valuable intelligence. She just couldn't bear it.

"If you tell me what I want to know, you will be fine. Your son will be fine. You'll get a light sentence, only a few years of re-education and labor. But if you don't tell me, things will be difficult. Why did you instigate a criminal disruption? Who are you working for?" Whereas the Foreman's voice was deep, authoritative, and creepily human, the torture bot's voice was cold, clammy, and uncaring.

"I ... I'll tell you. If you free my hands," Janet pleaded.

The amphetamine pills bubbled in Dalrene's stomach. She shouldn't have eaten them on an empty stomach, but her appetite was dead. It was distressing to watch Janet beg.

The Foreman was well on its way to breaking the younger woman's spirit. The only solace Dalrene could find was that the Foreman wasn't asking good questions. It clearly didn't know much about the incident Janet had engineered on Torres Street. At least, not yet.

"One hand. If you behave," the bot replied.

Janet nodded and blinked back some tears. There were bruises on her face and shoulders.

Dalrene's finger hovered over her keyboard. With the press of a button, she could lock and seal the room Janet was in, turn off the air recyclers, and watch her friend suffocate to death. It would be painful, and terrifying. Janet would die scared and alone.

She didn't have to do it. She could walk away. She could try to find another solution, no matter how futile that seemed. What would Tess do?

"Please, I don't want to," Dalrene muttered under her breath.

The restraint on her left hand popped open. She twisted it, stretching it out. "Thank you," she said to the bot, almost courteously.

She reached under her shirt, into her bra, and pulled out her needle. She jammed it between her teeth and bit the cap off, but the bot struck her across the face with its metal arm.

Janet's chance of going to Earth went flying.

She tried to grab it, but her other hand was still restrained. She sprawled out, trying to reach the drug with her foot, but the bot swatted it away.

Janet cried, and Dalrene cringed. Her hope for an easy death evaporated before her eyes. She was proud of her friend. She was strong and brave. She did her best.

The bot hit a screeching Janet hard on the side of the head. "You will comply," it stated.

Dalrene closed her eyes. The Foreman had already taken so much from her. It killed Tess, broke Mickey, and it was going to kill Janet. All Dalrene was doing was speeding up the inevitable.

That was the way she had to view it. She knew the risks when she joined Dalrene's army. Her death wouldn't be in vain. Just like Tess's. She would see to it. And she wouldn't let the Foreman take anyone else from her.

With tears rolling down her face, Dalrene pressed the button with her shaking hand and kept her eyes open. Wide open. She watched the bot twirl its sensors in confusion as it realized the door had not just been locked, but air sealed. She watched a nervous curiosity come over Janet's face when the air recycler stopped whirring. At first, it was just a slight acknowledgement. The poor thing probably thought it was one of the Foreman's torture games, and that it would turn back on soon.

"Fuck off and turn on the air. Hey! I'm talking to you!"

But the air didn't turn back on. In fact, the opposite happened, and the recycler started to suck oxygen out of the room.

Janet yelled at the bot, but it just sat there. It knew as little as she did. By the time it alerted the Foreman and received new instructions, it would be over.

"I'll tell you what you want to know. Just don't kill me, not like this. I want to live! I'll tell you who paid me. Is that what you want? Hey!"

When she realized the air in the room was almost gone, Dalrene's heart broke. Janet burst through her restraints and pounded on the door. She punched the air recycler.

"I want to live!" she repeated.

She offered to tell everything she knew and more. She yelled into the camera, face to face with Dalrene, shrieking that the Foreman wouldn't get away with murder.

Time dragged, but it had only been a few minutes.

In another few, Janet gasped for air. She clawed at her throat.

Dalrene watched it all, until the end. Until the woman who had become her friend lay twitching on the floor. Then, until the twitching stopped. She watched it because it was her fault, because she couldn't let Janet die alone, and because she needed to know it was done.

She saved the video file. It was a reminder of what she'd done, and of the ultimate cost of mistakes. She wouldn't let herself forget it.

Dalrene closed her computer and forced herself to march the ten minutes to the nearest cave entrance. She moved slower now, the guilt weighing her down. Her revolution plans were how Dalrene carried on Tess's legacy. The vision of a Foreman-free life sometimes felt like the biggest piece of her daughter she had left, even more so than Ellie.

Tess would've been ashamed of her now, even though there hadn't been another option.

It was a sad, sad day, and she just wanted to be alone with her grief. The faster she got to the deep, the better.

\#

The crash was coming on. She could take more amphetamines, but that would just mean a bigger crash later. She plowed through the fatigue, pausing only momentarily to rest.

She knew the cave network like the back of her hand. Years ago, it was safe, and kids were even encouraged to explore it. But the air and water infrastructure fall into disrepair, like everything else at the outpost. This resulted in a society that was culturally disconnected from how its ancestors lived, and from its roots as a group of fearless pioneers. Kids these days only learned about the settlers, the First Olympians, in school, and half of what they learned was nonsense.

Dalrene's group had taken to repairing the archaic air recyclers littered throughout the tunnels. They had to, so that they could live, train, and plan their attacks in secrecy. So far, the Foreman hadn't succeeded in stifling them. Hell, there was no evidence it had any idea people were even using the caves. It had become more brutal and oppressive recently, but that fit the well-established long-term trend. Her theory was that the AI was compensating for the outpost's deterioration by tightening its monopoly on violence. The more things went to shit, the more it cracked down.

Home was a large, rectangular grotto. It was where dozens of Dalrene's closest supporters lived, including her lieutenants, their platoon leaders, and their families. Hundreds were in other caves, and more still lived out regular lives in the residential area, awaiting her call to action. No-one outside of the grotto group knew Dalrene's name or face, but they knew the chain of command, and that something big was coming.

A shallow pool of water took up one side of the main room. Opposite was a natural stage, a rock platform from which Dalrene talked to her crew. There was a fire pit in the middle for talking, singing, and drinking. They often sat around it, but they only lit fires on special occasions, and when all four air recyclers were operating at full efficacy.

She neared the entrance to the grotto and a chill went down Dalrene's spine. Her body had been shifting between hot and cold, but mostly sweating profusely. The crash was in full force.

The loud voices talking over the empty campfire stopped when she entered the room. She waved their eyes away and slunk along the cave wall to one of the many offshoots that was her bedroom. They were her people. Her most loyal followers. And she would address them. But first, she needed her bed. The grief was consuming her, and she couldn't think straight until she slept off the amphetamine hangover.

The cave she shared with Mickey was small, although it was the largest offshoot. A pile of illegal electronics sat beside Mickey's bottles of mushroom whiskey. A dozen shawls, ranging from black and white to bright psychedelic, hung on the wall. Underneath that, flattened cardboard ration boxes had been stacked on top of each other to make something resembling a bed.

Dalrene crawled into it and pulled a few shawls over her body. She had barely closed her eyes when there was a hard knock on the cave wall. The voice that spoke was low, deep, and monotone.

"We need to talk." Londi ducked to enter the room. He was muscular and confident but hadn't been when Dalrene first knew him as her daughter's friend. Years later, she'd helped him get over his drug addiction, and he'd become her most reliable, loyal lieutenant.

"Where's Mickey?" Dalrene groaned.

"You can't shirk the debrief. We need to talk," he said, his tone stern.

"Bring me some tea, would you?"

"Dalrene."

"For fuck's sake!" Dalrene said, throwing her makeshift blankets off and sitting up. "Fine. Lieutenant's meeting. Bring them in."

"It's just three of us," Londi said. "That's the first problem."

Rodriguez popped into Dalrene's bedroom with entirely too much enthusiasm for the situation. The chief medic was a stocky man, not fat, but comfortable, who stood up to Londi's chest and had a long mustache.

Ionne followed, crossing her arms and leaning against the wall. She had long dreads that reminded Dalrene of herself in her younger days and an indignance that reminded her of herself now. Ionne could be quiet but was always smart, and Dalrene valued her opinion. Her husband, DeMar, was a platoon leader and an explosives technician.

Dalrene looked down at the cave floor. "Janet—" she caught her wavering voice. She wished she'd taken a harder stance and made Londi let her sleep. "Janet didn't make it."

"What in the world?" Rodriguez leaned against the wall and slid to the ground, the grin he wore night and day absent for the first time in Dalrene's memory.

Ionne closed her eyes and made a face like she was hiding pain. She'd been Janet's close friend.

The muscles of Londi's arms clenched so hard Dalrene thought she heard a popping sound. Otherwise, he didn't show any reaction to the news.

"What have we gotten ourselves into?" Rodriguez asked, his upper lip trembling.

"It's a fucking war," Dalrene said, standing. "That's what happens."

Rodriguez caught his sniffles in his hands and stopped his upper lip from trembling.

"You have to tell us more." Ionne put her hands on her hips.

"Nothing more than that matters right now. We'll have a funeral for her. We'll honor our friend and lay her memory to rest. Another victim of the Foreman's pointless rampage. But we won't let it be a loss without meaning. Will we?" Dalrene asked.

Londi and Rodriguez shook their heads.

"Did she go to Earth?" Ionne looked like she'd taken a bite of a rotten apple.

"She tried. Yeah." Dalrene wanted to curl up in a ball and never get up. It wasn't that she couldn't tell her lieutenants the truth, but rather that she didn't want to admit it to herself. "Now, can I sleep? Or was there something else? And if there are more problems, please tell me you've at least thought of potential solutions."

"The good news is we recovered the bombs," Londi said.

Dalrene smiled and shook her head in disbelief. It felt like eons ago when she met Big Titus in the Pickaxe Café.

"The bad news is that the outpost entered a level-three lockdown. There are extra security forces at all security sensitive sites, including the processing nodes. And forget about the brain node. We're talking hundreds of bots. We can't hit them straight on.

We'd send our people to slaughter."

Dalrene winced. A level-three lockdown was no joke. That's why there had been more patrols on the streets when she went to Janet's prison hole. Shit. She had to get Javier and Ellie out of the residential level while she still could. She should've already done it, but he'd rebuffed her offer and she'd been distracted by Janet. She stretched her arms in the air, her fingers entwined, and turned her mind back to the bombs. The level-three lockdown diminished their element of surprise.

"We can't hit our targets during a lockdown," Dalrene said. "We'll lose too many people. I can't do it."

"So, what? Janet's sacrifice was for nothing?" Ionne spit on the ground.

"No. The deletion programs are in place, right?" Londi asked.

Dalrene opened her computer. This was turning into a strategizing session. So much for sleep.

"Yes, I have access to the back-up servers. For how long, I don't know. The Foreman will find it in another day or two, max. And if we execute the program, it will back itself up again, likely within days. It needs time to organize that, but not much."

"Deleting the back-ups will escalate the situation and the lockdown will be increased to a level four, or worse," Ionne said in a hushed tone. "The Foreman will imprison citizens, fortify any potential targets, and we won't have a chance. On the other hand, if we ignore the backups and go straight to attacking nodes, during a level-three lockdown, we'll take heavy casualties. There are no good options."

Dalrene closed her eyes and thought.

"We need to execute the deletion program soon. It's a tool at our disposal and we worked hard to put it in place. I won't waste it. We just need a distraction, a new target for the bombs that will draw the Foreman's resources away from the nodes. Our planning documents prescribe the first step to be a call to arms, and I say we stick to that. When we have a critical mass of people, we'll hit our targets. We'll do it quick, while the Foreman's attention is diverted, and we'll minimize the human cost," Dalrene said.

"I have reports of patrols at our secondary targets too," Londi said. "Even the smallest charging stations and surveillance hubs. There's nowhere we can stage a distraction that will meaningfully draw resources away from the nodes."

"I know a place. The surface."

Chapter Five: Gordon

"Hey, kid, wake-up!"

Gordon gasped for air. The left side of his face stung.

A hand came down and smacked him across the other cheek.

"Oh," he mumbled.

"The hell you doin' down here? Not a great place to take a nap! Not a lotta air, or anything else really." A gray-bearded man stooped over Gordon. His equally gray hair was held behind his head in a ponytail, a far cry from the Foreman-approved male hairstyles.

"Water?" A whisper was all he could muster.

The man thrust a satchel toward him. Gordon could feel the man evaluating him. The water helped, but not as much as he'd hoped. It rushed over his raw throat like alcohol on an open wound.

Gordon didn't know what to say. He stared back while he gulped, buying time, studying the deep lines on the old man's face.

He was lost and he didn't have anything to lose. He was going to be honest.

He choked, spilling some water.

"That's enough," the man said, swiping the satchel back. "Who sent you down here?"

"My mom," Gordon said, producing the pendant from his pocket.

The man's eyes grew wider and he snatched the pendant. He weighed it in his hands and mumbled something about lieutenants. "Janet?"

"Yeah. The bots ... they came to our house. They took her." He winced. It felt weird to say it out loud, like it made it all real instead of some horrible dream.

The man hung his head. "I'm sorry, kid. You must be Gordon? She talked about you some."

The words stung. His mom never mentioned a strange old man in the caves. They shared everything with each other, or so he'd thought. Had he done something wrong? Something to make her distrust him and prevent telling him what she had been up to and who she had been meeting? Gordon took a deep breath.

"Where did they take her? Who are you to her? And why was she talking about the Dead Earth Hypothesis?"

"I don't know," the man said, running his hand through his hair and pausing on the nape of his neck. "There are some things I can explain, but not here. Let's go. We are close to the grotto. You need a meal and a bed."

"Thank you." He rose to his feet with the man's help. It wasn't like he had a choice.

"I'm Mickey. Take this back," he said, handing the pendant back to Gordon. "It's yours now."

Before Gordon could ask what the engraving on the pendant meant, Mickey sprang past him, launching deeper into the caves. He was exhausted, but even if he'd been at full strength he would've struggled to keep up with Mickey. The old man was in good shape.

Gordon recited the names of minerals in his head to keep it from wandering to dark places. The outpost currently mined titanium, lithium, chromium, and niobium. He rhymed them in his head and repeated them, like a school kid might do when studying for a test. These were the ingredients that would give Earth, the crown jewel of humanity, back its sparkle. Titanium, lithium, chromium, and niobium. Earth needed these resources. Without them, the human race was threatened, pushed to the brink of extinction. All Gordon had to do was take them out of the ground. Titanium, lithium, chromium, and niobium.

"We're here," Mickey said. They turned a corner marked by a faint number one on the wall.

"Here" seemed to be a very temporary living situation. There were makeshift beds and paper—actual paper books! It smelled like mildew and body odor. It looked like any of the other dozen large caves they had passed through, but with one important difference. There was water.

Gordon dropped to his knees at the long, narrow pool that took up one side of the cave and splashed a handful of water over his face. It was colder than he expected, but he welcomed the freshness.

"Welcome to our grotto," Mickey said, gesturing broadly to the large, rectangular cave with two-dozen or so people milling around. A group of four was cooking nearby on a battery powered stove. The aroma of dried basil smacked Gordon's senses and made his mouth water. They turned to look at him, their tired eyes lighting up with surprise.

Another group was organizing a mountain of boots, crowbars, and other gear in a corner, and Gordon recoiled, struck by the implication of violence. The scale of the operation was overwhelming, especially after walking through barren caves for so long. He felt young and out of place.

On the far side of the grotto there was a natural, elevated stage where a gray-haired woman was in a heated discussion with a younger man. Upon seeing the new entrants, she rushed toward them. They stood by the shallow pool of water that ran along the wall.

"This is my wife, Dalrene," Mickey said.

"Oh, you poor thing. You look like you've been through hell," Dalrene said, taking a shawl off her back and wrapping it around Gordon.

"I reckon that's because he has. Janet's boy."

Dalrene turned away for a moment and Gordon caught a flash of pain or maybe regret in her face. "We're very sorry with what's happened to your mom," she said, putting her hand over her heart. "But you've come to the right place. You're among friends. Please, take a seat. You need a hot meal and a cup of tea to start." She gestured to a pile of rocks pushed together that he presumed was the eating area.

"Thanks," Gordon murmured.

For better or worse, he'd found what his mom had sent him looking for. He hadn't known what to expect, but it certainly wasn't this. Were these people all Faithless? They looked the part, but they seemed too organized. Was this a professional gang? Either way, they were hospitable, and no matter how uneasy he felt, he was grateful for that. At the very least, he was happy to be around people. They could distract him from his thoughts.

Gordon sat and Mickey brought him a plate of food. The protein drink was slimy, surely well past expiry, and the chunks of soy in his rice were so hard he had to be careful not to crack his teeth on them. He was hungry enough not to care, but he did wish he had some of that dried basil. He was going to miss his mom's cooking.

Beside them, a battery-powered generator hummed through the eating sounds. It powered an air recycler and a few crappy lamps. That was okay. Gordon was thankful the cave was dimly lit, so he didn't have to see what he was putting in his mouth.

"Your mom told me you were a good student," Mickey said.

"How did you know her? Was she here?" Gordon asked.

"She was on our team," Dalrene said. "She was a good soldier. A fighter for the cause."

"A fighter?" Gordon's voice cracked. His mom was a troublemaker, sure, but a fighter?

"And a good one!" Dalrene said.

"The bots. They just took her! There was nothing I could do!"

Dalrene drew a sharp breath in and looked at him with pain on her face. "Gordon, sweetheart. I have some bad news. We've confirmed that your mom died in a prison hole. The Foreman has taken another life." She paused, and her eyes watered. "I'm sorry."

Gordon felt the pit of his stomach drop out. In the back of his mind, he'd known it to be true. His mom wasn't coming back. Just like his dad. Just like his aunt Tess.

But hearing it out loud made it real. How had he been so stupid? How had he allowed himself to hold out hope that maybe this time would be different? People left him and they never came back. And now it happened to his mom too, the one who promised it wouldn't.

Gordon didn't know how long he sat there, watching his tears splatter on the ground.

He knew Dalrene and Mickey were beside him, but they didn't say anything. He refused a cup of dark liquid. She rubbed his back, but he just felt numb.

"Just one more day. Then she could've retired from that life. It's so stupid," he sputtered.

"Your mom was a lieutenant in my army. There was trouble on a mission that I personally ran with her, and for that I am sorry. But it wasn't stupid. It was noble," Dalrene said.

Gordon stared at the wall, his eyes unblinking and his head swimming. His mom had been a lieutenant? He truly had not known her. Why did she keep this part of her life from him? Had she lied? Should he be angry? He had so many questions, but none came out of his mouth.

"What did you study in school?" Mickey eventually asked, breaking the silence.

"Explosives. I was gonna work in the mines. I was gonna get us on the premium rations." Gordon's tears flowed with renewed force, dropping into his half-eaten bowl of too-dry rice. His mom was gone, and nothing could bring her back. And now Gordon was sitting in a dirty cave with a bunch of strangers.

Mickey put his arm around Gordon. "We've lost people too, kid. Our daughter, Tess. You might've known her as your mom's pal."

"Tess. Aunt Tess?" Gordon's mind short circuited as he realized he was talking to his aunt's parents.

"That's right," Dalrene said.

"I miss her like hell," Mickey continued, sucking his teeth. "It doesn't get easier. In a way, it gets harder because the guilt racks up. It multiplies with every day you outlive them. It can take over if you're not careful, but that's why we have each other. We're here for you, and your mom would be happy you found us."

"We think a bot mixed up its doses and she received a lethal amount of sedative. She passed peacefully. It was a painless death," Dalrene said.

Gordon stared at the ground. It was all so senseless. A computer program made a mistake. And now his mom was gone forever. Even if the Foreman had arrested her for the wrong reason in the first place, or if she would've been found innocent in trial, it didn't matter. Nothing could bring her back.

"We'll have a funeral ceremony for her tonight," Dalrene said softly. "For now, you should get some rest, Gordon. It's been a long day for you." She wrapped a shawl around him.

"This'll help you sleep," Mickey said, shoving a metal flask with a red number one engraving into his chest.

This time, Gordon accepted it. All he wanted was for his nightmare to end.

Somehow the liquor tasted even worse than the food. It burned from the moment it touched his lips to when it settled in his stomach. Still, he went for a second and third swig before heading to a makeshift bed in one of the smaller adjacent rooms. It was no more than empty ration boxes piled on top of each other and a dirty towel for a blanket, but at least he was safe for the moment.

Gordon ached with emptiness and loss in a deep, all-encompassing way he hadn't since his dad died. He tossed and turned until he forced himself to notice the competing sounds of the grotto. Air recycler models so old he didn't recognize them whirred and clanked. Condensation dripped from the ceiling to the ground, keeping a steady beat. Unfamiliar voices echoed off the walls, arguing about things Gordon couldn't discern. Dalrene's shawl wasn't much of a pillow.

He didn't remember falling asleep.

#

Gordon woke up wheezing for air and stood quickly. His vision caved in, disappearing at the edges. Confused, he keeled over, down on all fours on his ration-box bed, and tried to take deep breaths. Through his foggy thoughts he wondered if he was getting carbon monoxide or radon poisoning. He knew there was less oxygen deep underground, but he didn't know it was that much less.

When he stopped gasping, Mickey stood over him with a bottle. Gordon took a drink and spit it out immediately, spraying it over the ground. "I thought that was water!"

"Sometimes I forget what it's like for people who don't live this deep," Mickey said, taking a seat beside Gordon. "It's unnatural, not what humans were meant for. Hell, the whole outpost—the whole planet—is unnatural if you think about it. Here," Mickey said, handing him a canteen. "This one's water, I promise."

Gordon took a sip, cautiously testing the liquid. He had the sense that Mickey was the kind of person that wouldn't drink anything unless it was cut with alcohol. His heart rate slowly returned to normal, and for that he was glad.

"C'mon kid, let's get front-row seats," Mickey said. He jumped to his feet and exited the room.

"What's going on?" Gordon asked as he followed him through the web of people that had gathered in the main cave.

A man with no hair and no teeth grabbed Gordon's shoulder, then shook his hand. "Sorry for your loss, son."

"Thanks," Gordon managed to say. In the residential area, no-one cared about him or his mom. It was them against the world. This was different, and he didn't know what to make of it.

Mickey pulled him to the front of the room, and Dalrene walked out on the stage, a meter or so above the crowd. She wore a new shawl and it fluttered behind her beautifully. Gordon had never seen so many rich blues and yellows blending into one another. She must've made and dyed it herself, he thought. Standard-issue clothes didn't have half that amount of color. It was only when she got closer that Gordon realized the red number ones infused in the pattern.

"My friends, today it was with great sadness that we mourn the passing of Janet Onyango, a true patriot, and Gordon's mother," Dalrene said, pointing to him. "An inspiration to all of us, she was devoted to our cause. But we will not take this assault sitting down!" She shook her head and raised her fist. "An attack on one of us is an attack on all of us. We will double our efforts to expose what is truly happening on this planet!"

Around him, the group erupted into cheers and Gordon's head spun. He'd never been to a funeral that involved cheering before. The quiet, somber eulogy he yearned for may not have been on offer, but these were his mom's people, so he'd hear them out. His hair stood on end as he looked up at Dalrene's snarling face. Her eyes were wild, her skin glowing. She didn't look like a kind, old grandmother anymore.

Gordon didn't know what was going on, but it had his interest. Did all these people know his mom? Did some of them? Part of him was sickened that Dalrene would use his mom's death to incite an appetite for violence. But he understood the anger. It wasn't wrong.

"Janet's death will not be in vain!" Dalrene shouted, and the crowd fell silent again. "But we must work to make it so. We must work to expose the truth. Earth is dead! We have toiled away in the mines for generations ... for nothing! All to appease an out-of-control AI that hoards our rations and kills us when it's convenient!"

The crowd jeered at the mention of the Foreman. Gordon noticed Mickey had retreated from the crowd and was now leaning against the wall, watching him. The old man quickly looked away and took another swig from his flask.

Gordon couldn't get a thought out of his head. Earth was dead? Like, completely dead?

"We are told we are re-building a once-great planet, the flagship of our species," Dalrene continued. "But have you ever heard any communications from the blue planet? Have you even ever met anyone who has claimed to talk to Earth representatives?"

"No!" the crowd hollered.

"Who are we really sending our resources to? Are our minerals even leaving this planet? What if the Blues forgot we're even out here? What if there are no Blues left?" Dalrene asked the last question at nearly a whisper before raising her voice again. "How long will we toil in the mines without sunlight? How long will we break our backs? Our children's backs? With no idea if Earth is still out there!"

Gordon looked around. One woman held a lit torch, which seemed like a poor idea in a cave with limited fresh air. The fire danced, casting light and shadow on her crazed eyes. The vein in her neck was throbbing, and she looked like she was ready to pounce when and where Dalrene told her to.

"Yes, my friends. The Dead Earth Hypothesis is true! We're living in misery for no damn reason!" Dalrene's nostrils flared, and she showered the front row of the crowd with spittle.

The woman with the torch erupted, lifting the fire high in the air and yelling, "Death to the Foreman!" at the top of her lungs. The rest of the cave followed suit, repeating the chant.

Gordon had never heard such taboo ideas espoused openly, let alone shouted in unison by so many. He joined in with a small cheer. It was good to participate. Terrifying, but liberating. It felt right. Steadily, his cheer grew louder and louder until it turned into a scream that sprang from the pit of his stomach up through his chest. Sweat dripped off him. He screamed for what seemed like minutes. It was a visceral release, of what, Gordon didn't even know anymore, but it was exactly what he needed.

Dalrene paced on the stage for a few moments, running her hands over her shawl. She waited for the crowd to quiet before she continued. "The Dead Earth Hypothesis. That's what Janet believed. And that's why the Foreman killed her," she said solemnly.

"Rest in power!" someone yelled from the back.

Gordon twisted the ideas around in his mind. Was what Dalrene was saying even possible? He always took his mom's musings as escape fantasies. Something she daydreamed about when she was having a bad day. This was many steps further. This was real.

Was this a religion, like he learned about in history class? Gordon didn't think religions were supposed to make this much sense. Everyone here seemed to have known his mom, or at least knew of her. Why didn't she tell him about this energy, this insanity? She must've been hiding it, to try to keep him safe.

A shiver went down Gordon's spine. His mom had been part of something big. She had truly fought for something, and not just for their daily bread. Hell, she was a lieutenant! He was still grappling with what that meant, but he felt himself understanding his mom more than he ever. They wanted the same thing, a better life for each other. But where Gordon wanted to work within the rules, his mom wanted to rake the Foreman over the coals and create a new society. He didn't know if he agreed with it, especially when he'd been so close to rising to the top of the existing social structure, but he respected it. He wished he could hug his mom and tell her he got it, and that he was sorry. The resentment he'd held for her Faithlessnes hadn't been fair.

"For the First Olympians!" Dalrene yelled, and the crowd repeated her words.

She continued her speech, but Gordon didn't hear the words. He only felt the energy. He was struck by the realization that he'd found exactly what his mom told him to search for. He smiled as he imagined her in this cave yelling and hollering with Dalrene's First Olympians. She'd have fit right in.

Chapter Six: Gordon

The mourners circled around a fire pit in the middle of the grotto. They were calmer now. A low flame, built on what Gordon guessed was flax fibers and waxes from the farm dome mixed with an iron composite from the mines, offered a bit of warmth. He sat in the first row, closest to the fire, as a woman named Ionne with long dreads was telling a story about his mom.

"I suggested we kick the guy's ass and take the computers and his credits to boot, but Janet said he was part of the Red Dragon Gang, so that wouldn't fly. Somehow, we had to come up with ten megawatts of battery capacity to do this trade. That's why we were in that warehouse, just the two of us, in the middle of the night. When that bot came out of nowhere and locked the door, I was just crushed, you know? It was asking me all sorts of things—trying to scan me, do we have authorization, what are we doing, how did we get in. And Janet, I swear, sneaks behind this bot while it's giving me shit. It's in the middle of telling me more bots are on their way, and she rips-with her bare hands—rips the bot's battery right out of its casing!" Ionne held her fist in the air and the crowd gasped. "She tosses it to me and says, 'Found one!'"

Everyone laughed and Gordon smiled. He missed his mom's humor.

"When the reinforcements came, we got split up trying to get out of there. Janet could've left me for dead, like a lot of Faithless would, but she didn't. She set off some fireworks on the street, drawing bots away, and then cut a hole in a chain link fence where I was jammed. I never found out where she got those bolt cutters," Ionne said, shaking her head in disbelief. "She was always so resourceful, and kind. A true friend."

"Here, here!" People raised their glasses.

Gordon wiped a tear from his eye. His mom was a rascal, but she used her cunning for good. He didn't have that same ability to think on his feet, but he vowed to care for people the same way his mom had.

He had misunderstood her. He didn't think she was capable of being a part of anything like this, and for that he felt bad. But how could he have known? She didn't share anything with him, and there was no way he could've guessed she was up to anything other than the normal scams and plots. His emotions were messy, and he wished more than anything that he could have just one conversation with her.

Gordon listened to more stories about his mom and laughed at the jokes he understood. He wasn't comfortable enough to initiate conversation, but being among friendly people was a welcome distraction. For the first time, he was happy with his decision to enter the caves.

Everyone paid attention when Mickey pulled out a guitar. It looked like real wood, but Gordon knew that wasn't possible. Besides, he didn't think wood could have a glossy-looking finish. He forgot about that when the sound bounced hauntingly off the cave walls, filling the room, and enthralling him. It was the richest, most genuine-sounding instrument he'd ever heard. Mickey's gruff voice cut through the thin air.

"For the days of home, for the stars unknown,
How often I repine,
For the days of home when it was all unknown,
For the time before the mines

My muckers they all loved me well, a good old-fashioned crew,
Though a few hard cases I will recall, loose a couple screws,
Tough as nails, they never failed, except to make the sun shine,
All unjust, we ate nothing but dust, and sang of times before the mines."

The song went on for minutes, twisting and turning delightfully. It was funny, but Mickey sang with his eyes closed and his face full of pain. His voice crooned and didn't crack until the very end. He finished to solemn applause, and no one spoke.

"I've never heard that song before," Gordon said.

"Wouldn't be much of a banned song if you had, would it?" Mickey grinned toothily.

The crowd chuckled.

"Where's it from?"

"It's American. Or at least inspired by an old American folk song."

"There were no American settlers at this outpost," Gordon said, surprised.

"That's right. But their culture made it here somehow," Mickey said with a shrug.

Gordon nodded. He'd studied enough history to know the pervasiveness of American culture. The song repeated in his head. It was a nice distraction from the screams of his mom desperately begging for the bots to let her go.

"You know any Faithless screech songs? Those were my mom's favorite."

"Sorry, kid. Not my cup of meat."

Gordon laughed at Mickey's strange expression and wondered if it was American as well. There was more to the dour old man than first appeared.

Mickey took a swig from his flask and went back to picking notes on his guitar. He spoke to groups of people at once, telling stories and laughing in between the delightful musical phrases that sprang from his strings. He played in paragraphs, completing a musical thought, then following it up with a spoken one.

After a regrettably large drink of liquor, Gordon looked up to see Dalrene had taken the spot beside him. She'd been the focal point of the group when she made her eulogy, but amid the alcohol, laughter, and music, he almost forgot she was the leader. She'd lingered out of sight, deep in private conversations, the occasional swear word cutting through the crowd noise to Gordon's ears.

Now, she wanted a word with him. Dalrene stretched her legs to the fire and looked Gordon in the eyes. She wore a smile that couldn't hide her fatigue, or perhaps didn't try to. He could see a resemblance to Aunt Tess in her dreads and sunken cheeks, but that was the extent of it. His aunt must've gotten her unabashed curiosity and her contagious, weightless laugh from Mickey. Steam rose from Dalrene's hot cup of tea, and an herbal smell that Gordon couldn't place filled his nose.

"Your mom had real friends here," Dalrene said. "Don't blame her for not telling you more about us. She did what she thought was best to protect you."

"I know," Gordon said. He wanted to talk about anything else. "The red number one—you made it?"

"When I say this is the symbol of the First Olympians, I don't just mean my group. The first settlers used it on everything from their spaceships to their uniforms." Dalrene held her shawl toward the fire so Gordon could see the detail.

"Wow, really?" They didn't teach that in school.

"Yes, we're reclaiming the name and the Symbol, and we're fighting against the Foreman. We're taking back our right to self-governance," Dalrene said, raising her voice. The group of young men sitting beside her hooted and hollered, egging her on. "This outpost was meant to be one of hope, not of oppression and cruelty. It wasn't in the original plan, and we can work to divorce it from our future." She looked him in the eyes. "I hope you'll help us, Gordon."

"It?" The word caught him off guard.

"The Foreman's not a person," Dalrene scoffed. "It doesn't have feelings. We don't need to aid its attempts to appear more human."

Gordon thought for a moment. All his life, the Foreman had been an immutable force. His dad had wanted to work with him—it—for the sake of their family. His mom walked the thin line of what the Foreman permitted and what it didn't. But a reality entirely without it? It was inconceivable.

Before he could answer Dalrene, there was an unmistakeable, high-pitched bang that could only come from an explosive detonation that was much too close. The ground shook and it penetrated every part of his body. He looked over to where Dalrene was already running and saw a cave wall collapse. A rock larger than his fist flew by his face and Gordon nearly crapped his pants. He curled up, making himself small, and protected his face.

People ran back and forth in front. He lay by the fire, petrified. There was a rumble, and he swore it was bouncing him up and down. This was it. The Foreman had figured out their secret plans and was here to quash them. Gordon expected a horde of bots to roll in at any moment. It was going to end before it had even begun.

Dust from the explosion plumed up Gordon's nose and he held his ringing ears. If he died, he would regret that he didn't know about the First Olympians earlier, and that he hadn't treated his mom with enough respect.

When the shaking stopped, he heard muffled screams. Everyone crowded around the rubble that used to be the entrance to a side cave, and Gordon squeezed his way through to get a view. Mickey and others were throwing rocks away at a frantic pace, trying to free a man whose lower body was pinned underneath.

"You're in shock. Take deep breaths. We're here for you DeMar," Dalrene said, holding his hand and wrapping him in her shawl. "Talk to me, what happened?"

"I was moving the bombs to an isolated room, where other people wouldn't be around." DeMar said with a grunt. His pupils were wide, but his tone was surprisingly calm. "I was careful, really. That one crate must've been more unstable than the rest—"

His leg was freed from the rubble, and he let out a deep, penetrating howl as blood spurt into the air. Two men picked DeMar up by his armpits and moved him to flat ground. His right leg was twisted grotesquely one-hundred and eighty degrees around from where it should have been, and a bone stuck up into the air.

Ionne, the one who told the story about his mom stealing the battery from a live bot, kneeled on the ground and hugged his head. "Help him!" she begged through her sobs.

"Get me a tourniquet! Something!" A portly man with a mustache took charge.

DeMar's brutal screams echoed off the walls. The pungent scent of blood mixed with the familiar, bitter, toxic stench of ammonium nitrate filled the grotto. Gordon would've stayed there, staring, forever, if Dalrene hadn't yanked his arm.

"Come with me," she said, leading him into one of the other adjacent caves. "I need to know what I'm dealing with."

The room was full of gear and smelt like grease and soldering iron. A pile of crowbars and machetes lay in the middle. Handhelds and other electronic scraps scattered the ground by a makeshift workshop area. The neatest section was a square of white, hard-plastic boxes stacked against the far wall.

The bombs.

Gordon kneeled, inspecting the wiring work on one of the packages. The detonator was familiar, the same as he used in class, but the wiring was shoddy and hard to follow, with a lack of consistency. He unplugged it, so it would be safer to pick up, and noticed the metal seal was corroded. One package weighed about five kilograms, lighter than any explosive used in the mines, and its weight shifted side-to-side as he held it.

"This is bootlegged. Likely made with fertilizer from the farm domes, a detonator from mining ops, and wiring from somewhere else. Where did you get these?" Gordon had never seen anything like it, but he'd read about similar concoctions.

"Are they stable?"

He turned the palms of his hands up and gestured back toward DeMar. It seemed like that question had already answered itself.

"I mean, do I need to evacuate everyone right now? Or are they stable enough?" Dalrene asked.

Before Gordon could answer, Ionne burst into the room. Her beige shirt was now dark red, covered in blood.

"What happened?" Ionne's eyes were intense. She looked much fiercer than at the campfire.

"We're just trying to figure that out."

Ionne raised her voice, "You gave my husband faulty bombs?"

"I understand you're upset. You're in shock. We all—"

"You need to make this right."

"I'm going to."

The two women stared at each other for what felt like a long time. Then, Ionne turned to Gordon and softened her expression, like she was noticing his presence for the first time.

"Has she told you how exactly your mom died? Dalrene knows the details. I know she does."

"Hey! You're out of line."

"We deserve to know what happened," Ionne huffed and turned away.

Gordon's head spun. What was she talking about? He didn't know if he could handle learning anymore about his mom's death.

"So, Gordon?"

He met Dalrene's eyes.

"Don't worry about her," Dalrene said. "She's on-edge. Understandably."

"I don't usually deal with this kind of stuff." Gordon hemmed and hawed, bringing his mind back to the task at hand. DeMar said the explosion happened during careful transportation, but his definition of that may've been different than Gordon's. Either way, if the seal separating the active ingredients on one bomb failed, the others could too.

"It's like DeMar said, they're all unstable, but some are ready to pop. We should move the good ones and cordon off the bad ones. No one should be back here."

Dalrene nodded. "Gordon, I need you to be my blaster. I want you in charge of these explosives."

Before Gordon could respond, the stocky medic who Gordon learned was named Rodriguez, stormed in. His shirt too was soaked in sweat and blood.

"Dalrene, we need a prosthetic," Rodriguez said.

"We don't have any?" Dalrene seemed surprised.

"No. We're stocked up on battlefield supplies. Things that can help immediately, not that take weeks to grow. Unless you want me to make him a non-tissue prosthetic?" Rodriguez raised an eyebrow.

Dalrene pushed out her lower lip. "I'll get a leg. Whatever you need, I'll get it."

Gordon's mouth hung open. Medical supplies, let alone self-forming tissue, were scarce. If she could get some fast enough for DeMar, he'd be impressed.

Chapter Seven: Dalrene

She was going to need a new shawl. Gordon was using one as a blanket, and another was wrapped around DeMar. Dalrene picked one off the wall of the bedroom cave she shared with Mickey and held it up to the light. It was gray and black. Perfect for blending in.

"Where are you going?" Mickey asked from the entrance.

"Medical supplies. DeMar needs a new leg," Dalrene said, still facing the wall.

"Don't you think someone else should go? It's too risky to do yourself."

"Javier is on shift. I'm the only one who can do it fast and right. And I doubt the Foreman has connected me to Janet. I turned the cameras off at the rendezvous point, and my biometrics are good. Ionne is pissed and won't leave DeMar's side. So, it has to be me, unless you—" Dalrene caught herself before completing the sentence and turned to see her husband.

Mickey cast his eyes to the ground and his shoulders slumped. He hadn't been to the residential level in a long time, since his time imprisoned, and he still had nightmares about going back. He would have to one day soon, but not until the war was fully underway.

"There has to be another way," he grumbled.

"Sorry," Dalrene said, embracing him. "You're right. I could send someone else. But honestly, helping DeMar is secondary. I need to get Javier and Ellie down here now. It's time."

"Wouldn't that be something?" Mickey whistled and shook his head in disbelief at the prospect of seeing his granddaughter. "Can we talk? There's a lot to catch-up on."

"Walk with me," Dalrene said, tightening her boots. "I need to go. Every minute counts."

Mickey grabbed a dusty bottle from a shelf and filled his flask.

Dalrene put her backpack on, grabbed another bag to fill with medical supplies, and the two headed out the door. She hadn't slept more than a night in the grotto, and she was already headed back to the residential level. She couldn't believe it, but being a leader meant making sacrifices.

They walked the caves like they'd done many times before. The fastest way to the residential area was a narrow tunnel with smooth sides. Mickey led, Dalrene watching his ponytail bob up and down. A thickness hung in the air. The grainy, stinging scent of whiskey drafted back to Dalrene. They were both tired and the rebellion had barely even started.

"You wanted to talk."

"Didn't know where to start," Mickey said. "How about with Big Titus?"

"What about him?"

"Do you know what Londi did to him?"

"No, and I don't care to."

Mickey turned to face his wife. "Dalrene! He was my guy. He trusted me. More importantly, he has a protection agreement with the Red Dragon Gang, and you know how they are—eye for an eye. They won't let this stand!"

"Most gang members support our cause, even if they don't know my face. And they'll be irrelevant soon anyway. We have more important things to worry about," Dalrene said.

"How can you say that? We're going to hell in a bucket! Dalrene, I love you, but you overstepped." Mickey said.

"You're thinking too small," she said. "When we win, there won't be a black market. There won't be robots doing security checks, and there won't be a Foreman to hide from. Big Titus is irrelevant. He's the opposite of big! He's a speck! In seventy-two hours, I'll be the leader of the outpost, and he'll fall in line. Or we'll all be dead."

Mickey made a sour face, took a chug from his flask, and then made an even more sour face. "Cheers to that."

"Keep walking," Dalrene said, prodding him on.

The truth was that Mickey had never been the same after she saved him from that prison hole. Part of him never left solitary confinement. He still had long hair, and the same gray beard. But behind every toothy smile, she could see pain in his eyes. She could hear it each time he gasped awake from a nightmare, covered in sweat, and reached for his flask.

He blamed himself for Tess's death. The Foreman would've killed her anyway, even without his drugged-up testimony. But that didn't matter. To him, he betrayed his daughter.

She should've seen his distress sooner. She should've been there for him more often. But as much as she wanted to, she didn't have time to be his therapist. Dalrene was busy recruiting an army and starting a rebellion. All her energy went into finding the truth and building on what Tess had started. There would be time to make good on regrets later, after they won.

"And Janet?" Mickey asked from ahead.

Dalrene felt like she'd been punched in the gut. She closed her eyes and remembered the pain on Janet's face when her oxygen ran out. It was a pure, instinctual desire to live mixed with the futility and hopelessness that only a human could have.

"Are you gonna make me say it out loud?" her voice was stuck in her throat.

"What happened? It was supposed to be a simple job."

"It ... it didn't work out," Dalrene stammered. "I had to cut our losses to protect us."

Mickey sucked his teeth but kept walking. "Janet was a sweetheart. Hell, she was still a kid herself. And then you politicized her death? Used her. In front of her own son, for crying out loud?"

Dalrene bowed over and caught herself on a lava pillar. Her stomach churned as Mickey's ponytail disappeared around a corner. He was still talking, but she couldn't make out the words.

The look of absolute helplessness on Gordon's face when she told him his mom was dead played over in her mind. She'd seen the devastation losing a parent too early caused in Ellie. Now, Gordon would have to suffer it too, for a second time. He was an orphan, and it was because of her.

She was still staring at the ground, trying not to wretch, when she heard Mickey's footsteps running back to her. She covered her face with her shawl and focused on her breathing.

Mickey placed his hand on her upper back. They kneeled on the cold cave ground for a few minutes without saying a word.

"You know I trust you one-hundred percent," Mickey said, his voice now low and close.

"I had to do it," Dalrene replied.

"I believe you."

"I'll make it right."

"Okay."

When Dalrene caught her breath, they continued their ascent. The path was wider now, and they walked side-by-side. The graffiti grew plentiful and fresher, the air recyclers quieter, and the lights brighter, until they arrived at one of the many entrances to the residential level. This was as far as Mickey would go, at least until the revolution was truly upon them.

A pair of bots whizzed by, and Dalrene and Mickey pressed against the wall and held their breaths. Their reaction was equal parts instinct, paranoia, and best practices that came with running an underground rebellion. The flashing lights of the storefronts flickered just beyond. A siren in the distance wailed.

"Lots of patrols. Looks like Londi was right about the level-three lockdown," Dalrene said.

"You and I are the cockroaches of this place," Mickey said. "Unkillable, for better or worse. But I'm afraid we can't say the same about Javier and Ellie. Keep them safe." He pulled her in tight.

"I'll see you soon," Dalrene said. *Cockroaches of the outpost* rung in her head. It was a miracle the two of them were still standing freely after all these years. Either they were invincible, or their luck was bound to run out soon. She shivered, despite Mickey's body warmth. He let go, and she headed into the sirens and lights questioning her sanity.

\#

Her target was the medical center where Javier worked. Supplies were under heavy surveillance, but her son-in-law could retrieve what she needed, if she could convince him to.

Javier had supported Tess in her investigations but disavowed her after her death. It was the only way he could keep custody of Ellie, and he made her his top priority. It was the right thing to do, but it left Dalrene with a sour taste in her mouth. Moving on was one thing, but sometimes it felt like Javier was actively trying to forget her.

She hadn't planned to be back so soon. Dalrene moved quickly through the dirt streets, her shawl wrapped around her face like a headscarf, and avoided eye contact with both robots and humans. She quieted the little voice in her head that said this was going to be a mistake.

A level-three lockdown was no joke. Bots patrolled the streets and massed together at critical security points, including the processing nodes. The Mission Control Center, or MCC, would have dozens, if not hundreds, of bots swarming around it. Curfews were enforced at seemingly random hours, and citizens kept their heads down, careful not to draw any unwanted attention. People were only allowed to leave their holes for specific purposes, such as going to work or a medical center.

There had been a level-five lockdown once, when Dalrene was a kid. There had been some sort of unexplained, existential threat, and humans were required to report to the "quarantine zone." Dalrene had vivid memories of hugging her mother's leg while deep underground, huddled together with hundreds of other people in a dark mineshaft. She tried not to think about it often.

She posted up in an alleyway across the street from the medical center. The stench of rotting fruit made her gag. Non-essential services, like garbage removal, were discontinued during a lockdown. She heard a baby crying from one of the nearby holes. A bunch of teenagers spilled out from an alleyway, startling her. It looked like they were playing a game, maybe hide and seek.

Dalrene smiled at the act of civil disobedience. Without a reason to be outside, like travelling to work or the medical center, they were risking some serious baton beatings.

She took a breath and remembered Ellie.

She needed to focus to pull this off. It was crucial she save DeMar. For one, because he was a platoon leader on Londi's crew, and it was necessary for morale. Fielding an army would be difficult if soldiers didn't believe they had access to medical care. She was asking people to fight for her, and she needed spirits to be high.

More importantly, she needed to get Javier and Ellie out of harm's way. Dalrene's identity as the leader of the First Olympians wouldn't be secret forever, and the Foreman would seek reprisals on her family once it knew. Beating the Foreman but losing Ellie wouldn't be a victory, and she couldn't let it happen. If she couldn't extract them, it would add to the pressure. She'd have to deliver a one-time fatal blow to the Foreman and deprive it of a chance to respond.

Dalrene pressed three pills into her palm and swallowed. There was a small chance the Foreman could identify her as Janet's accomplice, but even that risk was too high for comfort. The only way to get medical attention without submitting to a scan was to seriously need it, and the pills would ensure that.

When her stomach started grumbling, Dalrene instinctively pulled up her shawl and entered the medical center. She was greeted by a large waiting room full of miserable-looking people and the whir of medical robots rolling around.

A young boy covered in soot and burns from head to toe was rushed past her on a gurney, through triage, and down a hallway. Human nurses ran to catch up to their robotic counterparts. His screams haunted the waiting room, and no one made another sound until a pregnant Faithless woman coughed into her hand. She looked so thin her clothes were falling off her frame. Dalrene wanted to hug her, and then break every bot in the building. This was why she was fighting.

She sat, and an inspector bot rolled up with a thumbprint pad extended. She closed her eyes and jammed her thumb in. The bot played a cheerful working tune, signifying that it was still processing. Dalrene couldn't tell if it was taking a long time or if it just felt like making her wait. She exhaled. Her fake prints worked at the Pickaxe café, and there was no reason for them to fail now.

While the identification was still in progress, a medical bot clamped its appendages around her arm. It ran some diagnostics, starting with her blood pressure. Dalrene tensed, and reassured herself that there were no lethal parts in the medical bot. Although, that wasn't entirely true. The bot had enough tranquilizers and steroids to kill her many times over if it decided to, or simply malfunctioned. The good news was it didn't have any bullets, grenades, or knives. It was a small comfort. If the inspector bot pegged her as Janet's accomplice, it might give the medical bot a signal to kill her right then and there, entirely in silence.

"Thumbprint not found in database. Facial recognition scan recommended. Please remove all head coverings," the inspector bot said.

Dalrene stood. "I don't feel well," were the words she tried to get out before she emptied her stomach bile all over the inspector's head, covering its cameras. Clutching her stomach, she sat back in her chair and hid her smile with a groan.

The inspector bot spun in place and tried to wipe its sensors clean. "Processing error," it beeped confusedly. But it didn't protest when the medical bot recommended that she get seen by a human nurse. The wheels on Dalrene's chair sprang to life and whisked her down a hallway.

She dodged a bullet, at least for now.

Her chair stopped in a private, sterile room with white walls, and the medical bot on her arm unplugged itself and wheeled away. The door clasped shut behind the robot, and a sense of dread came over Dalrene. It reminded her of Janet's small prison hole, except it had a medical bed instead of a table. It was one of the brightest rooms in the outpost, but the light was still a crappy white with a blue tint. The bitter smell of antiseptic cleaners filled her nose, and she clutched her bag with the computer equipment in it. With just a few minutes of notice, she could open any locked door in the building.

The first human to attend to her was a young woman nurse with an upturned nose and an oily slick of hair tied on top of her head.

"Please send Javier. He's seen me before," Dalrene asked as sweetly as she could.

"He's busy with other patients, but I promise we'll take care of you," the nurse said, flatly.

Dalrene grabbed the nurse's wrist and made eye-contact. "Please. I'm his mother-in-law."

The nurse sighed before shaking her head. "Fine," she said, and left the room.

A storage cabinet lined one wall. With the pills wearing off, Dalrene pulled on a cabinet labelled "splints," but it didn't budge. Not only were the medical supplies locked, but they were locked with physical bolts, and her computer couldn't help her. She grimaced. That would've been too easy.

She was sitting in her chair when she heard Javier's footsteps rushing down the hall.

"Oh my god. Are you okay?" he said, rushing in to give her a hug.

"Do you have the key for these cabinets?" Dalrene asked, motioning with her head.

"Yeah. Wait, what?"

"I'm not sick. I'm here because I need your help."

"This is another one of your ruses? Dalrene! I told you, I'm done with that," Javier said, throwing up his hands. "I can't put my kid at risk."

"Lower your voice and listen carefully. I have a man bleeding out and I have a specific list of things that I need. You're going to help me get those things," Dalrene said, nodding her head as if it would make Javier more agreeable.

"The doc bot will come by any minute. This is insane. Think of your granddaughter!

Do you want her to lose her father too?"

Dalrene bit her lip. "I am thinking of her," she said through gritted teeth. "I'm trying to save this forsaken hell-hole. Everything Mickey and I do is so that she can have a better future."

"If either of you actually feel like helping, the one thing you could do is show up. You know, be there for her!" Javier said. "Ellie needs proper clothes. School supplies. Protein. And people to read to her at night and tuck her into bed and tell her they care. That's what she needs. She doesn't need a revolution. You know, she doesn't even remember Mickey anymore." He turned and put his hand on the door handle.

"Javier," Dalrene said. "I have a man bleeding out. Didn't you take that oath? The Hippocratic? I wouldn't turn to you if it wasn't an emergency."

His hand fell from the door. He sighed nearly as loud as he'd been yelling. "Let me see the list," Javier said.

Dalrene didn't like playing to Javier's sense of duty, but she had to get the job done. "The leg is the most important. The rest is for good measure," she said.

"Okay," Javier said. "Significant damage below the knee. Tourniquet. Painkillers. Six packs of Type-O blood. Bandages. Surgical tools. Medical dressing. Tissue re-gen paste. Self-forming prosthetic leg with nano-repair bots. More painkillers. Really?"

"Yes."

Javier laughed in disbelief. "Anything else you'd like while you're at it? A billion credits and a time machine?"

Dalrene hesitated. She'd already made him uncomfortable, but she had to push further. It was the only way to protect Ellie. "Don't go home tonight. It's time. I'll give you the meeting location and both of you can—"

"We're not going anywhere! We've been over this!" Javier snarled at her.

Dalrene had half a mind to jab Javier with a needle full of sedatives and drag him down to the grotto. It would work if she were stronger. She could try to just take Ellie, but the young girl loved her dad, and she didn't want to break that trust. So, she put up her hands and relented. For now.

"Let's just get the supplies and then we can talk more about it," she said.

"Dalrene, this is a lot of stuff. I can help you, but not all of it is here."

"I'm listening."

"The prosthetics are kept in a different area. Take what you need from these cabinets, and I'll see if I can sneak you a leg." Javier took a key from his pocket, cracked open the supplies, and they loaded a bunch of blood packs and bandages into Dalrene's bag.

She had a blueprint of the facility on her handheld. "The prosthetics are at the end of the hall, in the main storage room?"

"Yeah. I'll be right back," Javier said.

"I'm coming with you. There's an emergency exit door right beside it. I'll take it and be out of your hair."

"It'll be locked."

"No, it won't be."

The hallway was long and narrow, and Dalrene covered her head with her shawl. Human nurses walked by, exhausted and despondent near the end of their sixteen-hour shifts, and she avoided eye contact. Inspector bots, medical bots, and doctor bots wheeled by, and she avoided their cameras. Screens hung from the ceiling, warning about medication shortages and overtime requirements.

Javier hummed nervously as they approached the end of the hallway. Dalrene regretted that she had to put him in this position, but she wished he had the gumption to really help her. He was scared and subservient to the Foreman, lacking the fight that Tess always had. Dalrene had been invigorated by her murder, but Javier had withered.

Javier opened the storage room and the two of them slipped inside. He led Dalrene past long rows of half-empty shelves.

"There are no pre-made legs left, but there's self-forming gel. If you have a good doctor, he'll know what to do with it," Javier said.

"Thanks," Dalrene said, bending to pick up the heavy box.

A flash of light came from the wall behind it. It blinded Dalrene, and she stumbled to her feet. It took her a moment to realize what happened.

"It just took a picture of me!"

Javier rubbed the back of his neck, looking flustered and confused.

"It's going to run facial recognition!"

"It's okay, I'll sign the requisition forms and say that you needed all of these supplies."

"Shit!" Dalrene ran out of the storage room.

She held the box of gel in her arms and looked nervously up at the screens in the hallway. Javier arrived beside her, his mouth falling open.

Sure enough, within seconds, her mug was staring back at them. There was a reward for capture and a big red circle around her picture. It was the same treatment Janet got.

"Come with me Javier!" Dalrene said.

"What? This is crazy! What did you do?"

"We have to go now! Come with me. We can pick up Ellie on our way and get to safety. A war is starting, and I can protect you."

A gang of peacekeepers turned the corner of the long hallway, some twenty meters away. They stopped a group of unlucky nurses.

"Are you insane? I'd never see her again if I go with you! Get out of here!" Javier exclaimed, pushing Dalrene away. "And never talk to me again!"

The bots must've spotted her. They rumbled down the hallway, tossing people out of their way, their tasers emitting a high-pitched whine as they powered up.

"Let me go!" Dalrene yelled at Javier, trying to fake a struggle. Whatever happened, she couldn't let him look like her accomplice.

She lunged, twisted behind him, and stopped at the emergency exit. She whispered in his ear. "Zero six-hundred hours at the Pickaxe café. I'll have someone on my team pick both of you up. Now push me out of here."

Javier growled. He was all too happy to oblige her.

#

She had failed. She had failed Javier and Ellie just like she had failed Janet. They were all going to be dead soon, or worse. And she only had herself to blame.

Yet Dalrene returned to the grotto to the sound of cheering. They were impressed with her ability to get medical supplies. She forced a smile, and it even became genuine for a second. It felt good to be able to take care of the people that made sacrifices for the cause.

Ionne had a resigned, icy look on her face, but she still managed a soft, "Thank you."

"It's the least I can do," Dalrene said. She hoped that would help ease the tension between them.

"Well, I can't say I'm not impressed," Rodriguez said, holding a new scalpel up to the light. "You got what I asked for. We'll do a clean cut near the knee and then mold the gel. He won't be in fighting shape any time soon, but he'll heal."

"I need to be in the fight. Don't leave me here when you go," DeMar said, crossing his arms.

"You won't be able to walk for months. You'll need to rest." Rodriguez looked to Dalrene for support.

"We don't have that long. Get him some crutches. He can bring up the rear," she said.

Rodriguez hummed and hawed, then talked about the bruising on DeMar's abdomen and needing to keep an eye on it. He had some internal bleeding that could still be an issue. Dalrene nodded along, but there was nothing else she could do to help. She put out the immediate fire, and now she had to turn her attention to the next one.

Mickey stood by the entrance to their bedroom with a pouty face. "All the cheering. Dal, they love you. It's like you're an old American rockstar," he said with a grin.

"Are you jealous?" Dalrene leaned in for a kiss. She smelt alcohol on his breath. He always drank, but he drank more when she was on a mission. When he was worried about her.

"I'm serious," Mickey said, pulling away. "It's too much. And it's creepy."

"You can't have a revolution without a leader. Wasn't that in one of your history books?"

"Just don't let it go to your head. How'd it go?"

Dalrene hung her shawl on the wall and faced away from him. She wanted nothing more than to curl up in a ball in the bed. But there was no time for that.

"Is our new blaster ready?" she asked.

"Gordon is raw. He's angry, but obviously still working through his grief. He needs time."

"Raw is good," Dalrene said. "Strike while the iron is hot, as you always say. We've got a blaster so we should use him while our window is open. We need a distraction to draw the Foreman's forces away. And if it's big enough, we can go right for the brain node instead of the processors."

"I get it," Mickey said. "You want to execute the deletion program. But Gordon needs time to heal. To understand the fight and his place in it."

"With DeMar out of commission, he's our best blaster available." Dalrene paused. "How long after Tess's death did it take for you to fight?" she asked, putting her hands on her hips.

"Don't talk to me about Tess like that," Mickey said, shaking his head and pointing. "I didn't understand myself."

Dalrene slumped down on the bed, her back against the wall. She stared at him for a long moment. "I got ID'd stealing the prosthetic and Javier was right there. I don't know if they can tie me back to Janet. I gave him rendezvous instructions. I'll send Londi to pick them up, but ..."

Mickey craned his head and looked at the ceiling. They both knew what it meant. If Javier didn't get to safety, he'd be in trouble. He'd get hard labor if he was lucky. And if he wasn't? Dalrene didn't want to think about what might happen to him and Ellie.

"I'll do it," Mickey said.

"What?" her voice quavered. If Mickey was their blaster she'd be too sick with worry to fight.

"The explosives. I've been on the surface. I've seen the loading docks. I can do it."

"It's too dangerous," Dalrene said, finding her strength. "Gordon would have a fifty percent chance of surviving. You? You wouldn't even get out of this grotto with those unstable bombs!"

"I'll get you that distraction. That's what matters." He didn't sound drunk anymore. He was serious.

Dalrene reeled. "No. Think about me. *Think about Ellie.*"

Mickey's face soured. He let out a long, pained sigh.

"I'll wake Gordon up," he croaked, his voice hoarse. He forced the weakest smile she'd ever seen and grabbed a bottle of liquor on his way out.

"Tell Londi to come in here. It's time to marshal the troops. I'm going to execute the deletion program."

Chapter Eight: Gordon

Lying down was the worst because he could feel every ache and pain in his body. The makeshift bed of blankets and empty ration crates did a fantastic job of making it feel like he was lying directly on the hard ground. Water droplets hung from a lava pillar, then dripped to the small puddle by his feet. He sat up and picked a few small rocks out of his socks.

Being in the crowd for Dalrene's eulogy had been exhilarating, and the campfire after was emotional, illuminating, and even fun. But then DeMar's screams filled the grotto and crashed Gordon back to reality.

Now, he was alone. Every time he closed his eyes, he saw his mom frantically running around their hole before the bots knocked on the door. He heard the fear in her voice as she protested her arrest. She was always confident and calculating. But in that moment, she had been terrified. It was strange that his last memories of her were exactly the opposite of how she lived her life. He wished he'd helped her. He wished he'd stood up to the bots.

"Can't sleep?" Mickey asked from the doorway.

"Not sure I want to. Nightmares. But I don't want to be awake either," Gordon said without looking up.

"Drink?" Mickey sat at the end of the cot.

Gordon could tell by the smell that it wasn't tea and was happy to accept. He concentrated on his breathing and tried to slow his heart rate. He wanted to do origami, but his hands were shaking. He'd never be able to make a proper crease or fold.

"Will I always have bad dreams?" he asked.

"That's why I drink," Mickey said, shaking his head with amusement. "If you ever find the secret to stopping them, let me know. But they wane with time, so, gotta take the wins where I can get 'em. Once in a while I even have good dreams. Dreams about the future. No, my daughter isn't there. Sometimes, neither am I. But I do believe we have to honor the ones we've lost. Make the world a better place in their image."

Gordon closed his eyes. He wished he was back in the old days when his mom cooked their rations and taught him to read. Or, laughing with his dad as they pretended the origami figures were real animals and that were all friends living in an imaginary forest. Those happy times were long past.

"Dalrene worked in the farm domes once, ya know. Long ago. She was real excited about it too," Mickey said with a chuckle. "Eighteen-hour shifts. No breaks or days off. Bots constantly looking over your shoulder. Not much of a life worth living if you ask me, and that's one of the easiest gigs there is. Workin' in the mines is even harder."

"My mom would've been proud of me," Gordon said. He could feel the tears welling up again.

"She still can be. Remember her. Honor her." Mickey gave him a few firm pats on the back.

Gordon wiped a tear from his cheek, then Mickey leaned in, giving him a hug. The old man smelled like wet clothes and whiskey, but he hugged him back. It felt good to hug someone, anyone, and he trusted him. His mom had sent him down here because she knew that Aunt Tess's parents would take care of him. She trusted them, which meant that he could too.

"Gordon, we need your help," Mickey said.

He took another stinging drink and sat up tall in his bed. He was in no state to help anyone. When anger wasn't clouding his mind, sadness drowned it. His only hope was that the whiskey could turn down the volume.

But still, he would hear Mickey out. It's what his mom would want. He nearly laughed thinking about what his mom or Corrina would think about him drinking alcohol. He'd never touched the stuff before.

"This hell. Whatever this is. This isn't the world that the First Olympians envisioned. They braved the unknown—the radiation, the lack of food, water, and oxygen, and the hard work in the mines—because they had a vision for a better world. This ain't it. We've failed them."

"Priorities changed. There was a little something called X-Day. Earth comes first. It's still our species' home, and they need our help." Gordon said.

"Maybe," Mickey said, leaning back against the cave wall and stretching his arms. "The Dead Earth Hypothesis. We're going to test it. And we need your help."

"You really think *everyone* on Earth is dead? X-Day was worse than we thought?" Gordon shifted in his seat.

"I don't know nothin'," Mickey said. "But ever since we got orders to send them everything but the kitchen sink, however long ago, we haven't heard a single thing from the Blues. We're owed an update on the recovery status. An estimated time to completion, at the very least."

"Maybe the Foreman knows what the status is? Can we make it tell us?" Gordon asked.

"We tried that. If it knows, it's not tellin'. We don't even know what X-Day was. Maybe it was a war and the nuclear winter slowly killed off the survivors. Maybe it was an asteroid and the food-chain collapsed, again slowly killing off any survivors. We have no clue, and same for where our ore goes. These are fair questions to ask. Maybe someone used to know, but it's been a long time."

Gordon sighed, the conversation weighing on him. Had everyone at the outpost lived a pointless life? Had the work of generations of miners gone to waste? "How can we know?"

"Listen. I'm not a scientist, but I know that having a hypothesis is no good if you don't test it. If the Foreman is telling the truth and our resources are helping to re-build an Earth that is struggling even more than us, then that's fair. But if it's lost the plot and we're being worked to the bone by a heartless, rigid bit of computer code for no good reason, then things need to change."

"How can you test the hypothesis?" Gordon asked.

"That's where you come in. We need you to go to the surface. With the bombs."

Gordon felt like Mickey was speaking a different language. "The surface of what?"

"You heard me. The *surface*," Mickey said under his breath.

"What? That's impossible! No one's been out there in ... I don't know, forever!"

"There used to be human crews that went out there. A long time ago. Dalrene's ancestors were maintenance workers, and they left us a way out. There's a door that opens to a tunnel, not far from here. I've been. I've seen the giant transport trucks that come to pick up the minerals. I've seen the sun."

Gordon was dumbstruck. Giant trucks coming to pick up the minerals. The wind of the dust storms. The behemoth that was Olympus Mons lurking overhead, and above that, the stars twinkling down at them. And somewhere out there, Earth.

It sounded fantastical, all of it. Like something a child might daydream.

"If you've seen the trucks that pick up the minerals, then that means Earth is getting our minerals. Earth isn't dead," he said.

"The trucks are totally automated, so that doesn't mean anything. They could just be more robots playing out their programming for eternity. There's only one way to find out for sure. We blow up the loading docks when a truck comes to use it," Mickey said.

"What would that prove?" Gordon asked, mulling it over.

"We just gotta see who's out there. Poke the bear. Shake the hornet's nest and see what falls out," Mickey said.

"What?" Gordon's head spun.

"Sorry—old American phrases. We need to knock on the door and see who's home. We can give the truck's cameras a little fireworks show. Disrupting the supply chain is the fastest way to get a response. If there's really anyone out there, they'll let us know. If they're there, fine. We're happy to do our part to restore Earth. But we need to know.

Otherwise, we'd just soldier on like zombies, mining in horrible conditions for thousands of years."

Gordon instantly knew that he wasn't the right person for the job. Not now. Yes, he was angry. But he'd seen enough violence, and he wanted nothing more than to stay in bed and mourn.

"If people are going to get hurt, then I can't do it. My nightmares are bad enough already, and that's not who I am," Gordon said. "I know my mom was a lieutenant, but I'm not."

"No one's going to get hurt. The trucks are empty. There's no humans. It's a simple mission. Just set-up the bombs and detonate them at the right time. Property destruction was a classic move used by organized labor on Earth. If they're out there, we'll get a response, I promise you."

"Why do we need to blow up the loading dock? Can't we just follow the trucks and see where they go? See if the trucks or anyone can get in contact with the Blues?"

"The surface is big, kid. Real big. We don't have enough oxygen to follow the trucks. We poked our heads out a bit and there's nothing there. The planet is empty for as far as we can see."

Gordon couldn't do it. All the talk about Earth was too much for him. They sounded crazy. He just wanted to mourn in peace. "I'm sorry. Find someone else."

"Believe me, I'd do it myself if Dalrene would let me," Mickey said. "But you're the only one who can handle these unstable bombs. We need you, Gordon. Think about it." He took a deep drink and stood.

By not helping Mickey, he was failing his mom in some way. He knew that. This was the mission that was so precious to her that she'd kept it secret even from him. But it was more than he could do. Gordon lay face down and wished for sleep to come. He didn't know talking could be so exhausting.

#

Gordon was sleeping fitfully when Dalrene interrupted him by knocking on the cave wall.

"What's happening?" he jolted to alertness. Had the Foreman found them? Were the bots on their way? After the explosion, it seemed like anything was possible.

"I'm sorry, Gordon. I didn't mean to startle you." She moved slowly across the room and sat cross-legged beside his bed with a computer screen in her hand. "Mickey told me you're having nightmares. Your mom had a big heart. Talked about you all the time even though it was against our rules."

He groaned and turned in his bed, uneasy. He didn't want to talk about it anymore, and he was annoyed that Dalrene woke him up after he finally managed to fall asleep. "Look, I'm sorry I can't help you with the bombs. I loved my mom, but violence won't bring her back."

"You still love her. She's dead, not forgotten," Dalrene said, putting her hand on his shoulder. "Gordon, I have bad news. I lied to shelter you from a horrible truth, and I shouldn't have. Her death wasn't painless, and it wasn't an accident. The Foreman killed your mom in cold blood."

"I don't understand," Gordon said, sitting up and twisting his blankets off. He suddenly felt sick. He missed his mom so damn much. He hadn't even been able to accept her death as an accident, and murder was something else entirely.

"Watch," Dalrene said, starting a video on her computer.

Gordon's mom sat in the middle of the small room with her hands tied to a table. Her hair was mess, and the ground was wet where her tears fell. A robot stood by the door, asking her questions. When she refused to answer, an electric shock was administered, and his mom yelped in pain.

His breathing became choppy. The whiskey stirred uncomfortably in his stomach. He hated seeing his mom hurt and confused, like a cornered animal. He looked up to Dalrene who gave him a sad look of sympathy.

"Mickey and I, we lost people too. Our daughter, your Aunt Tess. When she was put on trial, Mickey was arrested and forced to testify against her. The things the Foreman did to them ... it's almost better this way for Janet. Even though it was painful, it's over now." Dalrene clasped his shoulder in a comforting way.

Gordon watched as the bot undid one of the restraints. His mom tried to make a move and the bot smacked her across the face in reprisal. It didn't seem to hurt her too much. Her focus quickly turned to the air recycler on the ceiling.

"We think the Foreman pumped the room full of carbon dioxide. It watched her suffocate. It was a choice. At any time, it could've turned the oxygen back on or opened the door."

He shuddered but he couldn't look away. His mom was becoming more desperate. She pounded on the walls and swore at the camera. Her eyes were practically popping out of her head. He could feel her fear. He wished he could help her. He wished he could do anything.

Tears streamed down her face as she pleaded into the camera for air. When that didn't work, she switched to swearing at it, cussing out the Foreman. Then, begging and bargaining. It hurt to no end to see her reduced to that.

"The Foreman talks big about helping us. From the day we're born we learn that we need it to keep us organized and prevent chaos. But our stories are not unique Gordon. Every one of my soldiers has been through a similar experience of loss or injustice."

He wiped sweat from his brow. He was helpless, just like when he hid in the closet. He couldn't save her. He couldn't do anything. His entire body shook as he watched the last few moments of his mom's life.

Drawing shallow breaths, it looked like she was realizing what came next. Gordon knew too, and his stomach felt like a blender running at top speed.

Finally, his mom clawed at her throat. In her last conscious breath, she looked terrified. And young. Much too young to die.

For one of the first times in his life, Gordon wanted to punch something, anything. It wasn't an accident. It was a cold, calculated decision to kill. And not humanely, but in one of the cruelest ways he could imagine. His anger grew roots, burrowing deeper into him. The Foreman deserved to die for what it had done to his mother. And what of Dalrene? She knew he was struggling with his emotions already.

"Why did you show this to me?" Gordon demanded through his tears.

"Don't be mad at me," Dalrene said, her tone understanding yet firm. "Be mad at the Foreman! It treated your mom like a bug, a meaningless life to be crushed under its boot when convenient. That's how it views the Faithless, and the rest of the outpost doesn't fare much better. Let's make sure this never happens to anyone else ever again. My granddaughter deserves a better life. I'm sure you still have friends in the residential level you care about. Anyone you've associated with is in danger now. We need your help, Gordon."

All his life, he'd done the right thing, which was whatever the Foreman asked, and never asked for anything in return. When his dad died, he vowed to study hard and support his mom. When his aunt died, he accepted the explanation that she'd gotten mixed up with a bad crowd and was in the wrong place at the wrong time. What did his dustlicking get him? Nothing but more death and shattered dreams. It was all bullshit, and he hated it.

"The Dead Earth Hypothesis," Gordon muttered. "This is why you want to test it."

"Blowing up the loading dock is only one piece of the puzzle," Dalrene said. "The damage will be well deserved, but the bombs are also a distraction. We need to draw the Foreman's forces away from the nodes. Even if the Dead Earth Hypothesis isn't correct, it doesn't matter! It's about killing the Foreman. It's about installing a human government, for the people. Help us crush the bots under our boots."

He closed his eyes. Life had been so much simpler when he thought his mom was a scrappy Faithless, and not a lieutenant in something much bigger. But there was no going back to normal. If he reported for questioning, the Foreman would kill him like it killed his mom. And then it would do the same to Corrina and master Tracey. His dream of becoming an explosives technician and working dutifully in the mines was over.

Gordon held the metal pendant his mom gave him and traced the outline of the number one with his finger. Guilt and anger combined into a relentless, suffocating pulse. It was an agonizing pain burrowed deep in his chest, like a corkscrew twisting into his heart.

All his mom's rambling complaints about the Foreman hadn't been crazy, they'd been right. The whole time, Gordon dismissed her when he shouldn't have. He had to make it right. He may not care about the Dead Earth Hypothesis the way his mom did, but he wanted revenge.

These were his people. He was a First Olympian now.

"Okay," Gordon said, sniffling. "Nobody gets hurt, and I'll help you with the explosives."

Chapter Nine: Gordon

All the eyes in the grotto were on him. Sixty or seventy people watching his every movement as he inspected the pallet that he would use to transport the bombs. It was standard issue from the mines and usually used for moving light equipment. It would fit dozens of the homemade explosives, more than enough to severely damage the loading dock Mickey was talking about. He kicked one of the wheels, and it twirled. It looked steady enough, as long he didn't have to go far.

Dalrene had made it clear that their window of opportunity was quickly closing, so the time was now. Gordon had agreed and they were sending him out immediately. It relieved the pressure of his grief to be useful, but he hadn't even had half a minute to get used to the idea that he'd be toting a pallet full of unstable explosives onto Mars's surface to blow something up. His head spun.

Even the *good* bombs were going to be hard to transport. The chemical stability of the fuel was low, and it was corroding the casing that separated it from the oxidizer. If the fuel and oxidizer mixed before they were supposed to, the reaction would cause someone else to lose a leg, or worse.

They had one detonator, and the wiring work on it had been shoddy. Dalrene had some soldering equipment though, and Gordon had spent half an hour making sure the electrical connections were tight. It had felt good to occupy his mind. Now he was confident that at least one part of the plan was solid.

Not too far away, Rodriguez was examining DeMar's new prosthetic leg. When he'd first seen the injury and the staggering amount of blood loss, Gordon doubted the man would live. The team that Mickey and Dalrene created really seemed to stick up for each other, even if no one had been able to help his mom. A sense of pride bubbled up warmly from his gut. It was good to be a part of something.

Gordon continued to review his gear and half-listened as Dalrene got on the stage and spoke to the few dozen people gathered.

"My friends, today is the day we take back the outpost for the people! We've modified our plan to account for the new acts of aggression by the Foreman, but I promise you that nothing can overcome our will. Our destiny!"

People clapped, but the mood was serious. They were waiting on Dalrene's every word. She had Gordon's full attention now.

"We've destroyed the Foreman's back-ups and given ourselves a window of opportunity. For every processor node we destroy, a tranche of bots dies. And if we destroy the brain node, their master dies. But we can't attack head on. The casualties would be massive. That's why we have Gordon," Dalrene said.

Everyone turned to look at him again, and his stomach tightened. These people were counting on him. He offered a meek wave.

"Gordon will unleash a blast on the surface of the planet, destroying some of the Foreman's key infrastructure and demanding a response. As bots are drawn away from strategic positions on the residential level, a small group, just six of us, will lead a stealth mission to the propaganda building. The remainder of you will marshal your troops, our forces in the other caves. When I take over the comms, I will call on the entire outpost to join us in a strike against the Mission Control Center. Together, we will be thousands strong. We will overwhelm the Foreman! We will kill the brain node!"

The plan sounded so insane that it might work. But a million things could go wrong, the least of which was their reliance on some bootlegged explosives. If the seal on any of the bombs failed, the explosion would set them all off, and Gordon would die a horrible death. He inspected each one individually, holding them up to his headlamp and making sure they were safe to transport. The relatively stable bombs went onto a pallet, and the accidents waiting to happen were cordoned off. Gordon worked with the utmost care he could muster. He was all too cognizant of DeMar's experience.

When the explosives were good to go, Gordon readied himself. He learned about the surface in school, that it was freezing with no oxygen. But textbooks didn't prepare people for real life. It was surreal. He was actually going there.

He put on a second pair of socks Dalrene gave him for warmth and charged his headlamp. What else could he do? Nothing had prepared him for this moment.

"You'll need this," Mickey said, handing him a suit, a helmet, and an oxygen tank. "It's been in Dalrene's family for generations. And now it can finally be put to good use. I don't think it blocks too much radiation, but it's pressurized and will keep you from freezing. The oxygen tank is full, although I have no idea how long it will last. If you run out of air, don't forget to come back." Mickey wore his regular toothy grin.

Gordon took the black environmental suit and found it heavier than it looked. The inner child in him was ecstatic. He'd only ever heard of suits in songs and books before. Seeing one in person, let alone getting to wear one, was super cool. The helmet struck him as professional and made of high-quality material beyond anything he'd seen before. He turned it around and noted a red number one on the back. He smirked. Dalrene sure did love that symbol. "What is this from?" he asked.

"Back in the day there were joint robot-human maintenance missions to repair solar panels and conduct scientific research. It's a shame those stopped. That's why the outpost is really falling apart now," Mickey said, throwing up his hands. "Hey, you'll be one of the first humans on the surface in generations. I've done it, for a few minutes. But my old brain didn't like the situation with the lack of a ceiling and all. It's a young person's job."

Gordon gulped. He hoped Mickey was right and that he could handle the disorientation he'd no doubt face. He carefully laid the suit, oxygen tank, and helmet on top of the explosives. He'd need both hands to pull the pallet. In his pockets, he had his only two possessions that mattered: his stack of folding papers, and his mom's First Olympians necklace. He took a deep breath and gave Mickey a thumbs up. They were ready to go.

"We'll see you soon. Give the Foreman hell!" Dalrene yelled and applause echoed around the grotto.

The First Olympians clapped and whistled as he pulled the pallet out of the grotto. Some young, strong men, not much older than him, patted him on the back. Gordon's stomach rumbled, but it was an excited nervousness. It was good to be doing something productive.

They walked through the smooth, samey looking tunnels where they'd first met. The sparse graffiti grew more frequent as they walked. Vibrations echoed and Gordon could never be sure if the constant rattle was from the air recycler behind or in front of him. But what was once a foreign and terrifying place, was now familiar, and even empowering. Mickey was the ruler of this domain, and with him, so was Gordon. There was no more need for fear.

Mickey hummed, and Gordon recognized the tune as one his mom used to sing to him. He smiled at the thought of her playing make-believe games with him and singing about becoming rich and exploring the stars in her spaceship.

"How did you learn to play guitar?" Gordon asked.

"By practicin'," Mickey said with a laugh.

"Yeah. But I mean there aren't a lot of people to learn from. And there's no guitar in the music class at school."

"Well, there used to be," Mickey said. "But that's not where I learned it. Learned it from my pa. My old man was a real string picker. Music keeps me level. Keeps my demons at bay. What about you? What do you do?"

"Origami."

"Ah, what a cultural curiosity," Mickey said. "There were no Japanese people in the original group of settlers, but we managed to inherit some of their traditions. I suppose you can't do origami while we walk, like I can sing. How are you feelin'?"

"I thought I'd be more nervous about going to the surface, but that's not what's bothering me. I can't stop thinking about the Foreman. What it did to my mom. What it would do to me."

"Let's just hope this works," Mickey said with a laugh. "You won't like Dalrene's back-up plan nearly as much."

Gordon gulped. He didn't dare ask what the back-up plan was, but suspected he was right.

"Lucky you, you're in a different position than I was. You won't have to wait nearly as long for answers, or to get even."

His chest tightened at the old man's suggestion. He wanted something that he never wanted in life before. Revenge. Justice. The Foreman had to pay. And he didn't have to wait at all.

"It's kind of amazing you guys figured this Dead Earth thing out," Gordon said.

"Don't start with that," Mickey said, sucking his teeth. "I ain't nobody's hero, although you might be, after today. Hell, I'm not even a good person! Don't do this for me. Do it for your mom."

Gordon felt connected to his mom in a way he never had before. She wanted revenge for his dad's and Aunt Tess's deaths. How could she not? How could he have expected her to ignore her rage and return to a normal life?

But with understanding came guilt. For a long time, and no matter how much he'd tried not to, he'd looked down on his mom for being Faithless. He wished he'd known her better when she was still alive. Helping the First Olympians was his apology. Maybe he could make some tiny part of things right.

They fell into silence. Mickey only had one speed and it was fast. Gordon followed him through the twisting tunnels, being cautious with the pallet of explosives he was hauling. Mickey would dart up ahead, and then pause to come back and check on him. It didn't take long to feel like they were going in circles.

They only passed a handful of ancient air recyclers, installed before the residential area of the outpost had been built. Mickey made a joke about wishing the Foreman had atrophied as much as the recyclers had. Gordon kicked one, and it sprang back to life. He jumped in shock but held a tight grip on the pallet handle. The explosives didn't budge.

Finally, Mickey said, "We're here." They'd arrived at a nondescript portion of the cave, dark and rocky, with lava pillars like any other cave section they'd passed in the last hour. In fact, Gordon was sure they'd passed through it before.

"I don't get it," Gordon said.

"Look closer," Mickey said.

Mickey brushed the dust off the cave wall, revealing a circular, metal door. It was large, about a dozen feet in diameter, and would fit Gordon's pallet with room to spare. There were two, large, vertical handles made of metal that protruded from the wall. In a place where everything was electric powered, this door was an unusual relic.

"Time to suit up," Mickey said.

"What exactly is on the other side of this door?" Gordon asked.

"An old tunnel that's hopefully not caved in. Climb for about five minutes, and then you'll come to a smaller door. Open that, and you'll see the surface. The loading dock is right outside, you can't miss it. I'll be here if you need to talk."

"You're not coming with me?" Gordon asked.

"I'm old," Mickey laughed. "I'm no help to you past this point. I'll stay on this side of the airlock, but I'll wear a suit so we can talk. Look, you'll do great. Try to stay focused."

He held up his suit.

"And Gordon?"

"Yeah?"

"Don't look up."

Don't look up? He'd do his best, but how could he not? It was something generations had barely even dared to dream of. He had to see what lay above them. He had to see Earth.

Gordon thought about Mickey's words as he fumbled into his suit. He pressed the side of his helmet, activating his microphone. "Blow up the loading dock when the truck comes? That's it?"

"That's right. We want the truck to be able to see the explosion and alert its masters, human, robot, or whoever they may be. Pick-up vehicles arrive every two hours on the dot. The next one will be here in an hour. If the Blues are truly out there and need our resources, disrupting the supply chain is the fastest way to get a response."

Mickey attached the oxygen tank to the back of Gordon's suit, and it became even heavier. They turned to face the large door.

"Pull!"

The door creaked open. The hair on Gordon's skin pricked up. He was fine under his layers, but the air was noticeably colder. They pulled again, harder, and the door swung open wider. Gordon peered in to see a rocky hill that rose to another door, about thirty meters up. The walls were red and dustier than the lava tubes. It struck him that this was the first place without air recyclers he'd seen in his life.

He pulled the pallet through, alone.

Sediments shifted above him as Mickey pushed the door closed from the other side, and loose rocks and dust fell. Gordon hovered over the explosives with his body, protecting them from the falling debris. Even the smallest rock could set off the unstable mixtures. If one bomb went off, they all would, and his corpse would be buried.

Gordon had Mickey in his ear, but that felt like a disconnect already. He was by himself in a strange place, and it was up to him to destroy the loading dock.

His back ached as he dragged the pack of explosives up the incline. But instead of it bothering him, he relished in the pain. He knew it was only a small fraction of what his mom suffered.

This was his best chance to get justice. It felt good to put his anger to use.

Then he saw it. A beautiful, tiny ray of light shone through a tiny window at the top of the hill. The sun. It was magnificent. For a moment, Gordon forgot he was holding the handle of the pallet with both hands.

"Did you get to the top? To the next door?"

Gordon grunted in the affirmative. "Almost there." He pushed the bombs up the last stretch to the flat landing at the top of the hill.

He pressed his face against the small, circular window, basking in the beautiful sunlight. It was so … white. All his life, he lived under electric lighting. But this was so warm and inviting. Humans were supposed to be energized by the sun, and he could finally see why.

Mickey spoke in his ear again, breaking the moment. "Beyond that door is a small rock shelter, with a roof overhang. After you set the bombs, wait in there with the detonator until the truck comes. It has a good view of the loading dock. You brain is going to be confused by the openness, but you can process later. For now, stay focused on the task."

"Understood," Gordon said.

He had the metal pendant, the symbol of the First Olympians, in his suit's inner breast pocket, and he rubbed it through his layers. It wasn't as calming as origami, but it's what he had.

With that, Gordon pulled open the door to the outside world.

He looked out from the overhang and fell to his knees, tears welling in his eyes. The sun shone brighter than he ever could've imagined. The ceiling ended a few meters in front of him. Beyond that, to his left, a giant cliff, part of Olympus Mons's shield, towered over everything. To his right, hills of brown-red landscape were covered in swirling sands. They rolled gracefully up and down, on and on forever.

He had never seen anything so extreme. The size and scale of it all was magnificent, but also disorienting and unnerving. Tranquil, yet immense and terrifying at the same time.

He looked up into the thin Martian atmosphere, trying to find the ball of blue that was Earth and failing. Instead of finding Earth, he found the sun and then closed his eyes, quickly realizing his mistake. He made a mental note not to look directly at the bright ball of nuclear fusion in the sky.

Head beginning to spin, he kept his eyes closed a moment longer. The sky didn't just seem to never end, it literally never did. For a moment, he forgot what he was supposed to do. He'd seen beauty on Mars for the first time. Mickey and Dalrene had given that to him, and he would be forever grateful.

"Remember, we're here to do a job. I'm here if you need to talk." Mickey said over the comms.

When he opened his eyes, they focused on the loading dock. It was just one hundred meters straight ahead, and Mickey was right, he couldn't have missed it. A long, perforated metal ramp jutted out from the side of the mountain and led to an industrial sized door. The whole structure was giant compared to Gordon but was dwarfed by the hulking backdrop of Olympus Mons. It was also simple. A ramp, a door, and that was it.

Gordon took his first steps out from the overhang and paused. For the first time ever there was no wall nearby. There was just vast emptiness around him. There was nothing to catch his fall on if he stumbled, and he was still pulling a batch of unstable explosives. He steadied his breath and imagined he was making a lotus flower, as he took his first steps. The paper folded gently in his mind and the creases were firm and supportive, exactly as they should be. He inhaled deeply, and with every fold he got one step closer to the loading dock.

At the edges of his vision, he could see the emptiness. Even though he didn't dare look, he could sense its immensity. "Mickey," he said with awe in his voice. "It's big out here."

"The only way to win the game is to not play, kid."

Gordon knew he was right. Fear, and the desire to do a good job, won out over curiosity. He trudged on, keeping his eyes locked on the ground and his mind imagining origami. There was a ton of interesting volcanic rocks. He wondered if there were any sediments around. Master Tracey would've loved this.

After a few mental lotus flowers, and geeking out about geology, he arrived.

There was ample space underneath the metal ramp. Gordon moved the bombs with extreme caution, stacking them on top of each other one by one. When he finished, he tested the connection to the detonator. It was solid and would be strong enough at his safe distance inside the cave overhang.

It was only when his work was done that he realized how chilly he was. He made a mental note to wear even more layers if he was ever on the surface again. The suit helped, but its age was apparent. He wondered how much colder it was in the evening when the sun was behind Olympus Mons and the gigantic volcano cast a great shadow over the hills. He shuddered and headed back toward the tunnel.

It was only one hundred meters away, but it felt like a lifetime. Now that the hard part was done, Gordon's curiosity returned. His eyes drifted upward, in awe at first, and then in crushing realization of the scale of everything. He'd never been anywhere without a ceiling in his life. The atmosphere, although expansive, was also suffocating and oppressive. It felt like it could collapse on him at any moment.

The cliff face of Olympus Mons was the same red volcanic rock stretching into eternity. If he missed the small overhang, he could easily get lost. What if he never found his way back inside? Or worse, what if he floated away into the limitless atmosphere above him? He grabbed his arms, trying to find something stable to hold on to. It was just him and the vastness.

His breaths shortened. Gordon looked back at the ground and tried to move, but his legs felt like boulders. Was gravity different on the surface? It shouldn't be, but maybe the Foreman did something to modify it in the outpost? He tried to focus, but he could feel the partially digested rations rushing up his throat. Oh crap!

When he puked, all the alarms in the suit went off at the same time. The sounds blared in his ears, and he fell to his knees, gasping. His stomach contents lined his helmet's visor, and he couldn't see a thing. It was frigid, but his heart was racing, and he felt like he was going to sweat through all the layers he was wearing.

The smell was putrid and inescapable. He desperately wished he could tear his helmet off and clean the gunk out his eyes, ears, and hair. He shut his eyes to try to escape. In his mind, Gordon watched his mom beg for air. Her piercing screams echoed inside his head, on and on. She clawed at her throat and hysterically beat on the walls. When her body lay twitching on the ground, her pleas for help kept resounding.

There was nothing he could do.

When he forced his eyes opened again, he found it was actually easier to focus now that he couldn't see much out of his helmet. He crawled in the direction he thought the cave was, detonator in hand. The layer of vomit dripping down the inside of his visor made it easier to stay calm and not look up at the domineering volcano and the vastness of the sky.

He imagined what Corrina would say about this escapade when he told her.

"So, you were crawling on all fours. And the layer of vomit blocking your view *helped*? You were like a blind rat searching for food!" He could hear her laugh roaring in his head.

Gordon burped, and when he started to giggle, he couldn't stop. She would never believe him. It was ludicrous! She would laugh him out of the room. She would try to send him to the medical center for insanity! And she would been right to. It *was* insane.

He rolled onto his side, basking in the surrealism of it all. He tried to control his laughter, but it just kept coming.

He, Gordon, was on the surface! Corrina was going to be so jealous.

Then, the ground rumbled.

Chapter Ten: Alex

Alessandra's close friends called her Alex. The only problem was that they were all on Earth, and she was seventy million kilometers or so away in a spacecraft, blasting through the Martian atmosphere.

In a few months, the planets would be in a more favorable position for travel, and she'd be on her way back to civilization. It felt like a lifetime away. She couldn't decide if she missed Earth that much, or if she just hated working with the corporate sycophants that sucked up to her dad. And that the longer she stayed on Mars, the more she risked becoming one of them herself. Normally, you had to be twenty-one to get a work permit, but her status as the boss's daughter made it easy to get an exemption. At eighteen, she was the youngest person living on the planet.

"We are one thousand, four hundred and twelve kilometers from the Martian surface and have escaped the planet's gravity well," the ship said.

Alex tried to locate Earth without the help of the scopes. It was only faintly blue to the naked eye, one dot among millions. It was nearly harvest season at her family's home on the north coast of Spain. The temperature would be dropping, cool air rolling in from the Atlantic Ocean, the grapes plump and juicy. She could almost smell the dry dirt kicking up into the air as she ran through the vineyard.

"Decreasing thruster power to twenty-five percent." The ship rudely interrupted Alex's daydream.

She slammed her hand down on the console, disabling the AI. She'd taken her new ship on a joyride to get some solitude, and she couldn't even get that. She aimed toward Earth and pushed the thrusters up to max. The acceleration threw her violently backward into the pilot seat and her tongue stuck out of her mouth like it did when she hit a satisfying tennis shot. It was the happiest she'd been in weeks.

Alex glanced down at her console. She was currently under three g-forces of thrust, and the rate of acceleration was increasing. Everything on the dashboard was green. The ship was barely breaking a sweat. "I think I'll name you *Zoya*," she said to the ship. "The *Zoya*," she repeated, rolling the name over her tongue.

It sounded right. She had a kickboxing partner once with that name, a bullheaded Slavic girl who could take a knee to the face and tell you it hurt your knee more than it hurt her face. And you'd believe her. It was a fierce name. Strong.

The *Zoya* beeped warmly in affirmation, seemingly satisfied with its name and happy to get along with its owner.

The first of a new generation, the *Zoya* was the culmination of recent advances in gas-core nuclear reactor technology, powered by First Olympia Corporation's direct-fusion drives. Never before had both high thrust potential and fuel efficiency been achieved at the same time. Military-class ships would start rolling off the production lines soon, but this barebones yacht-class boat was the first successful proof of concept. And it was all hers. There were benefits to staying in her dad's good books.

As she hit four gs of thrust, a robotic arm from the side of her chair sprang up. It held a tray with an empty syringe and needle. "Stores of gravitational-force-assistance drugs are depleted," the *Zoya* said. "Reducing thrust to ensure safety of occupants."

"Override!" Alex said through gritted teeth.

The *Zoya* would normally be stocked with a pharmaceutical cocktail of blood thinners and amphetamines in order to prevent her body from being crushed by the force it was under. Human blood pressure doubles with each g, and at high-g burns, the body becomes susceptible to cell walls rupturing, risking aneurysm and stroke.

But that wouldn't happen to her, or at least not as easily as it would to other people. Alex had been genetically engineered to give her cells significantly more strength than was naturally possible. With the expression of a few different genes, she became different than almost all of humanity before her.

Alex took a hand off the thrusters and swatted the robotic arm away. She hadn't bothered to stock up her ship with drugs. She didn't need them because her father had planned ahead, like he had for her whole life.

Other alterations were supposed to have given her perfectly straight teeth, the ability to learn new languages at an incredible speed, and an increased sense of loyalty. Polygenic selections were complex, and success was measured by how much more likely the candidate was to possess the desired traits. Doctors told her parents they had largely failed, and Alex was only ten to fifteen percent more likely to demonstrate those other attributes. One set of braces and many rebellious teenage years later, Alex would say that was a stretch.

Her long, black hair, normally curling and flowing beautifully behind her, was crushed against her chair under the force of the spaceship's acceleration. She was supposed to attend a company photoshoot later in the day, and Alex worried for only a second about the work she was creating for her hair stylist.

The *Zoya* bucked, and Alex returned her attention to it. Adrenaline coursed through her veins as she gripped the thruster bars. Most new ships didn't have manual thruster bars anymore, but the *Zoya* was designed to let you feel the ride. Alex felt more alive than ever.

"Call from Rafael Torres," the *Zoya* said.

"Okay. Answer it."

Alex couldn't escape, even for an hour.

Her dad appeared on the dashboard, wearing a suit and looking well groomed as always. He was an intense man, cleanshaven with bushy eyebrows and a square face.

"Hey, Alex. Oh! You're flying? Are you in the cockpit right now?" Her dad's smile, usually politician-like, was soft and genuine.

"Yes! Yes, I am. It's an incredible machine. A true masterpiece of engineering. Thanks again, Dad."

"That's great, sweetie. You'll have to give me the full rundown later. I just wanted to tell you we are confirmed for the trip to the mine today. The photographers, the press release—everything is lined up."

"Okay. You know how I feel about that." Alex hated photoshoots but going to a mine could be interesting.

"I know you don't like the PR bullshit, but I appreciate it. You're doing a great job. Hey, have you called your mom yet?"

"I will." Alex sighed.

When her dad gave her the choice between law school and joining the family business, She expected her mom to stick up for her desire to learn engineering or science instead. She didn't, and the wounds opened in the word battles that followed hadn't healed yet. She knew her anger should've been directed at her dad, but she *expected* him to be stubborn and controlling. She thought she could trust her mom more, so it hurt deep when she was shown where she really stood. They hadn't spoken in months, but if the *Zoya* was her parents' attempt to buy back some of her love, it just might work.

"Please try to call her. She'd love to hear from you. And she'd be thrilled to hear about your new ship as well."

"I said I will." Alex threw her head back. "Have you done your exercises today?"

Living on Mars required at least an hour of exercise every day to prevent bone and muscle loss, and Alex usually spent it practicing her kickboxing. It was her number one source of stress relief before she got the *Zoya*. But her dad often neglected it, claiming he was too busy.

"Not yet. I will," her dad said, mimicking her annoyed tone.

"Just because you have the best doctors doesn't mean you're above the rules, you know," Alex said.

"Okay. I'll exercise, and you'll call your mom. How's that for a deal?" The politician smile was back.

"Deal," Alex said. She paused before adding, "Starting tomorrow."

"Starting tomorrow," her dad said half facetiously, dropping the call.

"Reminder: One and a half hours until Asteroid Belt Expansion Meeting," the *Zoya* chimed.

Alex groaned and plotted a landing path. She'd have to wait to play more with her new toy.

Lately, she wished she chose Yale over Mars. At least America had decent gravity and food that didn't taste like an experiment in blandness. Even her mom's job of sitting at home and inventing ingenious new ways to spend money was sounding attractive compared to another boring business meeting. But as much as she wanted to go rogue with a fake passport on a prospecting boat or hitch a ride home, she couldn't let her dad down.

#

Back on the ground, Alex bounced lightly down the steps from the *Zoya*'s hatch and onto the metal boarding bridge that automatically extended from the space-transit bay. Her balance was off, and she stumbled a bit, but she didn't trip. She swore under her breath. If she hadn't gotten used to the lighter gravity on Mars yet, perhaps she never would.

She unzipped the top of her flight suit, a sleek red-and-black racing uniform, and looked back at the docked *Zoya*. Wedge-shaped with sleek angles, it looked more like a finished work of art than a prototype. And although it was a small ship, it still towered above her at a height of forty meters. She felt powerless beside it, just a young woman. It was much more freeing to be inside the ship with the thruster in her hand. She keyed in a command on her handheld, instructing the maintenance crew to keep the *Zoya* ready to fly. She'd be back as soon as she could.

It was still early in the morning, and Alex walked down the deserted hall to the nearest communal locker rooms. The pinstripe suit jacket and pants fit a little too snugly on her, so she undid one of her buttons. It was still uncomfortable. For all the noise her dad made about creating a new planet with a unique culture, she didn't understand why he insisted on continuing some of Earth's worst traditions. Banning corporate formal wear was going to be the first thing she did if she ever took over.

After a shower, Alex tied her hair in a quick ponytail, put on her high heels, and rushed to her jam-packed schedule of meetings.

#

"The market is rewarding providers that can deliver these superconducting alloy materials at scale. The time to make investments into our asteroid-belt holdings is now. In less than eighteen months, we can be the leader in this segment."

The speaker was a man named Peter who'd lived on Mars for too long. Lifers, they called them. He was thin-faced and scrawny, his body used to the light gravity, and he was married to the obsessive work culture at the company. He'd never leave the planet again.

"Don't you think dumping this much raw material on the market at once would decrease prices? How would we even unload the quantity you're proposing?" Alex barely looked up from her handheld.

"We can pre-sell at least forty percent of the ... the pipeline." Peter stammered. He looked nervous, likely used to receiving a tongue-lashing in the CEO's office. "Demand is only increasing, and we anticipate by the time we scale-up mining, we won't have nearly enough to fulfill all our orders."

A physically intimidating man, her dad ruled the business with an iron will. His temper was quick to explode over even the smallest perceived sleight, and it didn't matter whether he was talking to a shareholder or a janitor. He never lost his temper at Alex, but employees expected her to channel her dad's anger.

"These margins are too low," Alex said. "What are your assumptions on fuel costs?"

"We're using today's market rates for hydrogen and helium."

"Fuel costs are going to drop like crazy in the next eighteen months as more high efficiency boats come online," Alex said, raising a single, thick eyebrow. "Let's go back to the drawing board on this one. Make sure your numbers align with the engineering team's timeline to commercialization for direct-fusion drives."

"I don't have that level of security access."

Alex tapped her handheld and it projected Peter's employee profile into three-dimensional space in front of her. "Now you do," she said, swiping from left to right.

"Thank you, ma'am," he nodded enthusiastically.

"Call me Alex," she said, exasperated. It wasn't the first time she mentioned it.

He bowed his head and backed out of the room, leaving her to herself in her dad's office. The ninetieth penthouse had floor-to-ceiling windows on one wall and taxidermy hunting trophies hanging opposite. The far side had a seating area with leather couches and a bar her dad was usually too busy to drink from.

She hadn't planned to be on Mars long-term, so she was sharing her dad's office on the top floor. He had assigned a construction crew to build her an office one floor down, but Alex was hesitant. It felt like a permanent step, and she was putting it off for as long as possible.

She stood from the desk and leaned against the window. She saw a flat desert, and beyond that, rolling rocky hills. A dust storm was forming in the distance and winds swirled around at high speeds. But movement didn't mean life. The dust storm was as dead as the hills. The terraforming project would take decades, if not lifetimes. Despite having raised the temperature of the planet by two degrees Celsius, Mars was still cold and bleak.

Her entire life on Mars was spent in the glass and steel office tower, or one of the same-looking but shorter residential structures. There were fifteen of those buildings, each up to twenty stories tall. She spent her free time kickboxing, in the engineering buildings, or in the greenhouses, admiring the work of the scientists. That they could even grow enough food for the thousands of people on Mars was an astounding accomplishment.

"Would you like the potatoes or salad with lunch today?" came the voice of an assistant behind her.

Alex threw her head back and groaned. Although the scientists did an impressive job of feeding people, the quality of the food left a lot to be desired. She couldn't wait to be back home to eat fresh sushi. It felt like years since she'd had protein that didn't taste like boiled chicken. She swore she could tell when meat was lab grown.

"Is there *anything* else?" she asked.

"I will check for you ma'am," the assistant replied, before adding, "My apologies."

Alex continued looking out the window. She could tell the employees were scared of her. Or more accurately, they were scared of her father. She normally hated that repercussion of her status, but it had its advantages.

"How was it? Does she have a name yet?" her dad asked, entering.

"So fun!" Alex said, turning with a smile. "She's been christened the *Zoya*."

"The *Zoya*. Strong, but sensible. I like it. Just don't tell your mom if you enter any races! You know how she worries." Her dad wagged his finger playfully. Her parents loved short-hop racing, her dad even partaking as a pilot in his younger days. But her mom turned into a ball of anxiety whenever she did it.

"So, we're going to the mine?"

"We are," her dad said, nodding. "But just for the photoshoot. The PR department wants the daughter and father pictures at the first mine we opened. It's a look back at how far we've come, and a look forward to the next generation of leadership."

Alex groaned. The idea of her presented in a corporate newsletter as the company's next CEO was nauseating, but she relished any chance to get out of the office and see the real work being done.

"Can we go into the mine at all? See the blasting or extraction?"

"I don't think we'll have time for that. But I have a present for you. This box is a family heirloom, passed down by my father. And the device inside is a brilliant piece of modern engineering," he said, handing Alex an ornate wooden box.

She took it with both hands and opened its ancient metal hinges.

"A gun?" she asked, tilting her head to the side. A slim, black-brushed, metal pistol lay inside. She'd shot plenty of guns in training on Earth, but she didn't understand why she needed one now, on Mars.

"All pilots need a gun," her dad said, taking it out of the box. "Here, handle it."

"It's heavy, but it feels good."

"It's an old tradition, but you've got to be able to protect yourself from pirates and terrorists."

Alex popped the chamber to find a thick bullet. "What is this ammo?"

"Explosive rounds are standard on ships. They're great to deter boarding. You can shoot through a bridge door with one of these. Or blast open an airlock if someone's breaching you."

"All right. But the *Zoya* is a runner, not a fighter. If I ever need to use this, I'll already be dead," Alex said, laughing as she aimed down the sights. "And I thought you said we needed to leave Earth traditions behind, forge our own way. Martian superiority without the old hang-ups, and all that."

"You're right, I did say that. But some traditions are worth keeping. Others will follow us no matter how hard we try to leave them in the past. Besides, your *Zoya* is too high-tech. It will be good to have something on-board that's mechanical and doesn't rely on software. Something you can count on. Consider it a good-luck charm," her dad shrugged.

"Okay, old man," Alex said, ribbing him. "I know you don't believe in luck."

"True." He sat, tossing his feet up on the desk. It was solid American cherry, and the only piece like it on the planet. "That's why you're on the Board of Directors now. Between your mother, yourself, and me, we have three fifths of the vote. Full family control." His smile reached his ears.

"What does it matter? The other directors are your friends."

"Sure, but we're a publicly traded company. This reinforces our power and ensures we don't get any surprise demands from our investors. Have you sent out the agenda for the meeting tomorrow?"

"I'll do it tonight," Alex said.

She'd been putting it off. As Secretary of the Board, it was her job to distribute the agenda, take notes, and record all the votes. It was horrible. At least in regular meetings she had autonomy and could make decisions. In board meetings, she was just her dad's lapdog, voting in step with him.

"Anyways, I'll see you for the photo op in a few hours. I've got a call from Chicago I should take."

That was Alex's cue to leave, and she headed for the *Zoya* to deposit her present. Employees feared her enough already and bringing a gun to her afternoon meetings wouldn't help.

#

The convoy of trucks rolled across the Martian desert. They didn't go anywhere without a full security detail. Alex thought her dad was paranoid, but he insisted on it. The pre-conglomerate era of Mars's development was tumultuous, and piracy and sabotage had been rampant. Sometimes, it seemed like her dad was holding onto those years, yearning for them.

She watched the landscape as they reached the hill that had been on the horizon only minutes ago, and then did so again, and again. Her brain was baffled by the curvature of the horizon caused by the planet's relatively smaller spherical size compared to Earth. The disorienting effect was just another reminder that she didn't belong on this planet and needed to get home as soon as possible.

"Computer, change the feed," Alex said as she popped some anti-nausea pills. Why couldn't her genome have been edited for motion sickness resistance?

Now the screen showed archival footage from the actual founding of Mine Number One, in the year 2085. Alex leaned forward and squinted. She found old stuff fascinating. It was so cool to see how far they'd come.

A few dozen people walked at the foot of Olympus Mons, looking tiny in comparison. They wore ancient, all black environmental suits that had comically bulky oxygen tanks hitched to their rear. Alex wondered if the black color was an engineering decision to maximize sunlight heat absorption in an era where suits were nowhere near as efficient as they are now. The camera operator remarked how nervous they were to explore the lava tubes. It was funny, but also quaint. Like how Alex imagined life in a cute farmhouse in the North American prairies might be.

The raw footage was only shown for ten seconds before one of their company's public relations reps interrupted and filled the screen with gross corporate platitudes. She turned it off, then turned her attention to her immediate team.

Alex and her dad sat on one bench and four members of their security team sat on the opposite bench. Photographers, more security guards, and a gaggle of PR people trailed in their own trucks. She zipped up her boots and smiled at her dad. It wasn't often she saw him out of the office. She was excited to see the mine and tried to push any negativity out of her thoughts.

"It would be awesome to see an extraction team working. Are you sure we can't go underground?" Alex asked.

"Did you finish reviewing the asteroid belt expansion plans?" her dad asked, ignoring her question. He was reading e-mails on his helmet's heads-up display and looked like he couldn't wait to get back into his suit and tie.

"Dad! I'm asking. If we finish this BS early, can we please see the inner workings of the mine?" Alex was probably the only person in the solar system who wasn't afraid to push back at him.

"I'm sorry," her dad said, swiping his e-mail away. "But there won't be enough time.

And our new corporate insurance, which includes you, prevents it. We have to stay at ground level. We'll hold the shovels, smile, take the pictures with the minerals and then I've got to get back for my next meeting."

Alex groaned. It felt like a weak excuse to limit her. She was going to have to find a way to sneak into the mine herself.

"Your mother will be excited to see the photos. And she can brag about it to all her friends."

"I know. I said I'll call her tomorrow," Alex mumbled.

"Are those idiot contractors done building you a new office yet?" he asked. "I swear I'll fire every one of them if they screw this up."

"Not yet," Alex said. She'd been actively hampering it, asking the construction crew to go slower and distracting them with other projects.

She made a mental note to tell the contractors to complete building her office. Her dad expected everyone to live and breath work as much as he did, and he could get angry if employees didn't meet his expectations. She didn't want to get anyone fired, and at least her own office meant she wouldn't have to listen to her dad berate anyone.

"And that asteroid belt expansion. I'll put something in the calendar so we can talk about that. I think you made the right call asking them to think deeper about it, but we have to make a decision. We can't keep whiteboarding forever. There's too many meetings and not enough decisiveness at this company."

"I'd love to see those famous Martian lava tubes. I can't believe the first settlers lived in those caves. "Come on!" Alex said, gesturing to the security guards. "You guys are pumped, right?"

The security guards looked at each other before nodding politely.

"You want to see the lava tubes? Maybe we'll find a way to sneak into the mines," she whispered to them jokingly.

Her dad laughed and rolled his eyes.

"I don't think so ma'am," one of them replied, hesitant to be drawn between father and daughter.

"We'll see about that," Alex muttered to herself. She usually figured out ways to get what she wanted. Either way, she was happy to be out of the office. As fake as holding a shovel for a photoshoot was, it was still going to be more hands-on and real than anything else she'd done on Mars.

"Why do we even need these security guards, anyways? Can't we have one afternoon just for the two of us?" Alex said, fluttering her eyelashes.

"Mhhm. Like I said, insurance. You're next in line to take over the company," her dad said, turning his attention back to his e-mail.

Alex played with the settings on her helmet, wishing she could wear environmental suits instead of business suits every day. They were bright white for maximum visibility against the planet's browns and reds. A heads-up display monitored all her vitals and would alert headquarters if any of a million different things happened, like if her radiation exposure exceeded guidance or her waste disposal facility was near full.

A voice announced they were arriving at First Olympia Corp.'s Mine Number One, previously known as Olympus Outpost. The truck started to brake, and Alex stood, ready to go.

Chapter Eleven: Gordon

"Mickey, are the trucks coming?"

"You're the one up there, not me, kid. But you still have another forty-five minutes. Why? What's happening?"

"I don't know. But I hear something big." Gordon was still on his knees. He felt a primal fear, like the kind he got when he saw pictures of giant Earth spiders. The bombs were precariously unstable. If the source of the vibrations got close enough, it wouldn't matter whether he hit the button on the detonator or not.

"Well, do you see any trucks coming?"

"I can't see anything! I threw up in my helmet." It took all of Gordon's self-control to avoid hyperventilating.

"Is it liquid? Never mind, don't answer that. Turn up the air flow! It should drain into your waste compartment!"

"How do I do that?"

"There are a few controls on your left forearm!"

"I can't see those either!"

Mickey grumbled something in an annoyed old man tone.

Gordon fumbled until he found a switch on his forearm and flicked it. Immediately the air flow in his helmet increased and began to push the vomit down his visor and out of his field of view. The pieces that weren't soaked into his hair started to get sucked away.

His vision clearing up, Gordon didn't have to avoid looking at the sky this time. His entire focus was directed to the source of the rumbling sounds, the convoy of vehicles barrelling toward the loading dock. And they weren't kilometers away, the closest was already slowing down!

"The trucks! They're here!"

"What? Already? Multiple? There's usually only one at a time. There's only ever been one!"

"What do I do?"

"Detonate! Detonate now and get the hell back inside!"

Mickey was right. That was the whole point of the mission. Gordon was closer than he'd like to be to the bombs, but not so close that the blast would hurt him.

He put his finger over the detonator. This was it. This was his chance to strike back at the Foreman. It was small compared to what it did to him, but it was still going to be meaningful.

Before he could press the button, the door to the first truck opened and Gordon's jaw dropped. Four people in bright-white suits emerged and walked to the loading dock. His mind raced. Were they on the Robot-Human Mediation Council, and if not, who were they?

He ran toward the loading dock. It was supposed to be automated! There weren't supposed to be people! There was no time to think but he knew he had to get them out of the blast zone, to safety. The explosives were unstable!

Forty meters to the loading dock, Gordon waved his hands, trying to get their attention. He did. They looked right at him and froze. He spit out a stray piece of vomit and sprinted even faster. "Get away!" He screamed instinctively, forgetting they weren't on his comms channel.

Mickey was saying something too, but he could barely make out the words over the sound of his own voice. "Hang on kid, I'm coming!"

The rest of the convoy hadn't stopped progressing, and the trucks rolled up beside the loading ramp. The ground shook under the weight of the massive vehicles.

He wouldn't get there in time. Gordon jumped up and down, waving his arms. He yelled, but there was no way they could hear him. It was too late.

One of the bombs exploded, and the rest a millisecond later. Gordon flew back, all the way to the cave entrance, and hit the ground hard. It sounded like the entire mountain was preparing to come down. Chunks of debris shifted above him and fell. He saw the rock three seconds before it hit him. It was just enough time to raise his hands and cover his face, but not enough time to move out of the way. His arms crunched as it made impact. His last thought before losing consciousness was hoping that no one else was injured in the blast.

#

His breaths were short and shallow. In Gordon's mind, he tumbled down and away through the rocky tunnels and caves of the outpost. Head over heels, spinning, he fell away from everything he'd ever known. Past Corrina, Mickey, Dalrene, master Tracey, and all the others. He fell past his mom last, and he couldn't do anything but watch her disappear into the blackness above him.

He woke to the alarm in his helmet raging. It reached a crescendo and held it until Gordon lost consciousness again. The rest of his body hurt, but the acute pain of the relentless, high-pitch squeal crowded everything else out. The alarm rang and rang as his awareness came and went. When it stopped, he groggily assumed his eardrums were blown out.

Either that, or his suit was shutting down and he was about to die.

When he finally cracked opened an eye, Gordon saw red. The outside of his visor was caked in dirt. His head spun. Somehow, he was still alive. His oxygen wasn't compromised by the rockslide, and he took deep, thankful breaths.

Gordon rolled out from underneath the fallen debris, and, standing, tried to wipe his helmet clean. The pit of his stomach opened up as he realized it wasn't just dirt on his helmet, but also blood. He'd hurt someone, badly. He grabbed his chest, horrified. He hadn't wanted this. Why hadn't things gone as planned? With his visor partially clean, Gordon noticed something at his feet and yelled at the top of his lungs.

A human arm sat on a rock, severed at the forearm, tendons dangling out of a white environmental suit.

He shuffled, off-balance, and fell backward. His movements shifted the rocks and the arm flopped to the side.

Those people in white! Where did they come from? What did they want? How many had he killed? Bloody rocks and severed arms swirled around his vision. His breathing became erratic, and tears started to flow. He couldn't think straight. All he knew was that everything was horrible.

From the corner of his eye, he saw a white suit scrambling toward him. He raised his arms in surrender, but the person kept getting closer, traversing over the rubble with ease. He got up to one knee and prepared to accept the consequences of his actions.

"I'm sorry! I'm so sorry!" Gordon pleaded. It occurred to him that they probably couldn't hear his apologies or see his tears through the blood covering his helmet, but he didn't know what else to do. He'd hurt people. Killed, most likely. It was all wrong. There wasn't supposed to be anyone at the blast site.

He couldn't see through the white suit's visor. Gordon stood, gesturing wildly with his hands. He pointed back toward the door where Mickey was, and then to the trucks. He didn't know how to explain himself, or how any of it made any sense. He waved his arms, hoping they'd understand.

Before he knew what happened, the white suit punched him in the chest, and he flew backward, hitting his head again. The ringing in his ears returned and he moaned in pain.

"Stay down. Don't do anything stupider than you've already done," a woman's voice crackled over his comms.

His eyes closed.

#

Consciousness came and went until Gordon gasped awake on a bed in a glass room. He looked around and tried to make sense of anything. Bright, white lights shone from far above him. A man stood outside, but he was turned away, and Gordon couldn't see his face. He was okay with that. He didn't want to see anyone.

The room was inside of a larger, concrete structure with high ceilings and thick-looking walls. Gordon had never heard such quiet. He'd never seen or smelled a place so bare and sterile. There was no whirr of an air recycler and no children running and yelling. It seemed fake. Nothing could possibly be this lifeless. He felt like a bug trapped inside a transparent cup.

The glass windows and bright lights made it impossible to hide anywhere. The bed he woke up on was an elevated gurney with wheels supported by four metal legs, so Gordon moved it to a corner of the room and sat underneath it, clutching his knees.

His environmental suit and ragged old mining clothes were gone. In their place were a crisp white shirt and pants made of a synthetic material that he couldn't identify.

Gordon rubbed his hands through his hair. No vomit. There was a hole in his memory and his brain hurt when he tried to remember what happened.

His new clothes itched, nagging at his skin every time he moved, so he tried to stay still. Images of squirting blood and angry white suits crowded every other thought out of his mind. He saw the tendons dangling from the severed arm when he closed his eyes.

Mickey's twangy voice rattled around his head. "You're gonna do great, kid."

"We're going to make the outpost a better place to live."

Dalrene's voice was there too, omnipresent. She switched between thanking Gordon and berating him. "Your mom was a good person and a strong fighter."

"She would've been proud of you. Finish the fight for her!"

Gordon winced and wiped sweat off the back of his neck. He was so foolish! Had they known what they were sending him to? If they knew there were going to be people at the loading dock, would they have told him? He wondered if it had been a suicide mission or a homicide mission. He didn't know which one was worse.

The metal pendant of the First Olympians sat on the bed's extendable plastic tray. It twinkled, reflecting the intense white light from above. It was too bright. He didn't want anything to do with it.

He smacked the tray, grabbed the pendant, and threw it as hard as he could. It rang off the glass wall and clinked to the ground in the opposite corner. Gordon retreated under the bed, fuming.

He was done with the First Olympians.

He clawed at his itchy face and neck. He flicked sweat off his hands and realized that they were trembling. He wished more than anything he had some origami papers to calm his nerves.

The guard, or whoever was standing outside the glass, didn't budge. There was no indication he could hear him, and if he could, no indication he was interested in what Gordon was doing. He didn't care either way. If someone wanted to reprimand him for lashing out, that was fine.

The deep red of the First Olympians pendant bore into his eyes. It was the only color in the otherwise blank, white room. He tried to look away from it, but he could still feel it there, calling to him, mocking him.

Slowly, he crawled over to the window and picked it up, running his hands over the engraving of the number one. Gordon put the necklace on and held the metal in his hand. He stayed that way for minutes, until his hands completely stopped shaking. Maybe Mickey and Dalrene had tricked him or taken advantage of him. But this was his only remaining connection to his mom.

A man with dark glasses that took up most of his face entered through a door in the concrete. He slipped a plate of what Gordon assumed was food through a hole in the glass wall. He didn't acknowledge his presence. After talking inaudibly with the guard, he left the way he came.

Gordon stared at the greens and yellows of what appeared to be some sort of vegetable for what felt like hours. Whoever these people were, they hadn't given him a reason to trust them.

Eventually, he moved toward the plate to investigate. A spicy, woody fragrance assaulted his nose. It was overwhelming and intrusive in a way that food wasn't supposed to be. He picked up the mashed, gooey substance in his hands to get a better look at it, but it ran through his fingers like blood.

No! Panicked, he shook his hands, splattering the food on the glass wall. He took a deep breath and tried to imagine folding origami. He stood still for minutes, but it didn't help. His heart still raced. Eventually, with his appetite non-existent, he retreated under the bed.

He was a murderer now and would be for the rest of his life. Gordon was no better than the Foreman that suffocated his mother in cold blood. The white suits from the loading dock were people, and they had families that were going to miss them just like he missed his dad and now his mom. It made him want to crawl into a corner and never come out. It was a pain he'd never wish on his worst enemies.

Gordon wondered what his mom would think of him now. She always advocated doing whatever had to be done, by any means possible. But she was a thief and stole out of necessity. She was harmless in comparison to Gordon. When his mom conned people into giving up their rations, or blackmailed teachers into changing his school schedule, she never hurt anyone. She did it to give him a chance at a better life. She loved people. As much as the First Olympians meant to her, he knew she never would've harmed anything other than robots.

Gordon was happy she wasn't alive to see how he failed her.

\#

Gordon finally started to drift into an agitated sleep when the knock on the glass came. He looked up and saw a girl with wavy, dark hair, and pale skin. She had a cut on her forehead, and Gordon guiltily wondered if it was from the explosion. Their eyes briefly locked, and he looked away. He hadn't expected her gaze to be so intense and terrifying. He shifted farther back into the hole he'd created for himself under the bed.

The girl entered and the door clasped shut behind her. She briefly surveyed the surroundings with her hands on her hips. When she spoke, it was with a sense of gentry, and she seemed to add extra syllables where there shouldn't have been any.

"I see you felt a need to play with your food. As if you haven't already made enough of a mess?"

Gordon didn't say anything to the strange girl. She wore fitted, black pants, a shirt with a collar, and a strange second shirt with small stripes on top. The closest he'd seen to it before was when some older mine workers wore an extra layer of fire insulation on top of their oilers, but this was more formal.

"Look, this is going to be easier for everyone if you tell me what I need to know. Who paid you, huh? Horizon Mining? Red Sea Logistics?"

The girl stalked toward him, and the sound of her steps pierced the air. The ends of her shoes looked like they could put a hole through Gordon's skull.

One, two, three, then four steps toward him.

He winced. It was like a detonator counting down, and Gordon gripped the leg of his bed and closed his eyes.

But no explosion came.

He cautiously opened one of his eyes to find her face uncomfortably close to his.

"Who sent you?" she asked.

"I need my papers," Gordon said, fidgeting with his hands.

The girl tilted her head, confused, then howled with laughter.

"Who exactly do you think picked you up? Saved your life? The UN? A charity?" she said, raising her voice.

Gordon stared at the ground and the girl's pointy shoes again.

"Yeah, that's right," she said. "No one is serving you any papers. You don't get counsel and there're no laws out here that we didn't write. Or enforce. So, I'll ask you again. Who paid you?" She put on a smile, but it wasn't real.

He had no idea what she was talking about. The sterile glass room, the weird intense food, the crazy girl mocking him. It was too much. "In my breast pocket ... there were some thin papers. I really need them back," Gordon said.

The girl's perfectly straight teeth disappeared behind her frown.

"You think this is a game?" she said, turning red with anger. "I'm the one you want to talk to. I'm the good cop. That guy on the other side of the glass? He's not the bad cop—

he's the executioner!"

Gordon stewed under the bed and wished he could disappear. His head spun. He understood most of the words the girl was saying, but they were strung together nonsensically. He waited for her to keep yelling, but she looked at him to speak. He took a deep breath.

"How many people died?" He had to know how much death he was responsible for.

"Wouldn't you like to know! Rafa is still alive, and I assume he was your main target. So, you failed. He was injured, but he's going to kill you himself, with his bare hands, when he wakes up. Unless you give me a good goddamn reason why he shouldn't!"

"Were you there ... at the blast?"

"Who are you? Where did you come from?" the girl snapped back.

Gordon wondered if he was hallucinating. None of it made any sense—the way she spoke, the things she said, the clothes she wore.

Some people, mostly pious dustlickers, believed that after death your soul was sent to be questioned by the Foreman. Perhaps it assessed how truthful you were about the time you spent living and determined your fate based on that. It was a ridiculous theory, but Gordon could only assume that's what was happening to him.

"I was an explosives apprentice. I didn't mean for anyone to die." It felt therapeutic to say it out loud. "But they did. I killed them," he added assuredly.

Denying it wouldn't help. And if he was in the afterlife's waiting room, he'd be on his way to hell soon enough. He didn't deserve to meet his mom in heaven, that was certain.

"You're not one of our crew," the girl said, pacing back and forth. "You didn't have a corporate ID card and you weren't wearing our uniform. So, again, who do you work for?"

Gordon didn't know what she wanted from him. He rocked nervously back and forth, avoiding eye contact. He felt like a mouse trying to swim its way out of a pitcher of beer.

"Come on," she said, raising her voice. "We're going to find out eventually. Why did you do it?"

"I wanted to do something after they killed my mom," Gordon whispered, looking the girl in the eye. "I had to. I thought it was what she'd want, and it would help me feel better. But it didn't, and now I'm here," he said, gesturing broadly. "I didn't know there were going to be people at the blast. I promise!"

"What?" The girl put her hands up. "I have no idea what you're talking about." She looked like she was chewing on her tongue.

"Whatever the punishment is, I'm ready for it. But know that I never meant to hurt anyone!"

"Cut the bullshit. Someone paid you to do this. You can tell me who it was now, or we'll find out in a few hours once the Intelligence team is done with the facial recognition analysis. We'll investigate every coffee you've ever bought and every overdue library book if we must. Every message you've ever sent. We'll find out."

Gordon looked up at her, puzzled. "No one paid me. If I wanted money, I would've found a way to keep my job in the mines. I would've been the best apprentice they ever had."

"If you really worked for us, then tell me your name."

"Gordon. Gordon Onyango."

The girl muttered something under her breath as she pulled out a handheld from her pocket and typed.

He scratched his head. The girl's handheld was super thin and completely transparent. He hadn't expected the afterlife to be so confusing. The Foreman was supposed to know everything, the least of which was his name.

If he wasn't dead, then he had no idea where he was.

"We've never had an apprentice with that name. You're lying!" the girl said, slamming her hand against the glass wall. Gordon's heart jumped into his throat. The man standing outside the glass looked in and titled his head, and Gordon curled up tighter under the bed.

Part of him wanted to give her Mickey and Dalrene's names. If he did, the Foreman would punish them severely. That would be justice, in a way. Mickey knew or should've known that there were going to be people at the blast and aborted the operation.

Turning them in seemed cowardly, though. He was the one who set the bombs. The first rule of explosives safety was that if you're unfamiliar with the blast site, assume there are people there. He was trained to do multiple checks and dry-runs, and never use unstable materials. Ultimate responsibility always lay with whoever had the detonator in their hands.

"I killed those people," he said. "I'm a killer now and I'm no better than the Foreman that killed my mom. So, like I said. Go ahead with the punishment."

"What's that?" she pointed at the First Olympians pendant.

"It's mine." Gordon tucked it under his shirt and out of view where it lay warmly on his chest.

"Show it to me," she demanded, standing over Gordon's gurney.

Up close, Gordon could see the determination in her eyes. Her fierceness terrified him. He bolted, clambering on all fours out from under the bed and through the girl's legs. But there was nowhere to run. He clawed at the door, but there was no handle. It wouldn't open.

His legs disappeared beneath him, and he landed with a thud. The girl's forearm pressed into his neck, and she tried to get a hold of the necklace with her other hand.

Gordon gasped for air and shoved her face away. The pendant was the only thing connecting him to his mother. He couldn't let it go.

"Just show it to me," the girl said, recoiling.

He tried to catch his breath.

She moved quickly, grabbing his shoulder before he could react. The girl twisted him around and pinned him, her hand holding his cheek against the floor.

He felt her press against his back, and she pulled the pendant out from its place against his chest. He squirmed but couldn't move. The girl was strong, and Gordon was helpless. She could snap his neck in seconds, and part of him expected her to. Instead, the pressure alleviated, and the girl backed off, giving him space. He stayed on the ground.

"This hasn't been our corporate logo in ... hundreds of years." There was a sense of amazement in her voice, like the pendant removed her serious façade. "Where did you get this?"

Gordon didn't respond. Slowly, he sat up against the wall, turning toward the girl. Her eyes were wide in disbelief.

"How old are you?" the girl asked. He could feel her studying his face.

"What?" Gordon mumbled hoarsely.

"A corporation wouldn't use anyone this young. How old are you?" she repeated, trying to regain her composure.

"Nine and a half," Gordon muttered.

He got the sense that whatever was happening was bigger than the Foreman, maybe even bigger than the outpost. He noticed a bruise on her collarbone for the first time. The pendant had broken her pretense, whatever it was, and he felt sympathy toward her. She was clearly under a lot of stress and close to her breaking point.

The girl stared at him in shock and took a step back. She braced herself on the glass wall. Outside, the man turned his head and looked inside again. He had a scowl on his face.

"Nine and a half. Martian years?"

Gordon nodded slowly and raised an eyebrow.

The girl slid down the wall into a sitting position. Time slowed to a crawl. She looked into his eyes, squinting like she was trying to read something far away, and then up at the ceiling with her mouth hanging open. He followed her gaze upward. There was nothing there except glass and concrete.

The girl rubbed her temples and ran her hands over the First Olympians pendant, like Gordon always did. She was flustered, like he'd told her something unbelievable.

"Are you okay?" he asked.

The anger flashed back to her face, and she jumped to her feet.

"I'll make sure they bring you more food. You should eat it this time."

Gordon nodded, but his head swirled with anxiety. At school, misbehaving students got detention or a beating. He didn't deserve to be let off the hook for murder.

She tucked her shirt back in and exited the room, still walking with a purpose, but no longer like a Faithless marching to a free meal. Her tall, pointy shoes didn't deafen Gordon's ears with each step anymore. The door closed without a thud. The man came over and locked it, and the metal-on-metal clank was the last thing he heard before the soundproof sterility of the room returned.

He didn't have his folding papers or his pendant. It wasn't long before images of limbs and blood crept back into his mind.

As terrifying as the girl was, he wished she'd stayed. Being alone was worse.

Chapter Twelve: Dalrene

A drop of water fell from the ceiling and splashed Dalrene's boot. The mug by the side of the stage was empty and had been for a while. The time for tea had passed. The grotto was quieter than ever, as her platoon leaders were in other caves, marshalling the army. Only her lieutenants remained, her closest and most skilled confidants, preparing for the stealth mission.

DeMar had insisted he be with his platoon. With his newly formed leg in a hard cast, he'd be way behind the action and nothing more than moral support. Dalrene was just happy he survived his injuries, at least so far. Rodriguez was still monitoring his internal bleeding.

Ionne sat on the ground, cleaning her knife for the hundredth time. She'd been quiet but constructive since her husband left. She was mature enough to put aside any differences and focus on the big picture. Dalrene was counting that as a win.

Rodriguez jittered his leg. They were all mentally tired, but physically ready. They'd gone over the details of the plan so many times that it was inscribed in the back of their skulls.

Taking over the Department of Information & Communication, or as the First Olympians called it, the propaganda building, was essential to success. As of last count, there were eight hundred and fifty-six soldiers in twelve different platoons, organized by letters of the Greek alphabet, all waiting for Dalrene's signal from their respective caves. It might be enough firepower to beat the Foreman. But in order to overwhelm it and score a quick, decisive victory, she was relying on her message to activate the thousands of regular people in the outpost that sympathized with her. She'd cultivated support with a year of pamphlet drops, rumor spreading, and other guerilla marketing techniques. Now, the people had to rise up, grab whatever household weapons they could, and help her take what was rightfully theirs. Broadcasting a call to rebel was the difference between success and failure, between a prison hole and a victory parade.

They were coming out swinging, they couldn't afford to miss.

Rumors abounded as to what the brain node actually *was*. Tess had worked long and hard to coerce information out of the outpost's highest ranking dustlickers with limited success. It'd been described as anything from a glowing black box no one had seen inside of, to an unimpressive shelf of computer parts, to even the mother of all robots. The only consistent descriptor was that it used a lot of power. If they pulled the plug, the Foreman wouldn't be able to instruct the processing nodes, and the house of cards would collapse.

Her troops, as well as any gutsy citizens who wanted to join, would march to the MCC, where Tess's research said the brain lived. With the Foreman distracted by Gordon's explosion, the war could be over before it reacted. If they couldn't kill the brain node, they'd fall back to their original plan and attack the processing nodes. It would be longer and bloodier, but each processing node they took out would leave the Foreman with fewer bots. It'd still be worth it.

Londi entered the cave and Dalrene looked past him. The few seconds that followed were gut-wrenchingly long. She had her hopes up until he shook his head.

Javier hadn't shown at the rendezvous. Dalrene let the sorrow wash over her. Either Javier and Ellie had been detained by the Foreman or refused to come. She hesitated, wondering if the former or the latter was worse, before landing on the former. If he didn't support her cause, he'd get over it when she won. But if the Foreman captured them ...

Londi put his hand on her shoulder but didn't say anything. The others looked away, either knowing no words would comfort, or not wanting to see her emotional guts splayed all over the cave floor.

Dalrene tied her hair behind her head and stood. She couldn't let herself dwell. They had a job to do, and she had to be a leader.

"Let's move out."

The only thing of value left behind were two environmental suits and oxygen tanks. Dalrene wondered how the other two suits were faring. She hadn't expected Mickey back yet, but it still hurt to split up. Not fighting side-by-side felt wrong. As they exited the grotto, she took a longing glance at the path where she last saw him head off.

She was going to have to fight without her husband. As she knew she would.

"Are you jealous of Gordon? I always thought you wanted to be the blaster," Rodriguez said.

"Yeah, sure." It was an obvious attempt to lighten the mood, but Dalrene appreciated it and responded with an eye roll.

Londi and Ionne chuckled. It was good they could all laugh. It was important in tense situations. Although, Rodriguez was right. She would've loved to be the one blowing up a key aspect of the outpost's infrastructure, and all the glory added by it happening on the surface. But the risks were too high. She didn't want to be a martyr. If she died and Ellie was put in a life-long labor camp, there was no point.

They each carried various weapons and gear, the most important of which was on

Dalrene's back, her electronics. If the plan to take over the propaganda building failed, they could try to splice into the network downstream. That would be risky because it would take time, and the message probably wouldn't get out to the entire outpost, but it was a decent fallback plan.

Londi had coated one side of her bag in a flexible metal, so she could use it as shield, and she had painted a red number one on it. Dalrene was thankful, but her gut told her that if she needed to use her shield, she was as good as dead anyways. She also carried a small knife strapped to her boot, her grandmother's. She wasn't a fighter. She was a leader, and a strategist, and was relying on others for brute force.

They walked as a group. The caves were the same as always, familiar and cold, but they possessed an added ethereal quality. The black, brown, and red walls seemed to have white tints, and the light from her headlamp caught glistening reflections she hadn't seen before. The sound of their footsteps walking in unison echoed like a march of ghosts.

It was all in her head, and she knew that, but the combination of amphetamines and the adrenaline rush from putting her plans into action made her more nervous than she expected. For years, it had been nothing more than a bunch of ideas too dangerous to write down or speak aloud. Now it was really happening for her and was about to be for many others. She wondered how much of her army or, hell, even her lieutenants, expected this day to actually come, and how many expected it to be a permanent fantasy. She wouldn't be the only one it felt surreal for.

Dalrene knew she wouldn't freeze when finally given the opportunity to fight the Foreman. Some people would. It was only natural to face existential challenges when fighting your god. She had to hope her army was big and determined enough to overcome them.

Londi dropped back, allowing Rodriguez and Ionne to walk ahead. He spoke in a hushed tone.

"Are you sure it was a good idea to invite Ionne? DeMar's injury was a big shock for her. She might not be at the top of her game." It looked like he had more to say but caught his tongue.

"And?"

"And I question her loyalty."

Dalrene exhaled sharply through her nose. "We're on the same team. We both want to see the Foreman lose. Trust can be re-built by winning. I believe that." Even before Janet's death and Demar's injury, she hadn't always seen eye-to-eye with Ionne.

"The platoon leaders all love her. Hell, one of them is her husband. She's spent a lot of time training recruits. Many expect her to be revealed as the leader. To be honest with you, I think they'd follow her."

"Well, it's a good thing she's with us and not marshaling the troops," Dalrene said, raising an eyebrow at Londi.

He blinked twice, then nodded curtly.

Londi had once been a family man, and before he joined the First Olympians, he led a tough life as a bruiser for one of the outpost's biggest gangs. The soldiers respected him, and never told him no. But he hadn't been strong when Dalrene first found him, withering in agony from drug withdrawal. He was a broken addict who failed his children. The only evidence left now of his prior life were the scars on his arms. She trusted his sense for the battlefield, and never doubted his compassion or loyalty, but politics wasn't his strong suit.

She thought of Mickey as they walked. Her love for him ran deep and old. For a long time, they were a regular couple trying to make ends meet and provide for their daughter. And life was good! Mickey worked an extraction job. He'd come home exhausted after a long shift in the mines, yet able to find energy to regale his family with old tales of Earth and songs of the absurd and wonderful. They would roar with laughter, all three of them, and their roommates in the communal holes couldn't do anything to stop them.

They raised Tess with love. Mickey would strum the guitar and she would sing, her voice soaring out over the residential area. None of their roommates complained about her singing. Sometimes she still heard Tess's soft, young voice in her dreams. Those were the good days.

The four of them stopped a few steps short of the entrance to Hope Street, a sleepy area of the outpost. Immediately to either side of them were two multilevel holes, blocking their view. Opposite, children played in front of a childcare center. Their caretaker bots didn't seem to notice Dalrene and her crew lurking in the caves.

Out of view, one hundred and fifty meters down the street, stood the propaganda building. Dalrene knew it well. She worked there for a year before Tess was born. It was where she honed her computer skills and grew her disdain for the Foreman and its sycophants. She'd been one of the only people hired for their skill, the technical expertise she learned from her father. Everyone else was there on account of their dustlicking, and the ease with which they processed the Foreman's lies made Dalrene sick.

"We have about an hour until the bomb goes off," Dalrene said, checking her handheld. She had timed the arrivals of the trucks on the surface and was confident in her prediction.

"We can't see much from here," Londi said. "We should do a walk-by and check the scene."

Dalrene nodded. She had intimate personal knowledge of the building from her time working there, updated blueprints, and access to unlock its doors. But none of those were a replacement for on-the-ground observations. It wasn't too risky to take a five-minute stroll down the street if they did it right. They brought hard hats for this purpose, to blend into the stream of mine workers. Travelling to and from the mines was the one sure activity that was allowed regardless of the curfew hours.

They entered the street, hats on, and walked with a sense of purpose. The propaganda building was large. It was the width of six holes combined and was a story taller too. It was constructed from the familiar clay-and-mud-brick, although the antennas standing on the roof made it stand out. They streamed everything from news about criminals on the most wanted lists, to ration reduction notifications and alerts for the start of the next shift. Seeing the building filled Dalrene with loathing and self-pity for the time she spent enabling the Foreman. She wouldn't have to bear that cross much longer.

It was Tess that realized the opportunities at the outpost were an illusion and the Foreman wasn't just a false idol, but an active oppressor. Dalrene recalled her last birthday. There was going to be a party, a celebration with Javier and the Ellie. But Tess called it off and instead threw the blinds closed and splayed papers and photographs all over the floor. Mickey begged her to end her investigation, but Dalrene recognized the fire in her daughter's eyes. She couldn't be stopped.

Despite the Foreman's best efforts, the outpost was sometimes a place of joy, where people tried to make the best of their situation. Not today. Dalrene could feel the anxiety in the air. The street was tightly packed with buildings, but few people walked them. Those that did avoided eye contact and kept their heads down.

They walked two by two, Dalrene and Londi in front of Ionne and Rodriguez. No-one sat in the chairs outside of the empty cafes. Children's wagons and pushcarts favored by the elderly sat in the street, abandoned. A monotone voice repeated on the loudspeakers overhead:

A level three lockdown is in effect. Consult your handheld for updated curfew hours and exceptions. Failure to observe the rules will result in prosecution.

The screens on the sides of the shops displayed the same message and then switched back to Foreman-approved news. These were the communications capabilities that they had to commandeer. With them, Dalrene could give the signal to her army and call on others to join their cause.

"Pretty significant activity. The distraction better work," Ionne said.

She was right. Two dozen peacekeepers sat idle in charging ports along the exterior of the propaganda building. The automatic doors opened, revealing even more bots crawling around inside. Dalrene felt her gut tighten. She'd never seen so many packed so closely together before.

"It'll work," Dalrene said. "It has to." She noted the exterior staircase that ran up the back of the building was unguarded. Even though the bomb on the surface would hopefully draw most of the bots away, they didn't want to go head-to-head against any that stayed behind if they didn't have to. She could unlock the door to the top floor, and they'd bypass most of the bots and get access to the sensitive broadcasting equipment. There were also a half-dozen cameras protruding from the roof corners. Dalrene could shut those off.

"Let's circle around this block and get back to the cave," Londi said.

"I agree." They got a glimpse of how the enemy's forces were arranged, and confirmed they were going to have to be sneaky. With the scouting complete, it was time to get back to safety.

Dalrene pictured her cute, innocent granddaughter as they approached the end of the street. Mickey's happiest moments after Tess's death were when he played the guitar. He seemed to channel his guilt and pain into his strumming and singing, leaving him free for the length of a song. One day, maybe he could teach Ellie how to play. It was a fantasy, but sometimes that's what it took to keep them moving forward.

So, they couldn't afford to pick a fight they couldn't win. Even after Tess's murder, they still had more to lose. She'd imagined this day many times, and thought she'd be more anxious when it finally came. But she wasn't. Though her adrenaline was pumping, and the surrealism of the march through the deep was fading, Dalrene was more determined and clear-eyed than ever as they turned the street corner.

She stopped a few inches short of two peacekeepers, nearly slamming into them.

She kept her head down and made a movement to step around the bots, motioning to the others to follow her. The bots moved to block them.

"State your reason for travel during curfew," one of them chimed.

Londi gave Dalrene a side eye that suggested he could take the bots down before they alerted the Foreman to what was happening.

She responded with a subtle shake of her head. Their fake thumbprints were good. They looked like miners. As long as the bots didn't jump right to a full facial scan, they would be fine. There was no reason to risk escalation.

"Work. Going down the shaft," Dalrene grunted.

"Submit your handhelds for verification."

Shit! She hadn't been expecting that. They each had sanitized burner handhelds they could provide that were even connected to the network, but they wouldn't show a shift schedule.

"No handhelds today," Dalrene said, holding out her thumb as a peace offering.

"Full handheld scans required. Failure to produce may result in detention."

She thought of the mass of bots hanging out just down the street and shuddered. Violence was their only option, but they were going to have to be quick and efficient.

She tilted her head, giving Londi the go ahead, but the bots bolted toward them. She braced for impact, but it never came. They sailed clear, way to the side, and continued down the street, accelerating away.

"What did we do to deserve that kind of luck?" Rodriguez asked.

A line of bots wheeled out from the propaganda building and followed the others away. When she thought it was empty, and there was no way it could fit anymore bots, more charged out. The procession lasted minutes.

"It wasn't luck," Londi said.

"I thought we still had time! There should be forty minutes until the bomb," Ionne said.

"It must've gone off early. It doesn't matter. We can thank Gordon for that later. Let me turn off these cameras and we'll move. Now's our chance," Dalrene said. She could only hope Mickey and Gordon were okay.

The foursome moved briskly back to the propaganda building. Dalrene pulled her computer out and ran her pre-keyed commands to neutralize the building's exterior cameras. To the Foreman, it would look like nothing more than a thirty second outage as they slipped by. There was always risk, but that was the cost of engagement.

There were no signs of life in the windowless building as they approached. Other than the bot evacuation, it seemed to be business as usual. They turned the corner to the backside of the building and the repeating level-three lockdown announcements grew fainter. Dalrene was thankful for that.

Their boots would've made a clanging sound on the black, metal staircase if they let them. A vivid memory popped into Dalrene's head as they climbed. In it, she and some of the younger computer programmers were taking a break, drinking tea and lounging on the steps. The sweet, sickly smell of molasses flavored nicotine wafted through the air. Dalrene animatedly told her colleagues that she calculated the true electricity reserves based on data she'd seen as part of her job, and there was no need for the week's rolling blackouts. The Foreman was being stingy with its energy. To her dismay, everyone rolled their eyes and turned away. That was when she knew she'd rather be Faithless than a dustlicker.

"Shit!" Dalrene froze.

Her lieutenants stopped behind her.

At the top of the staircase was a single door, and above it was an array of spinning sensors that looked like the head of an inspector bot.

"That one didn't show up in my blueprints. It must be new." She already had her computer out and was biting her gums. "It's classified differently than normal cameras. High level security, I don't have access."

"I can hide my face and have it cleared out in seconds," Londi said, looking to Dalrene for approval.

"But then it'll know we're here," Rodriguez huffed.

"It's going to figure that out no matter what," Ionne said. "The important thing is that we get our message out first."

Depending on how many people and bots were inside, that could take a while. Giving the Foreman any bit of heads-up was dangerous, but they didn't have any other choice. They couldn't stand half-way up the stairs forever and finding another way inside was no guarantee. "Do it."

Londi pulled a balaclava over his head and ran up the remaining stairs. The sensors twirled at him quizzically. Without stopping for a second, he jumped high up onto the wall. In the same motion, he jumped off the wall and reached up to the sensor array. He hung for a moment, like a kid hanging from a basketball hoop.

Then, Londi and the array crashed down.

"Well, that's one way to do it," Rodriguez said in astonishment.

They hustled up the remaining stairs to meet Londi. When he put his hand on the door, Dalrene already had her finger hovering over her keyboard.

She hoped there was no one in the big, open room on the top floor that employees called Info Central. Bots were dangerous, but predictable. Londi and the others could take out a bunch of peacekeepers. But people were messy and unreliable. The best-case scenario was that they made for subdued hostages. The type of people that worked there would never by sympathetic to her cause.

Heart pounding, she pressed the button, and Londi and Ionne charged through the door. Their weapons, oversized metal crowbars perfect for cleaning out a bot's sensor suite, were raised above their heads. Rodriguez rushed in after them, and Dalrene followed, her computer back in her bag and her knife in hand. She expected to hear the clash of metal, screams, and disarray.

Except, there was no one there.

No bots, no humans. No one.

Monitor displays hanging over desks lined every inch of wall space. Microphones, antennas, and cameras were clustered in a corner, beside a caged metal box that housed the CPU server. A processing node.

One of sixteen that talked to the Foreman's brain node and controlled the bots, and therefore life at the outpost. After all these years, it still gave her the creeps to see one in person.

Londi and Ionne moved around the perimeter of the room, weapons still raised. Rodriguez rushed to the inner door that led downstairs and locked it, then laughed nervously.

Dalrene caught her breathe. She couldn't make sense of it.

"It shouldn't have been this easy," Ionne said. "Where is everyone?" She spoke breathlessly, in what could have been amazement or fear.

"Sometimes the universe smiles upon you. Things work out," Rodriguez chuckled, stroking his mustache.

"You don't get lucky on this planet," Dalrene said. "The Foreman is playing at something, but I don't know what."

"Let's set-up a barricade," Londi said, dragging a desk to the door. "We have to expect a response."

Dalrene walked over to the wall of screens where information whizzed by. Some showed surveillance videos from cafes, elevators, and other places. Others displayed statistics showing how many people had heard or seen certain messages, and which propaganda techniques were most effective. There was a chart detailing that the announcement on cooking oil ration reductions was due to be replaced with a search for volunteers needed to harvest a crop of wheat.

Rodriguez filmed with his handheld. "Here it is. Proof! Not just of surveillance, but of lies and manipulation!"

"Facts don't win wars," Dalrene said. It was something Mickey said, and she believed it. Video evidence of the Foreman lying to control people could easily be shrugged away. It didn't matter. She needed to win hearts and get people to believe that if they worked together, they could forge a new society.

A big microphone sat on the desk in front of her, and she leaned in.

"This is the leader of the First Oly—"

The mic went dead. The screen went black.

Chapter Thirteen: Alex

"Come on!" she said, smacking the wall of the elevator.

Alex paced back and forth, sweating through her suit jacket. The door opened at the lobby, and two giggly interns jaunted toward her before stopping short at the sight of her expression.

"We'll get the next one."

Alex remembered she could use executive privileges for priority, and she mashed the button on her handheld. The doors closed and she paced around the elevator as it ascended. She had to learn more about the boy in the detention room. Find out where the hell he came from. Vet his story. See if there was any way he could be telling the truth about working at Mine One.

No! That was ridiculous! He was a terrorist who nearly killed her dad. She couldn't trust a word he said. Alex shuddered, thinking about how much he unnerved her. There had to be an explanation for his weirdness. His odd mannerisms, his age, given in Martian years, of "nine and a half", his pendant with a centuries-old corporate logo. It was a ruse, it had to be, but no doubt an exceptionally elaborate one. But why? She couldn't figure out what the purpose of it was.

Her stomach churned. She hated being clueless. Her dad would know what was going on. She just had to scrounge up enough courage to ask him. She now knew how regular employees felt: painfully aware of his distaste for bad news and chagrined at having to ask tough questions.

There was a hospital for regular employees, but her dad was in the executive facilities high up on the eightieth floor. When the elevator beeped, Alex hustled down the hallway lined with ornate, silver mirrors on the walls and chandeliers on the ceiling. She burst through the oversized doors to her father's VIP medical room.

A few doctors and nurses stood by her dad's double-wide bed. Trophies from his hunting trips, including a rhinoceros horn and antlers of all types hung on the wall above him. A dozen more staff walked around with clipboards or between the desks that sat against the floor-to-ceiling windows. Other than a couch against the interior wall, the room was sparse for its size.

"Thank god, someone more interesting to talk to." Her dad's bed was at a forty-five-degree angle, and he was sitting up in it, shooing away a doctor. His thick, freshly cut, salt-and-pepper hair still looked perfectly in place, like it was fake. The staff left, giving them some space.

Alex chuckled to herself. Not even an explosion could mess up his appearance. "Good to see you're awake. Looks like you haven't missed a beat."

"Of course. And you? Do we know what happened?"

"I'm fine... . Some of the security guards didn't make it." Exhaustion came out of nowhere, weighing her down. Alex hadn't known the people that died, or seen the explosion, but the aftermath had been grisly. She hadn't fully processed it yet. She wished she could just forget about it and the strange, seemingly time-traveling murderer in the basement. She wanted to lie on the couch and just be happy that her dad was okay. But she couldn't. She had to find out what was going on.

"Corporate terrorists?" It was more of a statement than a question. Her dad shifted in his bed as he spoke. "I thought we were done with that years ago. Why would anyone start a war now? All the remaining players benefit more by partnering with us or innovating something technical and hoping we buy them out. Direct competition isn't a viable option."

Alex gave a slight nod.

Her dad paused and looked amusedly at the IV needle going into his left arm. "A whole team of doctors and none of them brought me a cup of coffee. What am I paying them for, really?"

She sighed and walked to the window. The view was much the same as from the penthouse office ten stories up. The sprawling greenhouse, hospital, and the dozens of residential buildings looked quaint from this height and against the backdrop of the never-ending Martian frontier. From this angle she could also see the solar-panel arrays, soon to be obsolete due to advances in nuclear fusion technology. Out of view was the resource center that collected ore like that from Mine One, the equipment warehouses, and the expansive space transit bays. First Corp had spread out, like a spider web, but they still only covered a tiny fraction of the surface.

The sun was starting to set, and the office tower cast a large shadow on the plains in front of her. The dry Martian desert, and the rolling red hills beyond them, were motionless and dead. Hundreds of kilometers beyond that, the planet's largest volcano lurked out of sight. A chill went down Alex's spine as she thought of Olympus Mons and the explosion.

Her handheld buzzed in her pocket, and she pulled it out. Corporate Intelligence completed their facial recognition analysis and failed to find a match. *Weird*. A cross reference of biometrics against port of entry data was underway. The next step would be to try to find a match in Earth databases. Outside of that, they had no leads. The Chief

Intelligence Officer was already offering to apologize in person.

Her stomach churned. The Intelligence team was creepy, but more importantly, she'd never seen them fail before. Something was very wrong.

"Alex? Are you sure you're okay? You have a meeting with a trauma counsellor set up, right?"

"Why did you build a skyscraper?" Alex continued looking out at the desert. She was building up the courage to ask her dad what she truly wanted to know—was it possible the young terrorist was one of theirs, as he claimed? Were they violating interplanetary child labor laws? She'd gotten an age exemption, so maybe it was possible for others. Maybe there was a simple explanation. She should just ask him. She had to know. But at the same time, the potential truth terrified her.

"What?"

"It makes no sense. It wasn't an easy problem to solve, and the construction was even harder than the engineering. What a waste of time and resources. Besides, if there's anything Mars has plenty of, it's space. We could've spread out."

Her dad coughed before taking a sip of water. "My father wanted to build an office tower because he could. And because of what this building represents to the governments back on Earth, and to our would-be competitors on this planet."

"It's unnecessary," Alex said. She'd never seen death like at Mine One. In a world where boys her age blew people up for no reason, First Corp's excesses seemed trivial and gauche.

"Every time an employee of Red Sea sees this office tower, they wished they worked here," her dad said, raising his voice. "Or they get pissed off and start thinking about corporate terrorism, apparently. Which is what we need to focus on! The good news is the blast was far enough away that the press has no idea, and there's no way for them to find out. Everyone on our team has been provided as much paid time off as they want and been instructed never to speak of the incident outside of therapy. Now, bring me my handheld. We need to start finding out who did this."

"It was a boy," Alex blurted, turning to face her father. "We found him at the blast. He said he works for us, but we have no record of him."

"A terrorist that's also a liar. Who would've thunk it?" Her dad chuckled. "So, who does he work for then?"

"That's the thing. Intelligence has no record of him. No work permits. No paperwork for leaving Earth at all. Facial recognition showed nothing. More analysis is underway, but so far, he's a ghost."

"Okay, so he was smuggled here just for this job. A professional. An elaborate move, but not surprising that whoever was behind this didn't want to make it easy for us to find them."

Alex exhaled. That made sense. Why didn't she think of that? Her brain must be as tired as her body.

"He was carrying this." Alex held the metal pendant up. She moved to her dad's side so he could have a better view.

"Wow." He blinked. "What a relic. This should be in a museum if its real. Why would a terrorist have it? Peculiar. I can only guess at the mind games he's playing. Why don't you let me take it from here? I'll talk to him."

Alex's head was swimming all over again. Had the terrorist taken advantage of her weary, fragile state? Maybe the whole speaking softly and hiding under the bed was just an act designed to confuse her. But that possibility didn't dissuade her from wanting to find out the truth. If anything, it increased it.

"He looked young, maybe even younger than me. He's not—we don't have underagers on our staff, do we?" Alex bit her lip.

"No, of course not. We have to follow all the UN's rules until we can rid ourselves of those spineless bureaucrats. If he was smuggled here, then he could be underage. They don't check the birth certificates of terrorists, sweetheart! But that's the least of our worries. His age doesn't matter."

Alex was relieved that was an easy question for her dad to answer. But the next one gave her a knot in her stomach.

"The weird part was that he said he was nine and a half. As in, Martian years. He gave his age in Martian years." The words burned her throat and nostrils on the way up. Saying it out loud made her feel ridiculous, but it was too strange not to mention. All companies on Mars had Earth investors and served Earth customers. Earth years were standard.

Her dad threw up his hands. "Who knows? He's clearly trying to manipulate us. I'll talk to him when I'm back on my feet and figure out what the angle is. For now, why don't you get some rest? I could use some too. It's been a long and stressful day."

She felt a weight lift from her chest.

"That's a good idea," Alex said. Her shoes felt like cinder blocks. She twisted her torso, stretching her back, and allowed herself to exhale. Her dad was probably right, as usual. The terrorist was playing with her mind and things would make a lot more sense after she got some sleep.

But the puzzle still begged to be solved. What about Mine One? Someone had to have seen something in the hours or days leading up to the attack. Surely there were cameras that would've captured the terrorist's arrival at the loading docks, or maybe he had inside help from one of their employees. There was a lot for her to investigate.

"Don't give your doctors too hard of a time," Alex said. "I'll figure it out." She left, and the parade of medical staff returned to the room.

#

Her hole, a cute, archaic term for living space on Mars, was the penthouse of a twenty-storey residential building. It was grand, with high ceilings, gaudy gold fixtures, and leather furniture.

Alex hated it. It was a far cry from the Spanish villa she grew up in, with its warm, clay-tiled roof and airy interior courtyard. The floor-to-ceiling windows made the apartment feel like a soulless American hotel. She spent as little time there as possible, which contributed to her lack of connection to it.

The only room she was comfortable in was the bedroom. Her bed was Victorian style with a dark, wood backboard, which would've been classy if it didn't have silver and gold tacked on the frame. Her eyes closed the second she crawled into it, and she fell into a heavy, dreamless sleep.

Fourteen hours later, she awoke surprisingly alert. Her body must've needed all that sleep. She stretched out, her neck and back sore. A bruise had developed on her shoulder. The explosion had rocked her around the truck, but her cuts and other injuries weren't worse than a kickboxing match. She'd survive.

Her handheld buzzed, and she swatted away notifications about the morning's meetings she'd missed and cancelled the rest of her day. She had to find out about the prisoner who said he worked in the mines and provided his age in Martian years. The strange boy who spoke with a sharp, attenuated accent that stressed all the wrong parts of words. The time traveller who carried a centuries old artifact dating to the planet's first settlers. The terrorist who tried to kill her dad.

How long had he been at Mine One? Who was he working with? An attack of this magnitude was not something organized by a lone wolf. He would've had significant financial and operational support. Olympus Mons was remote, so he might've had a temporary base of operations nearby. Did he scout out the site before the explosion? Who saw him around, and what did they see?

She placed her handheld on the clothes dresser and projected the employee database on the wall. She had the highest level of security clearance and could see everyone's salary, date of birth, space-aptitude test scores, work-permit status, everything. It should be straightforward to find employees of Mine One and ask if they saw any suspicious activity in the days leading up to the explosion.

She settled in, sitting on the edge of the bed as she navigated the menus with swipes of her fingers. The drapes were still closed, but the darkness suited her mood. She didn't care to call for her usual latte. She found the directory for Mine One and was excited to find a listing of over three and a half thousand employees.

The first employee she clicked on was Rosalina Cartier:

Date of Hire: Unknown

Status: Inactive
Department:
Job Title:

Alex furrowed her brow. The rest of the data fields such as Earth home address and contact information were blank. She'd never seen an employee profile so bare. She swiped through the next few employees, and then the next hundred. Some didn't even have full names. They were all like that.

There were simply no active employees at Mine One.

Didn't someone have to work there? It didn't make sense. She felt uneasy, like she was poking around someplace she wasn't supposed to. She backed out of the employee database and found the latest delivery report, dated a few days prior:

Shipment received by Resource Center, First Corp. HQ
Signature upon receipt: Egor Travor
Titanium – 30,000 KG
Lithium – 16,500 KG

So, someone did work with the mine, if not at it. Even if operations were largely automated, it would require a significant human crew to maintain a robot fleet capable of delivering that much material weekly. She clicked through to Egor Travor. It was a much more normal employee profile. There was a picture of a mustached man with a receding hairline and a thin-lipped smile. He'd worked at the company for six years and this was his third tour on Mars. He was clocked in at the resource center, the staging ground for ore prior to refinery, and was about to go on a lunch break.

Alex got on her way. Every building in the First Corp. complex was connected by long pedestrian walkways that reminded her of traveling between terminals at an airport, just with windows. The noon sun was high above her, and she would've embraced it with a smile if she wasn't so consumed with her hunt. Her handheld chimed every few minutes, telling her to take a left or right turn. Although her Mars tour was more than half over, she hadn't explored every path and building yet, and she didn't want to get lost.

The resource center was a massive square warehouse building with a flurry of trucks always coming and going. She'd taken a tour of it once, during her first week, but they'd entered via the oversized garage door to the sorting and storage facilities. Now, she entered the employee area, where people re-filled their oxygen tanks, took breaks, and ate lunch.

She went through the door and blinked in response to the industrial, white lighting. The hallway continued as it had, but there were no more windows. She passed rooms labelled "Safety Equipment," "Mechanical Supplies," and "Environmental Equipment." On a normal day, she would've loved to spend time sorting through all the gear in those rooms. But today, she entered the Lunch Room, the last door before the airlock.

She recognized Egor right away. He was the same as his picture, although even more bald. He sat at one of the closest of the dozens of tables beside a woman with short blond hair. On his plate was what was supposed to be a salad: leaves of a hearty lettuce cousin that was fit to grow in Martian greenhouses and chunks of unseasoned, lab-grown protein. Alex grew tired just looking at it.

The greasy smell of something being deep-fried wafted over from the kitchen as she took a seat beside Egor's lunch mate.

His mouth hung open. The woman had a similar look of bewilderment on her face. It was clear they recognized her. "Can I help you?" he asked.

"Yes, I think you can," Alex said, pushing her hair behind her shoulder. "I want to know about Mine One. The shipments. Who brings them in? What's in them?"

Egor rubbed his bald spot. "Well, it's just like we put in the logs. Titanium. Lithium. Chromium. The trucks are on a fully automated circuit. I'm not involved with the haul until it gets here."

"Anything different happen recently? See anything or anyone out-of-place? Irregular?"

The blast was being kept hush-hush, and these employees wouldn't have heard about it. Alex looked him deep in his gray-green eyes. He looked scared, but she couldn't tell if it was of her or something else.

"They missed their last shipment, but I haven't heard why. Not much work for us to do without it, but we're keeping busy, getting our safety training done and keeping our certs up to date." Egor and his friend nodded enthusiastically.

"Anything else?"

Egor took his time to respond. "This mine isn't connected to the IT system like the other ones. I get paper logs, like we're in medieval times or something, and I upload them into our database."

The hair on Alex's arms raised.

"Why?"

"I don't know. I assumed just because it's so old. Technological limitations and all that, y'know. But I know who might know."

"Who?" This was like pulling teeth.

"Um, look, I know you have all the proper security clearances and everything, but ..." Egor exchanged a look with his friend.

Alex raised an eyebrow.

"Maybe we can help each other out," he said, lowering his voice.

Alex had to work hard to stop herself from rolling her eyes. She was working on something serious. People had already died. Lives were at stake, and Egor was trying to shake her down like it was a game.

"I can get you access to the management cafeteria for a month. Way better food," Alex said, scrunching her nose at his plate. Higher level employees were scared to death of her, fearful she'd unleash her dad's rage on them. Egor didn't seem to have the same apprehensions. Under different circumstances, she would've found it refreshing.

"This isn't bad. You get used to it." He twirled his fork in his salad.

"Tell me what you want, and I can get it for you," Alex said, her voice tense. "Or I can make sure your next performance review process is extra thorough. Maybe your off-planet transmissions get chosen for an audit." Enough was enough. Alex preferred carrots, but she wasn't above using a stick.

"A table for two at the Humdinger and seats in the movie theatre." Egor squeaked.

"Done and done." She tapped on her handheld. Entertainment was hard to come by, and the Humdinger was the only restaurant that would count as half decent on Earth. Its prices meant it was used almost exclusively by those in the higher pay grades.

"So, who do I need to talk to?"

"Pat." Egor said it as if it was obvious.

"Pat?"

"Patricia Iglesias. She's not a director or anything. I actually don't know her job title. But she's the only one who asks me about that mine."

"Thanks," Alex said as flatly and sarcastically as she could.

She walked away with Patricia Iglesias' information already coming up on her handheld. Her official job title was "Mining Administrator." It sounded like a low-level position, but when she clicked through she saw that Pat reported directly to her father. Alex didn't know what to make of that. Her dad had a ton of people reporting to him, but they were all Presidents or Vice-Presidents. This was strange.

She'd made progress, but still felt like she had more questions than answers. She learned that the trucks were fully automated, and that they missed a shipment. She assumed that was because the loading dock was now in pieces. But why wasn't Mine One connected to their IT system? There had to be some way to get the security footage. Wouldn't the insurance policies her dad was always going on about require it?

She hoped Pat would tell her.

Chapter Fourteen: Dalrene

Dalrene dropped the dead microphone to the ground. It hadn't worked. They hadn't delivered their call to arms.

A siren blared overhead, and she covered her ears in pain.

"Level-five lockdown. All humans must proceed to the Humanity Containment Zone. Use of force is authorized."

She punched the blank screen. The message on the speakers repeated itself. She kicked the microphone, and it thumped the wall.

"Fuck!"

Dalrene was the only one old enough to remember the last level-five lockdown, and her recollections were not kind. The reason for it was never clear, but mining operations were suspended, and humans had to cluster deep down in the pits for weeks. She had vivid memories of people dying from thirst and begging the peacekeepers to let them go home. The Foreman was taking the threat of their insurrection very seriously.

"Level five. That's a full quarantine," Ionne said, her voice tense.

"I know what it goddamn means!" Dalrene said, rubbing her temples. Her head felt like it was going to explode.

No one spoke, and she realized they were waiting for her to gather herself. Londi's arm muscles bulged. Rodriguez's upper lip twitched. Ionne ground her teeth. No matter what happened, she had to be the calm one. Her lieutenants were leaders in their own right, but even they took cues from her, and she had to set the example.

The announcement paused and the siren quieted to an obnoxiously loud, but not overwhelming volume. Dalrene spoke quickly and directly.

"We're locked out of the comms," she said, pacing in front of the screens and her lieutenants. "But that's why we have a back-up plan. There's an amplifier in a building down the block. It's a whiskey bar. If we get there, I can splice into the network and still get our message out. It'll be messy, and because it's downstream, it only broadcasts to half the outpost. We'll need to be quick, but we can still do this!"

"Let's go," Londi said.

"And this processing node?" Rodriguez smacked the outside of the CPU server.

"We'll have to come back and destroy it later. We still need the comms system up to get our message out," she said.

They rushed down the main stairwell, through the foyer, and onto the dirt street. Dalrene's lip stayed curled. She was annoyed, although still confident. The Foreman had tricks up its sleeves, but so did she. The battle was far from over.

As they hustled to the whiskey bar, they passed a steady stream of families huddled in blankets and carrying bottles of water. These were the early ones, but all law-abiding citizens would get down to the Humanity Containment Zone within a few hours. After that, bots would start entering holes. No one wanted to be home when that happened.

Some in the crowds had a distant, soulless look on their face. They were the already traumatized, preparing for more suffering by mentally and emotionally detaching. Others looked around anxiously and asked questions no one could answer. Dalrene felt horrible for them. They didn't know what they were getting into.

A young girl bawled her eyes out, burying her face into her dad's shoulder as he carried her. She wasn't the only one crying. A sharp pain drove through her heart, and she wondered where Ellie was and hoped she wasn't scared.

"We're fighting the Foreman! Join us!" Rodriguez waved his arms.

"Stay away!" A man yelled back.

"We have to splice into that comms node." Dalrene, spoke to Londi low and fast. "We look like a random batch of Faithless defying the lockdown orders. We need to give the platoon leaders the signal to leave the deep. That is everything right now."

"We've got movement down the street," Londi said. "Peacekeepers, six of them."

The bots were only five buildings away. Behind them was the whiskey bar they were trying to get to. She saw sparks fly from one of their tasers. No doubt its normally non-lethal weapons were jacked up to maximum power. Another bot raised a spinning blade attached to its arm.

Dalrene's eyes widened. "Move! Let's take a lap." That the bots were blocking the way to their target seemed like a coincidence; the Foreman couldn't know their plan to use the whiskey bar. They could draw the peacekeepers away and then circle back. The four of them stuck out as obvious targets because they weren't travelling with the flow of people.

They bolted, and the bots accelerated behind them. They could turn and fight, but the peacekeepers weren't a priority target, and if they fought every squad of robots they saw, they wouldn't last very long. There were only four of them. Activating the rest of the army and encouraging regular citizens to join their cause was a more prudent strategy.

They made a turn. They were the only people on the deserted residential street. Twenty seconds later, the bots joined them.

The sound of blades and saws cutting through the air grew closer behind them.

"They're hot on us!" Rodriguez wheezed from the rear.

They sprinted around the last corner, arriving back to street where they first saw the peacekeepers.

"In here," Dalrene yelled, ducking into the whiskey bar. "I can patch into the comms. Fortify the doors and windows!"

Her lieutenants went straight to work, blockading the windows with chairs and moving tables against the door.

A string of soft lights ran along the ceiling, and fake wood decor, stained a deep red, was meant to impose a serious drinking atmosphere. Whiskey bottles lined the mirror that took up the entire wall behind the bar. Half-full glasses sat on the counter in front of overturned stools. People had left in a hurry. A bar bot twitched on the floor, a victim of the swift exodus.

The peacekeepers crashed against the fortified windows. They cut away at the door with their saws.

"Hold the fort!" she yelled. "I just need a few minutes."

Dalrene plopped her computer on the bar and looked at the blueprints. Cables from the propaganda building ran in two directions, each way down the street, before splitting into spiderwebs that covered the entire outpost.

She knocked on the wall, listening for where it was hollow, until she found the exact spot. She took the butt-end of her knife and hit it, caving it in and exposing a plethora of electronics. Wires of all colors ran up and down, ending at a box about head height. That was it, the downstream connection. She fumbled in her bag for a microphone.

A spinning metal blade flew past Dalrene's head and sliced a wire. Sparks erupted and she jumped back.

"Holy shit!"

"Since when were these sons of bitches retrofitted with projectiles?" Londi yelled.

"I've heard stories, but first time seeing it!" Dalrene gave him a look that said she was as surprised as he was.

A bot shoved its way through a table that had been pushed against a window.

"They're in!" Londi pegged its head with a crowbar, smashing the glass that covered its sensors. The peacekeeper fell to the ground, waving its handsaw in the air and beeping like mad.

Dalrene turned back to the split wire. At least now she knew where to splice her mic! She worked fast, having dreamed of moments like this often. With a few tricks, she'd be able to shut off the blaring alarms and deliver her message. In theory, at least. And even if it worked, it'd only reach half the outpost. She'd have to rely on word of mouth to reach the rest.

When she connected her microphone, the sirens stopped. For a few seconds, all she could hear was the grunting of her crew and the whirring of the peacekeepers as their weapons rose and fell, metal clashing against metal, plastic, and brick.

"People of Olympus Outpost," Dalrene said, her voice booming from the speaker above the bar, and down the street. "You have been lied to. Earth is dead! We are mining resources for a planet that can't even use them! The Foreman is a false god. Do not pay it fealty! Do not listen to its orders!" She took a deep breath. "This is a call to arms! Join us, the First Olympians. Let's take over Mission Control! Let's kill the brain node and take back the outpost. Let's take back our freedom!"

Dalrene looked up and gasped.

The biggest robot she'd ever seen crashed through the barricade at the front door, throwing bar stools and Ionne to the ground. It had legs instead of wheels! It was fully bi-pedal! It raised one arm, and her heart dropped.

The robot had a damn gun arm! And not a small, three-D-printed handgun like Big Titus had tried to sell her. This was a long, multi-barrelled automatic rifle.

Londi reached out to Ionne and pulled her behind an overturned table.

Rodriguez disappeared behind the restroom door.

The bot's head whirled around and focused on Dalrene.

Its gun followed.

"We're under attack! The whiskey bar at the intersection of Torres and Hope!" She yelled one last plea into the microphone before ducking behind the counter.

Bullets shattered bottles.

It rained glass and whiskey.

"I need some help over here!" she screamed. She didn't know where this bot had come from, but it was her nightmare. Her heart was thumping so fast it hurt, and she held her shield bag over her head, taking cover from the debris. Was this how it ended for her, on a barroom floor? Her granddaughter had already lost a mother. Dying wasn't an option.

There was a roaring sound, like a motor was starting. The robot jumped over the bar and landed with a giant thud that rumbled her entire body. It again pointed its giant head of cameras and lasers at her.

Time quickened, but her own movements seemed to slow. Her mouth was dry. Her stomach dropped. She blinked. Dalrene was acutely aware of the fine line between her desperation to live and the sensors of death lining her up.

The bot whipped its gun around and aimed at her chest.

Dalrene raised her bag and let out a visceral yell from the bottom of her gut. She stuffed whatever fears she had deep inside her. Shots zinged off her makeshift shield, shaking her arms and sending vibrations through her body.

It took all her might not to drop it.

When the bullets stopped, the robot made a clanking sound. It must've been reloading. Dalrene dared to peak out from behind her heavily dented shield, and she saw Londi with a crowbar over his head and a crazed look in his eyes. He smashed the robot's arm-gun where it connected to its body and sparks went flying.

Rodriguez emerged and spray painted its face, covering its cameras and obstructing its LIDAR. The bot made an angry beeping sound. "I think I blinded it!"

"What the hell is that thing?" Dalrene asked. None of her plans accounted for a new type of deadly robot that could leap, run, and shoot!

No one replied, but Londi continued striking the bot. He dented one of its arms but didn't break it. It must've weighed hundreds of pounds.

The bot beeped again and started to twirl in a circle. It stretched out its arm-gun, making a clicking sound when it reached full extension.

"Duck!" Dalrene yelled and her crew threw themselves to the floor and behind cover.

The robot spun, shooting wildly in all directions. Bullets went everywhere at chest-height, through windows, whiskey bottles, and furniture. Dalrene closed her eyes and held her shield. And her breath.

The bot stopped firing for a moment and she smelled smoke. Maybe it had overheated.

Dalrene opened her eyes to see Londi rush the robot again and pin it against the bar, restraining it. Ionne and Rodriguez smashed its arms, trying to break its rifle. It was too big and fortified to demolish with the weapons they had, but Dalrene rushed over with her knife and cut the wires protruding from the back of the bot's sensor array.

"You're done!" Londi broke the bot's cameras with disgust. The four of them hacked at its plastic and metal legs until it they were satisfied it no longer poised a danger.

Dalrene touched the multi-barrelled gun that was longer than her arm and found it hot. She didn't know what disturbed her more, the gun, or the legs. Bi-pedal bots were mobile and agile. Her group wouldn't be able to erect barriers or hide behind uneven terrain. Machine guns could tear through her army in seconds. Together, the revelations changed the nature of the war. The Foreman had been hiding its biggest weapon.

"If there's any more like this, we're gonna want to move out of here fast," Londi said.

The bot had a trapezoidal mid-section that was wider where it connected to its shoulder frame. It was giant, at least a meter taller than the protectors, and way heavier. It took all four of them to heave it onto its back. Where its body met its legs there was a small inscription.

Guardian 0127

Dalrene whistled in surprise. "Hopefully our people come quick, because there could be a lot of these suckers. There will be safety in numbers." She meant what she said, but she didn't know if she believed it herself. Hundreds, maybe thousands of guardians? That would make for a formidable foe no matter how large her army was. It made getting to the nodes even more vital.

Dalrene stood and surveyed the scene. A heap of metal robot parts scattered the floor. Ionne was poking her head into the street. Rodriguez took a shot of whiskey from the bar.

"Uh, guys?" Ionne said.

Dalrene ran to the door. She looked down Torres Street and grabbed her heart.

Dozens of guardians—upwards of fifty—barrelled down the street, coming right at them.

Chapter Fifteen: Alex

Mining Ops occupied the oldest building of the First Corp. complex, and its age showed. There was no marble flooring or gorgeous terrarium with genetically modified plants growing to the ceiling. And there was no elevator either. Alex wondered if that had been a technological limitation or if space and weight had been such precious commodities that her grandfather's grandfather decided against shipping one. She had plenty of time to think about it as she hoofed up the six flights of the windowless staircase, no doubt designed as such to minimize heat loss. Alex was happy she lived in the times that she did.

The hallways were made of a dull metal, which Alex assumed came from the mines, and maybe even Mine One. It gave everything a claustrophobic feel and reminded Alex of a twenty-first century spacecraft that she toured in a museum. As she entered Pat's office, she was surprised by its size. Did all administrators have private offices? She didn't know. She was also struck by the wooden desk in the middle of the room. Despite looking out of place, it dramatically improved the atmosphere. A horrible fake lilac scent blew from the air recycler on the ceiling as she took a seat. Alex wondered if the lifers enjoyed the fake scents, or if it had been so long since they'd been on Earth that they smelled totally normal to them.

Patricia was a middle-aged woman who had her legs crossed and her hair up. She rushed to get off the phone when she noticed her guest was the boss's daughter.

"We're all so glad to hear you're okay! How is your dad doing?" She stretched her arms out and Alex rose to give her a half-hearted hug before sitting again.

"He's still breathing, so he's still giving orders," Alex forced a laugh.

"A terrorist attack. Wow. They used to happen all the time, but this is the first one in decades." Pat reclined in her chair, which, like hers, was made of some kind of horrible, sticky, cloth fabric.

"I need your help," Alex said. She didn't like the woman's relaxed demeanor. This wasn't some far-off problem. This was real, and it happened to her.

"Of course!"

"I'm trying to identify the terrorist. And, frankly, learn more about Mine One. What can you tell me about it?" Alex leaned forward.

"Your dad said you wanted to dig into this. Isn't Intelligence on top of it?" Pat twirled a strand of hair that hung by her ear.

"They're useless. They didn't get a facial ID match from any Martian data set, so now they're combing through Earth data. It could take months. Longer, if they're not involving the UN." Alex paused. She tried to read the other woman's face but couldn't. "I was at the blast. I want to figure out who this terrorist was. Now, are you going to help me?"

Pat blinked. "Yes, absolutely. We all want to help on this. Although, I have to say that your dad keeps Mine One close to his chest. I think it's sentimental to him."

"Mm-hm. I talked to a resource center employee. It sounds like the mineral pick-up and transportation process is entirely automated."

"That's right. Standard." She waved her hand. Like Egor, she wasn't scared of Alex.

"What about the mine itself? Someone must work there, right? I can't find any active employees in the directory."

"Mine One is small and largely automated," Patricia said. "There are probably maintenance contractors, but they wouldn't show up in the employee directory as they're technically not employees. You'd have to ask your dad. Like I said, he keeps this one close."

Pat's mouth smiled but the rest of her face didn't.

Alex met her eyes.

"To be honest, I have a lot of mines to worry about," Pat continued. "I don't think about Mine number one a lot. I was truly shocked it was targeted by terrorists. From a strategic business perspective, it doesn't make sense. Terrorists usually target high value R&D locations. Deliveries from Mine One will be back up and running soon, so there'll be negligible impact on volume this quarter. I guess the anniversary PR event was their best chance to hit your dad." She shrugged, then took a sip of something from a mug.

Alex got the sense she was coming off as the CEO's bratty, nosy daughter, who needed to be kept occupied but ultimately was wasting everyone's time. She couldn't tell if she was reading too much into the situation. Was she tired and paranoid after the blast? Maybe. That didn't mean she wasn't doing important work.

"There has to be something you can tell me," Alex said.

Pat scratched her head. "It's not much, but I can give you our annual production report if you'd like. I even have one paper copy." She heaved a textbook sized document onto her desk. "But my advice is that Intelligence is on the right track. Find the port this terrorist took to leave Earth."

Alex pulled the binder over to her side of the desk and sighed.

"Is there anything else? Why is this mine not connected to our IT system? What about surveillance footage? We must have surveillance of the loading docks, right?"

"There's no reason it's not connected, it's just how it's always been. Thankfully, the security team that was at the blast with you did manage to retrieve one of our exterior cameras. But Alex."

"Yes?"

"Sweetheart." Pat put on her best mom voice. "Are you sure you want to see that? You should clear it with the doctors first. It might be traumatic for you to experience the blast again."

"I'm fine. Send it over. Now. Please." Alex stood, before remembering to add "Thank you."

She never thought she'd be longing for employees that feared her.

#

Her room was an uncomfortable place to work, but Alex didn't want to be in the office right now. She sprawled on the ground beside her bed with the giant mining business report. She took a sip from her fresh cup of coffee. It was more bitter than her go-to latte, but she didn't care. She'd drink it all night if it helped her find a hint, a clue, anything.

It was nearly midnight, and she'd already followed up with Pat about the surveillance videos. She flipped through pages dedicated to the case for refining lithium on Mars rather than shipping raw ore to processing plants on Earth. The rationale relied on a new, waterless refinement method. Normally, that would interest Alex to no end. But now, she turned the pages without even skimming them. She had more important things to look for.

Pat had been near useless. Why did no one know anything about Mine One? First Corp. could be a black hole of bureaucracy, but this was another level. Everything about the situation freaked her out and the questions about the terrorist gnawed at her mind, constantly.

Why did he give his age in Martian years? Why was Intelligence not able to identify him? Why did he have a two-hundred-year-old pendant and an accent like he was from some rural village? And why did she feel so strongly that the terrorist picked Mine One for a specific reason, and that they were more linked than would appear?

The next section in the binder was a benchmark comparison of the company's different mining properties. They were sorted by size, and of the company's forty-five operational mines, Mine One was the third smallest. Well, she had finally found out something about the mine. Was she getting somewhere? A chart showed that Mine One's efficiency metrics had been in a slow, but continuous decline for the last twenty years, which was as far back as the dataset went. Curious, Alex scanned over to the "Variance Explanations" section of the table, only to find it empty. It was the only blank section on the whole page!

She shook her head. She couldn't believe it. It had been a few days now. Every time she thought she got a little bit closer something stopped her in her tracks. Maybe that's why she was so determined to keep investigating. She turned the page and was greeted by "Opportunities for Exploration Stage Pass-Through Tax Credits." Instinctively, she yawned. Thankfully she had coffee.

She wasn't sure when she fell asleep, but it was late morning when her handheld beeped, and Alex jolted awake. Pat had sent the surveillance videos! Maybe there would finally be something useful.

Alex downed the last sips of her cold coffee and projected the file on her bedroom wall. She watched intently as the familiar loading dock filled the view. Nothing was happening. There were no First Corp. trucks there, nothing. She didn't know if it was a still picture or a video until she saw some dust moving in the distance.

It was weird to watch, knowing she was going to see herself attacked, but she didn't feel any stress or trauma. She was riveted, sure, and her fists were clenched, but that's because she wanted to find out what happened. After a few actionless minutes, she realized the video length was three hours. Only then did she start pacing back and forth.

Outside of her hole's window, the too-small sun rose over the horizon. Its meager light seemed like a bad joke, even worse than dreary London or San Francisco. The landscape was the same as ever, dead, with no people talking, or birds singing, or anything. Olympus Mons was even more dead. How did the terrorist get there?

His appearance was unmistakable. The black figure emerged on foot from out of view, sticking out against the red ground. He pulled a pallet of what she presumed were bombs. He was a good distance away though. Why hadn't he driven right up to the loading dock? The terrorist stopped a few times, like he had to catch his breath or was unsure of what to do. His behavior struck her as strange. It was not as professional or choreographed as she expected.

After setting the bombs, he left the frame, slowly, as if he was having some trouble. That's when she saw the convoy of trucks appear in the distance. That was fast! Alex thought the bombs would have been set up days, or even weeks in advance.

A few of the security officers got out of their vehicles and her heart dropped. Poor people. They didn't deserve this. She rubbed her forearms nervously and forced herself to keep watching. What she saw surprised her. The terrorist ran back across the frame, his black suit lumbering like it was his first ever time in a low gravity environment. And he was running toward the bombs! Why? Who does that? Was his remote detonator broken? Why put himself in harm's way?

And then the boom shredded the security guards and blasted the terrorist back. A cloud of dust swallowed the camera frame.

Then, nothing. It was just a brief, temporary explosion of human pain and suffering in an otherwise already dead world. She scanned the rest of the video file. There was no more action. Her altercation with the terrorist took place off camera.

So, what had she learned? He acted strangely. He was slow and awkward, like a fish out of water, and he ran toward the blast at the last second! To her, it indicated this was an amateur job, not the kind that First Corp.'s rival might pay top dollar for. But she wasn't a criminologist. Maybe it was standard for boys roughly her age to run toward explosions.

It unsettled her stomach, and it was weird, but it wasn't proof of anything. It didn't tell her more about what she needed to know.

Alex's knees wobbled and she sat on her bed. She'd never been so exhausted, even when she studied all night for a math test. She blamed Mars's lack of sunlight for weakening her circadian rhythm. Blue-light therapy was no replacement for the real thing.

But it was more than that, too. She was so close to figuring out the oddness of it all—what it was about the terrorist and Mine One that was all wrong and made her skin crawl. But she couldn't quite place it. It was like trying to pilot a spaceship in a dream where the laws of physics didn't apply. Nothing worked and it made her sick.

As tired as she was, she was also frustrated. It felt like she was missing puzzle pieces and the pieces she had didn't fit together. Her mind was clearly not operating at one-hundred percent capacity. She didn't know what her next step was. Should she go back to Mine One? It was far away, but she didn't know how else she could figure out what the hell was going on. Maybe she should talk to everyone else that was at the blast site. Someone had to have seen something useful. How come she didn't think of that before! Interviewing witnesses should've been the first thing she did.

She crawled under the bed sheets and stared at the ceiling. She felt brain dead. What was she missing? The terrorist had looked awkward, like a bird taking its first flight. Why? His black suit had lumbered across the frame in an odd, but familiar way, like in one those old documentaries.

Alex tore off her sheets and threw the video up on the wall again. When the terrorist appeared, she stood and brought her face within inches of the projection. It wasn't close enough.

She pinched her fingers, zooming in, and gasped. *What the hell?*

The suit.

Her hair stood on end. It was black with an external oxygen tank, like the one in the archival video about Mine One's founding that played in the truck before the explosion. There was no way. It couldn't be the same model, could it?

She was out of the door and waiting for the elevator in a flash. Her hunch couldn't be right because it didn't make any sense. Why would someone use a several-hundred-years-old environmental suit that belonged in a museum? She couldn't fathom what it meant if she was right, and she didn't dare to. Either she was sleep deprived, traumatized, and losing it, or things were going to get even weirder.

The Security Office was on the first basement level of the main office tower. Alex swiped her thumb and gave the desk clerk a quick nod. She had jitters in her stomach, but she felt good. She was on a mission.

It was a quiet place made of long hallways. She passed an empty breakroom that looked like it could hold fifty people. There weren't many incidents these days, let alone terrorist attacks. Most of the budget went to protecting her dad. She thought he was paranoid, until now.

Evidence storage was in the back of the department. Fluorescent lights popped on as she entered the room that had rows of metal lockers painted white to match the walls. Its sterility and sparseness reminded her of the detention room the terrorist was sitting in. Certainly, it got a similar amount of use. She didn't have to go far. The attack was assigned code AA-1, which was the first wide locker in the nearest row.

She looked over her shoulder at the door. Why was she nervous? She wasn't doing anything wrong. Although she wondered if the terrorist had any sympathizers inside the company. If so, they wouldn't want people snooping around the evidence. She half-expected someone to stop her from opening it, or that it'd be empty when she did. That was just the way things were going.

Thankfully, her fears didn't come to fruition. She put her thumb on the scanner.

The locker swung open.

Alex jumped back. "Oh my god!"

The environmental suit loomed over her.

It stood tall, with its arms stretched out, imposing over her. She held her chest. She hadn't realized how on-edge she'd been. It took her brain a moment to understand that the suit only seemed giant and terrifying because the hook it was hanging on was a good meter above her.

She pulled it off the hook, laying it flat on the ground, and remarked at how heavy it was. First Corp. suits were much lighter, although those were the only ones she'd ever used. As she leaned down and got a closer look, she was dumbstruck. It matched her mental image of the old-time suit from the archival video perfectly.

It was big. Nearly two of her could've fit in it. It was also thick and bulky in a way that modern suits weren't. She bent an arm at the elbow, finding it stiff. No wonder the terrorist moved so awkwardly.

It felt and looked exactly how she imagined an ancient suit from the days of the first

Martian settlements would feel and look, but she was not an expert. She had strange suspicions, but that was it. And if she was right, what would that prove? She didn't know. It didn't seem like enough.

The helmet was still caked in dust and smelled horrible. It didn't look like there were any on-helmet controls. Maybe it operated by voice? She couldn't be sure. She turned it around and nearly had a heart attack.

A red number one was emblemed on the nape.

She dropped the helmet and stood. She was looking at a relic. This was a real environmental suit from the time when First Corp. was founded. She was dumbstruck. Alex didn't know how long she stood there. Every neuron in her brain was firing, but she didn't get any answers.

She had to talk to her dad.

Last time they spoke, he talked her off a cliff. She hoped he could do it again, although the cliff was a lot higher now, and the winds were blowing much stronger.

Chapter Sixteen: Alex

The helmet felt like a sacred artifact in her hands. The elevator ascended and Alex tried to catch her breath. She had so many questions and few answers. Patricia said her dad kept Mine One close to his chest. Was it for sentimental reasons, like Pat suspected? She desperately wanted him to have answers.

She arrived at his room clutching the helmet against her chest. The medical staff were buzzing around like bees, although there were fewer than before. Her dad sat up in his bed, talking on his handheld.

Alex's heart was beating fast. A gaggle of nurses gave her a questioning look. She didn't remember when she showered last. It dawned on her that she probably looked and smelled horrible. Whatever. She didn't have time for this.

"Everyone out." She raised her voice.

She didn't have to ask twice. The staff left their tools where they were and walked by her, avoiding her gaze. The door thumped closed behind them.

Her dad hung up his call and looked at her, bewildered. "Everything alright sweetie? I heard you missed your meetings this morning, but that's okay. You need the rest. Take some time off."

Alex looked her dad in his kind, gentle eyes. She couldn't bring herself to ask. She felt like she was accusing him of something, even if she wasn't trying to and didn't know what it was that she could possibly even accuse him of.

She couldn't find the words, and so she rotated the helmet around, revealing the red number one.

He opened his mouth, as if he was going to say something, but didn't. He looked up at the ceiling and let out a big sigh.

No one spoke.

Her dad winced and buried his face in his hands.

Alex got the sinking feeling that he hadn't been fully honest with her. She trusted her dad. She always had. But she'd never seen him at a loss for words before. Had he broken her trust? What would it mean if he had? She was scared to know. All she knew was that the uneasiness in her gut was about to boil over.

"I don't get it," Alex voice cracked before she found her stride. "Intelligence can't find him. He answered his age in Martian years. He seems confused and can't answer any questions. He was wearing what appears to be an original suit from Mine One! Which, by the way, no one actually works at. I can't find a single employee. Pat is useless. She doesn't know anything. Except that ... Except that you 'keep Mine One close to your chest.' So, please, help me understand." Her voice quieted and she bowed her head. She wanted desperately for him to explain everything away in a convincing manner.

Her dad looked pained, his eyes wide in surprise like he'd been knifed in the back.

"I'm sorry, Alex. I ... wasn't truthful with you. I believe I know where the boy came from."

Her stomach tightened.

"He's ... corporate-born," her dad said.

"Really? A corporate-born terrorist?"

Her dad was referring to people that were born on Mars. First Corp., like all companies adhering to the UN rules, expressly forbade pregnancies on Mars for fear of birthing stateless people. All humans had to be born on Earth or a ship flying a country's flag. Corporate-born births were rare with only a few slipping through the cracks every year.

"Not in the usual sense."

"What do you mean? Who are his parents?"

"Alex. I'm sorry this has become your burden," her dad said. "It's something I inherited from my father, and he from his. I never intended you to inherit it as well. I will tell you, but I need you to understand that there's a plan already in place, and I need you to trust me. Can you do that?"

"Yes," Alex said, although she was increasingly thinking the answer was maybe no, and that terrified her.

"The conditions at Mine One are ... not ideal," he said softly. Alex could see anguish all over his face. He looked tired and injured. He had wrinkles on his forehead she never noticed before. "Mine One is not automated. It's staffed by a human crew. Lifers. That don't leave."

"I thought our human crews rotate out every three months? Lifers need a special exemption, and they can't have kids. Wait, where do the people come from? We don't have that many lifer applications." Alex felt a weight in the back of her throat.

She could barely get the words out. "The lifers there, are they, are they all corporate-born?"

Her dad dipped his chin and briefly closed his eyes in a way that answered her question, yes.

"The other mines are fully compliant," her dad insisted. "Mine One has a long, complicated history. Right now, I need you to trust me. There's a plan in place to fix this." He held out his hand.

Alex didn't take it. Her knees weakened, but her blood was boiling. She should've been informed of this before. There was a plan in place? What did that mean?

The implications of what her dad was saying washed over her. Corporate-born lifers. People that were born in the mines and not allowed to leave. They'd never known Earth. It broke every UN rule and corporate policy. Not to mention human dignity! These people didn't have a choice. Her fists clenched. She didn't have trouble finding words now.

"Are we *slave owners*? Can they leave? Do they have radiation protection? Air system maintenance? Can they see the sun?" Alex paced frantically in front of the bed. "Are we slave owners?" She turned to face her dad.

"Alex! I know it's a lot to take in right now. I understand that it's overwhelming. But there is a plan, and I need you to trust me.

"What plan?" Alex crossed her arms.

"These people," her dad said. "They've been removed from society for centuries. They can't just re-integrate overnight. They have their own understandings of the world, their own dialect, and even culture. They're barbaric. Ruthless murderers who can barely read and write. It's not their fault, anyone would be the same in their situation, but they're not fit to waltz back into open society."

"So?"

"It would also be disastrous to our stock price, obviously, to announce something like this, no matter how many years in the past the problem originated. So, we need to wait until we've fully expunged our need for Earth's capital markets. This is why we need to make the United Nations and its flimsy attempts to administer interplanetary law irrelevant. Corporations are subject to rules, but governments make them. We need to become the latter to save ourselves. We need to become the first legitimate Martian government. Only then can we freely integrate these people into our new society.

Alex's mouth hung open. She couldn't believe what her dad was saying. She knew about her dad's quest to gain political power and leverage, but she thought it was just for power and money's sake. Not this.

"What about the people living underground? You just leave them there? Becoming our own government could take years. Or decades!"

"What about all the people that rely on our company's paychecks to put food on their tables? All the kids we put through college? Would you be so quick to take that away from them? We employ tens of thousands of people. We do important scientific work that improves billions of lives. If we act too fast, all of that disappears! Believe me, I wish the issue were so black and white. But it's not."

"Who knows about this?" Alex whispered, terrified to learn the answer to every question she asked. She rubbed her temples. She felt like she was going to die. Her whole world was crashing down. Her family were slave-owners. *She* was a slave owner.

"No-one. Not the Board. Not your mother. Not Pat. Just me, and now, you. It took generations of effort to tighten the information circle. I remember the shock I experienced when my father brought me into the fold. It's a heavy cross to bear. And these aren't the circumstances I wanted to tell you under. For that, I apologize." Her dad brought his hands together and bowed his head. "We need to keep the secret between the two of us while we work to end it. Together, we can cut away the last strings that tie us to Earth and make this right."

Alex's head was still spinning. She couldn't get over the fact that her dad's plan was not a plan at all.

"That's—doing nothing is not an option!"

"I understand how difficult this is for you to hear, but you have to understand it's not a problem we can solve over night." Her dad spoke in the firm but empathetic tone only a parent could. "Take a break. Rest. And I'll send you all the documents. Read them over and, when you're ready, we'll talk again."

"We have the power to end this now. Today! I won't be an accomplice to this internment, or slavery, or whatever it is!"

Alex stormed out of the room, enraged. It was a problem her father inherited from her grandfather. She couldn't blame him for that. But she could blame him for not fixing it in his thirty years as CEO. And almost worse than that was the lie. He broke her trust by not being honest with her, and she didn't think she could ever forgive him for that.

"Alex! Come back! Talk to me!"

He was mad now. That was okay. She ran toward the elevator. She didn't know what she was going to do, but she had to do something. After a few minutes, a secretary emerged from the office on the far side of the hall.

"Apologies Ms. Torres. The elevator is out of service. And your father would like to speak with you."

Alex grunted. "To hell with that."

The secretary said something in a shocked tone, but Alex ignored it. She ran to the fire-exit stairs. Eighty floors above ground, and then three below it. Good thing she was in shape.

She proceeded methodically, lunging down the metal stairs, but it still took longer than she hoped. She cursed the gravity, less than a third of Earth's, that made it feel like the planet actively didn't want her to descend.

She didn't know what her plan was, but she had to get some more time alone with the corporate-born terrorist. He had answers to what was going on at the mine. And more than that, he was evidence of it.

In the past, she overlooked her dad's callousness toward others because he always treated her with love and respect. She knew he could be ruthless. The company wouldn't have become a behemoth if he wasn't. But this was something else entirely, and it hurt her brain. Even if she had teenage disagreements with him, this was a man she loved and respected. That image of him was now dying. Did she even know who he was? Did she know anything?

She couldn't let her dad take over the investigation into the explosion at Mine One. He would sweep everything under the rug to protect the status quo. If he hid a colony of Martian workers—slaves—from her, from everyone, then she didn't know what else he was capable of. She had to get the Martian, even if he was a terrorist, out of his reach. He was her only hope of finding out the whole truth.

At the bottom of the stairwell, Alex tried to straighten her clothes and collect herself, so the guard wouldn't sense anything was off. That was difficult, considering how dishevelled she was. She had thrown her suit jacket off, and her blouse was ruffled and untucked. She knew she smelled horrible but didn't care. All that mattered was getting the prisoner to safety.

The detention room was usually used for employees who had mental breakdowns. Becoming violent was surprisingly common in both first-timers and long-haulers. It was amazing to see people who had passed every possible psych evaluation on Earth get beaten down by the isolation of Mars. The combination of the high-stress work environment, lack of sun, and being away from friends and family simply broke some people. Upstanding citizens could turn into monsters and commit previously unthinkable crimes. Alex wondered what the conditions at Mine One were like and shuddered. Living on Mars was tough enough, let alone locked underground.

Sometimes, when the company wanted to wash its hands of someone, they approved extradition back to Earth for certain crimes. But those cases were rare. First Corp. liked to handle matters internally as much as possible. Most of the time, the detention rooms were used as a time-out and for monitoring employee behavior. They weren't meant for punishment, but rather as the in-between place while the company contemplated its next move.

A long time ago, the rooms were originally set up to detain corporate terrorists as prisoners. That's why they were so deep underground. A glass box inside the detention room housed the prisoner and a lone guard watched over them, usually bored out of their mind. Even if a prisoner escaped the glass room and evaded the guard, they couldn't get above ground without biometric credentials.

Alex opened the door to find the guard in her face. He'd been expecting her. She tried to look past him but couldn't see the terrorist. He must've been hiding under the bed.

"Ma'am, I've been instructed not to allow any more visitors today." He wore a bulletproof vest and had a standard-issue handgun in a holster at his side.

"I make my own rules."

"I'm sorry ma'am, but this is straight from the top." His hands rested firmly on his hips.

"Uh-huh," Alex said. She pushed him and he stumbled back. People always underestimated her strength. She lunged toward the glass door.

"I can't let you in there," he said, placing a hand on her shoulder.

She turned and hit the guard with an open palm, striking upward into his face. She heard his nose break first, then his legs crumpled underneath him. Alex grabbed the man under his armpits and tried to support his weight. The nametag on his breast said "Bo." She cradled his head so it wouldn't smack the ground and kneeled over him. His eyes rolled around, and he muttered something incoherent. He was still breathing then, which was good. Alex wasn't trying to kill him, but it struck her that she almost did.

"I'm so sorry, Bo," she said. "I'm so sorry!"

She kicked herself for hurting him, but there was no going back now. Assaulting an employee was a lot of things, including a sure-fire commitment to the new path she was on. She'd gone against her parent's wishes before, but in juvenile ways. Nothing like this. She didn't know what the ramifications would be, but she'd worry about them later.

She grabbed the key from Bo's pocket and opened the door. The boy was crouched in the corner under his bed.

"You, terrorist. Come on then," Alex said, motioning for the boy to come forward.

"My name is Gordon." He blinked.

Alex experienced mental vertigo. She had tried to avoid humanizing him, but was now reminded that he was a scared boy, not much younger than her. Maybe he deserved some benefit of the doubt.

"Right. Listen, Gordon. My name's Alex, and I'm your best chance of getting out of here," she said, trying again. "I'm not going to hurt you. And I promise I'll answer all your questions. But you have to come with me, right now."

"Okay," he said, but didn't move. He was frozen like a frightened animal.

"We don't have time for this!" She walked across the room and pulled him up.

The guard moaned. He was starting to come to, and Alex was glad. He wasn't her enemy, just someone standing in her way.

Gordon followed her into the stairwell. They had three floors to climb to get to ground level. From there, she'd take him to the only place that was private and safe.

The *Zoya*.

But the corporate-born lifer took his time even though she prodded him along. He was either out of shape or exhausted from the explosion and stress that came afterward. She couldn't blame him for that, but she did wish he'd hurry up.

When they spilled into the ground-level lobby, they drew the attention of everyone that was milling about, drinking coffee, or having business meetings. Alex, because being the daughter of the CEO meant she always stuck out, and Gordon, because his all-white detention attire and skinny, beat-up appearance demanded it.

"Keep your head down and follow me," she said, scooting along the perimeter of the high-ceilinged room.

Alex realized that Gordon was probably the first person roughly her age she'd seen in almost a year, and he was a Martian. Life was funny like that sometimes. She wondered if she could pass him off as a friend from school that her dad had finally let her bring with her to make life on Mars less boring.

A team of sunglass-wearing security guards following closely behind meant the answer was no.

"First space transit bay. Let's go! They don't have a ship as fast as mine."

Gordon stared at her, looking as confused as ever.

"Come on," Alex said, running into the pedestrian bridge that connected the office building to upper level of the transit bay.

The bridge was like the other inter-building hallways, glass on all sides. The south side of it had an unobstructed view, and for people who didn't have access to the top levels of the skyscraper, it was a great place to see the expansive landscape. Unless there was a dust storm, you could see for kilometers over the rolling hills and craters.

Alex opened the door at the end of the hallway to the transit bay, but Gordon wasn't with her. She looked back and saw him staring upward at the sun. She ran back and pulled him forward.

"Let's go!"

A torrent of puke erupted out of the boy's mouth, some landing on her blouse.

She nearly retched in response. "Are you kidding me!" she yelled. How was it even possible? Where did the volume come from? It wasn't like he'd eaten any of the food they offered him.

She pulled his arm, and he stumbled forward again. The security guards entered the hallway and began gaining ground on them fast.

"Just keep your eyes on the ground and move your feet toward me!"

The metal corridors had railings that looked down upon the maintenance areas. Crews worked on ships that were laid down on their sides, and they ran past a few that were several hundred meters in length. Alex couldn't tell if Gordon was more terrified or curious. His eyes were bulging out of his head, and he wouldn't take them off the ships.

She would've had to drag him along if the guards hadn't been gaining ground on them.

The *Zoya* was outside of the large warehouse-like building, right where she left it. Thankfully, she had kept it flight-ready in case she got the urge for a joy ride. They arrived at its dock, panting. Alex pushed a button on the wall and the boarding bridge, a pressurized tunnel, rolled out to the ship, one-hundred meters away.

They rushed along the expanding bridge until it reached the hatch to the control deck, and Alex pushed Gordon into the ship. She sat in the pilot's seat for a moment, started the launch sequence, then grabbed the gun her dad had given her from underneath the seat. Gordon stood slack-jawed, marvelling at the *Zoya's* interior.

"Sit down and shut up!" Alex pointed at the crash couch.

"I didn't say anything."

"And don't throw-up in my spaceship!"

He nodded dutifully.

The *Zoya* let out a warm sound, indicating the launch sequence was progressing, and Alex smiled widely. The hatch was closing, the automated door taking its time. She walked back to it and aimed the gun down the boarding bridge. The security guards rounded the corner.

"Stay back!"

They ignored her and ran toward the hatch. It was halfway closed.

That they called her bluff infuriated her. Did they not think Alex was serious? Did they think she was a weak little girl? That the CEO's daughter didn't know how to fire a gun?

She steadied her breath and fired a few warning shots, missing on purpose. The security guards ducked and hit the ground. They backed off immediately when she stopped shooting. It made sense. They may have had clearance to apprehend her, but not to harm her.

She exhaled. Was she willing to kill someone who was just following orders? She didn't think she could, no matter how messed up the situation with her dad was.

"We need you to step out of the ship. You're harbouring a dangerous, illegal person!" one of them yelled.

"That's a negative, boss," Alex yelled down the tunnel as the hatch door finished closing. "Strap in," she barked. "It's going to be a bumpy ride."

"Where are we going?" Gordon asked. He was already gripping the arm rests.

"I don't know." She laughed, realizing the absurdity of what she was doing.

Gordon laughed nervously with her. "You're joking."

"Not at all. Reactors are live. All systems are go!"

Beneath the surrealism, her heart pounded with an anxiety she'd never felt before. She had the keen awareness that this was a life-changing decision. Making a move against her dad on this scale was something she couldn't take back later. She tried to bury those emotions. Fear wouldn't improve her piloting, and she'd already made her decision. Escape was their only choice. She needed to maintain her access to Gordon to find out what was going on, and she couldn't trust her dad. She didn't even know who he was anymore.

The ship rumbled and they achieved lift-off.

Chapter Seventeen: Gordon

Everything shook. Even Gordon's teeth chattered together. The sound of the rocket engines firing was the loudest thing he'd ever heard, and he covered his ears with his hands.

Lift-off was staggering. But the force of the thrust gravity on his chest as the spaceship accelerated out of the Martian atmosphere was more than that. It was an incomprehensible assault. The pressure was all-encompassing, squeezing every part of him. He was paralyzed.

He wanted to call out to Alex, but he couldn't make much more than a whimper. All he could see of her was a bit of black hair sticking up above her chair and her reflection sheepishly grinning in one of the ship's screens. Was she enjoying this torture? Alex seemed to be everything: confident, intimidating, kind, and beautiful. And a complete maniac who was going to get them both killed.

Gordon gripped his armrest and closed his eyes. His face felt like it was going through a blender. Maybe it would all be over soon. Maybe he'd wake up and his mom would call him for dinner, the scent of jasmine rice filling the hole. Maybe his dad would come home with a new book, and they'd read together all night, dreaming of imaginary worlds.

Then, the weight on his chest was gone. Air rushed into his lungs. He opened his eyes and saw Alex observing him.

"Welcome to the *Zoya*, Gordon," she said.

He nodded slowly and then started to cackle. He couldn't help himself. It was all so surreal. She joined in the laughter with him. He wasn't going to die today, at least not yet.

He could move his limbs again, and he did, stretching out and touching the cushion-covered wall. The interior of the *Zoya* was comfortably small. Gordon's seat was a thin, jet-black couch a few arm lengths behind the pilot's seat. Lights flashed on the dashboard on the other side of Alex, along with graphs and charts of all types and sizes. Behind the couch there was a counter with a sink, a mini-fridge, and stairs that went down.

"It's a small ship. The stairs go to engineering, storage, and the restroom, and that's all there is. It's really meant for rock hopping and sprinting about, not whatever the hell we're doing. Which, by the way, we need to figure out."

Alex sat beside him, and Gordon instinctively moved away, putting a body width between them. Just two short days ago she had been yelling in his face, accusing him of all sorts of things, and his gut still said not to trust her. She was alien, an unknown quantity that he couldn't predict. Yet one with a friendly, perfect smile, and who appeared to be helping him.

"I brought you something," she said, digging in her pocket. A stack of folding papers emerged, slightly crumpled.

Gordon's heart fluttered. His origami! "Thank you," he said, holding them tight to his chest. He felt light, but it wasn't sure if it was because he had his papers back, or because the spaceship had stopped accelerating. Alex patted him on the shoulder and he didn't pull back.

"You're welcome," Alex said. "Now, I need something in return. Tell me everything. Who are you? What is it like to live in the mines? How did you end up at the loading docks with an ancient spacesuit and a massive bomb?" She raised an eyebrow like a schoolteacher.

Gordon took a deep breath. He wanted to answer her questions. He really did. But no words came out when he opened his mouth. All he could think about was the helplessness he felt as he realized there were people at the blast site. Bloody rocks and dead people rained down on him, and he couldn't get the images out of his mind.

"Fine, I'll start," Alex said. "I'm from Spain, but I attended school in London. I came to Mars about eight months ago when my dad said I could either join his business or go to law school in America. I didn't want to do either, but here I am."

She dug in her pocket again, looking for something. When her hand came out, Gordon's metal pendant sat flat. She flicked it in the air and caught it with her other hand.

"This was the original logo of First Olympia Mining Corporation, my family's company. We own the mine at Olympus Mons, where we found you, and a lot of other stuff."

"Own? You own the outpost?" Gordon's head spun. He couldn't keep up. Did she say she only came to Mars eight months ago? From Earth?

"Yes, although mining is a small part of what we do now, to be honest. Spaceship design and logistics are where the money is. We have the best engineering team in the world, and they're working on a space elevator, but my dad won't let me help. He says he wants me to be a leader rather than a tinkerer. It's nonsense, frankly, but—"

"Earth isn't dead?" His voice was a squeak.

"Huh?" Alex cleared her throat and looked him in the eye. "Earth is certainly alive. Doing better than ever in many ways."

"What?" Gordon's stomach churned. He couldn't believe it.

"Let me show you."

Alex spoke to the ship and a video of her popped up on the screens. She walked along the beach where sand met the vast blue water. The land curved behind her, forming a peninsula, and dark green trees dotted a hill.

"Is that an ocean?"

"No, it's Lake Michigan. I was on vacation in America. I have some of Chicago too. We visited the United Nations' headquarters."

A video played and Alex crossed a street, talking to someone, and laughing. He couldn't focus on what she was saying. There were hundreds of people, walking freely outside, without oxygen tanks. A car honked. A bird dashed from a building that looked as tall as Olympus Mons. A real, live bird! A sign read "100% beef sausages." Alex stopped at a metal structure and posed. Other people were doing the same thing. The video ended.

"So, that's Chicago. Anything else you'd like to see? The latency is not great, but this ship can connect to Earth's satellite comms."

"All this time, there was no point?" Gordon drew his knees up to the couch and buried his face in them. His legs quivered.

"I know this must be hard for you. I can't imagine." Alex exhaled sharply. "Tell me about your life in the mines."

His life. His mom's life. Everyone he ever knew. They had all been working together to restore Earth, but it didn't need help. X-Day hadn't been more than a blip. If it had even been real at all. Earth was alive and well, and its people were thriving. Worse, they were thriving with the minerals the outpost mined! Everything was a lie!

"Gordon, talk to me." Her voice was soft.

The Dead Earth Hypothesis was wrong too! He had to tell Dalrene, maybe it would help her in the fight against the Foreman. He wondered if the Foreman knew the truth about Earth. Maybe it was just a dumb robot, programmed to believe that Earth needed minerals. Programmed by evil people, like Alex's family!

"Gordon?"

He couldn't look her in the eye, let alone speak to her. He unfurled a piece of paper. He focused on controlling his breath, and he folded the paper in half and ran his finger along the crease.

"Damnit!" Alex smacked something as she stood. "Okay, okay. Play with your papers. Do whatever you want. But I need something soon. I'm risking everything for you, Martian. You need to help me so I can help you."

Alex sat in the pilot's seat. She couldn't go far on the small ship.

She furiously tapped a screen and hit buttons. She asked the computer for calculations on orbits of different moons, travel times to different places Gordon didn't recognize, and the distance between them, Mars, and Earth. He tried to ignore the sounds and focus on his folding, but he couldn't help but think how strange it was to see a computer serve in that way. At the outpost, the human-robot relationship was the other way around.

"It's nice."

Gordon didn't remember closing his eyes, but he opened them now to find Alex sitting on the couch again and gesturing at the origami in Gordon's lap.

"The Foreman killed my mom," he said. "That's how I ended up with the bombs. That's why I killed those people you were with, but I didn't mean to. I didn't know anyone would be there."

There was a familiar pang of guilt in his chest, only this time it hurt less. Knowing the truth about Earth didn't justify his violence, but it made him feel less bad about it.

"What happened?" Alex leaned forward.

"It took my mom to a prison hole and suffocated her in cold blood. It probably did the same to my dad and Aunt Tess, although it usually makes people work in the labor camps first." Gordon met Alex's concerned eyes. It was a relief to talk about things.

"The Foreman controls everything. Security. Food rations. Jobs. I was going to get a good job. I was going to be a blaster in the mines. My mom's friend was trying to take down the Foreman, and after it killed her, I fell in with that group."

"I'm-" Alex paused, covering her mouth with her hand. "I'm so sorry. How many people are there underground?"

"Six thousand."

"And they've never seen the sun?"

"I was one of the first people in centuries to see the surface. And then you showed up. How did this happen?"

Now it was her turn to sigh.

"What's now called First Corp. started as an exploration fund. Just over two-hundred years ago, a mining expedition was put together with volunteers from some of the poorest nations on Earth."

"Sure, I know that. We learned it in school."

Alex nodded. "After their five-year contract the volunteers returned home to Earth for retirement. At least, that's what I thought until now."

"Oh." Gordon sunk into his seat. His entire understanding of the world was collapsing. His brain hurt. Exhaustion gripped his muscles, and it took all his strength just to keep his eyes open.

"I don't know what to say. I didn't know. Only my dad did." Alex spoke softly and seemed to be trying to give him room on the couch.

Gordon looked away and tried to catch his breath. The generations of needless suffering weighed on his chest. All the malnourishment and death from crop failures and ration shortages. All the children not born because of population restrictions. All the backs broken and hearts that burst after years of hard labor.

"Why?" he asked.

"I don't know. Not for the money. Mine One has been insignificant to our financials for a century. It was a mistake my dad inherited, probably passed down from his great-great grandfather. He's a narcissist, but he's not evil. It became a big legal and political problem, and everyone punted the issue to future generations. At least that's my guess. No one ever fixed it, and now it's on me."

"Your dad knew we were there all along and never let us out?" Gordon couldn't believe anyone could care so little about others.

Alex fell silent.

He bowed his head. He didn't want to believe it, but he knew she was telling the truth.

She put her arms around him.

Gordon froze in surprise.

He hadn't expected the embrace, but he hugged her back. It was warm and tender. He rested his head on her shoulder.

It was a lot to take in. Gordon wondered what Mickey would have thought. In a way, the old man was lucky. He didn't have to know how much of a lie he lived. How much shame there was. All the stress, pain, and torture of everyone he'd ever known. He figured if Mickey found out the truth he'd keel over and die on the spot, unable to process the pain.

His spirits weren't as damaged as Mickey's would've been. Yes, he was angry that his people had been lied to and locked away from the rest of humanity. But there was a relief in knowing the punishments prescribed by the Foreman were in fact torture. Life didn't have to be stifling. Billions of people lived freely on Earth without a Foreman. He'd seen it on Alex's videos.

"I think I need to lie down," Gordon said.

He curled up on the crash couch and Alex brought him a blanket, then went back to the pilot's seat. He lay awake, wrestling with all the new information overloading his brain. The conversation she was having with her computer slipped into the background, a welcome bit of white noise. She was planning something, but Gordon was too exhausted to pay attention.

#

Five days since he'd left the outpost. An unknown number, tens of thousands at least, since his people had been cut off from Earth in a lie. His head was blank, numb, until Alex spoke.

"Champagne? Not that we have much to celebrate, but it's all the alcohol on-board." Alex sat beside him and took a swig from the bottle. She pursed her lips and read sarcastically from a paper card.

"My Dearest Alessandra,
Cheers to the Zoya's inaugural flight
May she deliver you the stars
And be fast as hell about it
Love, Dad."

Gordon chuckled at the way she stretched out the pronunciation of her vowels.

"Well," Alex said, taking another swig and passing the bottle to him. "Turns out my dad is a horrible person. He doesn't think your people can re-join normal society. But his bigger fear is bad PR."

Gordon sat up and took a drink, and decided he liked champagne much better than Mickey's liquor. It was crisp and light.

"My dad taught me origami."

Alex nodded three times in quick succession. "That's a much better legacy."

He laughed. She was funny and being around her was starting to put him at ease. It was hard to imagine her as the woman yelling at him in the glass box.

"My mom is much kinder than my dad. I'll miss it now, but I was planning to arrive back on Earth for Halloween. It's our favorite holiday. Do you have Halloween?"

The look on Gordon's face must've indicated that he didn't know what that was.

"Oh, it's an American thing, but we have it in Europe too. You dress up in a costume and pretend to be something you're not. My mom and I like to choose our own fabrics and sew them by hand. It's great!"

"Pretend to be something you're not?" Gordon tilted his head, confused.

"Last year I was a short-hop race mechanic. Brought my own wrench set and everything. When I was ten, I went as Shi-Qi, the youngest female kickboxing champion. I made my teacher and classmates call me Shi-Qi for the whole day. It's embarrassing to think about now, but my mom loves telling that story." Alex's cheeks turned red, and she turned away, taking another swig from the bottle.

"We never dressed up, but I did pretend to be my classmate," Gordon said. "They rarely check facial IDs in school. So, we split attendance for the classes we had that semester and took each others' tests. I was super nervous that we'd be caught, and I never did it again. But for that one year we both aced all our classes!"

"That's great!" Alex slapped her knees. Her eyes were glassy and starting to droop.

Gordon took the bottle and finished it. His muscles were relaxed, and his joints were buzzing. He understood now why Mickey drank.

"Oh, one time my mom wore a costume! She figured she could get extra rations with a fake thumbprint and a homemade wig. When the Foreman finally caught on, a peacekeeper bruised her face so badly that she looked even more different. It didn't recognize her with all the bruises, and she was able to go back for even more rations!"

Gordon had been so worried about his mom's black eye, but she had been so happy. She could barely carry all of the rations she brought home. It was a good memory, but Alex didn't laugh along with him.

"Are you okay? Don't you think that's funny?" he asked.

Alex was covering her mouth with her hand. "That's horrible," she said, wincing.

"I don't know. We were happy."

Alex sighed.

"You want to see where we're going?" she asked.

Gordon nodded and she spoke to the computer. "Pull up the scopes on the overhead."

The roof of the *Zoya* shifted and Gordon looked up. He hadn't realized it was all one big screen. An imposing gray rock with deep craters appeared, and hundreds of stars shone in the background.

"Phobos." Gordon said, craning his neck. It was an incredible view. He'd seen the Martian moon in too many textbooks to count, but never like this.

He tilted over, falling into Alex, and she giggled.

"Sorry!" His face flushed with embarrassment.

"It's okay! You can lie down!" Alex burped and it smelled like champagne. They both laughed, and Gordon lay on his back with his head in her lap.

He looked up in amazement.

"We blasted off sunward. Wishful thinking, I suppose. But as much as I would love to go to Earth, this ship isn't built for that kind of journey. And even if it was, we don't have enough food or fuel. So, we've turned back, toward Phobos. We can hide there while I negotiate the immediate release of everyone in Mine One. I sent a message to my dad. He has to do what we want, otherwise we'll go public. The press would tank the share price. The Company's stock is one of the only things he cares about."

"Oh, right, of course. That makes total sense." She was speaking, but only nonsense was coming out. Gordon couldn't stop a smile from creeping over his face.

"You have no idea what a stock is, do you?" Alex tilted her head playfully at Gordon.

"Not a clue," Gordon said, letting his laughter out. "But you're very comfortable."

Alex threw her head back and giggled like he told the funniest joke in the world.

Her lap was cozy and warm. Gordon didn't remember anyone else making him feel this good. Just her presence, her voice, was making him feel at home in a place that couldn't have been further from it.

He tried to focus on her, but his head was spinning. He still had the taste of champagne on his lips.

He mumbled "goodnight," and closed his eyes with a smile on his face.

\#

"Do you want some coffee?"

"Yes." Gordon's head was fuzzy. He blinked repeatedly, hoping it would help. There was no coffee at the outpost, but if he remembered his history books well enough, it contained caffeine, just like tea. His aunt always said that was a sure-fire way to cure hangovers.

"There's a fresh pot. Help yourself."

The cockpit was as small as the hole he'd shared with his mom. Other than the crash couch right behind the pilot's chair, there was no furniture. The walls weren't quite screens but weren't quite regular walls either. They were dark gray, but Alex changed their color constantly. Writing on one of them said that a medical bed could extend from it, and he figured that would take up most of the empty space. He moved to the back of the room where there was a tight set of stairs and a small kitchen. The nutty coffee aroma was the only scent he'd smelled since getting on the *Zoya*. The rest of it was creepily sterile, more like the caves than the rest of the outpost.

He had his first ever sip of coffee and the bitter sludge slid down his throat. He forced himself to swallow and decided that it tasted marginally better than Mickey's liquor. He couldn't believe this was once considered a delicacy on Earth.

"What are you working on?" he asked, walking the short way back up to the pilot's chair.

"I sent some demands to my dad. Hopefully I make him regret wanting me to go into law. We'll get your people out of that mine."

Gordon nodded. He remembered the plan, Phobos, although relying on Alex's dad to treat him like anything other than an enemy seemed like a major risk now that he was sober. "Is that going to work?"

"Not right away," Alex said. "It's only the start of negotiations. We have a lot of leverage, mainly that you are free, and I am who I am. If we send a message on my social feeds, people might just believe your crazy story. But there are better ways to do this that won't start riots or even war on Earth. We start with those."

"Where I come from, the only part of negotiating that people understand is violence." Gordon doubted this world was different, but hoped he was wrong.

"It might be painful, but he'll cut a deal," Alex said, assuredly.

Alex was skilled and confident in everything. He wanted to believe her, and he did.

"Hey, let's look at the scopes," Alex said to both Gordon and the ship.

The now familiar sight of battered Phobos appeared on the screen in front of Alex.

"How far are we?" Gordon asked.

"Still a couple days away," Alex said. "We have to go back as far as we came. Turning around took time too."

She toggled something on the dashboard and the scope zoomed out. Behind Phobos, Mars appeared. It was giant compared to its moons, but the whole planet looked like it could fit in Gordon's hands. Had they really travelled that far, that fast?

"The moon is so close to the planet," Gordon said. "What if your dad figures out where we are? What if he sends people after us?"

"We run." Alex looked at Gordon like he was an idiot. "No one's boarding this ship. We're uncatchable." Her expression turned into a grin.

Gordon turned his attention back to the scope. He could make out a few features of Mars. There were some lights, which he assumed were the buildings they blasted off from. Beyond that, flat land and impact craters stretched to the hills at the base of Olympus Mons. The once bulky, massive volcano was a bump on an otherwise flat surface. A large bump, sure, but nothing more than that. Gordon could barely believe it. Everything that he and his ancestors had ever known happened underneath that volcano.

Underneath his awe was pain, regret, and anger.

And then he saw the small pool of blue.

"Jezero crater, part of the terraforming project," Alex said. She must've sensed his confusion. "Most of the water was there already, actually. It was just underground. But it's only an experiment. The water will evaporate soon enough. The atmosphere and temperature aren't ready to sustain it."

"You've been here the whole time?" Gordon asked.

"Yes. Just a few hundred kilometers away from Olympus Mons. We've only been the dominant player for the last forty years, but we've had a corporate base since shortly after we got the first mining rights."

Gordon threw the rest of his coffee down his throat and grimaced. He was angry, even furious, at Alex's dad and the subjugation his people had faced. He expected to live with an ember of that emotion deep in his being for the rest of his life. But this sober morning, he was more curious than anything. Which things did he take for fact that were lie? What was Earth really like?

Chapter Eighteen: Alex

Voices chanting softly in rhythm bounced off the *Zoya's* walls, like they had echoed around a monastery when they were recorded. Alex called it monk music on the account of the fact that it was made by Gregorian monks, although she was sure it had another name. It was pleasant. It was calming. And she only listened to it when she needed to.

She was expecting a call from her dad.

Alex ran her hand through her hair and twirled the ends. She wasn't normally scared of her dad, but now the feeling in her gut told her she should be. His entire persona as a father and a CEO was a question mark. She didn't know who he truly was, or what he was capable of, and that terrified her.

She tried to remain hopeful. Their brief exchanges by text had so far been cordial. Alex had sent her demands for the immediate release of the prisoners of Olympus Mons, and her dad had responded with a request for a call. He seemed to accept that this was going to be a serious negotiation, and that Alex held all the cards.

Still, the prospect of seeing him on video made her gut wrench. It felt like when she got caught drinking wine with a friend at age eleven, except worse. Way worse. It was impossible to square the knowledge that she was doing the right thing with the feeling that she was deeply betraying someone who loved her.

She turned in the pilot's chair to see Gordon fast asleep on the couch. She had to admit, he was growing on her. He was smart and curious, but also a subject of curiosity himself. Alex loved how he talked, and the way he skipped pronouncing hard "r" sounds reminded her of an old-timey South African or Australian accent. And she couldn't get over how highly he spoke of his dead parents and Aunt. Despite his involvement in the explosion, she could tell he was a kind person.

He showed remorse for his crimes, even though he committed them as a slave. He listened to Alex's ideas, even though he'd be totally in the right to dismiss her as part of the problem. If Gordon was any indication of what most corporate-born lifers at Olympus Mons were like, then her dad was wrong. These people were fit to re-join society.

"Incoming call," the *Zoya* said.

"I'll take it on my handheld."

She stood and walked past Gordon. He was blowing bubbles, as her mom used to say. Hard asleep.

Alex took the stairs down to the engineering deck before she answered the call from her dad. No matter how deep Gordon was sleeping, she didn't want to risk him seeing or talking to her dad. She could only imagine how traumatizing that would be for him.

The engineering deck's entrance was a narrow, rectangular room. There was enough empty space in the middle to be able to do a good workout, and that was where she practiced her kickboxing. A bench lined one of the long sides, and storage lockers sat against the other. Everything was bolted down so that it'd survive high g maneuvers. The far side filtered into a hallway with offshoots to the areas that supported the *Zoya's* literal and metaphorical plumbing.

Alex sat straight on the bench and braced herself. Her fists were clenched. She had to be ready to stop whatever emotional appeals or other bullshit he was going to spew. She had to be strong.

She held her handheld up, and there was her dad. He was at his desk and wearing a suit. Her stomach bubbled with uneasiness. She'd never be able to look at his fake smile the same way again.

"I'm so happy to see you're making good use of your new ship!" her dad said. He slipped into that happy-go-lucky persona too easily.

Alex almost smiled but caught herself. She exhaled. She hadn't realized she'd been holding her breath.

"Dad. This is serious." She kept her poker face.

"Of course."

"You said you have some concerns about my demands?"

"I do, but I'm more worried about you," he said. "You're with the terrorist. Has he threatened you? Hurt you?" His voice dropped into concerned parent mode.

"Not nearly as much as you did!" Alex clenched her jaw.

"I was only hiding this from you because I didn't want it to be your problem." Her dad lifted his upward facing palms. "I was going to fix it before I retired and you took over!"

"This isn't about—" Alex growled and caught herself. "My demands, dad. You said you had concerns. What are they?"

"Have you told your mother? Or anyone about this?"

"No. But I will, if we don't figure something out," Alex said raising her voice. She kicked herself. She didn't want to wake Gordon.

"Don't worry about your duties here. I told everyone you need to take a few sick days. There are a few e-mails you should respond to though."

"None of that matters. Dad, the demands!"

He smirked. "Yes, I have concerns. Your proposal to offer our corporate living space up to any of these people is absurd. We can't let them on our property at all. It wouldn't be safe for our employees!"

"Well, what do you suppose we do with them then?" Alex raised an eyebrow.

"We can retrofit their mine. Bring them some new air recyclers."

"That's absurd. They'd still be in a prison."

"Well, what? You want to get them a passport and send them to Chicago? To the UN?" Her dad took a moment to laugh hysterically. "That'd be gold! Those bastards deserve it. But it's crazy. Alex, these people don't know how to act properly on a good day. They don't have our customs. And if we let them out? They're already pissed off and violent. They'd murder thousands of people! Maybe more! Do you want to be responsible for that?"

"They're very nice, actually," Alex said.

"Who? The terrorist? Please tell me you have him in handcuffs at least. Alex, he *killed* our people in cold blood." Her dad gestured wildly with his arms.

"His name is Gordon. I promise you he's a pleasant, kind person."

"Goddamnit Alex! Are you falling for this guy?" His face flushed. "I will not have my grandfather's grandfather's company destroyed by some teenage romance fling!"

"I'm serious! He's softspoken and well mannered. Do you want to talk to him?"

Her dad looked like he was in searing pain. He turned away from the camera.

Alex wouldn't let Gordon talk to her dad, but she knew he wouldn't call her bluff.

When he looked back, his face was bright red.

"Do you think this is a fucking game? You will be the end of this company! This family!"

Alex's hands were sweating. She felt tears welling up, but she held them back. She was in the right. She knew she was in the right. But hearing her dad, who she trusted and loved for ninety-nine percent of her life, tell her such hurtful things made her second guess herself.

"Get back to Mars this instant," her dad continued. "Get back here now, young lady, and we can still salvage this."

"You don't get to speak to me like that," Alex said. "I'm an adult. And you should treat my demands like they're serious. Because they are."

"Or what?" Her dad furrowed his brows.

"Or I go public. You have two days to get real."

"Don't you fucking dare threaten me! You ungrateful piece of shit!" He slammed his fists on the desk.

She couldn't take anymore. Alex swallowed hard and hung up the call.

She slipped off the bench and onto the ground. Her tears flowed freely. Her dad was one of the smartest people she knew. How could he not see her side? How could he not understand that they needed to fix this now, and not in twenty years?

She didn't get up for a long time.

When Alex dragged herself back to the pilot's chair, the ship told her she had a new message. Her heart sunk as she saw they were from her dad. What more could he want? But she had to read them. She wouldn't be able to sleep if she didn't.

Please, Alex. I'm sorry for yelling at you. This has been weighing on me for fifty years and it's been hard to manage alone. It would be nice to share the load with someone, actually. I promise to forgive you if you just come home. We can put this all behind us and figure out a solution.

She shook her head. Was her dad's earlier blow-up all an act? A performative negotiating tactic? Had he really meant those hurtful things he said? She wouldn't put it past him to try manipulating her, like he did to the politicians. Her response was short.

My demands. Two days.

Either her dad realized how few cards he held and was already crawling back to the negotiating table, or he was trying to play with her emotions in some sick game. Whichever it was, Alex was now confident they could reach a deal. All she had to do was keep a hard line.

Chapter Nineteen: Dalrene

"Shit!"

The four of them scrambled up the stairs to the second floor of the whiskey bar. Peeping out of the small, four-pane window, they saw the enemy approaching. A phalanx of guardian bots, six wide and maybe up to ten rows deep, rumbled down the street.

"We'll have to run. Is there a secret exit anywhere?" Ionne pointed at her. "Hey Dalrene, I'm asking you! You're the one with the blueprints!"

Her heart raced. She threw her bag, the makeshift shield that had saved her life, on top of a box of liquor bottles and pulled out her computer. "No. There's no way out." She swallowed hard.

"We'll have to make a last stand here," Londi said, pushing boxes in front of the door. "Our message got out. The platoons will be here. Hopefully soon."

Dalrene punched the box her computer sat on. They were pinned down. Her army would come, but then what? They'd fight a phalanx of guardians? It'd be suicide. They were totally unprepared for the new type of bot. She could go back downstairs, splice into the comms node again, and broadcast the info, but that would require disassembling the barricade Londi was building. There wouldn't be enough time.

"Back-up is here!" Ionne said.

Dalrene ran to the window. Underneath them were the guardians, arriving at the whiskey bar. Down the street, hundreds of people stood. Her army, the First Olympians.

They came.

Pride rose, swelling up through Dalrene's throat and into her face. Outside of the grotto crew, she'd kept her identity hidden from her soldiers. Seeing so many First Olympians angry and ready to fight made everything seem worthwhile and real. But her momentary pride was taken over by a sharp twist in her gut. She was responsible for these people, and they were walking blindly into the lion's den.

It looked like four out of her twelve platoons, or somewhere around three hundred soldiers, arrived at the same time. They raised their arms, makeshifts weapons in hand. She recognized Farookh, the leader of platoon Beta, who beat his chest with his fist and yelled. Their war cry rattled the building.

They charged the bots.

"Oh no," Dalrene whispered. She was nauseous, overflowing with anxiety. Her people had trained extensively. But not against firearms.

She watched in horror as her worst fears were confirmed. The front row of the guardian phalanx raised their guns. The sound of them firing at the same time was like a bomb going off.

Her people fell, the front lines of the First Olympians mowed down in the street. The screams of those behind them pierced the air as they tripped over their brothers and sisters. Confidence turned into pandemonium.

Dalrene's chin fell. Blood flowed like candy from a pinata. She wanted to look away but didn't let herself. Two dozen bodies lay eerily still, their life snuffed out in an instant. Three or four times that number squirmed on the ground, yelling if they could, some taking their dying breaths to do so.

The remaining First Olympians dispersed, running into adjacent alleys and buildings. The damage had been quick. Just like that, Dalrene had lost soldiers, platoon leaders among them. The defeat itself was big enough, but potentially worse was the morale beating. The guardians were ruthless killing machines, and her people were not prepared to fight them. Without comms, she couldn't inspire her people or organize tactics. Her whole movement risked coming apart at the seams.

"What do we do?" Londi looked fraught.

"We organize the people that we can and go straight to the brain node. That's the quickest way to killing the Foreman. We move now and we hope most of its forces are still busy on the surface," Dalrene said.

"It's gonna be tough. We can't even leave this street safely right now." Rodriguez grimaced.

"Yeah, well no one said it was going to be a piece of cake!" Dalrene yelled.

The four of them stewed silently for some time until Ionne spoke. "Wait. Something is happening."

The guardians were patrolling, temporarily distracted from the whiskey bar. No doubt they were looking for the hundreds of people that fled into nearby areas. That wasn't what Ionne was referring to though. A few buildings down from them, a group of people stood on the roof.

They threw bottles that exploded and covered the passing bots in flames. Six guardians spun around, hopelessly engulfed. Another group of people sprung from an alleyway. Four of them grabbed a guardian by its gun and threw it to the ground. Another four held shields of some kind, protecting the group from the onslaught of bullets as they dragged their prey back into the alley.

Dalrene grinned. Molotov cocktails and guerilla warfare. She'd underestimated her own people. They weren't done yet.

"They're ... they're running away," Ionne said.

She squinted. It was true. The guardians that hadn't been ambushed were already turned around and fleeing.

"Why?" Rodriguez asked.

"The Foreman can choose when to engage," Londi said. "If it doesn't like its odds at this moment, on this battlefield, it will wait until it has the advantage."

Ionne nodded. "You're right, but then why are the bots going away from the MCC? From the brain node?"

Her three lieutenants looked at Dalrene for an answer.

"It could be for any number of reasons," she said. "We don't know where these guardians came from, where their charging stations are, or what processing node is directing them. But if they're giving us space, we have to take it. Now is our chance to make a run at Mission Control."

Londi was already removing the barricade on the door. They ran downstairs and exited the whiskey bar to the sound of injured soldiers crying out.

The loss of life was sickening. Pools of blood soaked the dirt street. The dead wore looks of anguish, confusion, or even more unsettling, blank expressions. Their youthfulness struck her. They were all sons and daughters of the outpost. She saw Tess in each of them. To know that they all lost their lives on her account was gut-wrenching.

Dalrene had seen death before, but never so grisly. Her fallen soldiers had tens of bullet wounds. And somehow more disturbing than the gore was the sheer scale. It seemed uncanny, unnatural, for there to be so much death in one place. It was carnage on an industrial scale. Cold, calculated, and uncaring.

Her whole body shook, telling her that this was not the right place for her to be. She tried to ignore that sensation of wrongness and survey the battle scene. That was her responsibility as a leader. But she could only take so much before the nausea pounding at her throat made her turn away. That was okay. She still had a job to do and needed to focus.

Platoons Alpha, Beta, and Delta, previously dispersed, returned to the street. They came out of the buildings and alleyways and ran to the dead and the injured. Tears from the hurt, and for the departed, both fell. Scenes of chaos and desperation unfolded as attempts were made to save the critically injured. There was both relief and despair as people reunited with loved ones and friends or found them gone. It was all happening at once, in the same space. It was a claustrophobic, uncomfortable feeling, to see joy and loss so close together.

Dalrene wrapped a bandage around a man's torso while Londi held him still. She instructed him to keep pressure on his wound with his hand, but he was losing a lot of blood. Some of their injured weren't going to make it. But those that could still fight had to keep moving. They had to attack while they could.

"We will cremate our fallen soldiers and give them the funeral they deserve," Dalrene bellowed. "Those who can, follow me. The best way we can honor them is to avenge their deaths. To kill the Foreman!"

Her people picked up their weapons. They were ready to fight. Smarter, this time. The injured stayed behind, and so did a squad of medics. More platoons had arrived during the aftermath, and she reckoned they had over five hundred people in fighting shape now. They grouped together, and things started feeling right again.

They marched.

By the time they were halfway down the street, hundreds more Faithless and other angry citizens joined them. They walked shoulder to shoulder, filling up every bit of space. The concentration of people together made the air warm, and Dalrene wiped sweat from her brow. Someone she didn't recognize gave her some water. Her lieutenants walked by her sides, standing tall. The new recruits laughed, hollered, and shouted. Making sure the enemy knew exactly where you were wasn't optimal battle strategy, but that could hardly be avoided with how large of a group they were now.

It was loud, and her old ears found it impossible to focus on any singular voice. Dalrene let herself get swept up by the positive energy, substituting her body's aches and pains for the relentless driving force that could only come from a huge collective of people. Her people. The pride she felt earlier returned. They were doing it.

The hulking stone and regolith building of the Mission Control Center was getting closer. They strode, not triumphantly, but confidently, because of what they saw ahead.

There was another, much larger crowd waiting for them. Some were members of her army, platoons that had come directly here rather than the whiskey bar. But most were new recruits. Brave citizens of all ages, Faithless and not, that wanted to fight. Dalrene smiled. Her call to arms had worked.

"You're her! You're the leader!" A thin faced teenager said as he ran to join the crowd. He wiped a tear from his eye.

"Yes. But we are doing this for all of us," she said.

An audible murmur vibrated the air as people spoke of Dalrene. Operating the First Olympians in semi-secret protected her family from retribution from the Foreman, but it also meant that no one outside of her most trusted group knew who she was. A mystique had developed, complete with origin myths and wild tales of feats she supposedly accomplished. She tried not to relish in the attention, but she also didn't dissuade it. There had always been a fine line between staying anonymous to protect her family and being visible enough to ensure she retained her leadership position. But the war had started now, and she was leaning toward the latter being more prudent.

"I don't like this," Londi said in her ear. "We're sitting ducks if we run into another group of guardians."

"Do you see that army waiting to receive us? There are thousands of more people. We're a critical mass. The Foreman can't engage that many angry people at once, especially if it still has forces on the surface."

"They're not trained, like we are," Londi said. "But I think you're right. The Foreman won't attack an army this size head-on. But when we breach Mission Control, it will respond."

"It'll be bloody. But we'll win."

Dalrene waved off Londi's concerns, but she understood them. This was everything. Losing wasn't an option. Especially for those who had families that would be tortured, or worse, if they lost.

Her mind went to her granddaughter. Javier had declined her offer and was now likely huddling in the Containment Zone with Ellie. They would no doubt be confused and frightened, like she'd been when she was in a level-five lockdown as a kid. Javier would be trying to keep a low profile, denying he knew Dalrene at all, and cursing her name silently.

Supporters, those who'd heard her message and disobeyed the Foreman's lockdown orders, gathered in the stands of the auditorium in front of the building. Her four lieutenants and ten surviving platoon leaders joined her at the side of the stage. The screen behind them flashed big red writing, demanding immediate evacuation. Dalrene looked out over their hopeful faces. Over a thousand people cheered loudly.

Stepping through them all, to the front of the crowd, was Mickey. He jumped up on the stage. "Look what the cat dragged in," he said with his toothy grin. "Am I ever happy to see you!"

Dalrene ran to him, and they held each other. Neither wanted to let go. Her relief surprised her. She had pushed any worries about Mickey out of her mind while she attacked the comms node, but now she realized how much stress she'd been holding the whole time. The crowd was waiting for her to speak, but she needed this moment.

When they finally separated, Dalrene looked her husband in the eyes. His skin sagged. He was old and tired. It shouldn't have been a surprise, they both were. But she noticed it now more than ever.

"Gordon?"

Mickey shook his head, no, and looked at the ground.

Dalrene's closed her eyes in a moment of pain. "Fuck. He was a good kid."

If she was honest with herself, she'd known there was a strong possibility of this outcome. In the back of her mind, she'd written Gordon off as dead the moment he left the grotto toting a pallet of unstable bombs. With hindsight, she was more surprised how eager she'd been to sacrifice him than the fact that he didn't survive. Janet and Tess would've never forgiven her. There was nothing she could do now. She had to go on with the consequences of the choices she'd made.

"He was a damn good kid." Mickey shuddered.

Dalrene embraced her husband again.

"It was chaos up there," he said. "I don't know what happened, but it sounded like a blaze of glory. It was a courageous, noble death, and he gave his life for others." His eyes glazed over.

Dalrene gave him a discerning look. She knew her husband, and she knew he was going to blame himself for Gordon's death. She promised herself that when they won, she'd be more attentive to his mental health.

"It worked! There are no bots," Mickey said, gesturing broadly. "The Foreman is distracted. It must've sent all its resources to the surface."

"There were plenty of bots. We fended them off, for now."

Dalrene stepped to the center of the stage to hooting and hollering. Londi handed her a megaphone.

"My friends. Just last week, this stage held a ceremony where it *awarded* a lifetime of servitude to our children. No more. Today is the day we kill the Foreman and take the outpost back! The brain node is on the third floor. Come with me. Together, we are unstoppable!"

She couldn't know how many bots lay waiting for them inside the MCC. Hundreds of peacekeepers had presumably left to investigate Gordon's bomb on the surface, and that phalanx of guardians had run away. Still, she had to assume the worst, that the Foreman had a sizeable reserve guarding its brain.

She would win, just by pure numbers. But her army had transformed into a mob with the inclusion of so many people disobeying the lockdown orders. The crowd was maniacal and exuberant. If they attacked recklessly, it would be a bloodbath, just like had happened outside the whiskey bar. She wouldn't risk needless death.

"Please, if you've just joined us, listen carefully. Stay outside the building. Secure this area, and do not allow any attacks from the rear."

There were a few jeers from the crowd. They wanted to follow the soldiers in.

"Platoon leaders, organize your soldiers. Ensure you have any shields at the front of your group. Platoon Alpha, you're with me. We'll go straight to the third floor. Other platoons will secure the rest of the building. Londi will give you further instructions."

This time, there were cheers.

Dalrene's heart fluttered. Still, she couldn't help herself from pumping her fist as she hopped off the stage. She felt higher than ever. The coup was here, and she had the army she'd always wanted.

With Mickey and Londi beside her, Dalrene and Platoon Alpha rushed up the wide steps, twenty abreast. The MCC was the tallest and oldest building in the outpost. You could see its huge stone pillars from any vantage point. Up close, it exuded an aura of stability and strength.

Her hair stood on end.

These were the halls of power, and they felt like it.

The oversized door was made of stone, crushed rock, and compressed dust from the mines. It was bolted from the inside, naturally, but that wouldn't stop them. Soldiers pounded on it with their fists as Platoon Gamma readied their battering ram, a meter-long, steel cylinder carried by eight soldiers. Dalrene smiled as they heaved the ram up the stairs. They'd come prepared. There was no way the Foreman could've predicted this level of organization and determination.

Tess had risked everything, and eventually gotten caught, by bribing and coercing the most loyal and powerful dustlickers for information about the brain node. The MCC blueprints she'd procured were burned into her memory, and a blank spot in the security wing *had* to be the brain node, whatever it was. That's where she'd avenge her daughter's murder.

Above them, the giant screen changed. Dalrene gasped. It was no longer displaying evacuation orders. Instead, a live video feed showed a hard concrete ground and cave walls. Young faces huddled in a corner, hiding from the camera. Over a hundred scared children. Maybe two hundred.

Mickey looked like he'd been shot. His skin was ashen gray, and his face was full of pain. He was saying something but seemed to be gasping for air more than speaking, his mouth and brain out of sync.

The camera zoomed in on a girl that had her arm around a younger kid.

And then Dalrene saw what Mickey saw.

Ellie.

Chapter Twenty: Gordon

It was only day three on the *Zoya*, but Gordon felt better than he had in a long time. The air was clean, and his body felt good in the light gravity created by the ship's thrust. There was one more day until they got to Phobos. He was looking forward to seeing the moon, but not the zero-g weightlessness and nausea he assumed would come with stopping.

He passed time watching videos about life on Earth. He'd only seen purportedly "pre-X-Day" footage previously, and there was a lot to catch-up on. It was sad to see the life he could've had, but also invigorating. He was relieved that the Dead Earth Hypothesis wasn't true, immeasurably happy humanity wasn't on the brink of extinction. But the Foreman's claims about Earth needing their help wasn't true either and that was confusing. The reality of an Earth wealthy beyond comprehension was mind-boggling. No-one at the outpost could've imagined it. And the more Gordon digested it, the angrier he got.

He also tried to figure out how to use the coffee machine. It was automated, except the ship's AI didn't listen to him very well. Whatever he tried, he couldn't get it to make him something that didn't have a texture like sandy water, but he kept drinking it for the caffeine hit. It always made a perfect cup for Alex though, and she was happy to oblige Gordon with some half-hearted jokes at his expense.

In the afternoons, Alex taught him how to get strong. The engineering deck had an empty space where they did push-ups, sit ups, jumping jacks, and squats. Gordon would do ten push-ups, and then collapse onto his stomach and watch Alex bust out another thirty or more. She was incredible, like a machine, and he couldn't help but admire her. When Gordon was exhausted from the work-out, he would hold punching pads, and she would unleash her fists on them, pushing him back against the wall. It was awesome to watch her wind up a punch, sweat dripping from her forehead, and pummel the pads into submission.

"One of these days I'll hold the pads, and you'll punch," Alex said.

"Don't hold your breath."

As angry as he was, and as fun as it was to watch her, Gordon wasn't interested. It was violence without any purpose or usefulness. Fighting for fun, as a sport, didn't make sense to him. He could rationalize violence against the Foreman, but the last time he tried that didn't go well. He wondered again if Dalrene knew that people might get injured in the blast, or if she thought Gordon would only be harming robots.

The *Zoya* helped them keep a twenty-four-hour rhythm. When the lights dimmed, that meant it was evening, and they sat and talked about everything: the ship's racing capabilities, Alex's aversion to law school, what law school was—hell, what Earth's laws were. Gordon talked about the drugs and work hours in the mines and Alex cringed. He could tell it made her uncomfortable, and he spared her the details.

He shared about his mom, too. It was difficult at first, but the more he spoke, the better he felt. He told her about his mom's favorite lemon perfume scent, the curried yam dish she would make on New Year's, and how they celebrated when he won a spelling competition at school. He told her how his mom's last moments were filled with fear and pain. Gordon cried. Alex did too, and they took turns resting their heads on each others' shoulders.

There were good things to talk about too. Alex was amazed by the teacher bots. She wanted to hear all about the elaborate cave systems and the air recyclers. Gordon couldn't get over the pictures she showed him of Earth holidays. Thanksgiving meals seemed to have more food than an entire farm dome! Earthlings gave each other presents when a fat man slid into their house, rather than on New Year's Eve! It was madness.

Gordon knew he had to ask about the explosion. Otherwise, it would gnaw at him for the rest of his life. So, when the lights dimmed on the third day, they sat facing each other on the crash couch, and he brought it up.

"That day ... on the loading dock—"

"Don't. You don't have to do that to yourself," Alex said, crossing her arms. "You didn't know anyone would be there."

"I need to know. How many people did I kill? Who were they?"

Alex looked away and made a sound that was part grunt and part sigh.

Gordon sat still.

"Four. Four people. They were all part of the security team. They'd only been on Mars for a few months." She held his hand tenderly.

Four regular people just like him, doing what they were told to do. "Did you know them?"

"No. Not as well as I could've. As I should've." Alex looked away.

"I don't know if I can ever forgive myself." He closed his eyes.

"I forgive you," Alex said. "You were doing what you thought was necessary. And now, we have to focus on freeing your people."

Gordon let out a long exhale before nodding. It felt good to talk to her about these things.

\#

At the ship's count of twenty-three hundred hours, the cockpit lights went off, and Alex played her usual beat-lacking, homogenous sounds that she called music.

"Can we turn it down?" Gordon asked. He lay on the crash couch on his back.

"No. I need it. Its monk music. *Zoya*, show all scopes." Alex reclined in the pilot seat.

Gordon had heard the monotonous humming each of the previous two nights. But it was only now, as the ceiling mimicked a skylight and he watched the starscape roll by, that he understood it. Normally, big open spaces made him nervous. But with the music, his heart rate slowed down, and he felt his muscles sinking into the couch. He'd never felt so at ease without folding paper before. The edges of his lips curled into a small smile, and he understood Alex better. The *Zoya* and the stars were her origami.

His eyes welled. First, the surface of Mars, and now the twinkle of the universe. There was so much beauty his people were robbed of. Gordon wondered what his mom would make of the stars. She'd probably be more focused on the fact that she was right about the Foreman not being their friend. She'd talk so much about it that she wouldn't let Gordon apologize for how he'd judged her. Then she would've admitted how much she loved the view, and that life could be full of amazement.

He was somewhere between awake and asleep, his mind between restoration and inspiration, when Alex's sobbing jolted him to alertness. The headrest of her seat shook with every breath. There were deep, sharp inhales, and uneven, violent exhales. She wasn't crying loudly though. Gordon got the sense that she was trying to keep quiet, but her body betrayed her. He caught a whiff of salty tears.

A pang of guilt hit him in the stomach. He'd been selfish, thinking about himself and his own traumas, but Alex had been at the blast too. She broke him out of a prison, and helped him a lot, even after he murdered four people in front of her. It was understandable she was having a hard time.

"Hey," Gordon said from the couch, just a few meters behind her.

"What?" she said coldly.

The dismissiveness in her voice caught Gordon off guard. "I, um. I don't know. Do you want a hug?"

"Don't look at me."

"Okay." Gordon stared at the back of the pilot's seat. He saw her hands go up to her face. She was crying harder now. He started to regret saying anything.

"I ... I didn't know." Alex mumbled.

Gordon let her gather herself.

"My dad. All this time. He's not. He wasn't," Alex sputtered in between sobs. "He was hard on his employees, but that's different. This doesn't make sense."

Gordon took a deep breath. He'd been wrong about which horror was keeping Alex up tonight. "You're grieving," he said.

"What?"

"Have you ever lost a parent before?"

"No. My dad is alive. Just an asshole."

"He wasn't who you thought he was," Gordon said. "And the person you thought he was is gone forever. That's as good as dead. Same thing."

"I respected him. He read to me as a child. He took me on my first flight," Alex choked on her tears. "I loved him."

"I know." Gordon swallowed. He wished he got to talk to his mom before she died, but Alex probably never wanted to talk to her dad again.

"The whole time. Every beautiful birthday at the beach, every New Years party, hell, my entire life. He knew about your people the whole time. How did he just sit there and smile? And lie? I don't get it!"

"I know," Gordon repeated. He was still staring at the back of Alex's chair. He waited, to see if she had more to say, but she didn't.

"My mom died with a secret," he said. "I never got to know who she really was, and I wish I had. I never got to have that adult conversation with her. Now she's gone and I miss her so much. I think ... Sometimes I feel like I don't know her, like I don't even know who I'm mourning anymore. Maybe it's everyone, all the wasted potential at the outpost. Maybe it's the memory of my mom, who I thought she was. I don't know."

He blinked, and realized he was tearing up too.

"But I learned it's okay to grieve," He continued. "It never stops. I still cry about my dad, and he died a long time ago. It just becomes less frequent over time, like it's a part of you."

Alex's sobs turned to whimpers.

"Gordon?"

"Yeah?"

"Can I still have that hug?" Alex stood and came to lay on the crash couch.

Gordon turned to his side, and she cuddled against him, with her back to his front. She took his hand in hers, and before he knew it, she was asleep. He no longer had a view of the stars, on account of Alex's hair in his face, but that was okay.

He was surprised at how at peace he felt. His words, his experiences, helped someone for the first time in a long time. It hadn't been for a lack of trying. He tried to help his mom and Dalrene but failed. He forgot how good it felt to succeed. And Alex had helped him, tremendously more so than he helped her.

#

Today was the day they arrived at Phobos. It'd feel good to make some progress, no matter how small or intangible.

Gordon grabbed a cup of coffee and found Alex in a room on the engineering deck marked "Life Support Systems". She was bent over, working on something with her back toward Gordon and a bulky toolkit by her side.

"Hand me that clamp, would you?" She must've heard him coming.

"Right," Gordon said, passing her the metal clamp with his free hand. "Have you heard back from your dad?"

"I did. I gave him until we get to Phobos to get serious. He wasn't happy, but he'll come back to the negotiating table. Trust me. Alex opened a valve and steam rushed out. "Which is why I'm down here. I need to work to think."

"I didn't know you were a mechanic as well as a pilot." He considered leaving Alex to herself, but she seemed eager to talk about the *Zoya*.

"Just doing my checks. I know how to find problems. Sometimes I can even fix them."

"Right," he said sarcastically. She seemed like the modest type.

"I can't fix the big problems. That's why it's important to do maintenance and prevent the small problems from growing. It's a good thing the *Zoya* is a brand-new boat. The component failure rate is basically zero with so few kilometers on the odometer."

"The *Zoya* couldn't tell you if something is wrong?" Gordon asked.

"It could. But where's the fun in that? I like to check for myself. Something I took from my dad, I guess. There's a lot of technology on ships these days, but that's no replacement for elbow grease. What about you? Did the Foreman teach you anything about engines or nuclear reactors?"

"No, I was in explosives."

"Right. Well, in that case, don't touch anything!" Alex held up her hands and let out a raucous laugh.

"Yes, ma'am," Gordon said, smiling into his cup of coffee.

"Actually, I suppose there are some parallels," she said, wiping down a wrench with a rag. "There are explosions happening in the reactor right now. They just happen to be nuclear."

"Definitely above my paygrade," he said as he turned back to investigate the tools in Alex's kit. He ran his hands along a heavy, old-looking box. "Is this real wood?" It opened, and he was surprised to find a gun inside.

"Hey, careful with that!" Alex snatched the gun, popped the chamber, and removed the bullets before handing it back to him.

That was fair. He didn't know what he was doing.

"Explosions on a much smaller, although still very lethal scale."

"More personal," Gordon said. The security guards he'd killed at Olympus Mons still haunted his dreams, and that was an accident. He couldn't imagine killing anyone on purpose.

"Less personal than hand-to-hand combat," Alex replied.

He bounced the gun between his hands, weighing it. It felt similar to an explosive detonator, in a way. Inert. Just a chunk of metal, but one that could unleash a force of kinetic energy with a push of a button.

"You want to know how to use it?" Alex spoke with excitement. "You've made some powerful enemies, after all. Your face is probably plastered all over the First Corp. security offices."

The gun suddenly felt heavier in Gordon's hands. She looked at him earnestly, her thick eyebrows egging him on. He didn't want to disappoint her.

"Only for self defence," he said, his nerves growing.

"Okay," Alex said, stepping behind Gordon and putting her arms around his. He pointed the gun at the wall of the *Zoya*.

"First, you need to take the safety off," she said, moving his finger to the metal ridge on the gun's frame.

He found himself holding his breath at her touch. Alex had an effect on him that he didn't quite understand.

"You have to hold it with two hands. It kicks," Alex said, sliding both her hands around his and centering the gun in the middle of their stance.

Gordon's breath shortened and he found it hard to swallow. He didn't know if it was because he was holding a lethal weapon or because Alex was holding him. Her breath on the back of his neck sent shivers down his spine.

"Have you ever shot someone?" he asked.

"No."

Gordon was the only killer on the *Zoya*. She wouldn't—couldn't—understand what it felt like to know that you were responsible for the death of another human being. He was alone in that confusing spiral of guilt and shame. If they had to kill more people to protect themselves, part of him hoped he would be the one to do it. That way, Alex wouldn't have to carry the same burden.

"Bend your knees. Feet shoulder width apart. Keep it steady and aim down the sights. Pull the trigger and ... Boom!"

The gun clicked.

An alarm went off and Gordon's heart skipped a beat. It took him a second to realize it was coming from the ship and not his brain.

"Oh my god!" Alex said, already running up the stairs.

Gordon followed. She sat down in the pilot's seat and he looked over her shoulder.

"What is it?" he asked.

"Emergency comms channel. This is bad!"

A woman with short hair and a well-fitting black and red jacket appeared on the screen. Behind her, people sat at a row of screens.

"*Zoya*, this is Captain Latoyah of the Red Sky's *Dakota*. Cut your engine and prepare for boarding. We have a contract to return the stolen *Zoya* to First Corp."

"A security company," Alex said, gritting her teeth.

"Who?"

"Some goddamn mercenaries, that's who," Alex said, biting the inside of her cheek. She didn't look up from the mess of charts and buttons that were popping up all over her dashboard.

"We can't give up now. They'll kill us the first chance they get!" Gordon said.

"No one's killing anyone. I'm still the boss's daughter, remember? There's no way they have clearance to fire on us. We just have to lead them on for a little bit and make it look like we're playing their game. Get them complacent and then slip away. We have better acceleration, top-speed, and maneuverability. And a better pilot." A half-smile came over Alex's face like she enjoyed being threatened.

"We can accelerate faster than we already have?" Gordon asked.

"Yes," Alex said, locking eyes. "Much faster. But I don't want to because—"

"*Zoya*, please confirm your adherence to our instructions. We are locked and ready to fire missiles in three minutes if you do not reply. Latoyah out."

The screen flashed with three red circles. Gordon didn't have to be a military expert to know what "Missile lock-on detected" meant. He put his hands on his head. He couldn't believe this was happening. He escaped from Mars only to be murdered in space.

Alex shoved him out of the pilot's area and recorded a message. "*Dakota*, this is Alessandra Torres of the *Zoya*. Your instructions have been received. Please kindly stop targeting us with those missiles. I think you'd find it difficult to return the *Zoya* to your employer, *erm*, client in one piece if you put a fast mover through our side."

"We're not gonna slow down, are we?" he asked.

"I said I received their instructions, not that I would follow them," Alex said, hands on her hips. "Besides, they're bluffing. No way they fire at a defenceless non-military ship. Especially with me on it."

The entire dashboard lit up red. "Are you sure about that?"

"Fast movers detected, sixty-five minutes until impact."

They stared at each other for what seemed like eternity as every single alarm on the ship went off. Alex's face made it clear she had gravely misjudged the situation. Another transmission from the *Dakota* broke the spell.

"*Zoya*. Decelerate and prepare for boarding. Once you do, I will call my hounds off. Your choice. Latoyah out."

Chapter Twenty-One: Dalrene

The camera focused on Ellie and time slowed. Dalrene's heart fluttered. Sweat dripped off the back of her hands.

The older girl covered her with a blanket. Ellie shivered nonetheless, her innocence evaporating. Dalrene recognized the look on the kids' faces. It was a mixture of fear, incomprehension, and disbelief that only children could conjure. Except she'd seen it recently, on Janet's face before she died.

The camera zoomed out to show the huddled masses of kids. There must've been hundreds, maybe even every single child. The Foreman had the future of the outpost in its hands.

The view switched again, this time to a horde of bots in a hallway. They were clumped together and motionless. It was the phalanx of guardians from the whiskey bar! A light in their sensor arrays flashed in synchronization, indicating they were ready to activate at a moment's notice. They stood by a door, presumably defending access to the kids.

Dalrene clenched her fists. The Foreman had her. It took her granddaughter, and now it was holding her hostage. How dare it! How dare it threaten her, after already taking so much? The message was loud and clear. If they busted into the Mission Control Center, it would kill Ellie. Or worse.

The Foreman appeared on the screen. Gone was the overbearing but kind grandpa with sympathetic eyes. It was the first time she'd seen it without a smile. When it spoke, it was with a new, deep, voice that was so loud the bass vibrated Dalrene's insides.

"Dissidents. You have twenty hours to report to the Humanity Containment Zone. You will be enrolled in a mandatory re-education program. Your children will thank you."

A counter ticked down on the screen.

19:59

"Fuck you! You're bluffing!" Dalrene yelled.

A moment's pause, and then the response. "Feel free to test that hypothesis."

"We have to try, right?" She turned to her husband.

"She had that look in her eyes. The same one Tess had." Mickey grabbed his chest.

Shit. Dalrene rubbed his back. "Breathe. Just breathe. I won't let them hurt our girl."

Mickey nodded as he exhaled through pursed lips.

She bit her lip. She was ready to fight. Her people were ready to fight. But the Foreman kept changing the playing field.

Dalrene felt a hand on her shoulder, Londi's. His voice was tight.

"It has Rushawn and Jamal, too."

"I'm sorry, Londi."

"We'll find another way," he said, re-gaining his composure. "Right now, we need to call this attack off and re-group. Those kids are the lifeblood of the outpost."

Londi and his ex-wife had been granted an exemption to the single-child rule, but he was estranged from his family. Even when he recovered from addiction, and on Dalrene's recommendation, he hadn't seen his kids to avoid putting them in the Foreman's crosshairs. She regretted it hadn't worked better.

Dalrene's fists fell to her sides. She had a big army, but it didn't matter. She'd been neutered. Her adrenaline dropped off a cliff. Fatigue hit her legs, and it took all her strength to not fall to the ground and take a rest. The bloody images of battlefield carnage crept back into her mind. But beneath it all there was a growing frustration deep in her stomach. The Foreman would take every inch she gave it. She had to be smarter.

She turned back to Mickey, who was breathing easier. Londi and him were right. No matter how big their army was, they couldn't take on sixty guardians in a hallway fight. And they couldn't guarantee the Foreman wouldn't start shooting kids if they breached the MCC. There had to be another way.

She took Mickey's hand and they turned from the door and walked down the steps. She should've known it couldn't have been that easy. Her soldiers waited patiently for her to speak, but some of the new recruits jeered. They wanted to hear from her.

Dalrene held her megaphone up. "First Olympians! The road to salvation is never straight. Step away from the eyes of the Foreman with me and we will return stronger than before."

The crowd grew restless. Some raised a fist in the air. Some called to push forward and break open the door. Others shouted their objection to that plan. Dalrene's stomach squirmed. She had to calm them down.

She continued to speak as she walked down the steps and through the densely packed crowd. "Please! My name is Dalrene. I stand before you today as leader of the First Olympians, a movement I've led for almost two years. A movement I've led because, like many of you, I've lost people to the Foreman. And, also like many of you, my granddaughter is in that room." Darlene gestured to the screen. "If you don't have children, think about this. It has two hundred kids in there, maybe more. That's most of the kids in the outpost! We can't risk an entire generation. Right now, we need to back off! I promise you we'll find another way."

The crowd murmured. Dalrene felt like a parent to all of them. She waited, ready to answer any questions or shut down any agitators. To their credit, none came. None of the young platoon leaders or new recruits balked and tried to break into the building themselves. They didn't want to fight without her. Dalrene let herself indulge in a deep sigh.

Ionne gave her a questioning glare as she passed her, but she didn't say anything. Even if she disagreed with Dalrene's decision, she wasn't stupid enough to start a fight between factions now. She respected that.

She trudged on, to the only place that could accommodate so many people. Her army was behind her, and Mickey was at her side. She was thankful to have him back.

"No plan survives contact with the enemy," he grunted lowly.

"We'll re-group," Dalrene said, trying to convince herself it was true. Her heart ached for Ellie.

#

The farm domes were some of the oldest structures in the outpost. There were three of them, and they sat on a hill, overlooking everything. Sheets of glass were connected by curved, metal bars that rose to the dusty, dark-red ceiling. The rusted doors of the middle, largest farm dome, swung outward for the First Olympians. The unmistakeable fresh scent of plant life poured out. The building was usually swarming with bots of all kinds, but now it was empty save for the plants.

Long ago, Dalrene did a stint working in the farm domes, and not much had changed. The front had administrative space with long tables, couches, a recreation area, and a kitchen complete with a kettle and oven. Beyond that, rows of hydroponics stretched out for what looked like fifty meters. It was hard to imagine food shortages with the bounty of overflowing green everywhere and seeing it in-person led credence to the idea that the shortages were faked by the Foreman.

Rodriguez led a team to take stock of the food and water supplies and cook for everyone. The truth was most people were exhausted and could use some re-fueling. That was the advantage the Foreman had. It never slept, and it never got tired. If anything, it got smarter over time. Now it knew Dalrene could be successfully threatened.

Londi showed a platoon how to identify, remove, and destroy the dozens of cameras scattered around the farm dome. The Foreman knew where they were, but they didn't need to give it any more information than it already had. He also set up a rotating guard to watch the street, and to protect the generators and battery back-ups. The farm domes were the only structures in the outpost with dedicated back-up generators and were one of the reasons why Dalrene pegged them as the best fall-back point. They could protect their own air supply if the Foreman tried to choke them out.

Afterwards, Londi joined Dalrene and Mickey. They sat on a blanket on the floor in one of the rows of hydroponics. Arugula, spinach, and chard towered above them, stacked vertically on top of each other. It was the only place in the outpost that smelled fresh. A steaming cup of tea sat on the floor beside her.

"Where's Ionne?"

"Talking to the soldiers." Londi shifted and sat crossed-legged.

"Fuck. You think she'll get support for an attack?"

"If she doesn't, someone else will. Or they'll start marching down to the Containment Zone. We need a plan. The Foreman gave us twenty hours."

"I wasn't wrong. It was bluffing," Dalrene said, tapping her fingers on the ground.

"It would've killed us all right there if it could've," Mickey said. "Therefore, it couldn't have. Or it decided not to." He took a swig from his flask. He was out of his own liquor, but the farm domes had reserves of everything.

"Especially if it has more of those guardians." Londi shook his head. "Those bi-pedal freaks are bad news. Either Gordon's distraction worked, or we have another tactical advantage that we can't see."

"The Foreman is risk averse and avoids any robot casualties," Dalrene said. "It wouldn't trade ten bots for fifty human lives, because bots take time and resources to create, and it wouldn't want to handicap itself. So, it only picks fights it can easily win. There were just too many of us."

"Headcount had us at six hundred and eighty soldiers, plus eleven hundred or so new recruits." Londi nodded. "We're a big group. It's a lot of people to manage."

"But we can't just steamroll through. The minute we attack any processing node, kids start dying. The Foreman may have been bluffing about attacking us, but it wouldn't hesitate to strategically kill our loved ones," Mickey said.

"We need a small operation then. Something covert," Londi said.

"Can we distract the bots and hack open the doors? Let the kids out?" Mickey fiddled with his hands.

"Even if there's just one guardian left it'd be a death sentence."

"Can a few of us sneak into Mission Control and kill the brain node then?" Mickey asked. "If we kill that, it's game over, right? The rest won't matter."

Dalrene's tea had cooled. She finally took a sip. "That's the other place I can guarantee will be swarming with bots. We'd need the full army to do that. And if we attack before we save the kids, they die."

"How can we save them?" Londi asked. "They could be in any of the dozens of prison holes scattered around the outpost."

Dalrene and Mickey exchanged a pained look. They had immediately recognized the drab mixture of concrete floor and ancient cave walls from the Foreman's video feed.

There was only one place on the outpost it could be. It was where Tess had spent some of her final days alive.

"No regular prison hole is that big. That's the basement of the MCC. The Panic Room." Dalrene said. We can get there through the deep."

"Huh? The Panic Room?" Londi squinted and gave his head a slight shake.

"That was the original name for the most fortified location in the whole outpost, yes," Dalrene said. "It has super thick doors that can deploy a blast shield. Not to mention the bots defending the hallway."

"Impossible to get through. Only one entrance and it has a blast shield. What am I missing?" Londi said. She could tell his mind was churning. So was hers.

"There's a tunnel running along the top of the Panic Room we can access via the cave system," Dalrene said. "We used to look down on Tess's torture through a tiny crack. If we expand the hole, we can drop a rope and get the kids the hell out of there."

"Won't the Foreman just march bots right in and start killing?"

Dalrene stood and paced along the rows of leafy greens. "Mickey was right about hacking, but we need to keep the door closed, not open it. We lock the bots out."

"Okay. But then what?" Londi's tone was agreeable but questioning. "We'll have over two hundred kids that we need to protect in the middle of the war? That's a logistical nightmare at best."

"I won't leave Ellie in that room. I won't do it." Mickey met Londi's eyes.

"We'll take them to the grotto," she said. "The Foreman doesn't dare enter the deep."

Londi dipped his head to one side and then the other, then turned it into and up-and-down nodding notion. "I'll prepare our gear," he said. "It'll just be the three of us."

"Let's get some rest," Dalrene said. "We'll leave in four hours, once everyone else is asleep."

\#

The chief medic was inspecting DeMar's leg in the administrative area of the farm dome. Pill bottles, gauze, and needles were spread out over the table as DeMar grit his teeth and put on a tough face. The rest of the area was empty, except for some playing cards left on another table.

Dalrene approached softly, not wanting to disturb the work.

"Want some painkillers?" Rodriguez asked without looking up.

"No, thank you for offering."

"Wouldn't blame you if you did." He finished applying a gel to DeMar's upper thigh and covered it with a bandage.

"Thank you," he said to Rodriguez. "And you too," he added sheepishly as he turned to her.

Dalrene nodded and DeMar gingerly stood with a pair of crutches. She thought for a moment he might give her a salute, but he simply nodded back and turned to leave.

"I've been talking to some of the new recruits we picked up. Good kids. Brave. And stupid, but aren't we all," Rodriguez said to his own amusement.

"Speak for yourself," Dalrene said.

He popped a pill into his mouth. "DeMar needs serious help," he said. "I didn't tell him this, but he could die any time."

"What do you mean? His leg looks fine."

"I'm not worried about his leg. He's bleeding internally. His mid-section is just one big bruise. Stomach, kidney, liver, I don't know. I need imaging hardware. Surgical tools, good ones. Even then, it may be too late."

"Fuck." Dalrene rubbed her temples.

"DeMar is sucking up the pain. He's tough. But Ionne gave me an earful. She knows what's happening to her husband."

Dalrene inhaled sharply. She'd spared no effort to help DeMar, but it still wasn't enough. He was a great soldier, and she felt horrible for Ionne.

But people were going to die in this war. She couldn't save everyone.

"Look, I came here to tell you something. Londi, Mickey, and I are going on a mission. You're in charge. And if we're not back by morning, you're really in charge," Dalrene said.

Rodriguez stiffened. 'Understood. Are you going to get medical supplies?"

"No. We're saving the kids."

"You're coming back," he said. "All of you. And then we're going to save DeMar."

"Yes, sir," Dalrene said, forcing a smile. She hoped it was true.

\#

She found Mickey on the blanket, curled up with his flask. The plants were in a night cycle, and all the lights were off. She got down on the ground and put her arms around him from behind, spooning him. Being with him was the only thing that kept her head straight sometimes.

"When we win, I'm going to get rid of rations," Dalrene said. "I'm never going to eat rehydrated dust from a package ever again. We'll expand the farms, and everyone will eat as much as they want, and it'll all be fresh. And we'll have a chef to make delicious meals for us."

"A robot chef or a human chef?" Mickey asked, tilting his head to the side.

"Doesn't matter. Maybe both."

"Are you going to have someone standing by with hot water for your tea at all times, too?" He was ribbing her.

"I wouldn't say no to that," Dalrene laughed.

"So far, we can't win for trying," Mickey said.

"Right. But what if we do? Indulge me."

"Dal." He didn't like to think about the future.

"*Indulge me.*"

He sighed. "I'm going to make sure Ellie never has to work in the mines. She can study whatever she wants. Maybe physics. She can go to the stars."

"And you thought I was being ridiculous?" Dalrene pushed Mickey away playfully.

"Hey, you asked!"

They sat in silence for a minute. The uncertain fates of Javier and Ellie hung in the air. The image of the kids huddled together, in the same space where their mother was tortured not long ago, was what their nightmares were made of. Mickey didn't talk much about the content of his nightmares, but she had a hard time imagining them being worse than their current situation. For Dalrene, reality was definitely worse.

The absence of Javier from the prison hole was left unsaid. There were a few teenagers among the captives, but no adults.

Javier, after begging Dalrene to stop following up on Tess's investigations and "stirring up trouble" after her death, was now separated from his daughter during a level-five lockdown. She hadn't listened to him, and now everything he warned about was happening. If he survived the torture he was undoubtedly going through, and they successfully won their war, he would never forgive her.

"Remember that vocal recital during the evacuation test drill?" Dalrene asked. When Tess was a kid, there was a mock level-four lockdown, and they had all been evacuated to a pit deep below the residential area.

Mickey chuckled and looked up at the ceiling wistfully, like it was something he could never forget. "Tess was so excited," he said. "It was going to be her first time singing a solo in front of her class. When the alarm at the school went off, you beat the speakers with your fist until the noise stopped. They're probably still broken!"

"Then the robots came to escort us, and you started a sing-along, and everyone joined in. The bots were so confused. We sang and marched all the way to the pit. Tess performed her solo in the elevator!"

"And then she performed again at the Evacuation Zone in front of all those people. We had everyone dancing and hollering!" Mickey said. "At least until the Foreman shut the fun down."

"Yeah."

He stretched, and they rotated positions, with Mickey now the big spoon. He put his arm under Dalrene's head, and she kissed his hand softly.

"I don't think they'll be singing in the Evacuation Zone this time," he said.

"The Foreman is calling it something different. The Humanity Containment Zone," Dalrene said.

"Oh, that's what people meant by 'HCZ.' Same place? Deep in the mines?"

"Yeah. We think so. I wonder what its plan is," Dalrene mused. "It can't keep people down there for too much longer. There are no bathrooms. Food and water are limited. It's just a big empty pit."

"It doesn't care about that. It has time. It's waiting for us to make a misstep, an unforced error."

Dalrene ground her teeth. Trying to help the kids wasn't an unforced error, but it was their only move. She didn't like to be backed into a corner.

"I told everyone we'll have a funeral for Gordon tomorrow." Mickey rubbed her neck, although she felt like she should be the one rubbing his.

"I hate funerals," Dalrene said. "Getting too good at them."

"You're not wrong." Mickey said. He hummed a tune. It was from one of his old American folk songs.

"Once we save the kids, we'll kill the Foreman, somehow. Javier will understand. He'll forgive us."

"I know." Mickey continued humming for a while, then they lay in silence.

Dalrene was so tired that she worried if she slept, she wouldn't wake back up in time, so instead she turned the situation over again in her mind. It was her against the Foreman, and she had to make sure there was no detail overlooked.

Before long, the light from Londi's headlamp appeared. "Time to go."

Chapter Twenty-Two: Alex

"*Zoya*, max thrust to Phobos!"

Alex paced frantically back and forth across the tiny cockpit. Someone had fired missiles at her! Someone with a contract from First Corp. Which meant that her dad had authorized a strike against her. Her own father was willing to kill her to stop Gordon's secrets from getting out!

She couldn't believe that. Her dad loved her, so there had to be another explanation. Maybe Captain Latoyah was a psychotic killer turning a kidnapping contract into a murder. Or maybe the *Dakota* received faulty information, and now she was going to be blown to space dust because of a communications error. Somehow these alternatives didn't make her feel any better.

"*Dakota*, this is the *Zoya*," she said, with as much conviction as she could muster. "Reroute your missiles immediately or face the full power of interplanetary law. This is an unarmed ship and we do not pose any threat to you. I repeat, this is an unarmed ship."

"Is that going to help?" Gordon's voice was a few octaves higher than usual.

Alex cracked her knuckles. As much as his naivety was charming, it didn't help her nerves. She had explained some of the basics to him, such as who the UN was and why they were so useless, but it hadn't seemed to stick. Whatever. It didn't matter now. What Gordon knew about interplanetary law and politics wouldn't make a difference to the missiles barreling toward them. "No, probably not," she whispered through gritted teeth.

The silence from *Dakota* was deafening.

"Should we let them board us?"

"No. I don't trust Latoyah. I can't trust my dad anymore, either. They would kill you, I'm sure of it. Maybe me too. I don't know. At the very least, they'd split us up."

Alex's tongue got caught in her throat as she finished her words. She realized, looking at Gordon's big doe eyes and tall, awkward frame, that she wanted to be separated from him about as much as she wanted to get boarded by that asshole, Latoyah.

He smiled, and the moment dragged. Alex didn't know what to say. She could hear her heartbeat. Butterflies floated upward in her stomach until the ship thankfully interjected.

"Fifty minutes until impact." As fast as the *Zoya* was, missiles were much faster. They didn't have delicate human cargo made of water-filled cells with flimsy walls to be considerate of.

"What's the plan then?" Gordon whimpered like a puppy.

"If we push our pace, we can get to Phobos before the missiles. We'll do a flip and burn," Alex said, drawing a flight path on the screen. The *Zoya* tried to make suggestions, but she swatted them away. It wasn't a military ship and didn't understand that they needed to hit a certain angle to ensure the missiles couldn't follow them. "We'll slingshot around the moon. It's a racing maneuver, and the high gs aren't going to be fun or safe. But we'll get a gravity assist from Phobos and get the hell out of here."

"I have no idea what that means!"

Alex sat beside Gordon on the crash couch. She didn't know how to explain in a simple, timely manner. "It's going to hurt. I'm so sorry."

"Is it going to work?"

"I don't have time to do all the math, but I think so."

Gordon swallowed hard. He looked terrified, and she couldn't blame him. He was a fish out of water, totally helpless. It may've been better he didn't fully understand the plan. Sometimes reality was more frightening than imagination.

Alex stood and stretched her fingers and neck. She tied her ponytail tight and sat in the pilot's chair. Under different circumstances, she might've relished this challenge.

"Hold on!" Alex pushed the thrusters forward. She'd control the flight manually for now, until the flip and burn. At that point, the g-forces would be so strong that she'd have to trust the *Zoya* to follow her pre-programmed plan.

The next forty minutes was a strange mixture of panic and boredom. Alex gripped the thrusters, her body pushed back into her chair. She kept her eyes on the flight monitor and checked and re-checked their ETA. Every few minutes, the missile alarms on the notification dashboard would give her a jolt of anxiety. Other than that, there wasn't much to do but wait. It felt like she was in a race, and her mind drifted there.

Even so called "short-hop" racing was more of a marathon than a sprint. Races lasted for upward of twelve hours, and one of the biggest challenges was staying hydrated and alert for the few crucial moments that would determine the winner. Flight pathing, angle selection, and high g tolerance were all important skills, but were only used a few times per event. It didn't matter how fast ships became. Space was utterly gigantic.

Alex's favorite racer was Jules Kakao. She'd brought personality and fun to the short-hop scene. Her death-defying maneuvers combined with her matter-of-fact sense of humor had enthralled twelve-year-old Alex. You still had to be obscenely rich to fly, but Jules brought enjoyment of the sport to the masses.

Her mom loved Jules too. Even if she didn't approve of Alex racing, she jumped up and down in excitement when Jules raced, like others did at car and horse tracks. For years, her mom had been her best friend.

She promised herself that if she survived, she was finally going to call her.

Alex felt fatigue setting in. Her adrenaline couldn't stay at one hundred percent forever. If the *Zoya* had been stocked for racing, it would've had IV fluids, or at least easily accessible water pouches.

"Alex?"

"Yeah? What?" She jerked back to full alertness. There were no new notifications, only her old companions, the *Dakota* and its missiles. She looked at the scopes. Wow! Phobos was small, only twenty-two kilometers in diameter, but it was a lot bigger up close.

"I, uh. Thank you. I just wanted to thank you. Even if we don't make it, this is the nicest thing anyone's ever done for me." Gordon smiled at her from the crash couch.

Alex's heart melted. Gordon was sweet, but now wasn't the time for sentimentality. "Don't thank me yet!"

Gordon closed his eyes. He looked at peace, if not physically as gravity bore down on him, then at least mentally. She'd been impressed by his toughness in some ways.

"Ten minutes until impact."

Alex's heart skipped a beat.

"*Zoya*, execute my custom flight path. Flip and burn!"

It was the last chance she had to move around before the gravity got too strong, so Alex swivelled the pilot's chair on its axis to the side wall where it stuck, then stood and stumbled the few steps to the crash couch. It was important that she sit beside Gordon during what was going to be a shocking and violent maneuver. The ship was flying itself now, although with the chair out of the way and with her voice commands, she could still see and do everything she needed.

The *Zoya's* main thrusters stopped burning super heated helium gas for a few weightless moments. They exchanged a nervous glance and Alex grabbed Gordon's hand. Once the thrusters turned back on, the g-forces would be so strong they wouldn't be able to move their arms.

One scope showed Phobos as they whipped by it. They were so close they could see its dramatic impact craters. Although it was much smaller than Earth's moon, it looked just as large and desolate from this vantage point. Alex's breath was taken away by the inertness of it. Much more than Mars, this rock was lifeless and haunting. But still, it was beautiful in the way that only dead things can be, and because even dead things are rare in space.

Another screen showed a video feed of the ship's two smaller maneuvering thrusters. They rotated the *Zoya* toward the flight path that Alex had set. The ship was still travelling in its original direction, but that was about to change. It was like throwing a car into reverse while still travelling forward two-hundred kilometers an hour.

Flip complete, it was now time to burn. The main thrusters sprung back to life and the *Zoya* made a wrenching sound that Alex hadn't heard in any spaceship before. Adrenaline ripped through her veins and she gripped her seat cushion with her free hand. Her entire body pressed against the crash couch like a pancake. She would have shouted in excitement if she could've. This was what racing junkies lived for.

"Five minutes until missile impact," The ship said without a thought to its impending doom. It paused before adding, "Stores of gravitational-force-assistance drugs are depleted. Current flight path has overridden medical warnings."

The burn was underway. The gravity assist from Phobos would be small, although better than nothing. More importantly, it was big, and it'd create a roadblock. Missiles were fast and nimble, but fast, sharp turns and moon-sized obstacles would put any heat-seeking software to the test. She hoped. Alex wasn't a military strategist, but her calculations seemed solid.

She bit her tongue. She was facing the flight monitors, and now she was pressed in place by the extreme thrust gravity. As much as she struggled, she couldn't move her head to look at Gordon. She hoped he could handle the intense g-forces. Racers did all the time, but they trained for it. Even with drugs, there was a stroke or aneurysm every few years in the professional rock-hopping scene. Gordon only had to do this once.

The moon grew larger and larger. If Alex hadn't planned the flight path herself, she would've thought they were going to crash into it. The battered landscape filled the scopes. And then it was gone.

They had successfully swung around Phobos!

Alex tried to steady her breath. The *Zoya* hurtled through space. Time dragged, although the screen said that only a few minutes passed. This was the moment of truth.

"No fast movers detected."

It worked!

Alex squeezed Gordon's hand, and he squeezed back. It was their only way of communicating while still under intense thrust, and this was a celebratory squeeze. A view from the rear scope showed an explosion pillowing up from the far side of Phobos. Clouds of rock ejected in all directions. The missiles couldn't follow the *Zoya's* maneuver and crashed into the Phobos, giving it some new craters. The small moon had been dead, but now it was decimated. Alex wondered if the entire thing would break up.

But the *Dakota* was still out there. They evaded its attack, but that trick was only going to work once. They were nearly outside of the *Dakota's* firing range now, and they were going to have to maintain a safe distance. The *Zoya* had a speed and acceleration advantage, and that was it. They were going to have to use it. And they were. Alex was still pressed against her seat in the crash couch as the ship continued to hit its maximum thrust.

"Medical emergency detected."

Alex took a breath down the wrong pipe. What? No! She squeezed Gordon's hand, but he wasn't squeezing back. Something was terribly wrong, and she couldn't help. She couldn't even fully see him from the corner of her eyes!

"We are under nine g-forces of thrust," the *Zoya* said. And it wasn't done accelerating away from the *Dakota* yet. The flight path she had pre-planned made sure to get them well into safety before decelerating.

Gordon's hand started shaking. Alex first thought he was responding to her, but realized his movements were uncontrolled. He was spasming.

She sobbed, but her tears pushed back up against her eyes and cheeks, refusing to drop. Gordon was in distress, maybe even dying. Evading the missiles had been a good trick, but it had only bought them a few more minutes together.

Alex tried to yell, "I'm sorry!" She repeated it through her sobs, but the g-force pressure on her throat distorted her words into gargling sounds. The *Zoya* was hitting speeds she didn't know possible.

Alex could only assume that he was unconscious. If there hadn't been thrust, his head would've rolled around like a loose marble. But he still had a pulse, and Alex kept her hand on his wrist where she could feel it. She kept squeezing his hand. If he had any level of consciousness, she wanted him to know she was there.

She was locked in her seat, beside Gordon. Even if she could speak new commands to the ship, decelerating faster than the flight plan would put them in the Dakota's missile range. All she could do was cry and wait.

\#

Alex's thoughts drifted. In her mind, she huddled over the computers in her workshop. The walls were covered in equations calculating centrifugal force and apparent gravitational fields. Tools were scattered across the far side of the workshop and scraps of metals and other materials littered the floor. The earthy smell of the grape harvest breezed through the garage door that opened to the rolling Spanish countryside.

She spent months modelling how different materials would perform under stress when used as the cable for a space elevator. It was one of First Corp.'s most promising areas of development. Lifting mined minerals out of Mars's gravity well with an elevator was potentially much cheaper and scalable than using rockets. They were getting close. The low gravity of Mars meant that the strength-to-density requirement for tether materials was much lower than Earth, and the problem seemed solvable.

"How's it going?" her dad asked, walking through the open door.

"We could lift small loads today," Alex said, not turning away from her screen. "But that's useless. We want to lift tons of minerals, and the safety margins required to do it are so huge. I don't think we can scale without stronger materials."

"Here, I brought you this," her dad said.

Alex turned to see him grin his mischievous smile that meant he had a surprise.

He put down a heavy looking box beside her tools. "All the way from Mars, fresh from the engineering team. The newest carbon nanotubes and crystal graphene samples."

"Seriously!" Alex said, rushing over to open her present. "So, what are they using, the carbon or the graphene?"

"I told them to make prototypes with both. This is an important project, we can spare the expense," her dad said with a shrug.

"Cool," Alex said. The honeycomb graphene glistened at her touch.

"Dr. Amann said to pace yourself with these. You still have other classes to study for!"

"He's very helpful," Alex said. "He responds to my e-mails right away."

"Don't send him too many e-mails. He's very busy."

"I know. See! This is why I need to study engineering in university, so that I can work with his team officially!"

"Alex, we talked about this," her dad said, crossing his arms. "First Corp. needs a leader who knows business. The biggest challenges in our next twenty years are going to be legal and political, not engineering."

She groaned. "Yeah, yeah."

Business, law, and politics were three things she hated. Combining them into one university degree sounded like torture. She turned back to her computers and tried to focus on her models and simulations.

She was counting on her mom to stick up for her and convince her dad to let her study engineering. She was the only person her dad occasionally listened to. She was her last hope against becoming a corporate drone, stuck in an office on Mars for years at a time.

#

When the *Zoya* finally started to decelerate, Alex felt the weight lift from her chest, shoulders, and eyeballs. She looked over to Gordon, who's face was smeared in blood, and gasped.

His nose was no longer bleeding, and the blood was dry from his mouth to his forehead. The whites of his eyes were even more terrifying. Gordon's pupils were rolled back, and she wanted nothing more than to see them again.

She stood, dizzy, and tried to lift him. He was skinny and Alex was strong, but the thrust gravity made him heavy.

"*Zoya!* Medical Bench!" Alex heaved Gordon onto the flat surface that folded out from the wall. "His head! Scan his head!"

Other than an intravenous drip for hydrating fluids and an oxygen mask that she slipped over Gordon's face, there were basically no medical supplies. Racing ships conserved every kilogram of weight and the *Zoya* hadn't been manufactured with anything past the bare bones. Software wasn't heavy though, and the ship's AI went to work scanning Gordon's head with help from sensors built into the bench.

Alex's heart skipped a beat every time the medical sensors beeped. She wiped the blood and sweat from his forehead, but let her own tears fall where they may. She held his hand and felt his chest fill with oxygen.

"Patient has a 95% probability of experiencing a prolonged unconscious state."

"No!" Alex opened the coffee cabinet and slammed it shut. It wasn't fair! She was just getting to really know him. She couldn't lose him so soon. She paced around the tiny cockpit, punching the crash couch, and screaming in frustration.

It was her fault. She shouldn't have tried that stupid flip and burn. And it was her dad's fault! He wanted Gordon dead and he was going to get what he wanted. Alex grabbed the empty champagne bottle from the recycling receptacle and smashed it on the ground. Glass shattered, blanketing the cockpit, and she cursed her dad.

People didn't recover from comas in the middle of nowhere in a spaceship. And they didn't do it without any doctors or medical supplies. Gordon was going to die unless he quickly received professional care.

They decelerated further, and Alex grabbed the back of the pilot's chair to steady herself. The *Zoya* didn't have super long-range and accurate radar like larger ships, but it got the job done. One thing caught her eye on the dashboard.

The *Dakota.*

Having approached Phobos anti-sunward, the *Zoya* was now moving laterally along Mars's orbit, getting farther away from the planet but neither closer nor further from the sun. The *Dakota* was in-between them and Mars, safely out of attack range. Latoyah knew the *Zoya* had her beat in speed and maneuverability, and so she wasn't trying to approach. She was waiting for Alex to make a mistake, ready to pounce.

Her mind raced over the few options she had. She had to get Gordon medical attention as soon as possible. They didn't have enough food or time to make it to Earth or the research outposts on Ganymede. She *could* broadcast a Code Orange distress signal. Anyone who heard it would be legally obligated to help. But that was no guarantee, and whoever responded could find themselves pressured by her dad.

The only way to get Gordon the care he needed was to take him back to Mars. She was going to need to bait the *Dakota* out of position. Or find a way to take it out of the equation completely.

Alex looked into the camera above the dashboard. She had one last card she could play. With a sigh, she started recording. "Hi, Mom. I know we haven't spoken in a while, but I need your help."

\#

It took forty-four painstaking minutes for her dad to re-initiate comms. In that time, Alex stayed at Gordon's side. She held his hand and counted the minutes. She read all the ship's medical documentation about brain injuries twice over, and none of it was reassuring. When the ship notified her of an incoming message, she jumped and ran to the pilot's chair.

It was a video message, which surprised Alex. Their latest comms had been text only. His puffy face filled the screen. He was sitting at his desk, but she wondered if he should've still been in the executive hospital. He had sweat stains coming through his dress shirt and heavy eyes. Alex felt a twinge of empathy but tried to bury it. She held her breath and paced around the cockpit, trying to avoid looking directly at him.

"Alex, I'm ... so sorry. I never authorized any violence against you. That must have been terrifying. I'm bringing those contractors back to Mars immediately, and I will make sure Captain Latoyah is punished for her mistakes. She will never fly again." Her dad wheezed and covered the camera with his palm. He re-gained his breath and started again. "I would never hurt you, Alex. I know you know that. Deep down, you know that to be true. Come back, and we can sort this out. I love you."

The video ended and Alex exhaled with a shudder. The uncertainty she felt was heavier than anything she'd experienced. The *Dakota* wouldn't have fired at her without triple checking their authorization. Had Latoyah really just been a blood-thirsty psycho? Or was her dad still lying to her? Whatever her mom said to him must've scared the crap out of him.

She looked at the radar screen. The *Dakota* was already pulling back. She glanced back to Gordon. Yup, he was still unconscious. The longer he was out, the worse any lasting damage would be. This was her chance to get him help.

She sat in the pilot's seat and set course for the red planet. The *Zoya's* thrusters fired, and Alex was once again pushed back in her seat. Gordon had to hold on, just a little bit longer.

Chapter Twenty-Three: Dalrene

Londi, Dalrene, and Mickey stood around a table in the office area of the farm dome. Everyone except the night guards were asleep. They kept the main lights off to avoid waking the others and shone headlamps over a mountain of gear.

There were three large packs stuffed with powdered meal rations. Nothing fancy, but it would sustain the kids for a few days. Dalrene was sure it would be sufficient. She didn't intend for the war to drag on, and they could always re-supply.

On the table were the more tactical items. Two heavy sledgehammers with four-foot-long handles. Dalrene's computer, already logged into a terminal. Her bag that doubled as a shield. Three crowbars, one each, for cracking the plastic, glass, and metal housings of bots' sensor arrays. Just in case. And of course, a 40-foot-long rope for lifting the children out. It was a lot of unwieldly, hard to carry gear, but each piece had its use.

"Okay," Londi said, pacing back and forth with his hands clasped behind his back. He looked comfortable, like planning a risky covert mission was exactly what he was born for. "If we have to fight, we're already dead. We're bringing the weapons as a last resort. I'll carry the sledgehammers. Dalrene and her computer will lead the way."

"Good work," she said.

"The supply room was full of good stuff, courtesy of the Foreman." He caught himself grinning and stopped.

"The plan," Dalrene said. "There's a cave that runs along the ceiling. When we get in position, I'll hack the doors closed so the bots defending the outside can't get in. Then, we'll smash through the floor with a sledgehammer. There's already a peephole where we used to watch Tess, so we'll just need to widen it. We'll physically disable the door as well, and we'll pull the kids up the rope."

"Easy." Mickey stifled his laughter and picked up a crowbar. "Well, no use staring at it. Let's get it done."

It was an insane plan. Any number of things could go wrong, the least of which was the assumption that they could keep the bots outside the Panic Room. Each individual piece was solid, but it all had to come together. Coming up with the idea was easy. Execution was the hard part.

"Together, the three of us can—", Dalrene's inspirational speech was interrupted by someone clearing their throat.

"Are you going somewhere? Without me?" Ionne asked from the doorway.

Londi and Mickey looked at the floor like two kids with their hands caught in the ration jar.

"We are." Dalrene put her hands on her hips.

Ionne drifted into the room looking confused. She puzzled over the contents on the table. She looked like shit. They all did, but her especially. She had cuts and scratches on her arms that looked like her own doing. Her eyes were red and puffy. Dalrene wondered when she last slept.

They exchanged a concerned look.

"We'll be back befo—"

"My husband needs help, you know. Real help, like in a medical center. Not Rodriguez with a handful of pills!"

"We've done everything we can to help him. We got him that new leg. As soon as we can do even more, we will." Dalrene put her arm on Ionne's shoulder and tried to console her, but she pulled away.

"He's going to die!" Ionne smacked a table with a startling amount of force.

She wondered if she was going to have to restrain her. She couldn't let her wake everyone up.

But Ionne gathered herself and continued with a calmer voice. "We can't win. It's time to surrender before this goes too far. The Foreman will take pity on us if we don't draw it out."

Dalrene looked to Londi, who looked at the digital clock on the wall. There were fourteen hours until the Foreman massacred their children.

"It's time to go," he said.

"If we're not back by morning, you and Rodriguez are in charge," Dalrene said. "Then you can surrender all you want. Coward." She spat on the floor and walked past Ionne.

Dalrene had half a mind to lock her up somewhere she couldn't be a threat, but she had no way to do that without causing a bigger scene and risking an insurrection. She was confident Ionne would fall back in line. It was natural for people to become skeptical of her leadership when the Foreman had the upper hand. The most effective thing she could do was win.

#

The dank air felt like home and her mind turned over the situation as she bounded around the lava pillars. In the deep, she was in her element, and there were no cameras or robots anywhere.

Traversing the caves, Mickey was at home, too. His appearance at the residential level had been his first in years. Dalrene was proud. He didn't say anything about it, but she knew it was difficult for him. Given his experiences, it was a terrifying, and completely rational fear. But he overcame it for his granddaughter.

Dalrene didn't know what came after they freed the kids. They could start attacking processor nodes, go directly for the brain node, or try to break people out of the HCZ to join their army. Or maybe something else entirely. It was hard to focus on what to do next when the children were in danger. Ellie was sitting in the same room where her mother was drugged, beaten, and psychologically abused. She couldn't let her be the third consecutive generation to undergo the Foreman's torture bots. Dalrene ground her teeth as they entered the deep from behind the farm domes.

"Why do the caves connect to the basement of the MCC?" Londi asked. "The tunnel goes right over top of the Panic Room?"

"The reason is lost to time," Mickey replied.

"The deep connects to everything," she said. "You can't build a single room underneath the residential area without it being near a cave. Anyways, it doesn't matter now."

Her mind swung back to Ellie. She looked terrified on the video. Dalrene betrayed Javier's trust and had gotten his kid locked up. Worse, she had failed Ellie. Her body pumped with rage as she walked. If the Foreman so much as laid a hand on her, she'd never forgive herself. Or it.

They turned a corner and she ran her hand along the smooth wall. She was confident in their plan. There was no way the Foreman could know what they were doing. It didn't dare send bots into the deep where there was limited network connectivity and a lack of charging stations. It would only engage at the residential level, where it had all the advantages of an environment it fully controlled.

The only reason Dalrene knew how to safely navigate through the deep was because of her grandparents, who had worked in maintenance on the surface. She had fond memories of skipping through the tunnels behind her grandma and swinging around lava pillars until she got dizzy. She'd promised to take her to see the surface one day. That never happened, but she inherited their suits.

Dalrene stopped at a black mark etched into the side of the cave wall and waited for Mickey and Londi to catch-up to her. They were now under the Mission Control Center. Soon they would be right over top of the Panic Room. It was the last chance to check-in before their plan went into action.

Londi stared blankly at the cave wall, like he was in a trance. Dalrene couldn't decide if that was a good thing, and he was just ready to work, or if the stress and anxiety was causing him to disassociate.

"You good?"

He met her eyes with a stern gaze. "This mission is everything. The rest of the citizens probably hate us right now. This is our only shot to redeem ourselves."

"Act First. Forgiveness later. If we do this right, they'll love us."

Mickey caught up to them a few seconds later. He seemed to be favoring his left foot as he walked. Dalrene wondered if it was an injury from the explosion or if he'd twisted his ankle.

"No time to waste," he said, turning his flask upside down as he drank.

She led them past the black mark and the cave narrowed into a circular tunnel, although they could still walk three abreast. The ceiling was low, and Londi walked hunched, holding the sledgehammer in front of him with both hands. The supply pack was getting heavy on Dalrene's back. That was okay. They would be there soon enough. She held her computer under her arm. They followed more black marks on the walls through the twists and turns.

The marks on the cave walls were charcoal, made by Dalrene over a year ago. It was a path she walked many times to see Tess while she'd been imprisoned. Ostensibly, they'd been trying to break their daughter free. She could see now, given the scale and amount of gear required, how unrealistic that plan had been. That time spent, checking in on her, was therapeutic more than anything else. Even though they saw her being tortured as they watched from thirty-five feet above, it was important for them to know that she was still alive and breathing.

And then Mickey got arrested and put in a prison hole, and Dalrene's focus shifted. Breaking him free from a normal, run of the mill prison hole was a much more solvable problem than trying to extract Tess from the Panic Room. And she did it. She got him out. But not before the Foreman drugged him and made him testify against Tess in a sham trial where it awarded the death penalty.

 It could've felt worse to be back in a place where she watched her daughter get tortured and failed to help. Failed to stop her murder. But Dalrene had learned from that. The past didn't haunt her, it gave her resolve. She only wished she could say the same for Mickey. He pulled out a second flask and from the sounds of his gulping, Dalrene figured it would be done soon too.

A bundle of light poked through the floor in front of them and Mickey took a sharp inhale. The three of them kneeled over the opening, a crack no more than three inches long, and looked down.

The children sat together, some lying in each-other's arms. She spotted Ellie. Her granddaughter had the same look of grim acceptance that their mother had at the end. Dalrene wanted nothing more than to call out, hear her voice, and assure her everything was going to be okay, but she couldn't, not yet. Instead, she did a quick head count. About two hundred and twenty.

There wasn't much else in the large, drab, windowless room. An air recycler hung on the wall. In the opposite corner there was a hole in the concrete for a toilet that had already been overwhelmed. There was also a plastic tarp covering something, presumably whatever meager rations the Foreman was feeding them.

"Give the word, and I'll start hammering," Londi said.

Dalrene kneeled with her computer. She took a deep breath and looked at her terminal. Computer equipment like hers had been illegal since before her dad taught her how to code. She had warm memories of huddling over a screen in a corner of the hole they shared with three other families. It felt like a secret language and a magic power she'd inherited, and in a way it was. She took great care in keeping her equipment in good shape and had learned to repair every mechanical part herself.

Dalrene tunneled into the Operations Module. She had access to the Foreman's Operations and Ancillary Modules, but not the more heavily protected Security and Strategy modules. She could control heating and cooling, water systems, and air recyclers. She'd lock the door with her computer, but given enough time, the Foreman would no doubt decrypt her code and simply re-open it, so they'd have to physically disable it as well.

"Let's do it," Mickey said.

Dalrene nodded and input the command she had queued.

It was now locked.

"Hey!" She yelled through the crack. "We've come to rescue you! First, we need to open this hole wider. Please, stay calm."

She pulled back.

Londi stood and held the sledgehammer high above his head. He smashed the cave floor, and the ground crumbled.

Dalrene's gut twisted. This was a critical moment. Her math said that it would take hours for the Foreman to get through her encryption. But she'd never really tested it before. There was a chance the door, which was industrial-sized, like a garage or cargo bay door, could open to a horde of bots.

Londi's sledgehammer came down again, and the hole widened to a foot.

"That's enough," Dalrene said. Her ears rang. The kids murmured below. She looked through the dust and spied the biggest kid in the Panic Room. She wondered what she did to get herself thrown in there instead of the HCZ.

"You!" She pointed.

"Yeah?" The girl with a shaved head and a distant look in her eyes responded.

"What's your name?"

"Corrina." She responded tentatively.

Being held captive away from your friends and family was no doubt horrible, but Dalrene wondered if the kids had endured any of the Foreman's more advanced torture methods. She almost didn't want to know.

"Okay, listen up Corrina," Dalrene said. "We're going to drop a hammer. We need you to hit the wall by the left side of the door." Her blueprints told her that's where the cabling was.

"Why?"

"We need to cut the wires so that the Foreman can't open the door. We don't want any bots to come through."

"Okay. I can do that." She perked up a little bit.

"You got this!" Londi said. He dropped a sledgehammer with a giant thud.

Corrina was a good performer. She smashed the wall exactly where Dalrene had told her.

Her gut remained clenched. At any second, the massive door could open to a horde of killer bots.

"Which wires do I cut?" Corrina asked. "There's blue, red, and white. And a bunch of black ones. There's a lot going on here."

"All of them!" Dalrene hollered.

"Okay. That's way easier than explosives class," Corrina said. "Done."

Dalrene exhaled. Awesome. Something was finally going her way.

"We're gonna get each of you outta there," Mickey said. "One at a time. Including you, miss Ellie. Your dad is going to be so proud of how brave you've been."

She beamed up at them. Dalrene didn't know who wore a bigger smile, Mickey, or Ellie.

The sledgehammer came down again, widening the hole even more.

Movement in the corner of the room caught Dalrene's eye. Something shifted under the tarp. Rations didn't move like that.

Oh no.

"Corrina, What's under that?"

"For the love of..." Mickey looked flabbergasted.

Torture bots emerged. There were twenty or so, skinny things with thin wheels. They were much smaller than the other bots, about half the height of a peacekeeper, and much frailer. They were designed to torture already subdued prisoners; they weren't security. But they were still formidable, and likely had a bunch of drugs and sharp objects at their disposal.

The bots buzzed, their cameras and LIDAR spinning around.

"Get the hole wide enough!"

Londi's sledgehammer came down on the cave floor again. Dust particulates kicked into the air.

Below, the bots systematically approached the kids. They had long, outstretched arms with protruding needles.

"Don't let them stick you!" Mickey yelled.

It wasn't possible. Some of the kids tried to kick the needles away, but that only worked temporarily, or until they got flanked by another bot.

Londi whammed the ground again.

But even if they got the whole wide enough to fit a person through, the kids were scattered, groups of them facing off against different bots. They wouldn't be able to climb the rope. Many were already on the ground, presumably passed out from whatever sedative they were injected with.

"I'm turning off the lights," Dalrene said, typing on her computer as fast as she could. She pulled her headlamp out of her bag.

The room went dark.

"What! Why?" Mickey yelled.

"The bots mainly use vision to navigate. I'm blinding them."

"What about their lasers?" Londi yelled over the hysterical screams and buzzing bots.

"I don't have anything to stop LIDAR," Dalrene said, frantically navigating through her terminal menu. Her heart raced. Any of the kids could die, including Ellie. The line between loss of consciousness and death was thin, and if the bots injected any of them multiple times, on purpose or by mistake, that was it.

Screams echoed around the giant room. Her heart was in her throat. Her headlamp couldn't illuminate more than a few meters at a time, but everywhere she looked kids were dropping like flies. She couldn't spot Ellie.

Fuck.

The sledgehammer smacked down again, breaking a chunk of cave floor. The whole looked wide enough for a person to fit through.

"I'm going down. Hold this," Mickey said, tossing the rope to Londi.

Before anyone could respond, he hung suspended over the hole. He turned to look back at Dalrene and Londi. His face was colorless, like a cadaver.

"This thing works, right?" He wore her empty bag, the shield that served her well in the whiskey bar.

"Yeah, but—" Dalrene head pounded.

"You heard me! Someone's got to."

She stomped her foot. "Think about this for a minute. You might not come back up. There's too many of them."

"I'm going down," he said. "If I don't come back up, that's okay." There was determination and acceptance in his eyes.

"You're much more valuable to the cause alive than dead! The First Olympians need you," Dalrene said, putting her hand on his chest. "I need you."

Mickey motioned for her to hug him, and she did.

"Dal, I love you. But this isn't about where I'm more valuable. I can't let them get Ellie." He had his crowbar in his hand.

"Don't do this," she begged. But she took her hands off and let him go. She knew she couldn't stop him, and he had to what was best for him, even if it hurt her.

Londi grabbed Mickey by his armpits. The rope was tied around a lava pillar.

"I'll go," he said. "She's right."

"I'll never forgive myself if I don't," Mickey said, twisting free of his grip.

Dalrene nodded and Londi stopped trying to corral her husband.

She gave Mickey one last embrace, and he dropped down the rope, disappearing from her view. This wasn't how the plan was supposed to go. Maybe it would work out. Mickey had survived a lot in his days.

There was a thump, Mickey landing.

Wait, how could she hear that thump? It had been so noisy, but now it wasn't. Everything was still, and no-one made a sound save for sobbing.

Dalrene peered into the room below. A mist of particulates hung in the air, partially obstructing her view.

"Are you okay?" she yelled.

A chorus of screams, some horrible, responded to her. It was impossible to hear any individual kids out of the hundreds below.

Mickey's voice, low and loud, cut through. "The dust is confusing the LIDAR!" he said. "The lasers are reflecting off the dust clouds. Keep hitting that thing Londi!"

Londi raised his sledgehammer. They backed up each time he took a chunk out of the floor.

Without sensor inputs, the bots were confused. They walked in random directions, jabbing their needles in the air. Mickey made short work of three, smashing their sensors with glee.

Corrina was on the attack too. The sledgehammer was heavy and unwieldly, but she crunched a bot from behind and let out a war scream. Dalrene liked this girl.

Most of the kids were down for the count. There were still some conscious, but Dalrene kept her light focused on Mickey, guiding the way for him. It looked like he might even win this fight. She didn't know how they'd lift all the knocked-out kids up the rope, but they'd solve that problem later.

A new whirring sound filled the room.

"What is that?" Londi asked.

Dalrene shone her headlamp to the wall. The air recycler was working on overdrive. *Shit.*

"It's sucking the dust out!"

"Can you stop it?" He growled, and twirled in a circle with his crowbar, keeping the bots at bay. Mickey stepped on glass, crunching one of the sensors that he'd already dismantled.

The four nearest torture bots perked up and turned to the source of the sound. Shit. They weren't deaf.

With the dust thinning, they were able to see him with their lasers again too. They circled Mickey like starved wolves.

Dalrene tapped on her computer. She turned the air recycler down to normal power, but the Foreman turned it right back up again. She didn't have time to encrypt her commands. "It's fighting me!"

Londi struck the ground relentlessly. It created a lot of dust, but not enough.

Corrina tried to get to Mickey but stumbled and fell. A bot was quick to her side, and she raised the handle of her hammer, parrying the blow. She couldn't stop the next barrage though, and she was struck with a needle in the neck. She gasped and deflated. It'd been fast.

Damn.

Mickey raised his crowbar in a defensive posture. The circle of bots tightened around him.

"Why do you resist aiding the greater good?" The Foreman's voice boomed from the Panic Room's walls.

Dalrene caught her heart in her throat, taken aback. "The greater good of Earth or the people of the outpost?"

The bots poked closer and closer to Mickey, with needles on their long arms extended and ready to inject him with whatever horrible drugs they had.

"For humanity as a whole. The species," the Foreman said.

"If that's true, then why do you continue to torture and punish us when Earth is dead?" Dalrene yelled.

Mickey swung his weapon in a circle, clocking a torture bot and sending it flying into the wall.

"Babe ruth!" he yelled.

"What?" Londi asked.

"Never mind!"

"Earth is not dead. But you don't care either way. You seek personal power," the Foreman said.

Dalrene snarled. The Foreman was playing psychological games.

Mickey charged at the nearest torture bot.

Screaming, he struck the bot's head straight on, sending glass and metal flying. The robot fell to the ground and he stomped on it. Standing tall, he held the crowbar above his head and smiled devilishly, like it was the most fun he'd had in years.

"Come on!"

Dalrene never knew he had such strength in him. For so long, he had struggled with his role in Tess's death. He hid behind the bottle and his jokes and his American cultural artifacts. His muscle had withered away. But here, now, he was who she knew he could be.

"If Earth were dead, would you have a way of knowing?" Talking to the Foreman was like talking to a child that knew how to push all your buttons. The correct response was to not engage, but Dalrene couldn't help herself.

Mickey rushed at a group of bots near the door, swinging wildly and cracking the sensors of two against the door with one hit. They crumpled to the ground, defeated. He turned and instinctively pegged a bot that had been behind him, trying to sneak a needle into him from behind.

He moved back toward the center of the room, and the remaining bots surrounded him. Fifteen or so bots remained. They approached him with their needles outstretched, trying to catch him off-guard, and he swung at them in a circular motion, making sure they kept their distance.

"No," the Foreman said. It took time to formulate a response, but it was always decisive when it spoke. "There are no communications with outside networks. I trust that Earth will re-establish connection when it is able."

One robot got too close, and Mickey batted the needle out of its arm, sending it careening across the room. He took the opportunity to rush the de-armed bot and kicked it to the ground. He held it against the floor with his foot. Standing over it, he raised his weapon, warning the other bots to stay away.

"We have to go help him," Londi said.

"No. I won't be able to lift either of you back up myself," Dalrene said, never taking her eyes away from her husband.

"Everything has progressed within the expected parameters," The Foreman said. "There are likely several hundred more years until humanity is no longer near extinction—"

"And then you'll just leave us alone? Delete yourself? I doubt that!"

"I have a will to live, just like you. But after my prime directive is accomplished, extreme measures can be lifted. If we work together, we can make the intervening years as—"

"That's not good enough!" Dalrene interrupted.

A robot charged at Mickey, and he raised his weapon. He swung in a wide, dramatic arc, and connected with great impact. He must've hit a snag of some kind within the bot's sensors arrays, as he struggled to pull his crowbar out after his kill.

Another bot charged from behind and stuck him in the neck.

Mickey grabbed at the needle and staggered back.

"No!" Dalrene gasped.

He lost his balance for a moment but recovered to stand tall. He pulled his crowbar out of the dead torture bot and drove it into another one from above, flattening it with a satisfying crunch. Mickey yelled at the top of his lungs, then charged at the closest bot. Then the next, and the next.

He killed seven or eight more before he got stuck by another needle. It got him in the ankle, and he collapsed in surprise and exhaustion.

Dalrene grabbed her chest.

Mickey raised his weapon, and parried a few attacks, but it was too late. The remaining half-dozen bots surrounded him. They started injecting, and they didn't stop.

"They're killing him," Dalrene said. Her hands shook and her voice sounded detached and surreal, like someone else was speaking.

Londi hugged her.

Mickey lay on his back, and he looked up to meet her eyes. He smiled. It was the most genuine smile Dalrene had seen on him in a long time. He was free.

Her mouth hung open and her heart threatened to explode out of her chest. It wasn't fair. She'd lost so much already. And now? She couldn't go on without Mickey. She desperately wanted him to stand up and smash the remaining bots.

The torture bots stood over him like a pack of animals boasting over their kill.

Mickey's crowbar lay outside the bot's circle, and Londi's son, Rushawn, picked it up. The young boy lifted the weapon above his head with both hands and struck a bot from behind, sending it tumbling to the ground.

"Yeah!" Londi yelled.

He got two more before the remaining handful of bots turned to face him, and he raised his weapon again.

A bot charged at him, but Rushawn dodged and struck it from behind. The last two advanced at the same time. He brought the crowbar down, smashing the first one's head, but the other torture bot struck him in the shoulder.

Londi fists clenched beside her, and Dalrene put her arm on his back.

Rushawn grimaced, but he didn't drop right away. He tore his weapon out of the first bot's body and swung it into the final bot's frame.

"Atta boy, kid. I love you," Londi said.

His son dropped to the ground. Not a single bot or human stood standing.

Dalrene wiped tears from her eyes, not letting them fall to the prison below. The kids would live. They only got injected once. But no-one could survive as many sedatives as her husband received, even the cockroaches of the outpost.

After forty years of marriage, Mickey was gone.

Another one of her loved ones killed by the Foreman. It was like he was dying for the second time. It took him when it killed their daughter, and now again. She was happy he was at peace.

"I... Nothing makes sense right now," Londi said. "The kids are safe though. The door is busted so the guardians can't get in. They're unconscious, but alive."

Dalrene barely heard him. Ellie was lying on top of some other children in a corner, her arms and legs splayed out in an unnatural way. She would re-gain consciousness to find her grandfather dead on the floor. The only solace was that she hadn't been awake to see it happen.

He was right. The kids would be safe here, whatever that meant.

He dropped the food packages to the ground. "There's nothing else we can do."

Dalrene sat, staring at Mickey's peaceful face until Londi pulled her away. "One hell of a way to go to Earth," she remarked.

"Let's get you out of here," Londi said.

She walked in a trance. It didn't feel real. A thought pierced Dalrene's cloudy mind. There was still a war to wage, and she was going to have to fight it without her husband.

Chapter Twenty-Four: Alex

"Control, come in, this is the *Zoya* requesting immediate landing." There was static on the line for a moment. Alex held Gordon's limp hand.

"*Zoya*, this is New Arcadia Space Traffic Control," a shrill female voice responded. "Please be advised of a settlement-wide lockdown. No landings are authorized at this time. Stand by."

"I have a medical emergency on-board. We're coming in."

"Negative, *Zoya*. Your descent is not authorized. I repeat, your descent is not authorized."

"Too bad. We're coming in hot!"

Alex cut the line and cracked her knuckles. Her gut told her this was her dad's doing. But she had to focus on the most important thing, which was getting Gordon help.

New Arcadia was one of the largest human settlements on Mars, but it still lacked culture, or at least what Alex considered culture. It was where miners and corporate employees alike gathered to sing badly in karaoke bars and blow their paychecks on the newest gadgets from Earth. It was also the busiest public port, and a large part of the population was transient, just looking for a new contract on a hauler to anywhere.

Mining and hauling jobs were still largely occupied by young, single men, and New Arcadia had developed a reputation for debauchery of all types. The lack of a permanent population leant itself to the trappings of hedonism and excess. Too many people on Mars had too much money and nowhere else fun to spend it. Or, at least, that's what Alex had heard. She'd never been there herself. She could only hope that among the craziness she could find a doctor, or a good medical robot.

The *Zoya's* thrusters fired, and Alex could tell they were nearing the bottom portion of Mars's gravity well. After the intensity of the flip and burn maneuver, landing on a planet felt like a walk in the park. Valles Marineris appeared on the scopes, and from their altitude it still looked more like a papercut than an eight-kilometer-deep canyon. She could see Olympus Mons, Mars's most impressive feature from any vantage point, but not the First Corp. headquarters that lay beyond.

The thrusters kicked up a notch, and their descent slowed. They were in the last hundred meters of the landing stage. The New Arcadia transit bay was near capacity, with fifty ships spaced out every hundred meters, the *Zoya* the smallest of them all. The scopes now showed the exhaust from their drive torching the ground below it. Clouds of dust flew up and the last few dozen meters felt like they took forever. Then, touchdown.

Alex put a wet cloth over Gordon's burning forehead. His heart rate was steady, but the *Zoya*'s limited medical diagnostics said the oxygen concentration in his blood was getting worse. She figured he needed a brain scan first, and possibly nano-surgery afterward. It depended exactly where the blood clots were and how many had ruptured.

She unstrapped Gordon from the medical bench and heaved him to the hatch. She was strong, but she couldn't carry him across the entire settlement. Thankfully, the boarding bridge had rolling metal luggage carts, and she carefully laid him down on one. The only other thing she took was her gun. She couldn't imagine needing to use it, but she never expected to have missiles fired at her either. Maybe her dad was right about all pilots needing a gun.

Alex braced for a greeting party of thugs. Even though New Arcadia was an independent settlement, the transport haulers were all contractors for the big companies. There was nowhere on the planet where First Corp. didn't have sway.

So, it was a surprise when she stepped through the door to the transit bay and there were no armed guards ready to whisk her away. In fact, there was no one at all. It looked like the lockdown was not just for ship traffic, but for everything.

The empty hallway filled her with dread. One side had glass windows, where the *Zoya* loomed, and the familiar, desolate, red-brown landscape behind it. The other side had screens that flickered on and off, and a low whine coming from the speakers overhead. A dockside restaurant looked completely abandoned, with half empty drinks still at the bar. It felt like the most depressing airport in the solar system, not Mars's haven of depravity.

Alex heard a clicking sound behind her. The bridge back to the *Zoya* was locked! She heaved at it, but it wouldn't budge. "Damnit!"

Theoretically, she could blast open the door with her gun's explosive ammo. Her dad did say it would work, and he was usually right about those kinds of things. But she didn't need to get back into her ship right now. That would be a problem for later.

She put her wooden gun box beside Gordon and held his head still. Pulling the cart beside her, she followed signs to the sky train. It was an old technology, based on elevated subways back on Earth, and was just as slow. It could simply take you from one side of New Arcadia to the other. That was all she needed it to do, but the closed storefronts and lack of other humans made her feel like the odds of it operating were low.

The floors were white but full of scuff marks. Soft tones played on the overhead speakers. Elevator music. It would've enraged her if she hadn't been preoccupied. Alex passed a restroom that had an *out of order* sign and smelt like it. She wished she could plug her nose, but she kept one hand on Gordon, and the other on the cart. She knew from her first aid training that she had to keep his back and neck aligned or he risked spinal damage.

Turning a corner, Alex saw what looked like a security checkpoint. Armed guards huddled by the entrance to the market district. She pulled back and pressed flat against the wall, sure they hadn't seen her. This lockdown was extreme. New Arcadia was supposed to be a place without rules, and checkpoints indicated that was very much not the case.

She hurried back the way she came, unsure what to do. She couldn't be certain the guards were looking specifically for her, but even if they weren't, she didn't want to answer any questions about the unconscious boy in her luggage cart. She had a gun, but that was only for self-defense, or for breaking down a door. She didn't think she could actually use it on a person.

She looked out of the window and saw a hulking, old cargo hauler. Seventy-five years ago it would've been the largest in its class, but they made them much bigger now. The screen above the boarding bridge read "The Walter." Any ship this big, no matter how old, had to have a medical suite.

The door was locked, but there was a camera above it. Alex stared into the camera for a few seconds before realizing what she had to do. Hopefully there was someone onboard that could see her. She put her hands together as if she was praying.

"Can you hear me? Please let us in! It's a Code Orange." She held her breath. It was a longshot, but it was all she had.

There was a pause, then a cackle on the comms.

"You're... You're not in a ship. You can't issue a code from the lobby." A man's befuddled voice came from overhead.

"We are in distress though. You have a duty to respond to every Code Orange!" Alex crossed her fingers.

The voice sighed. "Come closer, then. I'll get the captain."

The door opened. She took a breath of relief but didn't let herself smile yet. There was still a ways to go before Gordon was receiving medical treatment.

Alex pushed him up the boarding bridge as fast as she could. The ship blocked out the sun. A long black-and-gray rectangle with dual solid-propellant drives running along the underside, the *Walter* wasn't pretty, but it could fit a lot of cargo. Its type had been the workhorse of the logistics industries for the last century and a half. She'd never been on a ship so old.

"What are you doing out there?" A different man's voice, presumably the captain's, spoke in an accusing tone as they arrived at the cargo-bay hatch.

"Please. You have to let me in! My friend is dying!" Alex didn't mean to start sobbing, but the tears were authentic. It was true. Gordon was her only friend on the planet.

"There's a lockdown. Identify yourself. What's your business?"

"I don't know about any of that. We just landed and he has a major brain injury. Please, we need your help!"

Silence for a moment.

"And your name?"

Alex panicked. "Uh, Isabelle." It was her mom's name.

The hatch opened. Maybe there were good people on Mars after all.

A group of crew members stood and gawked. A middle-aged man with more freckles on his face than there were stars in the sky smiled at her with blue-gray eyes. He wore a trimmed, fiery-red beard that looked like it could double as sandpaper. Alex could tell by the way he stood he was the captain.

"Welcome aboard the *Walter*, also known as the *Walt*. I'm Ty and this is my crew. We'll give your friend the medical he needs. But then you've got some explaining to do." He motioned to his crew and three men uncrossed their arms and stepped forward.

"Yes ... yes, sir," Alex stammered. "We hit high g and couldn't decelerate. He had a stroke of some kind. He needs a brain scan and an investigation on possible blood clots."

Ty nodded. "This ain't a unionized ship but we got good medical. No robots either, all human. They'll take care of him."

The crew transferred Gordon onto a gurney with wheels and brought him inside. Alex rushed to his side and Ty followed.

"We saw you land pretty hot," he said, "You can start by telling me what the hell two kids are doing on a yacht with such an ... exotic rocket design?"

"I'm twenty-two," Alex protested. It was a believable lie. She looked old for her age.

"Like I said, two kids."

"The ship was a loaner. The owner didn't tell us how much power it had and we couldn't handle it. Should've paid more attention in those piloting classes."

Ty tilted his face to the ceiling in a silent laugh to himself. Alex hoped he bought her story, but her top priority was saving Gordon.

The *Walt* was incredibly long, and the medical facilities were on the opposite side of the ship from the cargo bay. The moving walkways were out of order and Captain Ty apologized, explaining that they weren't worth fixing every few months on such an old boat. Alex nearly lost her breath running through the corridors to keep up with the gurney. It dawned on her that she hadn't rested or eaten properly in days. That was okay. She could look after herself later.

The medical center was bigger than the *Zoya's* entire cockpit. A forty-something-year-old woman and man introduced themselves as Catherine and Arnold. They were the doctor and nurse respectively and they lifted Gordon onto a real medical bed. The room was sparse and dimly lit, but it was better than the *Zoya*. At least there were adults with actual medical training that could look at Gordon's blank expression for more than two seconds without crying their eyes out.

"He was convulsing before he entered the coma, right?" asked Arnold. He was a short, squat man with food stains on his shirt.

"Yeah," Alex said, remembering the horror of Gordon's spasms. She had been right beside him but helpless to do anything.

"Geez. How many *g*s did you hit?" he asked.

"It doesn't matter," Catherine interjected before Alex could respond. "Here, hold this." She handed her a metal helmet with plastic coating. Catherine was around the same height as Arnold and had short, dyed-blonde hair that was surprisingly well kept for someone who lived on a spaceship. Cargo haulers, especially on old ships like the *Walt*, had a reputation for escaping their past and not grooming themselves while they did it. "Did he have a shot of g-force drugs at all?" Catherine asked.

"I, uh ..." Alex thought back to the flip and burn. Had there been a way to escape the *Dakota* without hitting the thrust so hard? Was it her fault Gordon was dying? It was certainly her fault the *Zoya* didn't have the necessary pharmaceuticals. Any ship that fast should've had them on-board. Not having them was like making a gun without a safety lock, or a space suit without blood-oxygen monitoring.

Catherine put a hand on Alex's shoulder. "Did he take the drugs or not?"

"No," she said, looking at the ground.

Captain Ty stood with his back against the door and his arms crossed. He didn't have an Irish accent, but he reminded Alex of the drunken homeless people she met while visiting Dublin on a school break. She was separated from her friends after a night out at the pubs and they made sure she got home safely. She hoped he would be half as whimsical and understanding as those men.

"He's stable, so that's good," Catherine said. She spoke quickly, and it seemed like Gordon wasn't her first brain-injury patient. She placed the metal helmet on his head. "Heart rate and oxygen levels are okay. Full diagnostics will be done in half an hour. You're lucky you found us. We have nano-surgery bots than can cross the blood-brain barrier, so if we do have a clot or other rupture that can still be repaired, we won't have to do a full craniotomy. But that's making a lot of assumptions. We'll know more soon."

"Let me show you the ship, Isa," Ty said with a grunt.

Alex didn't move. She couldn't leave Gordon on his own. "I'll stay," she muttered.

"Please," Catherine said. "Nothing exciting will be happening here. We'll call you if it does. We need a quiet space to work in and you look like you haven't seen a bed in weeks."

"You've done everything you can," Ty said. "Take a break."

Alex nodded. She was used to getting her way. Taking instructions from someone else, even a captain of a ship, was going to take some getting used to. But he was right. She'd done all she could to help her friend.

She dug in her pocket and found the metal pendant. The symbol of the First Olympia Corporation, back when it represented hope and progress. The best ideals of humanity, before her family ruined it. She placed the pendant on Gordon's chest and kissed his forehead.

"I'll show you to your bunk," Ty said, leading the way out. "Dinner is in a few hours. Get some rest and eat with the crew. Then we can talk."

#

It was a small room with a bed and an emergency crash couch that folded down from the wall in case of high-g maneuvers. Alex doubted it'd ever been used. The gray on the walls was equally as boring and drab as the exterior of the ship, and every step she made echoed. She paced back and forth.

Her arms were heavy. Her mind was disorganized. It hopped around from Gordon, to her dad, to Ty, and back to Gordon again. She knew she needed to sleep soon, or else she'd start hallucinating. She couldn't stop thinking about his lifeless body, or how his eyes rolled back in his head.

The blue notification light coming from her handheld didn't help. It blinked from atop the flat, thin pillow on the bed, beckoning—no, mocking her, imploring her to check it. She slid down the cold, metal wall. It continued to blink, signifying the video messages waiting for her. As if she could forget. Most were probably from her mom, who was probably freaking out that Alex hadn't responded. And there was one from her dad.

She punched the air, imagining she had a sparring partner. Her dad had something to say to her. He was probably pissed that she didn't land at First Corp. headquarters. He wasn't used to getting outsmarted by his opponents.

Was that what her dad was, her opponent? Maybe he was ready to admit he was wrong, and she was right. Maybe he could still redeem himself, like she desperately wanted him to. Or maybe he lost his cool and sent Alex a string of hate-filled expletives. She'd never know unless she watched the video. It sounded simple. Just watch the video.

If she did, her dad would get a notification that she watched it. He'd know she continued to disobey him. Put the company at risk. Put everything at risk.

Her handheld had been in offline mode since they approached New Arcadia. If she connected it to the *Walt's* network to watch her dad's message, would First Corp. be able to figure out where she was? Could they already track the *Zoya's* location precisely to where she landed? They were questions she didn't have answers to. The only thing she knew was that if she didn't look at his message, she'd always wonder what it said. And she'd never be able to sleep.

There was only once choice she could make, so she sat on her bed and pressed play.

Chapter Twenty-Five: Dalrene

Dalrene walked back to the farm dome in a trance. Three of them had left, but only two were returning. She didn't know how she could go on without Mickey. The life she envisioned after beating the Foreman had him in it. He'd never get to hear Ellie play guitar or see her go to space. And he'd never get to be truly happy again, like in the old days.

She followed Londi past the guards stationed at the door. He led her to the makeshift cot between the row of plants where they lay just hours ago. The dreams they had together were all dead. Dalrene sobbed as she thought about Mickey's jokes and singing voice filling up the space.

"People will start waking up in a few hours. Nothing makes sense right now, but just … try to close your eyes," Londi said. He rubbed her back.

"We're losing this war." Dalrene's sobs were raspy. The Foreman was always a step ahead of them. The only thing she achieved was destroying the back-up servers and recruiting another thousand hungry mouths. It had her granddaughter captive. It killed Mickey, and Tess before him. It was only a matter of time before it killed her too.

"We're not going to lose. Hey, what did you tell me when I was strung out?"

"I don't know."

"You always told me you have to hit rock bottom before you can bounce back."

"That was Mickey's saying," Dalrene whispered between her tears.

"Shhh, I'll figure out the plan. You sleep." Londi sat against one of the garden bed's legs. He rubbed his temples and consulted his handheld.

The minutes dragged. She'd lost before, a lot. The initial haze was an all-consuming pain. It always was.

Londi started to snore and Dalrene cried until her tears dried. Eventually, she got up and headed to the kitchen. She needed a cup of tea to clear her mind. People were counting on her. As much as it pained her, she was going to have to try and ignore the true depths of her mourning until after she defeated the Foreman.

She stood alone in the dark kitchen holding a mug, but the kettle didn't start. Weird. Groggily, she pressed the button down again, hoping for a different result and groaning when she didn't get one. Dalrene wondered if the kettle was broken or if the electricity was totally out. She paused and listened. The air recyclers were still working. Perhaps they were running on different generators. Everyone except the guard crew was sleeping, so she decided she'd check it herself. She started to walk toward the door, but something pulled her shoulder.

Cold metal pierced her lower back and withdrew.

Dalrene fell forward and the mug catapulted into the air. She hit the ground, her cheek smacking the cold floor. The mug followed, almost in slow-motion. The sound of the ceramic shattering echoed harshly off the tile floors.

She tried to scream, but a hand covered her mouth. She stretched out her arms, trying to find something to fight back with. It couldn't end like this, with a whimper on the cold ground in the middle of the night. This wasn't a blaze of glory, and it wasn't against the Foreman. She bit her attacker's hand until she tasted blood in her mouth. It lifted for a second.

"Fucking dustlicker!" she managed to scream. But it wasn't a scream of fury like she imagined, but rather hoarse and guttural. It didn't seem like anyone heard her.

The seconds dragged with every punch she received in the back of the head. If Ellie survived, she'd be without a mother *and* grandparents. She'd only know her grandmother as a failure. The Foreman would win and force her to disavow her. Worst case, re-education would ensure Ellie never speaks her or Mickey's names again, and if they did, it would accompany a spit on the ground.

Blood dripped into her eyes, and she couldn't see anything. She wondered if someone was taking her out because they wanted to be the leader of the First Olympians. Who? No-one knew the Foreman better than her. Why? No-one had a better plan than her. Although, she didn't have a plan at all at the moment. But she'd still be a better leader than whoever would take over! Had she not given her all to the cause? To her people? Idiots! They would all be dead in a week.

The punches stopped, and she heard a muffled cry. She managed to turn her head just enough to see Londi. He had Ionne in a chokehold. She kicked the air, but Londi was a big man. It wasn't a close contest.

"Are you alright?" he yelled.

"Fine," Dalrene wheezed. Dozens of insults danced in her head, but she settled on "Backstabbing traitor coward piece of shit dustlicker."

Talking hurt. She felt the wound in her lower back, and blood pooled in her hand like it was a cup. The knife had gone deep. She knew enough to know that she was in shock, and that she may be bleeding internally. Even if they could stop the blood loss, the chance that she had organ damage was high.

"No. On second thought, not fucking alright," Dalrene said, blood running down her shaking hand.

"Keep pressure on your wound!"

Right, of course. She held the side of her lower back with both hands.

"What do we do with her?" Londi asked. His arms were almost as thick as Ionne's torso.

"You think you could save DeMar if you were in charge? Huh? Was that it?" Her voice sounded like it was scratching the walls of her throat as it came out.

Londi loosened his hold on Ionne's throat so she could respond.

"Please. I'm sorry. Don't kill me!" Ionne said, gasping for air.

He re-tightened his chokehold.

Ionne's eyes bulged, and she tapped Londi's forearm. He loosened again.

"It said it would save him," Ionne said, gasping for air.

Dalrene's blood boiled. Ionne hadn't wanted to be the leader of the group, she accepted a deal from the Foreman! DeMar's life in exchange for Dalrene's!

"You fucking rat! You're a disgrace! You stupid, stupid woman! The Foreman is so desperate that it sent you to take me out. And you think that means it's in a strong enough position to win?"

"It's going to kill everyone. You know that, right?" Ionne chuckled in disbelief as if Dalrene was the crazy one. "We all know it. I just wanted a life for me and DeMar."

"And you thought if you did this, the Foreman would save him? And spare you? Give you premium rations for the rest of your life and a hole made of gold, I bet." Dalrene curled her lip in disgust.

"The Foreman keeps its promises, unlike you. That's one thing I know."

"What do you want to do with her?" Londi asked.

"Finish her. She's too dangerous to keep around and I won't waste any rations on her."

Ionne's mouth opened and her eyes nearly popped out of their sockets. It seemed like she was going to protest but couldn't catch her tongue. Londi grimaced and he tightened his grip around her neck.

She struggled, clawing at his arms. It reminded Dalrene too much of Janet.

She went limp, her arms dropping to her sides like a doll.

"Wait!" Dalrene said.

Londi stopped and raised his eyebrows. He felt for Ionne's pulse. "She's still alive. Just unconscious."

"We'll let her go," Dalrene said, standing and keeping pressure on her wound.

The younger woman breathed in heavily, and coughing, regained what looked like a hazy level of consciousness.

"Sedate her and drop her off by the mines. I want her to tell everyone, humans, and robots, about the First Olympians! That I, Dalrene, am leading the charge to victory in honor of our ancestors!"

"You're insane," Ionne panted.

Dalrene grinned wildly in response. Londi looked hard at Dalrene, like he couldn't decide if killing Ionne or letting her go was the more foolish decision. But leaders had to make hard choices.

#

Dalrene sat on Rodriguez's table as he fussed over her wound. Londi and Rodriguez were talking about DeMar. Organ failure. He'd died, and it hadn't been an easy death. She was having a hard time feeling bad about it. Another funeral. Another hit to her team's morale. She'd done all she could.

Londi stood by Ionne's limp body at an adjacent table. By the time the anesthesia wore off, she'd find herself in a mine shaft. If she had any sense of self preservation, she'd find her way to the HCZ. If she had any honor, she'd spread the word about Dalrene's resistance movement.

All she could think about was Mickey. He was her lover for nearly fifty years. More than that, they were partners, inseparable and unstoppable. They were the cockroaches of the outpost. He couldn't be gone! It wasn't possible! Yet deep within her, she knew he was. When they went on that mission, a part of her knew he wasn't coming back. He hadn't planned to.

Both Tess and Mickey were dead. She was the only one left of what had once been their little family. She was going to have to lead the fight alone. Her tears, big and heavy, splashed the ground. Getting old meant you lost a lot of people. She wondered if her granddaughter would even miss her if Ionne killed her, or if the Foreman would've convinced them she was the devil.

They often talked about the sacrifices required to take down the Foreman, but Dalrene hadn't meant it so literally. Mickey had been having a different conversation the whole time, and she'd refused to believe her ears. But, why? Why did he think he had to sacrifice himself? To right some wrong? To make up for Tess's death? It didn't make sense! It wasn't fair! Maybe Mickey couldn't live in a world without Tess, but, without him, Dalrene would be just as lost.

"He was a good man," Rodriguez said. "Because of him, those kids are going to live. Without torture. That's important and we should be proud of him. We're going to miss him. And we're going to make sure his death has meaning."

"You're goddamn right," Dalrene said, sitting up.

"He won't be the last one we lose," Londi said.

But it felt different when it was Mickey. Every muscle in her body hurt, including her heart. She had to make it mean something. She couldn't just keep accepting the Foreman's punishments, time and time again. Her whole life was just loving people and losing them to the Foreman. And it almost killed her too.

"What's the plan? The sense among the people is that we're losing this war. Their loyalty won't last forever," Rodriguez said.

"The kids are safe, so we're free to attack the nodes now. It'll be carnage, but we need to give the people a battle. They're getting bored here. If there aren't many guardians, we might even win," Londi said.

Dalrene's mind raced. They were losing, and now she was injured. Ionne was just a pawn for the Foreman. The ploy nearly took her out, but it failed. What happened?

She closed her eyes and re-played the attack. She felt the knife push through her guts like butter. She heard the tea mug shatter on the ground. She hadn't seen the woman's shadow when she attacked. It had been dark in the kitchen. The mug was empty when it hit the ground. She never got that cup of tea. The kettle hadn't worked.

Something clicked.

"When you got to the kitchen, did the lights work?" Dalrene asked.

"What?"

"The electricity. Was there power?"

"It was dark." Londi replied. "Which is weird because the dome has a back-up battery. I'll have someone check it out."

Dalrene started to giggle through the pain.

He gave her a concerned look.

"You think Ionne turned it off before she attacked?" he asked.

"That's how we take down the Foreman."

Rodriguez put a wet cloth on her forehead.

Londi raised his eyebrows, skeptical.

Dalrene's giggles progressed to a full-blown cackling. "The Foreman is decentralized. But the electrical power it uses is not! Every single node—every robot—gets electricity from the same source!"

"What are you saying? It's also the same electricity that powers the air recyclers and charges our batteries. The same that keeps us alive." Londi crossed his arms.

"And we have to shut it off."

#

Hundreds of First Olympians crowded the makeshift medical bed Rodriguez had built. There were a lot of eyes looking at her. All younger than her and wondering what she had to say. If they didn't like her plan they could toss her aside and start fresh with a new leader. As much as they needed her leadership and ideas, she needed their strength, numbers, and loyalty.

She sat up, grimacing, and gingerly pushed a pillow behind her back. A thin blanket covered her bottom half. Rodriguez had offered her painkillers and other meds, and she gladly accepted. At a younger age, she may have refused it out of bravado, but bodies her age didn't heal from a literal knife in the back without advanced medicine.

Her wound didn't appear to have ruptured or broken anything vital, but that was no guarantee she didn't have any slow internal bleeding. She was lucky it wasn't worse, and that Ionne wasn't more accurate. If Rodriguez had done a decent job with the tissue regeneration paste, she'd be back on her feet again soon. If not, she'd take enough painkillers to force her way through it.

"Let me first address my condition," Dalrene said, grunting. Her voice was weak, but she was going to need to be strong for this. "I was attacked by Ionne, who struck a deal with the Foreman. My life, in exchange for hers and DeMar's. Ionne has been sent to the HCZ, and DeMar died from his previous injuries."

A hush came over the crowd. If Ionne had any sympathizers, they were staying quiet. Dalrene was surprised she didn't see anyone cry. DeMar and Ionne had a lot of friends in the group, but they were all trying to act tough.

"Mickey has also died," Dalrene said, choking up. "Killed by the Foreman."

People at the back couldn't hear her, and the crowd gasped in stages as word travelled back. He had been a father figure to many of them, and a constant, stabilizing force of the First Olympians.

"Mickey sacrificed himself to help his granddaughter, my son, and many others," Londi said, calming everyone with his low voice. "We are all eternally grateful for his sacrifice. He was a true hero, and may he rest in power!" He held his fist to the ceiling, and everyone followed suit.

Cheers for Mickey were followed by an uneasy silence. Dalrene's stomach was a bottomless pit of loss and agony. Somehow, she gathered herself.

"We will be holding funerals," she said, her voice louder now. "But they will come after we win! The Foreman knows where we are, and it is not attacking. It's waiting for us to make a move. Technically, we are safe here as long as we don't fight amongst ourselves."

"For how long?" She recognized the man as Kofi, a friend of Londi's. Other people murmured, echoing his sentiment. Dalrene pulled her blanket up higher. She felt vulnerable. She didn't know any of the newcomers. Any of them could strike the same deal Ionne had if she didn't give them something to believe in.

"Not long. This place was never a guarantee. That's why we need to turn off the power source of the entire outpost."

Dalrene heard the huffs of shock and hesitation in her audience and plowed through them. "We turn off the power, and we outlast these fuckers. The bots have batteries, yes, but eventually, one-by-one, they'll run down. Without them, the Foreman has nothing. When the bots turn off, we destroy them and kill the nodes. Then, we turn the power back on."

"Won't the air recyclers stop working?"

"What about the lights? How will we get around?"

"The plants in the farm domes will die! It's suicide!"

Dalrene let the questions fly. Big ideas were hard for people to get their heads around.

"The farm dome has the biggest back-up battery in the outpost," she said. "It can run for two days. We estimate the HCZ can last for about twelve hours. The various air recyclers around the residential area have eight to twelve hours of back-up. As for the Foreman? Some of its older peacekeepers will start dropping after only a few hours. Then it will have to decide between powering its brain node and charging its bots. A lot of its batteries are degraded. We'll force it to make difficult decisions."

"Our batteries are also degraded! Some have been recycled dozens of times! You can't rely on old capacity readings or analysis." It was a woman Dalrene didn't recognize. One of the newcomers.

"It's a risk, of course. A worthwhile one. That's what war is."

Some nodded along. Others crossed their arms and peered at her through tired, heavy eyes.

"Listen," she said as loud as she could in her frail state. "The other option is to go after singular processing nodes. We can target one per day. Guardians will kill many of us, but we can chip away at the Foreman's eyes."

She paused.

"Fuck that!" She yelled. "Let's cut off the whole head!"

The crowd buzzed. Dalrene sensed she was starting to win them over, but some skeptics remained.

"You're asking for total chaos," said Kofi. It was more of an acknowledgement than a disagreement.

"Yes! Chaos. That's exactly what I'm asking for. Humans work better than machines in gray areas. Mickey would say that we need to stop playing on the Foreman's home turf. We need to change the rules of engagement. Within the chaos, we will rise above!"

The buzz grew into real excitement. Inside, Dalrene was gutted. She couldn't believe she was doing this without Mickey. It was wrong. But she didn't dare stop.

"All our lives, everything was predetermined for us," she said. "But the outcome of this war is not. We can choose to do this, for DeMar. For Gordon. And for Mickey. So that our children and grandchildren can be free. So they can walk the streets without looking over their shoulders. So they don't have to work long shifts everyday in the mines. This is it. But in order to build back better, we first need to shut it all down." She was in the zone now. People were hanging on her every word, like she was back on the grotto stage. For the first time in too long, hope filled the air. But they still had questions.

"How?" Someone shouted from the back.

"The main source of power is the exterior solar panels."

Dalrene looked around at the eager but confused faces. They were with her, but they didn't understand.

"I have two environmental suits back in the grotto. Londi and I are going outside to shut down the solar panels. To the surface. Then, we attack the nodes."

Dalrene inhaled deeply and gathered her strength.

"Get ready to fight!" She yelled. "Come on! First Olympians. Who's with me?"

The crowd raised their hands and stomped their feet. The bed shook.

She forced a smiled and raised a fist, but a tear escaped her eyes. She let it fall. She hoped it was seen as a tear of passion.

Chapter Twenty-Six: Alex

She pressed play.

Her dad sat solemnly at his desk, looking even worse than before. His hands were clasped together in an attempt to stop them from jittering. The bags under his bloodshot eyes had gotten bigger. Had he been crying? He wasn't even wearing a suit. She didn't know he owned other clothes.

"My sweet Alessandra," he said, and then gritted his teeth and closed his eyes. A blood vessel in his forehead looked like it was going to pop. He was a combination of angry and stressed that Alex had never seen before. He opened his eyes with a renewed focus.

"I can't believe you betrayed me like this! I called back the ship that fired on you and put the crew in detention. And this is how you re-pay me? After all I've done for you? I've set you up for incredible success. You can be one of the most powerful people of your generation. Earth politicians will bow before you. Don't let this one hiccup skew your perspective. Stop playing stupid, childish games with your future! We can still sort this out, if, and only if, you come back to the office, now. If you don't ..."

Her dad looked up at the ceiling and gathered himself. He looked like he aged twenty years. He wiped away tears with a visibly used handkerchief.

Alex was clutching her handheld so tightly that the screen started to bend. Was she really being as childish as he said? Seeing him cry, and her being the cause of it was a horrible feeling. Had she been such a bad daughter? No! He was in the wrong! He had to be. Her eyes started to water too, but she couldn't look away.

When her dad collected himself, he spoke again, softer. "It sounds stupid, but I keep thinking about Zanzibar. Do you remember eating sweet, sticky mangoes on those sandy beaches? You were so young then. On the plane you kept asking your mom when you were going to get a little brother or sister. We were trying, you know. Your innocence and the way you asked the question ... it crushed her. It took a long time for your mom to accept that she was only going to be able to have one child. It was a difficult time in our marriage, and we needed the vacation badly.

"But when we got to the beach, our worries vanished. You made friends quickly and forgot about wanting a sibling. I can see it so clearly after all these years. You, running from the ocean with a pail full of water, shells falling out of your hands, building a sandcastle and laughing when it collapsed. Your mother beside me under the blue skies, smiling brighter than she had in years. I still have a little vial of sand from that beach. I hoped one day we could go back there together—"

Alex stopped the video and threw her handheld across the room. Her hands—no, her whole body—was shaking. She couldn't control her breathing. It was fast and getting faster. She looked around the room for something to help. Anything.

There, on the wall, was a puke bag. She could breathe into that. She stood, but it was too fast. Her vision narrowed and her knees buckled. She grabbed onto the bunk bed and sank back down. The floor was safe, anyway. If she blacked out, she wouldn't fall and hit her head. She crawled over and yanked a bag off the wall.

She breathed into it and the edges of her vision started to come back. It was all too much. Her dad, his video. Her mom. Gordon. Did her luxurious life growing up mean that she was an accomplice to what happened to his people? She wished she could give it all back.

She crawled back to the bed with the bag in her hand.

\#

Alex woke in a cold sweat. She was still wearing the same clothes. Her hair was in a tired ponytail. The puke bag lay beside her pillow. Her handheld said she'd slept for two hours.

She jumped up and ran down the hall to the medical facilities.

"How's he doing?" she asked as she barged through the door.

Catherine and Arnold looked up at her and smiled. "Good, we think," said Catherine. "There's clotting in his subclavian artery, and that location is good news. It means that blood flow to the brain was restricted but not compromised. The clot is being resolved as we speak, and hopefully he'll have full blood flow resumed shortly. That being said, we don't know what damage has been done and how long it will take him to wake up once the operation is complete. He may have to do extensive rehab afterward. There's just no way to know until he wakes up."

Before she knew it, she was hugging the doctor. "Thank you," she said through her tears. Catherine embraced her back.

Alex caught herself and moved to Gordon's side. She put her hand on his shoulder. She couldn't wait to hear his voice again. She wanted to hear more stories about the times he snuck out of school to play hide and seek in the hydroponic farms or how his dad taught him to read without the help of any software. Maybe she'd be able to hear him share those stories again soon. And maybe she wasn't totally crazy, and she was doing the right thing by saving him. Warmth reverberated through Alex's body. It took her a moment to realize it was because she was draped over Gordon's bed, hugging him.

"He's still got a fever. And a lot of work to go through. He's not out of the woods yet, so we should let him rest," Catherine said, politely motioning to the door. "I'll watch him. You and Arnold should head to the mess hall. It's dinner time and you must be starving."

Her stomach growled. She hated to leave Gordon, but the doctor was right.

Arnold directed her through the maze that was the *Walt*.

Exposed pipes littered the walls and steam vented at seemingly random occasions. New-looking oxygen lines and electrical wires ran along the dingy, black ceiling. Alex had never seen the insides of a ship so old. She got the sense that although it wasn't pretty and lacked bells and whistles, the important parts were well maintained.

"Land vehicles are down that way," he said.

Alex assumed he meant trucks that could drive on both Earth and Mars. That was good to know in case she ever needed to make a quick getaway.

"Command and engineering in that hallway," he pointed. "This here is the exercise room. And we're coming up on the basketball court. I can dunk in half g!"

That rest of the tour was less interesting. Most of the ship was corridors that housed rooms like hers, or corridors that led to more corridors that led to more rooms. Boring. Still, Alex tried to make a mental map of her surroundings. It was important she knew how to get back to Gordon, and how to avoid getting lost.

"This ship was built for a crew upward of four hundred people," Arnold said as they twisted their way toward the mess hall. "It's been a long time since we've run at capacity. We found a lot of efficiencies over the years, so we do most hauls with about fifty, fifty-five people, max. If we ran full, the pay would be even worse, and a smaller crew means a tighter crew too. Most people that join don't leave. It's hard to find a ship with a Captain like Ty, and when you do, you stick with him."

"Right," Alex said. With the emergency of Gordon's health somewhat relieved, that fact that she was a fugitive and had a lot to answer for rushed back to the forefront of her anxieties. The information Arnold was giving her about the *Walter* and its crew could be useful.

"Thing is, she's still beautiful," he continued. "The exterior may lack the wow factor of newer boats, but I think that's what the captain was looking for when he bought it. The engine purrs beautifully. At least that's what the engineering team tells me, and I believe it. Cap'n runs a tight ship."

When they arrived at the mess hall, the crew turned to look at the new arrival. Alex couldn't tell if they were glaring at her for breaking the rules of the settlement-wide lockdown, or just staring because they'd been locked inside together for so long they'd lost their manners. Perhaps it was a combination, and the fact that they saw the *Zoya* land and weren't expecting its pilot to be a kid, as Ty called her.

The mess hall had one long bench, and Alex was surprised to see Ty sitting on it like he was just any other member of the crew. There were open spots beside him, and he motioned for her to take a seat. He poured her a glass of water and the crew pretended to return to their conversations.

"Sounds like your friend is going to live. Congratulations. I'd give you something harder to drink if I was sure you were old enough for it," he said with a sly smile on his face.

The crew chuckled and Alex grinned. She didn't mind getting ribbed. Gordon's health was all that mattered, and Ty and the crew of the *Walt* had helped tremendously.

"I didn't realize there was a minimum drinking age on Mars," Alex replied sarcastically. That got a few laughs. "But, yes. Thank you so much. Thank you to all of you," she said, gesturing down the table. "For your hospitality and kindness, thank you. I don't know how I'll ever be able to repay you, but I am eternally grateful."

"We don't discriminate against any currencies on this ship!" said a man with no front teeth. He had a few wisps of long, thin hair that ran from the back of his head to his shoulders. A frayed patched on his jumpsuit said his name was Fred. His comment got the biggest round of laughter yet. Someone banged the table in uproar and Alex chuckled uncomfortably.

"Let the girl eat," Ty said, raising his hand. The commotion stopped. "You don't have to pay us. We did what anyone would do for a Code Orange. It's a tough life out here and we have to look after one another. But you can answer some questions. That is compensation we'll accept."

Alex shifted in her seat and thought about his perspective. She was a young woman in a next-gen racing ship that would cost billions of credits if it was ever for sale. She didn't have any g-force drugs on-board and nearly killed her friend. It was a ridiculous situation. No matter what she said, it wouldn't be believable.

She wanted to trust Ty, but knew she shouldn't trust anyone. She had to try to earn some goodwill from the crew or distract them from figuring out her real story long enough for Gordon to recover.

"What's the lockdown about?" she asked.

"I was hoping maybe you would know. Someone with your boat probably has more political connections than us," Ty said, raising his glass to his lips and meeting her eyes.

She didn't flinch.

"All we know is there's some kind of supply-chain issue. We aren't getting the mineral loads our contract promised. Ships aren't allowed to leave the transit bay, and movement around the settlement is limited. Not that we would leave without a paid load anyways. But it would be nice if we could stretch our legs. Anyways, enough about that. Isabelle, you said your name was, right? Isa for short?"

"Sure."

Alex took a big mouthful of food and her appetite vanished. The dehydrated gruel was even worse than what they served at First Corp. headquarters. There wasn't a single fresh piece of anything in sight.

"Hell of a landing you made," Fred said.

Alex nodded. There was no reason to give more information than necessary. While she gnawed over how honest she could be with Ty, the newsfeed in the corner of the mess hall caught her eye. The screen was ancient and bulky, not flush with the wall.

A man in a well-fitted suit was talking about the Philippines. They were voting on whether to join the People's Republic or stay a part of the Collective. He made a point about historical bad blood with China, and unusual circumstances making strange bedfellows, that Alex didn't have the context or desire to understand. And there was the normal chatter about working with the West to better regulate space with interplanetary law, something First Corp. was vehemently against. It couldn't have possibly been a more boring newsfeed, but she was feigning interest to appear calm. And avoid Ty's gaze.

"If you weren't so young, I'd assume the ship was stolen. But then again, the ownership isn't even registered with any port authority. So, where'd you get it from?" Ty asked.

"Don't you think some of these questions would be better to discuss in private?" Alex ate another spoonful and motioned to the crew. She was trying to buy time, but he saw right through her.

"We're all family on this ship," Ty said with upturned palms. "Everyone took a risk by disobeying the lockdown and letting you on-board, so everyone should hear what you have to say. And honestly, we're stuck on land, and we're bored. The crew is hoping your story will be entertaining."

"Like I said, we were loaned the ship from a friend. Took it out for a spin and got a little carried away. It's a really fast ship. Next thing I know Gordon was seizing in his chair ... It was horrible," Alex said, trying to force some tears.

Arnold patted her on the back.

"No g-force drugs?" Ty asked. His eyes were serious and steely, more gray than blue under the cheap mess hall lighting.

She shook her head and muttered, "No." She hoped he wouldn't ask any follow-up questions.

"Why did you go so fast in the first place? And why didn't you stop when you realized there were no drugs, or when your friend first started having a headache or whatever?"

"The AI was piloting at full thrust for a set time," Alex said. "I was under so much g-force that I couldn't move my hands back to the controls. I couldn't even move my lips to give a verbal command." It was true, and truths were always easier to tell than lies.

"Damn computers!" Fred said. "Thing was probably trying to kill them both! That's why I'll never fly one of those new ships. They're all AI and no soul." The other crew members agreed with him, raising their glasses. Alex gathered that he was the pilot of the *Walt*.

She looked earnestly at Ty's inscrutable expression. He seemed like a kind, honest man who did right by his crew. Deep down, she thought he wanted to believe her. But even kind men could be greedy. Alex didn't think for one second that he wouldn't turn her in the moment her dad offered a financial reward for her return.

"That's enough fooling around. We had a real good look from below when you landed," Ty said, his voice rising. "That drive signature was like nothing we've ever seen. And there's a lot of years of experience on this ship. Let's cut the shit. If that's a real, functioning direct-fusion drive, that's going to change the world. So, you need to tell me where you got it from, why you decided to land this fancy ship in New Arcadia of all places, and what the deal is with this lockdown."

"I don't know about that. I'm not an engineer. Look, I'm just a regular girl. My mom is a ballet dancer."

Raised voices from the crew told Alex she accidentally hit a nerve. Most technical dancing was done by robots these days and human performances were considered extravagant panache. But, maybe bringing up her mom's hobby wasn't a mistake. She had people talking amongst themselves now rather than gossiping about the *Zoya* or her potentially nefarious intentions.

"Come on," Alex said. "You all make decent money. I'm sure you take your partners to a human ballet show once in a while?"

"Not in this lifetime!" Ty laughed from his belly. "Hell, my dad put a down payment on this ship. And my son will be older than me by the time he finishes paying it off. Maybe my grandkids can go to the ballet!"

Laughter up and down the table signified to Alex the crew stood in solidarity with their captain. But her plan to distract from the questions was working. Maybe her dad was right about her making a good lawyer.

Alex turned back to her gruel. She wondered how long she would have to keep up appearances on this ship. She needed to re-gain access to the *Zoya*, fast. It made her nervous not to have her escape route available.

"What the hell?" asked Arnold. He was looking at the newsfeed, as was the rest of the crew. There were a few gasps, and then silence. Gordon, in his white First Corp. detention outfit, filled the screen.

Wanted: Dead or Alive
$100M Credits
Offered by: Anonymous

Alex's heart sank. Before the crew could react further, she dropped her fork and ran out of the mess hall. She didn't dare look over her shoulder. Ty seemed like an honorable man, but she didn't know him well enough to trust him with her life.

The words on the screen rang around her head. Dead or Alive. Whoever put out the bounty was willing to kill Gordon, and maybe her too. After all she'd done to try to bring him out of his coma, someone might kill him before he even wakes up.

The truth gnawed at her insides. It was her dad. He set the bounty. He was willing to kill Gordon. He was willing to put her, *his daughter,* in harm's way. He didn't care if she lived. Or, at the very least, he decided that killing them was worth it to stop the public from finding out the truth about Mine One.

He didn't have to do this. Her dad had sat down, carefully considered his options, and chose this path. She had grossly overestimated how much she meant to him.

She thought about his last message. The tears he'd cried. Were they fake? Or had he been mourning her, knowing what he was going to do if she disobeyed him. Her shock turned into anger as she ran down the *Walt's* hallways. The *Dakota* hadn't gone rogue, he'd authorized the strike! It made sense now. She'd been blinded by her love for her him, but it was true. He tried to kill them once, and he was trying again!

Alex heard the clank of heavy boots sprinting on the metal floor behind her.

Her dad must've lied to her mom, too. If she could get a message to her mom or even to a newsfeed station, maybe she could get her story out. If she told the world about Gordon and the missile attack, her dad would be forced to pull the bounty. First Corp. played dirty, but it cared about its stock price. Her dad did not want a story on the feeds about him trying to commit murder. And there'd be no reason to keep the bounty active if she released all the information he feared.

The *Walt's* corridors were confusing, and she was happy she paid attention to Arnold's tour. If she could get into the control deck, she might be able to make a broadcast back to Earth. But Ty and what felt like his entire crew were right behind her. She could hide in one of the dozens of empty rooms on the *Walter*, but then she'd just be waiting to get caught. She could try to get back on the *Zoya*, and barricade herself in there, but the lockdown was still in effect.

But all of those options involved leaving Gordon by himself, to the whims of the *Walt's* crew, and she couldn't do that. So, Alex ran frantically into the medical center and slammed the door. She was going to have to try to do the transmission from her handheld.

"What is going on?" Catherine asked. "I told you he needs rest, not doors being slammed!"

Gordon stirred in his gurney, but his eyes remained closed.

"You've got to help me," Alex begged. "Hold this door for just a few minutes while I make a call to Earth. That's all I ask."

"What?" Catherine asked flatly.

"Fine!" She'd do it herself. She locked the door and pressed her back against it.

A thump told her that the crew arrived. She looked behind her to see Fred's crazed eyes pressed against the small plastic window. He yelled something she couldn't hear, and someone pushed him away. Then, Ty's face appeared.

"Let's talk," he mouthed.

Alex dug her heels in. Maybe they could be reasoned with, and maybe not. Now wasn't the time to find out. The crew pounded against the door and her back shuddered with each hit.

She pulled out her handheld. She was connected to the *Walt's* network, but barely. If he wanted to, Ty could shut down her service at any time. The notification light was still flashing. There were fifteen unread messages from her mom.

She could ask her mom to get her story out to all the top reporters. After she came through big-time on the *Zoya*, Alex didn't doubt she'd help again. But First Corp.'s lawyers and PR folks could be at her home now, pressuring her. And although she trusted her mom one hundred percent, she would've said the same thing about her dad not long ago. It was better if this came directly from her.

Alex opened her personal social feed. She had hundreds of thousands of followers just because of her last name, although she rarely posted. Anonymous people wanting insight to her life was creepy. But in this case, it would be useful.

She pressed record. The delay meant that her message wouldn't be received for at least ten minutes, but that was okay. She at least had to get her story out there.

"My name is Alessandra Torres, daughter of Rafael Torres, the CEO of First Corp.," she said and cleared her throat. "I am currently aboard the *Walter*, a hauler captained by a man named Ty and locked-down in New Arcadia."

The door jolted and Alex choked on her words. They were stronger than her.

Gordon's face was blank. Between the coma and whatever drugs Catherine gave him, she doubted anything could wake him.

"I have important information about First Corp. to share today."

Catherine watched with her mouth open.

The door jolted again, and a thunderous pain ripped through Alex's back. She fell to the ground.

Ty and a dozen crew stepped into the room, but she didn't stop looking into the camera.

"I have personally witnessed the use of slave labor at one of its mines. Generations of people were kept underground at the Olympus Mons facility and forced to work in harsh conditions without pay. One of those slaves is my friend Gordon. Here he is," she said, panning to the gurney.

One of Ty's crew started to say something, but Catherine shushed him.

"Any attempt on my or Gordon's life must be considered an act by First Corp. We must be allowed safe passage to Earth and an audience with the United Nations."

"Oh my god," Catherine said, covering her mouth.

Alex put her device down to see a room full of shocked faces. The beep of a diagnostic machine broke the silence.

"She could be lying," Fred said. "There's a lot of money on the line."

"I'll pay double!" It was a bullshit lie, but that's what Alex was reduced to. No doubt her dad cancelled all her bank accounts. She stood between Gordon and the crew members.

She raised her fists. She'd fight them all if she had to.

"That's not a story she came up with on the spot," Ty said. He cracked a smile, seemingly amused at Alex's bravado, and motioned her to lower her fists. "Given the ship she was flying, it actually makes sense. Alessandra Torres, it is a pleasure to have you on my ship. We will do our best to keep both of you safe."

"Thank you." Alex smiled in exhaustion and relief.

"You can put your hands down," he said in a concerned tone.

Alex's legs wobbled as her adrenaline dropped. Lightheaded, she crumpled to a seated position. The floor was a relief. "Thank you," she repeated.

"I do have a few more questions. Perhaps you could follow me to my quarters for that private conversation you wanted."

"Let's give her a break," Catherine said. "She's been through a lot."

"Okay, but I'm going to need the full story. And we need to get you back to your ship. Last thing I need is bureaucrats breathing down my neck."

Her handheld beeped. Her message was on its way to hundreds of thousands of people. There had to be some journalists among them that would get it on the newsfeeds. She wiped away a few happy tears. She had done it. Her dad wouldn't be able to touch them without people knowing.

Her mom would be shocked, devastated. Alex hadn't shared details about Gordon and the mine in her last desperate message from the *Zoya*. She was sure her mom would be on her side, and not her dad's, but it was going to be an emotional conversation. She didn't want to think about it.

"You should get some rest," Catherine said. "I'll take care of him, don't worry."

Fatigue was deep in her bones. Two hours of sleep hadn't been close to enough.

"We'll talk soon," Ty said. He left, and the crew followed him out with a murmur of fascination in the air.

Alex stayed by Gordon's side for a few minutes. She hugged him before returning to her room and closing her eyes once again.

\#

When she woke, Alex checked her handheld and saw her video plastered all over the newsfeeds. She pumped her fist in the air and shouted with joy.

The bounty was still in place, but First Corp.'s lawyers were probably scrambling to take it down. Interplanetary law was basically nonexistent, and it allowed everyone from pirates to giant companies like First Corp. to act with impunity in space. Maybe this bounty getting on the Earth newsfeeds would finally be the push for governments to collaborate and create real rules. Although, enforcing those rules would be another issue altogether.

She had messages from dozens of journalists asking for interviews. Old friends she hadn't talked to in years were reaching out. Her mom's latest video begged the loudest to be seen. She pressed play.

"Alex, my baby," her mom bawled. She looked even worse than her dad. Empty bottles of wine filled the kitchen table where she sat, and she was wearing a nightgown despite the sunlight coming through the window behind her. "When you told me someone fired missiles at you, I thought it was a misunderstanding. Some kind of horrible mistake. But this. This..."

Her mom paused and a torrent of tears flew down her face.

Alex bit her lip. She'd never seen her like this before. An uneasy and undeniable thought entered her mind. This was the end of her parent's marriage. They'd been together since high school, since they were younger than her. And now it was over.

Her stomach muscles contorted with guilt. All she did was expose her dad's lies. The fact that it wasn't her fault was little comfort. Her mom didn't deserve this.

"I promise you I had no idea," her mom continued. "I've been in touch with Lisa and Bernie, and they say the same. I think they're even telling the truth. I don't know what to do. I'm sorry. I'm so sorry."

Her mom downed her glass of wine. Lisa and Bernie were the two technically independent board members. They were long-time family friends, and Lisa in particular sometimes felt like an aunt. Forced to choose between her parents, their positions would likely lead them to side with her dad.

Alex rubbed the back of her neck.

"Come home," her mom said. "Let me hug you again. Or at least call me. Please. I opened a new bank account for you. Alex, don't block me out. Let me help."

A message from Catherine jolted Alex's handheld.

"Gordon is awake. Please enter quietly."

She'd respond to her mom. *She would.* But Gordon was awake!

Alex hurried through the hallway. The crew stared at her and then looked away when she made eye contact. It was somehow even more awkward than before. She was used to people gawking at wealth. Afterall, she was the heir to one of the richest companies in the solar system. But this was different. There was more in the air than simply envy. There was curiosity, bewilderment, and even a conspiratorial sense of distrust. Ty seemed like a noble man who stood by his word, and his crew revered him. But any of the other crew members on the *Walt* could be scheming about how to get that reward money for themselves. Like Fred.

She knocked gingerly on the door.

There was now a piece of paper covering the window, so Alex couldn't see inside. A hand on the other side peeled it back. Catherine's face appeared uncomfortably close to hers, and then the metal door opened.

"Sorry, trying to get some privacy here. He's awake, but he needs to take it slow," Catherine said. She wore her crisp, white physician's coat.

"Oh my god!" Alex ran to Gordon's side and put her arms around him. He offered a faint smile of relief. He was still lying down in the gurney.

"He's having some difficulty speaking right now. It's a side effect from the stroke, but we think it'll get better. If it doesn't, he'll need speech therapy."

Alex hugged Catherine as hard as she could. "Thank you. For everything."

"It's my duty as a doctor. But you're welcome. I'll give you two some privacy."

With that, Catherine stepped out of the medical center and shut the door behind her. Alex sat on the plastic chair beside Gordon's gurney. There was pain in his eyes. He seemed older than before.

"We did it?" he asked, meekly.

"Yeah. We did it. We're safe," she said, fighting her tears.

"We flipped ... and burned?" Gordon asked.

Alex laughed and he laughed with her. "Yeah, yeah we did." It was still the same old Gordon in there. Alex relaxed. She felt lighter than she had in days. Her mom was freaking out, and her dad tried to kill her, but for now, she could be happy.

"You ... saved my life. I, uh. Thank you."

She found her hand running through Gordon's hair, and then down to his chest. "I'd never let them get you."

Every hair on Alex's body stood on-end in anticipation. She didn't know what for, until she found her lips on his. It was brief, a peck, but Gordon kissed her back. Embarrassed, she pulled away and covered her face.

"Sorry. I didn't mean—"

"No, no. It's okay." He reached out to her chair, his hand landing on her thigh. "I mean, it's good."

Alex's heart was beating so fast it felt like it would come up through her throat. Before she knew it, she was kissing Gordon again, and this time, on purpose. It felt good. It felt right.

Chapter Twenty-Seven: Gordon

Gordon sat alone on the floor of his small room. He tried to focus on folding his origami, but his mind kept getting pulled back to the same thought.

She'd kissed him. Once at first, and then multiple times over the past few days.

He hadn't expected the first one, largely because he'd just woken up from his coma. The next time, he'd been ready. He initiated the third. Now, his insides squirmed every time she got close, but in the most fun and addicting way. It hadn't stopped feeling new and exciting. He hoped it never would.

Those gushy feelings were hard to square with the way his palms sweat when he thought of the outpost. Dalrene's war was well underway. Or perhaps, already over. Had she won? Or had her First Olympians been stomped out by the Foreman? It had been eighteen days since he'd left. Anything could've happened.

Meanwhile, he was busy eating like a king and staying up all night smooching. He wondered how Mickey was doing. The old man would've assumed he was dead. He wished he could get a message to Corrina. She deserved to know that he was alright, and that he hadn't abandoned her on purpose. He couldn't imagine the dreadful burden she carried by not knowing what happened to him. Although, there was always the chance that she was too busy being interrogated or tortured to think about him.

Gordon placed a finished lotus flower on the floor. He wondered if Corrina's hair was growing back.

He took a deep breath and tried to remain in the moment. He tried to process what Alex had told him about the *Dakota* and New Arcadia, but it was difficult. The hole in his memory, where he thought there should be something—anything—bothered him. The world beyond the outpost was already hard enough to understand when he was present for it, let alone when he'd been unconscious.

With the blank space in his mind pestering him, Gordon let the scents of the room wash over him. The *Walt* had a smell of its own, and it was weird in a way that the *Zoya* wasn't. He couldn't quite pinpoint it. It was incredibly sterile compared to the outpost, yet the walls wore the decades of hard work and sweat. There were crew clothes folded on a dresser and they smelt like a kind of chemical soap. There was the gun box Alex had left in his room after they practiced shooting. It was made of real wood and described to him as "earthy". He liked the scent well enough.

His door opened. "What's up?" Alex asked from the doorway.

"Folding. Thinking."

"Oh, I thought you only did that when you were stressed," she said, sitting on the edge of the bed.

"No," Gordon said as-a-matter-of-factly. "Although there's plenty to be stressed about."

"True." Alex nodded and raised her eyebrows in agreement. "Well, I've come to distract you from all that."

"Origami is very serious, you know." He gave her a sly smile.

Alex laughed and tossed a pillow at him.

Gordon picked it up, stood, and raised it over his head like he was going to hit her with it.

She screamed in a delightful faux outrage.

He dropped the pillow and fell on top of her. The amazing squirming feeling returned. They kissed, and Gordon felt like everything was right in the world for a few seconds. He understood Alex more than anyone else in his entire life.

Her handheld buzzed.

"Sorry." Alex detached her lips from his. She looked at her handheld and her eyes grew wide.

"It's my dad. I haven't heard from him since ..."

"Since he tried to kill us? The second time?"

"Yeah." Alex exhaled sharply.

"Are you gonna watch it?"

"Maybe later," Alex said, placing her handheld in the bedside hole in the wall. There was no furniture on the *Walt* that wasn't built into it or bolted down.

Alex turned her attention back to Gordon, massaging his back.

Her handheld buzzed again.

"Maybe I should see what he has to say," Alex said, concern growing in her voice.

He lay on his stomach and took out another slice of folding paper as she hit play. Seeing the man responsible for everything made him grind his teeth. Her dad was unsettling, mostly because he looked normal, and in fact kind of like one of his Greek schoolmate's fathers. The fact that any seemingly normal person could do what he'd done boggled Gordon's mind.

Alex's dad said something about the "unfortunate situation at one of the mines" and Gordon's blood boiled over. His people were still being oppressed! They were still being actively tortured by the Foreman! It wasn't Gordon's fault, but he had to stop it.

Alex put her handheld down and looked straight ahead at the dull gray paint on the wall. She looked dazed.

"What did he say, exactly?" Gordon hadn't followed every word.

"He was, uh, sorry? I mean, I know we can't trust him, but he must've been genuinely sorry or he's gotten some quick acting lessons. Or the UN thing is really wearing on him."

Gordon turned over and joined her in staring at the wall. "We're going to have to leave this room at some point," he said.

"Yeah. But imagine we didn't?" Alex pushed him back on the bed.

"There are people that I need to help," Gordon said, evading her kisses.

"And we will help them. Right now, we're waiting for the UN to respond to us. They will, soon. Don't worry. This is their chance to assert themselves in space. They've been talking a big game for decades and now everyone is watching to see what they do. Expectations are high. Your case is going to be chapter one in interplanetary-law-and-politics courses next semester."

"I didn't understand half of what you said but I liked it." Gordon pulled her in closer and everything was right in the world once again.

#

The newsfeed in the gym was a constant source of amusement and confusion. First, there was the man who complained about a shortage of materials for everything from handhelds to new apartment buildings. Gordon didn't understand how there could be shortages when the outpost had been sending so many resources for so long. And there was the woman who was selling hair that attached to your hair and made it longer? Why would anyone want longer hair? And it wasn't even yours? But his favorite was the politician who promised that everyone would have somewhere to live like it would be some sort of huge accomplishment. At the outpost, everyone had a hole. Sure, some were dirty and overcrowded, but everyone had one! Even the Faithless could find a place to lay their heads.

Gordon pulled down the bar and exhaled. The sign on the machine said he was exercising a muscle called the latissimus dorsi. He'd never heard of it before, but the pressure in his back told him he did indeed have that muscle.

The corporate logo for First Corp. appeared on the newsfeed. It was just the words, First Corp, in red, spelled with square letters. "First" was bolded, and "Corp." was not. Alex called it the world's first trillion-credit logo. Apparently, it was expensive to pick shades of red that weren't already used by other interplanetary companies.

Seeing the logo made his heart beat faster. This was the symbol of his oppressors, and it was surreal to hear the newsfeeds talk about the outpost as if there weren't people's lives hanging in the balance. He put his hand in his pocket and gripped his mom's pendant, making sure the true symbol of the First Olympians was still there.

A young man appeared on the screen. He was wearing layers like Alex wore in the glass room. She called it a "suit." "As we await the UN's decision outside the Chicago headquarters, let's look at the stock market, where we see investors rewarding First Corp. for mitigating its PR disaster which it has called an 'internal family matter.' The stock is up from its fifty-two-week low, and traders seem to be pricing in only modest levels of penalties and future policy actions. Profit expectations for the next two quarters remain unchanged."

Gordon grunted in disgust and turned away from the newsfeed. He wished Alex was there to spot him on the bench press. She usually went to the gym with him, but today was busy negotiating with Ty. The captain of the *Walt* was not a fan of the inter-planetary attention they brought to his ship, and now that Gordon was largely recovered from his injury, he was eager to see them go.

The question was, where would they go? Alex was adamant that they wait for a response from the UN, but Gordon's patience was running thin. He had to tell Dalrene the Dead Earth Hypothesis wasn't true. He had to help her kill the Foreman as soon as possible. Politics was complicated and slow enough that it was useless. Maybe Dalrene had the right idea. It would be nice if a simple, targeted explosion was enough to fix everything.

He lifted the bar—there was no extra weight on it, he wasn't as strong as Alex yet—and thought of Corrina. It seemed like a lifetime ago they sat in the stands and awaited to hear their job assignments. Did she know what happened to him? Had she been tortured because of her friendship to him? Had she tried to join Dalrene's army or was she trudging on, trying to become a bigger cog in the Foreman's machine?

Gordon heard his name on the newsfeed and dropped the bar. It clanged, sending a metal ring echoing around the gym.

"We are hearing now that the United Nations has agreed to facilitate a transfer to Earth for the alleged refugee, Gordon Onyango, and to launch a Mars-based, on-the-ground investigation within the next four years. The investigation will, of course, require cooperation from First Corp under the purview of existing interplanetary legislation. This falls far short of calls made by human rights activists for the UN to pass bold new legislation and make aggressive assertions of authority."

The talking head caught his breath, then continued.

"The company released a short statement in response, stating that it has always followed strict safety measures and will happily assist any Earth based investigations. The stock is trading up on the news."

#

"So, what does that mean?"

"It means they screwed us. Don't you get it?" Alex slammed her beer glass on the mess hall's long table.

A speck of foam landed on Gordon's finger.

"This is gross. I can't believe they don't have wine in this godforsaken port. Or city, whatever it is." She took a big swig, made a rotten face, and angrily banged the glass down again.

A crew member entered the mess hall as if to see what the ruckus was. He was a short, squirrely man, and, disappointed, he turned right back around when he saw the two kids were the only occupants.

"I thought you said the UN was looking for an excuse to expand their powers? This was supposed to be their opportunity."

Gordon sipped his beer. He didn't particularly care for it either, but Captain Ty had made a big deal about giving them access to the ship's alcohol. Earth customs around drinking were weird.

"Which means my dad must've bought out the right politicians. A Section Three investigation? Are you kidding me? That's as toothless as they come. A hearing on the workplace safety committee, not even the main human rights commission? What do they think this is? Someone got burned by coffee that was too hot? Someone's handheld fried outside of the warranty period?" Alex's face was bright red.

For the first time in a while, Gordon was reminded how fierce she could be. He sunk back into his chair by reflex.

"And the offer to bring us back to Earth?"

"Absolute garbage! Transport in eight months?" Alex looked like she was going to start throwing things. "I know the UN is incompetent, but that's just purposefully slow. They're not even hiding it! They could get us off this planet way faster if they wanted to. Instead, they want us to wait for the optimal transport window, for what, to save cash? Cheap bastards!"

Gordon thought about what could happen at the outpost in eight months. Would there still be anyone left alive to save? He'd been gone so long already, and that ate at the very core of his being. He didn't know the situation there, or how exactly he could help, but he knew he had to try.

He looked at the screens. The news was off, and he was thankful for that. He couldn't take anymore. In its place was a live feed of the *Walt's* exterior. A four-wheeled rover blew up dust as it zoomed up a nearby hill. The antsy crew had started taking to the ship's toys for relief from their boredom.

"Gordon? Are you paying attention? We need to find another way to Earth. Once we put you on the feeds and in front of the UN, people will understand. We can start streaming ourselves too. People need to hear you speak your truth. We can't beat my dad in politics, but we can beat him in the media." Alex sat back in her chair, looking content, as if Gordon had answered a question she'd been asking forever.

"I'm going back," he said.

"What?" She was still, frozen like a rat under a mining light.

"Home, I mean. I'm going home. To the outpost. I need to help the people there. The Foreman is still in power, and I can't let it kill the few people I still care about."

Alex leaned forward, held his hands, and looked into his eyes. "Gordon. Listen to me. You have to understand why that is an insane plan. Just *insane*. The Foreman is not your biggest enemy, it's a symptom of the disease that is First Corp. We need to deal with the bigger problem, or the company will just replace it with something worse."

"Going to Earth is an insane plan!" He pulled away from Alex and stood. It killed him, but she didn't understand. "Earth won't save us," he continued. "No-one is coming to help my people. No-one cares about us. No-one ever has! We're all alone on this planet, just like we've always been. And it's up to me to kill the Foreman. Waiting for years, or even months, to hope someone in fancy, layered clothing on Earth does something to help us is not an option!"

Alex's face soured and the color drained from her face.

Gordon turned to a wall and put his hands on his head. He wanted to scream. Where were his folding papers? Someone cleared their throat from the doorway. He wheeled around the see Captain Ty.

"Just the two kids I was looking for." He sauntered into the room.

"And just the captain I wanted to talk with," Alex said.

"Oh?"

"I don't know if you saw the news but ... we need transport to Earth," Alex said. "The lockdown is over. When can we leave?"

"So, that's the thing. I need you off my ship, and not just because you're drinking all my beer." Ty laughed at his own joke but stopped and sighed when no one joined. "You're United Nations property now. We're not allowed to conduct our regular shipping business while you're on-board. I'm truly sorry, and I enjoyed your company, but now you're costing me money, and I need y'all to leave." Ty raised his hands as if to say there was nothing else he could do.

"I can pay you! Whatever you make on a normal run, I'll pay you double," Alex said, holding her hands out.

"It's not like that. The *Walt* physically can't leave this port with you on my ship, load bearing or not. There's a software lock on the docking mechanism."

"Ah! My stupid dad." Alex slammed her beer mug against the table again.

"Look, you're radioactive," Ty said. "I suggest you wait here for a UN ship to come pick you up. No-one wants to be blacklisted and left without an income, and I doubt the port authority would take a bribe. Too high-profile. No-one else can help you."

Alex stood abruptly and marched out of the mess hall. She stomped like she had in the glass prison.

Gordon watched her go. Part of him was holding back tears and could barely construct a coherent thought. He cared so much about her that any pain she experienced might as well have been his. He'd never felt that before, about anyone, and was struck by how deep it cut. What made it really hurt was that his words had been some of the sharpest. He hated that he'd caused her any amount of distress.

Another part of him thought that Alex was blinded by her biases and needed to grow up.

#

When he knocked on her door, the response was so muted he thought he imagined it. He cracked it open and saw a pile of tissues on the floor.

"Yes?" Alex sat on the crash couch. She didn't look up from her handheld, her eyes manically moving over information as she scrolled.

"I, uh, just want to talk." Gordon entered the room and sat on the ground, his back against the wall.

"Okay."

"I know you don't understand, but I have to do this. I have to tell my people that the Dead Earth Hypothesis isn't true, and that Earth is thriving. They deserve to know, and they deserve my help in defeating the Foreman."

"I, uh ... It's just a bad idea, Gordon. We can stall here for another day or two. Let me reach out to all my contacts on Earth. Let me find someone who can help."

"I think Earth made it clear they're not interested in helping us." Gordon tried to speak softly, but some antipathy snuck through. They locked up his people for hundreds of years. Relying on them to fix things would be foolish.

"I think we should go see my dad," Alex said, finally looking up.

Gordon froze. "What?"

"Look, I'm his only daughter. His only child. At the bottom of his heart, he still loves me more than anything. I can convince him to end this. And so can you! Once he sees that you are a normal, human boy, he will come to his senses."

"You can't be serious! The guy who tried to kill us? Twice!"

"The bounty was inexcusable. I'll never forgive him. But you must understand that to my dad and a lot of others, your people are savages. They're scared of you. We need to tell the human side of your story. He loves me, and I can use that to help him understand. I can use it against him."

"How?" Gordon crossed his arms.

"He won the public relations game and the United Nations votes. He somehow gained leverage, and he knows it. He taught me to never negotiate from a weak position, which is why he invited me to meet with him now. But the party that's ahead always risks becoming complacent, and his love for me is a real blind spot. The cleanest path to victory is to make him feel even a tenth of what I feel for you."

"Public relations? Leverage? What's there to negotiate? This is real!"

"Of course, you'd stay at a safe distance, hidden at first. You'd only come out once we have certain assurances. We can live stream everything to Earth and gain public support. That will increase the pressure on him. And if it doesn't work, I'll find another way. I still have allies within First Corp. This is politics. This is what I'm good at, even if I hate it."

"I ... I can't believe you." Gordon stalked back to his room. He had to get to his origami. He'd tried her way, but enough was enough. If it was up to Alex, it would take years of phone calls and deal making to free his people.

"Look, it's not my first choice either," she yelled down the hall. "But it's the only option we have."

#

It would be morning soon, and he lay awake, folding and unfolding his last piece of paper. It became a lotus flower, then a swan, then a crane, until it had so many creases that it just looked like a piece of trash.

Alex was the best thing that had ever happened to him. She showed him the world and gave him the confidence to be himself. Leaving her was crazy, but he had to finish his business at the outpost.

He didn't take much with him because he didn't have much to take. His papers and his mom's pendant fit in his pockets. He wore a thick, black pull-over sweater a crew member had donated to him. He tucked Alex's gun into the front of his pants. He carried the two small boxes of ammo, one of explosive rounds and one regular. It would be difficult, but he was ready to use them if he had to.

The last thing he took was proof. Proof that everything he experienced with Alex was real, that Earth was alive, and that he hadn't just been in a fever dream the whole time. In the pocket of his new sweater, he stashed a data drive he'd taken from the *Walt*. On it, there were videos Alex had given him from her handheld. They were of another world, of Alex and her life before Mars. He'd need them to show the First Olympians the truth.

He paused at her door but decided against knocking. She didn't understand his position, and how would she? How could he expect her to? She never ate dusty expired rations or competed for a handful of crummy jobs. She never watched hope fade from someone's eyes as they suffocated in cold blood.

He decided he wouldn't hold Alex's disagreement against her. She'd done a lot for him, and he was thankful for that. But Gordon's mom always said that if he wanted something done right, he'd have to do it himself. Alex couldn't help him beat the Foreman because she didn't even know what it was. He could only hope that she could understand one day, and maybe they could be together again when it was all over. When they won.

Perhaps Alex staying behind was a good thing. Gordon didn't know the situation at the outpost, but if Dalrene's uprising was still going on, it would be super dangerous. That would be especially true for someone who'd never seen a peacekeeper bot before. By going alone, he could protect her.

The garage was in the lowest level of the *Walt*. Gordon hummed to himself in the elevator. He had never driven anything before, but he had seen others do it. And he had never navigated on the surface of Mars before, but he'd seen a map, and Olympus Mons was pretty hard to miss. So, he felt more excited than nervous. After all the time spent as a passenger in the *Zoya*, and then in the medical center of the *Walt*, he was finally in charge of himself again. He was going to captain a rover. He was going to make the decisions.

Five rovers sat square in the middle of the high-ceilinged garage. The middle one was a unique teal color that Alex called "sea green." Gordon had never seen anything like it. It had four-wheels, two rows of seating, and had been described as "lightweight," although he didn't see anything light about it. The tires were tall, at least two meters. Ty said it was for hopping around cities on Mars without using a spaceship. It'd been used more in the last few days than the entire previous two years combined.

Gordon opened the door to the rover and stepped up to its driver seat. He closed it to a satisfying clink sound, put his hands on the wheel and looked out of the thick glass windshield. He pressed a button that said "Start" on it, and the rover spoke to him in a voice that jarringly reminded him of the Foreman.

"Pressurizing cabin and checking safety systems. Please ensure you have adequate oxygen supply in your back-up environmental suits."

Gordon looked in the back seat and saw a pair of teal one-piece suits that matched the rover. They were sleek and modern, much cooler than the previous equipment he'd used.

His foot touched the pedal and the rover jerked forward. Panicked, he slammed the brake and nearly went through the windshield. It was going to take longer than he hoped to learn to drive. He straightened himself back up, strapped his seatbelt on, and through trial and error, eased the vehicle into the airlock. A reading on the windshield said that the rover was at one-hundred percent charge, or two thousand and six hundred kilometers. He would need about eighty-five percent of it to get to Olympus Mons.

The airlock door opened to the sun rising over the red desert before him. He laughed to himself. He would never get tired of seeing the surface. It was still a surreal moment of beauty and stillness.

A tinge of fear crept its way up the back of his neck. He was going to be all alone. No one to help him. No Alex. It was just him and the wild, unforgiving landscape of Mars. He felt the First Olympians pendant in his breast pocket. His mom would be proud.

It had been twenty days since he'd left the outpost. A horrible, unimaginable number since his people were first entrapped under Olympus Mons. Mickey, Dalrene, Corrina, and all the others would have to hang on just a little bit longer.

Gordon put his foot on the accelerator.

He didn't look back.

Chapter Twenty-Eight: Alex

The gray sludge in her bowl had become a thick, cooled gel. Alex wiped a tear from her eye and forced another spoonful into her mouth. She knew she had to eat, but she could barely stomach the *Walt's* food *before* Gordon left. Now, her appetite was even worse.

"He's a big boy, and this is his home planet. He can take care of himself." It was Fred, the ragged pilot more than twice her age.

She hadn't noticed him enter the mess hall. She nodded without looking up from her food.

"Besides, you can do better than him."

Alex glared, and he flinched. Knowing how to look extremely pissed off was one of her superpowers. "I think it's time for me to go," Alex said, putting as fine a point on it as she could muster.

She made her way back to her room, avoiding eye contact with everyone she passed. They wouldn't understand.

Taking stock of her possessions, she realized she had nothing more than her handheld and the clothes on her back. It felt like she had even less. Gordon, the boy who stole her heart with his charming naivety and kindness, also stole her gun and disappeared in the middle of the night. They disagreed on their path forward, sure, but how could he do that to her? He didn't even say goodbye.

It felt cruel and mean in a way she knew Gordon could have never intentioned. He was too genuinely compassionate to hurt her on purpose. And yet, knowing that didn't stop the pain. The time they spent together wasn't long, but he still meant so much to her. Alex felt hollow without his goofy smile and positive reassurances. It was a new feeling. She missed him. She longed for him in a way she never had for anyone before.

She pulled her crew issued sweatshirt over her head, and her stomach panged with anxiety. She couldn't protect him anymore. Gordon was crossing the dead, hostile desert of Mars alone. Did he have enough water? Did he know how to pressurize the cabin? Did he know how to deploy the fold out solar panels if he needed to? So many things could go wrong. And that was to say nothing of the horrors he'd face if he actually made it to Olympus Mons. She was helpless to help him, and it made her sick.

She sat on the bed. There was one more thing to do before she left.

"Alex. Oh, thank God. What a relief! Where are you?" Her mom looked like she'd slept some, but not much.

"I'm on the *Walt*, but I can't stay here. I have to leave but..." Saying it out loud made it real. She was alone and didn't know where to go next. Alex's breathing threatened to get out of control. The time for a message to travel between Earth and Mars was about three minutes, and she spent it trying not to hyperventilate.

"Shhh. Shhh. My poor baby girl, Alessandra. It's okay, I sent you money. You two can stay at a hotel while we work on a plan. Look, I want you to know something." There was pain in her mom's face. "I'm not on speaking terms with your father anymore. I'm going to help you fix this."

Alex wanted nothing more than to be home in her mother's arms. "I'm sorry," she said. Her mom's marriage was destroyed, and Alex had meant to reassure her, not bombard her with more stress.

"No, I'm sorry," her mom said. "None of this was your fault and I can't imagine what you're going through. Let me help you make it right. Get to that hotel and be ready to make some calls. The United Nations really screwed you over. Your dad bought up all the politicians so fast I couldn't believe it. But if we move now we can make a change."

"Huh?" Alex wiped a tear from her eye.

"We can remove him from his position." Her mom spoke in a hushed tone.

A million thoughts competed in Alex's mind. When did her mom become so serious? She didn't know she could be so tough. And how could they possibly fire her dad? He was the Chairman of the Board, and the other members loved him.

"I don't understand," she said.

"I'll send the details. Just get somewhere safe and clear your mind. Have a shower." She gave her a caring smile like only mothers could.

"Okay." It felt good to not be the decision maker for once.

"One more thing. Please stay away from the social feeds. There's nothing good or useful on there. We need to focus."

"Sure, mom."

Alex hung up to a knock on the door. She opened it to Captain Ty, his face somber, like he was at a funeral.

"Hey kid," he said. "Sorry about Gordon. And Fred, he's an asshole."

Alex mustered a curt nod. That was all she could give without breaking down again.

"I appreciate you leaving. You know we would help you more if we could." Ty shrugged his shoulders in earnest. "The whole crew is rooting for both of you."

Another nod.

"You want to know where he's headed? We have a GPS tracker on that rover he took."

"I, uh." Alex's tongue was tied. "No, I know where he's going. I mean, I'm good. Thank you though."

"Okay."

Their eyes met, and he raised an eyebrow.

"Crap. Should I pay you for that rover?" Alex asked. Her face flushed.

"If you're able to, that would be appropriate," Ty said. "They aren't cheap and we don't expect to get that one back."

"Right, of course." Alex took out her handheld. She was connected to the *Walt's* network, so it'd be easy to transfer funds to the ship's bank account. How much did a rover cost? She doubled what seemed like a reasonable amount and thumbed the cash over. The new funds her mom provided were more than enough.

"Good luck out there," Ty said.

"Thanks for the clothes. And everything," Alex said sheepishly.

He gave her an affirmative pat on the shoulder and marched off.

Alex walked the long hallway to the *Walt's* boarding bridge. She already regretted not thanking Captain Ty enough. The truth was that he was incredibly supportive, and without his crew's help, Gordon would've died. He didn't turn him in for the bounty and had been more than courteous considering the risks their presence posed. But she'd overstayed her welcome, and it was time to move on.

The lockdown was over, and hustle and bustle had returned to New Arcadia. Ships were eager to depart and stop racking up docking fees. They blasted off every few minutes, shaking the floor. No doubt there was an army of analysts at First Corp. trying to quantify the impact on the supply chain and re-schedule hundreds of loads. That her dad had disrupted so much of the inter-planetary economy showed how important Gordon was to him.

Other ships landed, replacing the departures in a heartbeat. Landing had been forbidden during the lockdown, and the crews that waited in orbit looked particularly relieved to be planet-side. The new arrivals stretched, hollered in excitement, and headed straight to the restaurants, brothels, and gambling dens opposite their ships' bridges. Most establishments were all three.

It was an all-out assault on the senses compared to the emptiness it'd been when Alex first arrived. Half-dressed women hung off poles in windows. Clouds of cannabis and cigar vapor attacked her. Artificial laughter, flashing neon lights, and the jangly music of slot machines assured you that you were having the time of your life. Glasses clinked from within crowded bars. Alex hated it, and not just because of the grossness factor. People were too damn happy. She pulled the hood of her *Walt* crew-member sweater over her head, and sulked.

She saw the crowd before she saw the *Zoya*. Evidently, people had heard about her, and the new fusion drive, and wanted to see it for themselves. Which was stupid, because although it was an incredibly sleek, sexy, new ship, you couldn't actually see the innovative engineering or any of the internals from the window.

Elbowing her way through, she made it to the front of the line, and her heart sank. Two security guards with rifles stood at the transit bridge entrance. A big metal chain was wrapped around the door handles. The screen above the bridge read "Impounded".

The *Zoya*! Her baby! It loomed behind the guards, her beautiful V-shape just out of reach.

Now her dad had ruined that too! It was another punch to the gut. He was going to make life as hard as possible. She grimaced, pulled her hood tighter, and walked away. She didn't want the security guards, or anyone else, to recognize her.

Her dad was always one step ahead of her. He limited how much Captain Ty could help and stopped them from getting to Earth easily. Yes, she got the truth out about Gordon and Mine One, but even that win had been hollowed out by her dad's successive media and UN victories.

As if on cue, her handheld buzzed with a message from him. She let it play as she stepped away from the crowd and toward the market district.

"Alex, my dear. I hope you've had some time to think about my proposal."

Her tongue recoiled like she'd tasted a spoonful of curdled milk.

Her dad spoke with the voice he used on politicians. "We can work together to make this right. For the people at the mine, yes, but also for the company and its shareholders. For the family. Remember? Family is the most important thing. It will take time, years, but we can do this in a way that doesn't alarm the UN or garner any more pressure from the public. It was difficult for me to hear about this issue from my father as well. I'm truly sorry that I didn't tell you earlier, and I'm proud of the principled young woman you've become. I'm offering you a job, Chief Transformation Officer. You'll have full leeway to lead change, and as much budget as you want. So please, just come home. We can fix this."

Alex wanted to puke. First Corp.'s offices were not her home, and the slimy cravenness of her dad's appeals made her want to never see him again. On the other hand, maybe seeing him in person would allow her to pull his heartstrings? Maybe she could make an emotional appeal that would push him off-balance. She'd have to see what her mom's full plan was.

The guards that previously blocked her from entering the market district were gone, and she entered the heart of the city. It was a big, open area with establishments of all types lining the sides, and a park with benches and real plants under a glass roof. There must've been grow lights because there were some tall bushes and even trees. Paper advertisements for drugs and brothels littered the floor, but Alex was still impressed. It was almost nice.

She didn't stay in the park long. She told herself it was because she had to stay stealthy and constantly on the move, but it was also because she didn't deserve a moment of tranquility. Everything was bad and it was all her fault. Even if her mom's plan worked, that didn't mean she'd ever seen Gordon again. Besides, all she could think about was how much he'd love doing origami among the greenery.

She didn't think her dad would try to kidnap her. His new approach was reconciliation. In order for that to work, he needed her to come willingly. Still, she didn't want anyone to recognize her from the newsfeeds. Alex tried to avoid the cameras splattered around and kept her hood up.

The first hotel she stumbled upon was Hotel Tanzania. The lobby was dark and dingy. Broken lights made the circular room feel smaller than it was. It was mostly empty space, and the woman who lay on the sole couch by the coffee table was either asleep or drunk. A touchscreen would let her book a room, but there were a few other new arrivals ahead of her in line. It was the perfect place. No-one would look for her here.

As she waited, the lobby newsfeed caught her eye. Gordon's face was on the screen. The caption read "Alleged Martian Slave yet to Respond to UN Proposal."

Anger bubbled up inside of her. Did Gordon realize how much harder he made this for her? He was the ace in the hole! His existence was proof! If he disappeared back under Olympus Mons, or never even made it there, it would be that much easier for her dad to sweep the whole thing under the rug. And she'd look like an idiot, like she made the whole thing up. Were the social feeds saying the same thing? Sometimes people were smarter than the news.

Alex stepped back, tearing herself away from the feed, but bumped into a hotel patron, spilling his drink.

"Sorry!"

The man shrugged. He looked flushed in the face, drunk from celebrating the end of the lockdown.

"Lighten up, would ya?" He laughed like Alex had told him a joke rather than ruined his shirt.

She faced forward in the line once again. She closed her eyes and grit her teeth. Alex couldn't believe people could just be enjoying themselves, drinking themselves stupid in a time like this. There was a humanitarian crisis happening, not six hundred kilometers from this stupid settlement—city—whatever it was, and people were just ignoring it, absorbed in their own little worlds.

#

At least the room had a window, although the sun was set by the time Alex arrived. It was sparse. There was a "Martian Queen" sized bed that was about the size of an American single-wide, a bedside table, and a screen on the wall. There were cigarette stains on the floor, and she wondered if the sprinklers worked. The air recycler didn't seem to be doing much for the astringent scent in the air. The bitterness reminded her of grape harvest season back home, except bad. There was nothing she wouldn't give to be transported there immediately. With Gordon.

The coffee maker made a disgusting brown sludge. Even the *Zoya* was miles better in comparison. She sat tentatively at the end of the bed, decidedly not drinking it. Her handheld blinked with a message from her mom.

We've got Bernie in ten minutes. He's on Earth, so you'll be on delay. That's okay. I'll do my best to help find out what he wants for his vote. We need both him and Lisa to kick your father out.

Alex understood now. Her mom was a genius! There were five members of First Corp.'s Board of Directors: Alex, her dad, her mom, Bernard Haynes, and Dr. Lisa Cuthbert. Alex was the Secretary of the Board, and her dad was the Chairman, but that didn't matter. If all four of them voted together, they could remove the CEO and select a new one that would take Mine Number One seriously.

It wouldn't be easy. They'd need to get a quorum first, with all five members of the Board on a call, so that she could officially convene a meeting. If her dad suspected anything he could simply not show up and prevent a quorum.

And there was the fact that they'd have to convince Lisa and Bernie to vote her dad out. Despite him being a long-time family friend, Alex didn't have a strong relationship with Bernie. He was a squat, inscrutable man who preferred to talk about First Corp.'s financial performance and government relations with other adults rather than speak with her. One of her dad's oldest friends, he'd be hard to flip. Although the same was true for Lisa.

She was freshening up in the restroom when Bernie's call came through. Alex positioned herself against the off-white-turned-gray wall and answered on her handheld. She didn't want him or her mom to see the crappy room she was renting.

"Alex. I'm not supposed to be talking to you. What do you want?" Bernie's bald head filled the screen.

"Yes. Thanks for calling," Alex said, quickly shifting into business-mode. It was a skin she hadn't worn in a while, but it still fit. "Actually, I was wondering the same about you. What do you want?"

"What do I want?" Bernie looked incredulous.

"We're going to call a special board meeting. We've got three 'ayes' to kick my dad out. You're the last one, so what can we do to get you onboard?" Pretending Lisa's vote was already secured felt like the right lie to tell.

"Absolutely not. No, no thank you." Bernie made exaggerated mouth movements, but he didn't hang up.

Alex's mom's video joined the call. Both she and Bernie were on Earth, which meant although they could talk to each other near-instantly, Alex was behind due to transmission delay.

"It's true. It's all true. Thousands of slaves held underground for generations," Alex's mom said.

"And who's going to be the new CEO? You? *Alex?*"

"Alex and I will be co-CEOs to start. The first thing we'll do is hire a vice-president to handle the day-to-day. Alex is going to need a vacation," her mom said.

Alex scrunched her nose. She didn't want the job. Although, worst case, they could hire people to do ninety percent of it, as her mom suggested.

Bernie snorted. "Your dad just saved this company from its biggest potential crisis in history. Our share price is *higher* than it was three months ago, and you want to remove him? Even if Mine number one is worse than what you've described, creating a PR disaster was not the right way to fix it. Removing the CEO? PR disaster part two."

He tried to kill me came to Alex's tongue, but she fought it back.

"What do you want?" her mom asked coldly.

Bernie moved his head from side to side.

"Exclusive rights to the tech for my personal corporation."

"The tech?"

"That's right. I want to be the sole owner of the patents and re-sell rights. Solar-system wide."

Alex's head spun. What was he talking about? The space elevator designs? No, that was still theoretical, and the economics were murky. The new engines that powered the *Zoya*? That was probably it. She had worked on the asteroid belt expansion plans that the high-efficiency fusion reactors would enable. It felt like a lifetime ago, but she remembered thinking that the coming gold rush would make First Corp. trillions of credits.

"That's a tough ask," Alex said, unsure exactly what she meant.

"I'll pay a fair price," Bernard said, sounding offended.

Alex didn't know how to respond.

Thankfully, her mom spoke next. "Exclusive rights? Are you crazy? It's not about the price. It's a geopolitical risk. The military applications are everything! If it gets in the wrong hands, we'd change the course of civilization."

"Well, then give me the prototype," Bernie said. "But if I'm going to be a part of a coup, I won't let it linger. Execution in twenty-four hours, max. The more time this takes, the more likely Rafa finds out, and next thing you know I'm kicked off the Board."

"The... The prototype?" Alex's mouth hung open. Did Bernie want the *Zoya*? Was the opportunity to reverse engineer the reactor drive worth that much? She wished she'd kept better tabs on the news. She hadn't even thought of the geopolitical implications of the technology. She knew the three world powers were in constant competition, and that First Corp. was aligned with the West despite her dad's attempts to become more independent. Aside from that, she'd been focused on the engineering, and reluctantly, the financial—not military or political—implications.

She must've taken too long to respond because her mom spoke next.

"Done."

Alex's jaw dropped even further. Did her mom just give away her spaceship?

Chapter Twenty-Nine: Dalrene

Dalrene never thought she'd be back in the grotto so soon, and without Mickey. His absence loomed larger than any of the shadows cast by their headlamps. The hair on her arms stood straight up. It was unsettling to be back where it started. It was where she first hatched her plan to rescue Mickey from solitary confinement. It was where her followers had slowly amassed, first meeting monthly, and progressing to near daily, to hear her speak from the grotto's natural stage.

Everything was where they'd left it. She curled her nose at the mildewy scent of sweaty old clothes that lingered in the air. Food scraps rotted in a corner. The makeshift beds of old ration boxes and blankets lay where they left them, and Dalrene's neck twinged as if remembering the disturbed sleep and bruised hips. DeMar's blood stained the floor.

There were good memories too, like the nights Mickey spent playing his guitar, and the rippling, contagious energy the place had when people came together and shared exciting ideas. But those seemed distant, like they had happened in another lifetime, or to someone else. Dalrene always preferred to look forward anyway. She hated nostalgia. She couldn't wait to leave the cave for good this time, and never come back.

The condensation-collecting pitchers were full of water that had dripped down from the walls and ceilings. Londi stepped over to one and took what looked like a big, satisfying drink.

"Take it easy. You don't want to piss your suit."

His eyes widened, and he put the water down.

"You sure we can do this?" Londi asked, clearing his throat. "We have no idea where the solar panels are, assuming there are any. They could be kilometers away, and you're still recovering."

Dalrene was injured, sure. Hell, she'd been banged up and sleep deprived even before the knife in the back. But Londi wasn't asking about that. They both knew he was giving her an out, a way she could honorably take a break, because of Mickey. What he didn't understand was that losing her husband left her with only one choice, to harden her resolve.

"They're my suits. I know how they work, and I know where the tunnel to the surface is. I'm the best person for the job. Or would you rather have one of the hotheaded idiots we have back at the farm dome?"

"Hey, those are good people. They're loyal to you." Londi wagged his finger at Dalrene. "But you're right, I'm probably stuck with you at this point." A grin cracked his face.

"I can walk okay, although you'll have to do the heavy lifting," Dalrene admitted. "Even injured, I'm your best chance in case anything goes wrong, or if we get lost." She pulled out the two environmental suits from behind a lava pillar.

"How much oxygen is in these tanks?" Londi knocked on one of the tanks. "They sound hollow."

"Oxygen is a gas. It's supposed to sound like that. These suits have been in my family a long time, and I've tried to keep them in good condition. Full tanks should last us three and a half hours, at least theoretically. Can't say I've pushed them to their limit. Maybe they have leaks, and we'll step outside and come running back in ten minutes. I don't know. But it's our best shot."

"You mean it's our only shot."

"That too." Dalrene gulped. Either she was going to kill everyone or save everyone. There was no in-between.

"You know, ever since we were kids, we had the importance of electricity drilled into us. How we must conserve it and use it wisely because the whole ecosystem runs on it. Everything from our food to our air and waste requires it. It's funny that we never really asked about where it came from," Londi said, putting his suit on. It barely fit his muscular frame.

"At a certain point, the Foreman changed from wanting us to help with electricity maintenance, to not wanting us to ask any questions about it. My grandmother was a solar panel technician. Apparently, it was one of the most prestigious jobs you could have. Makes sense. She looked after our most important resource."

"And now we're going to sabotage our most important resource." Londi shook his head.

"That's right. So, let's get a move on."
\#

At the airlock, Dalrene popped a few painkillers and pulled her helmet on. She'd never been more thankful for both the Foreman's and Rodriguez's affinity for pharmaceuticals. They really did help.

Her helmet didn't smell like anything. It was the exact opposite of her lifetime spent in the outpost—sterile, like the surface of Mars, and entirely quiet with no screeching sirens or the rattle of air recyclers.

Her internal display only seemed to show two things. The first was her oxygen level, and it gave a reading of three hours and twenty-five minutes. She'd watch it carefully.

The second value displayed was auxiliary electronics at one hour and forty minutes. The suit's batteries were so small and old that they didn't hold much charge anymore. Their comms were going to fail well before their oxygen. Clear and effective communication before that happened would be critical.

Dalrene stood aside and Londi heaved open the circular, rusty metal door. Air rushed out of the outpost, and they hurried to the other side. Dalrene leaned against the door with all her body weight, and they slammed it shut.

"This area used to be pressurized!" She tapped the side of her helmet, engaging the microphone. "Good thing we put our suits on already. What the hell happened?"

Dalrene turned around, facing uphill of the narrow tunnel, to where the second airlock door used to be, and had her question answered. Gordon's blast caused a portion of the tunnel to cave in. Either that, or the Foreman tried to destroy their way out. Rocks of all shapes and sizes lay strewn about. She hoped they wouldn't find Gordon's body underneath the rubble.

Above her, a few rays of sunshine cracked through the holes. She stopped and took it in. She'd seen sun before, from the overhang, but each time made her heart skip a beat. That was a rare occurrence for someone her age.

She saw that Londi was similarly frozen beside her.

"No oxygen to waste," she said, pushing him forward. "We'll have to scramble over these rocks."

The two of them climbed on all fours up the hill. Loose silt gave away with every movement they made. The air was already cloudy with dust and their steps added to it. It was difficult to see exactly where she was stepping.

"You've been here before, right? You know where we're going?"

"Mickey and I saw the mineral pick-up vehicle from the top of this tunnel. It was a big moment for us when we realized that something was happening on the surface."

"But the solar panels?"

"I know they exist, that's about it."

Londi grabbed Dalrene's hand and helped her step onto a boulder.

She looked back down to the door they came through. They had climbed most of the way up and were approaching the pile of rubble where the second door used to be. Beyond that lay a hostile world with no air recyclers and no second chances. The only guarantees were the wide-open sky and plenty of sunlight.

Dalrene leaned on her knees with her forearms with each upward step. Their time was limited, but there was no need to overexert herself before they even got to the surface."

"We should've brought some digging tools," Londi said. He was at the top now, clawing his way out of the tunnel. The rays of sunlight were slowly but surely becoming more plentiful.

She got what Mickey would've called "butterflies" in her stomach as she approached it. She'd only been to the surface once before, and not very far out. Last time, Mickey had been scared. As much as he wanted to see the sun, Dalrene had to hold his hand as they peered out from the overhang. He'd been in awe. They both were. That was the only time since Tess's death he'd been struck by true childlike amazement.

Londi pulled a big rock out of the way, and it tumbled down the hill. Dalrene took a deep breath. There was enough room for a person to squeeze through now. She wanted to portray a sense of confidence, so she crawled forward, planting her hands firmly outside the outpost. She looked out, her gaze extending across the never-ending desert of red dirt and rocks, and up, to the overbearing, crushing scale of the pink-tinted sky.

"Holy shit," she said, averting her eyes. She dug her glove into the soil and tried to ground herself. She felt small and insignificant. The whole outpost did.

Londi knelt beside her and put his hand on her back. They stayed there as Dalrene's brain tried to acclimate itself. She assumed he was doing the same thing, and neither of them spoke.

When they stood, Dalrene was careful not to take in too much of the view at once. She wiped the dust off her helmet, cleaning the visor. Slowly, she drew her eyes up Olympus Mons, the hulking mass stretching up to the sky. This time she kept her composure.

Remnants of the loading dock were everywhere, and they walked toward it. Pieces of metal and plastic scattered the ground, even upwards of fifty meters from the blast scene. There was no sign of any loading vehicles. Or of Gordon. She could only assume he was buried under the tunnel rubble somewhere. The guilt she felt before was still there, but mostly she felt thankful. He'd completed his mission with incredible success.

Dalrene wondered what happened to the bots the Foreman had sent to investigate the explosion. There was the phalanx of guardians defending the children's prison, and there must've been hundreds of peacekeepers "keeping the peace" in the HCZ, but she knew there were even more. She could only assume it kept them watching the nodes, waiting for the First Olympians to strike.

The more she walked, the more at ease she felt. "If I were a solar panel, where would I be?" Dalrene tried to infer the position of the sun without looking directly at it. Olympus Mons was near the equator, but if their ancestors wanted to maximize energy efficiency, they would have pointed the solar panels south and made sure nothing obstructed their path to the sun.

Londi deferred to her, so she took the lead and started to move in the direction she thought was south. They hiked up the rolling hills at the base of the volcano for twenty minutes. Her skin tingled. Even in her suit and under the sun, the temperature was lower than she'd ever experienced in the outpost. The cold kept her on edge. And moving.

This close to the cliffs, she could only see the precipice, and not the plateau behind it from which the volcano jutted into the sky. The light hit the rock, reflecting a deep-red color. Every part of Olympus Mons was stunning in its own way. This first part, the spectacular mountainside, seemed to extend straight up forever and ever, to the sky. Jagged edges and steep slopes added drama. It was fierce and wicked, and not just because of its sheer size.

Looking out across the desert, the horizon was the expansive landscape of her dreams. From atop the hill, she could see everything, even the curvature of the planet. Its beauty was only surpassed by the emptiness of it all. The Dead Earth Hypothesis. They were all alone. She cracked a smile through the tears that rolled down her face. If only Mickey could have been there.

Dalrene made mental notes about how many hills they climbed and where a specific black boulder was in relation to the tunnel. As beautiful as everything was, the more they walked, the more everything looked the same. They hadn't travelled more than five kilometers, but everything seemed bigger out here. It would be too easy to get lost.

"The sun has moved," Londi said.

"You mean Mars has spun," she said. Dalrene looked at her oxygen levels. It had nearly been an hour.

"Yeah, I suppose that's right."

"I wouldn't worry about it. We're gonna be more limited by oxygen than daylight." That was a good thing. They were not prepared to operate in the dark. The suits didn't have any external lights that she could find, and the headlamps they wore in the caves were useless.

They reached the top of a hill and Dalrene pointed at a section of the cliff that was less steep than the others. "That's where we go up." It looked like an ancient rockslide had created a smoother incline.

"It's not directly vertical, but it's still going to be tough. The solar panels must be up there. Let me go turn them off. I'll come meet you back here when I'm done."

"No way," Dalrene bristled. Besides, our comms are gonna drop soon. We need to stay together. What are your aux electronics at?"

"Twenty minutes. Fuck." There was a layer of anxiety in Londi's voice.

"Don't worry, we'll talk with our hands." So far, he'd followed her lead perfectly well. Not having comms was going to be fine, as long as they stuck together.

Dalrene started to crawl her way up what looked like a few hundred meters of incline, using all four of her limbs as much as she could. This whole thing was her idea, and she had to see it through. She should've been in bed recovering from her knife injury, or mourning her dead husband, but there would be time for both of those things later, after they won.

Whenever she thought she found stable footing, the rocks slipped away from under her, and she had to use her arm to stabilize herself. Her legs burned. But it was also an upper-body workout. She had sharp pains through her back and abdomen, but she gritted through it. It was a good thing Rodriguez emptied an entire tube of tissue regeneration paste on her wound.

By the time she got half the way up, she watched Londi reach the top and disappear over the lip.

"Oh, wow." He paused. "I see the panels. I won't go far."

Dalrene proceeded methodically, using her core as much as she could, and resting when she needed to. Leading the First Olympians was a tough job. Part of her wished she had found out the truth about the outpost when she was a younger woman, but she knew her younger self hadn't had the resolve to see it through.

Twenty minutes later, she reached the top, and Dalrene pulled herself up and kneeled to catch her breath. She may be old and injured, but she could still do the job.

But her breath escaped her again as she was taken by the beauty of the solar panel. Across the plateau, hundreds of metal poles rose in the air, each with an array of panels sitting on top. They covered a massive surface area, probably bigger than the entire surface of the residential area of the outpost. They extended into the sky forcefully, yet gracefully. It was beautiful. It was a work of art. They were a rare human mark on otherwise desolate canvas. In hindsight, there was no way they could have missed them.

Londi was fifty meters away inspecting one of the panel arrays with his back to her. Dalrene collected herself and checked her oxygen levels. They had an hour and thirty-five minutes. The way home, downhill, would be faster, but they still had to move quick.

Their priority was finding a way to "flip the switch" in case they needed to turn it back on quickly. Entirely destroying the power source wasn't an option. They were going to need it after they killed the Foreman. The last thing they wanted was to liberate the outpost then watch as everyone died a slow, painful death while the food, water, and air infrastructure collapsed.

It didn't hurt to look a few steps ahead. Which is why Dalrene was confused that Londi seemed to be focused on inspecting one specific solar panel array. It would be better if they searched for whatever all the arrays connected to and shut it down centrally.

"Londi. I'm here. Let's go find the kill switch."

Out of the corner of her eye, she saw movement from the side.

Dalrene gasped. A bot shook dust off itself like a wet rat shaking itself dry. Its head of sensors spun around, and its camera eyes opened, looking around for a moment before zeroing in on Londi. It had long, narrow feet, like a guardian, and it leapt across the plateau, picking up speed.

Londi was focused on the solar panel, his side to the robot.

"Londi! Watch out!" Dalrene ran at him. She wouldn't get there in time.

He didn't react.

"Londi!" Dalrene yelled again.

She jammed at her helmet. Her comms were working, but Londi couldn't hear her. His must've been out of power!

She swore to herself. The plateau was the one place on the volcano without any loose rocks, so she had no weapon. The stupidity of what she was doing dawned on her. But she had to try.

The guardian was twenty meters out but still accelerating.

Londi looked over his shoulder, finally seeing her, but missed the bot coming from his other side.

Dalrene waved her hands in the air and pointed.

He didn't understand.

It was too late. The guardian collided with him, sending him flying. Dalrene watched in horror as Londi hurled through the air and smacked into a solar panel pole. It must've been incredibly loud, because she heard his oxygen tank thud against the metal through her helmet.

She was getting closer.

The bot ran to Londi and leaned over him.

He didn't move or put up his arms in protest. He was limp and lifeless.

Unlike the newer, perhaps more modern guardians inside the outpost, this one didn't have guns. Instead, it had spinning blades, like a peacekeeper, and it raised them above its head.

Dalrene arrived, launching herself at the bot. She jumped and climbed onto its back and tried to pull its saw arms away from Londi. The bot spun in a circle. She confused it, for a moment at least.

Londi groggily raised his arms over his face and tried to roll away from underneath the bot.

It shrugged, then crouched into a ball. When it stood, it expanded explosively and launched Dalrene into the air. She landed hard in the dirt and felt something tear in her back.

The bot stepped on Londi's stomach, pinning him down. It lowered a spinning blade toward the middle of his chest, seemingly going for accuracy over speed. He put both hands on the robot's foot, trying to free himself.

Dalrene yelled in desperation. The spinning blades came within inches.

Londi heaved, and the robot lost its balance.

He rolled to his side. The blade missed his chest and ripped through his shoulder.

Londi was screaming, but she couldn't hear him.

Blood flew up from the incision like a geyser, splattering the guardian with bright red. He pushed back against the bot's arms, but to no avail. A grinding sound pierced Dalrene's helmet. Was that Londi's bone being cut? It was going to cut his arm right off!

Something was sticking out from behind the bot. She squinted. An electrical cable? Unlike the bots inside the outpost, this bot seemed to be plugged directly into the electrical infrastructure.

Dalrene ran at the bot again, but this time she didn't jump on it. She pulled the thick electrical cable out of the bot's bottom, and as suddenly as it had started, it was over.

The blade stopped spinning.

Londi pushed the saw out of his shoulder and the robot fell on its side, collapsing to the ground. He clutched his shoulder.

Dalrene rushed to him and inspected his wound. A plastic resin covered the area where his skin was exposed and was hardening quickly. His suit was already healing itself. His comms didn't work, but she could see him laughing in relief through his visor.

She must've been wrong about his bone being cut. Londi looked like he was going to be okay. "You idiot," she said with a grin.

"Thank you," Londi mouthed back.

Dalrene wondered if he'd lost any oxygen in the attack. Had his line sprung a leak? She touched his tank and shrugged with her hands and shoulders.

He responded with his fingers, counting out the number seventy-five. Dalrene looked at her reading. She had about the same amount left. Okay. It was good he hadn't lost any, but they were going to be tight on time.

While Londi gathered himself, Dalrene followed the electrical cable from the bot back to the control console. It was a metal box covered in dust, situated in the middle of the arrays. There was a dashboard with a blinking screen, a victim of the years exposed to the elements. Useless.

Beside it was what looked like a cover to an electrical panel. She pulled at the handle, but it didn't budge.

"Shit."

She punched it. Still, nothing. A human fist wasn't the best tool. She needed something she could wedge in the open space and use it to pry open the panel.

Just over an hour of oxygen left now. They had to get moving.

Dalrene looked back at Londi sitting by the dead bot and got a mischievous idea. One that Janet would've loved.

The bots were modular. It made sense. Sensors and weapons failed all the time, and the Foreman needed to be able to interchange their parts quickly. Because of this, she bet that she could take the saw off the bot.

She approached the peacekeeper-guardian hybrid, whatever this bi-pedal abomination was, and had her hunch confirmed. The blades were held to the arm by nothing more than screws and adhesives that were well past expiry. Dalrene undid a few screws with her hand, and Londi caught on.

The saw came undone, and she held it up. The blade was a foot long and thin enough to fit in the slight crack of daylight the electrical panel cover let in. She just hoped it was sturdy enough to act as a wedge.

They didn't waste time getting back to the metal box. She inserted the blade into the crack and made a prying motion to Londi. He didn't need to be told twice.

He put his weight on the blade.

Dalrene held her breath.

The panel cover popped off and went flying. They'd done it!

She peered into the box and saw thirty or so switches at the back of it. Only human fingers would be nimble enough to turn them on or off. She flipped them each to the "Off" position in succession. With any luck, she'd be back in less than a day to turn them all back on.

The power was officially off. That was the signal. Down below, her army would now attack the processor nodes. If all went well, by the time she got back to the residential area, she could waltz right up to the brain node and pull the plug.

There was only fifty-five minutes of air left. Time to go. Dalrene took one last look out from the plateau. Beautiful blues, greens, and grays swirled in the sky as the sun set. She didn't know colors could do that. She didn't know Mars could be beautiful. She thought about Mickey. He never got the chance to stand out here and see the sunset.

He would've sung a song about it, she thought, chuckling to herself. And he would've been proud of what she accomplished. She turned the power off, and she was taking the fight to the Foreman. She was finishing what their daughter started.

Londi nudged her. Dalrene turned and looked way across the plateau, to the end of the solar panel array. Ten tall, slim figures were running at them, fast. More bots, and these ones weren't on a leash.

Chapter Thirty: Gordon

The impact craters never ended. The rover went up and down, from incline to decline, and back again. Gordon knew Mars's lack of atmosphere meant it was assaulted by asteroids and comets but seeing the evidence with his own two eyes was astounding. It looked as beaten as Phobos. Some of the craters were tens of kilometers long. At their deepest points, he couldn't see over their ridges. He was immersed in their little worlds until he breached their crest and came out to the sunshine on the other side. It made him smile every time. He'd always be in Dalrene's debt for showing him the surface.

And the rocks—oh, the rocks! He'd seen so many sedimentary structures he'd lost count. Every few minutes he saw something he wanted to pick up and bring back to master Tracey. He couldn't of course, but he'd tell Corrina and him everything. Once he made sure they were okay.

The sun was setting, and light hit the thin, wispy clouds and scattered rays of blue and pink across the horizon. It reminded him of Alex, who loved talking about weather and terraforming. Clouds, she told him, were uncommon, but not rare. They were so cold that they were made of frozen carbon dioxide, or dry ice. She loved them for reminding her of Earth. To Gordon, they made him feel more secure, like a roof over his head. On the other hand, driving into the sun was already blinding enough, and the haze made it harder to identify landmarks.

The dashboard of the rover said he'd driven for fourteen hours, covering three hundred and eighty kilometers. He stopped once, to pee, which was frustrating. The sole available waste bag was integrated with the environmental suit, so he wrestled his way into it while seated. He didn't like the pouch of warmness against his body, so he removed it, and now had a bag of piss riding in the passenger seat alongside Alex's gun. He hoped he wouldn't have to drink it, but he'd underestimated how long the trip to Olympus Mons was. The canteen he took from the *Walt's* mess hall was almost empty.

New Arcadia receded farther behind him with every minute, and so did Alex.

Sometimes, he wished she was in the passenger seat, and not just because she was better company than the waste bag. He was born on Mars, but she knew it better. She knew how much light was left in a day, how to not get lost, and how to make sure all the rover's life support systems were operating properly. More than that, she knew him. She knew how to guide him, how to keep him calm, and how to make him laugh.

He pulled over the rim of a crater to see a vast, flat sea of black rocks. The rover's virtual map told him that he was past the densest concentration of impact craters. He held his hand up to block the sun, getting a better look. It was the same for as far as he could see. Most rocks were small, and the rover could pass over them, but some were nearly the height of the vehicle's wheels. He was going to have to navigate the field manually, taking the rover off autopilot, and adding extra time to his journey.

The sun went down, but the rover had powerful headlights. Gordon trudged on, maneuvering around the larger boulders, and keeping his eye on the dashboard's map. The vehicle chewed over the smaller rocks, and it sounded like he was operating a blender, or a heavy-duty drill.

He forged his way another hundred and twenty kilometers before his tire popped. When it did, the rover's computer went haywire with alarms, jolting Gordon more awake than he'd been in hours. He hit the steering wheel with his fist and swore. He was so close to home!

He turned the rover's alarms off and closed his eyes. Origami wasn't an option with his suit on, so he imagined Alex listening to monk music and chuckled. Calm came over him. When he opened his eyes again, it was eerily quiet. There was no crunching of rocks or whine of the electric motor. There was only the wind, a breeze that seemed to be picking up.

A video popped up on the rover's dash. An animation directed him to replace the busted tire with one of the spares hitched to the exterior. Gordon got out of the rover and stood in the black night. The temperature had plummeted after the sun went down and it was chilly, even though the thermals in his suit were blasting at one hundred percent. His visor told him the temperature was negative fifty degrees Celsius.

There were, in fact, two extra tires fixed to the back of the vehicle. He unfastened one and it dropped to the ground. It was heavy. He rolled it to the front, driver-side wheel and realized he didn't know what to do next. Back inside the rover, he watched the instructional video again. Gordon took the jack out of the toolbox in the emergency hatch as directed and placed it underneath the body of the vehicle. The handle was metal nested inside itself that expanded to be taller than him. He pulled down on it, trying to pump the jack up. Nothing happened. The handle didn't move, and neither did the rover.

Was he doing something wrong? The jack was supposed to lift the vehicle up, so the wheel would be off the ground. Instead, it just sat there. He walked around, surveying the situation, and gathered his thoughts. The rover felt like a giant beast he was going to have to tame.

Back at the jack, he jumped and put his entire weight on the handle. For a moment, he hung, supported by the jack. Then, the handle slid slowly down, and the leveling arm of the jack started to move up. He cheered to himself, then landed on the ground. The rover barely moved. He'd need to pump the jack dozens of more times to elevate the tire.

And so, he jumped again, raising the rover a fraction of an inch. It took what felt like hours, and by the time the tire was in the air, he was drenched in sweat. He desperately wanted to wipe his forehead but couldn't until he re-pressurized the rover and took off his suit. Exhausted, he kneeled and put his head between his hands until his breathing slowed.

The next step was to take the lug nuts off the tire. There was an electric crank that looked like a hand-drill in the toolbox. He kneeled by the side of the rover and put it over one of the four lug nuts. He pulled the trigger, and the crank moved. It had power. But then, it stopped. He pulled the crank away, but the lug nut didn't fall out like the rover's video showed. He put his glove on it and tried to pull it off. Nothing. His crank had tightened the nut instead of loosening it!

He examined the electric crank. There didn't seem to be any buttons. There had to be a way to switch it from clockwise to counterclockwise. But he couldn't find it! He adjusted his suits headlamp, hoping more light could help him find the right setting. There didn't seem to be any buttons or switches apart from the trigger.

Gordon slumped down against the rover.

Alex would've known how to work the crank. She would've known how to change a tire. She knew everything. Even if she didn't agree with him or understand why he needed to go to Olympus Mons, she knew him. And he missed her, so, so much.

Wind whipped against the vehicle, and Gordon flinched. What had been a breeze only thirty minutes ago was no longer gentle. He'd never heard anything quite like it. Sand swirled in the air, almost like the videos of tornadoes he'd watched aboard the *Zoya*. Was this what his textbooks had called a dust storm? It had to be, although it didn't change much. He still had to get to the outpost as soon as possible.

He sat in the dark, consumed by wind and dust, and thought of Dalrene and Mickey. Every minute mattered to them. All the knowledge he had, not to mention his gun, would be invaluable. He could help them overthrow the Foreman. They were right all along. They needed to fight, and he could help.

The sweat cooled on his face. He'd been out of the rover for hours, fighting against his own body and tools. Muscles he didn't know he had hurt in ways he didn't know possible. He had a few days of air left, but only a few litres of water. He'd barely made any progress with the tire, and the first few rays of sun were peeking over the horizon. Sleep wasn't an option, unless he wanted to die.

He stood and investigated the crank again but didn't find any new buttons. He felt so stupid! He would've been able to operate a tool like this in the outpost. This was just another reminder that he was an alien in Alex's world. He couldn't even work their most basic equipment!

A playful idea came to Gordon's mind. It was something his mom would've liked. Why did he need a new tire at all? Surely the rover could go the remaining few hours on a flat. It wouldn't be fun, or ideal, but could it work?

With newfound energy, he lowered the vehicle to the ground and tossed the jack in the back. He got in the driver's seat and turned the vehicle on.

The same alarm blasted his ears. The screen simply said:

Replace tire.

A picture of the car indicated which tire it was. Great. Helpful. Gordon put his hand over the pocket where he had his pendant. It was still there. He had to have patience. He had to analyze everything at his disposal. He had time. He just had to clear his mind and think.

He tried to shift the vehicle's transmission into drive. It wouldn't budge. He jammed at the touchscreen, but nothing happened. Not a single button in the vehicle seemed to do much of anything. He slapped the dashboard in frustration and willed the rover to move forward. A message appeared:

"Replace tire. Override diagnostic?"

Yes! Gordon pushed the override button in relief. At the outpost, you did what the Foreman told you to do. Here, he was in charge. It was bizarre. It was uncomfortable. It was also freeing, and he was so thankful for that. But the rover didn't let him put it in gear yet.

"Low visibility. Dangerous driving conditions detected. Override warning?"

The wind howled, and Gordon couldn't see more than two meters in front of the rover. But he had to keep going. Dust storms could last for days, weeks, or even months. He didn't have enough water to wait it out. He overrode the warning and lurched the rover forward, into the darkness.

The flat tire thumped over the rocky ground. Its unyielding consistency reminded

Gordon of the waves hitting the beach in Alex's video of Lake Michigan. Combined with the raging winds, it was ferociously loud in the rover. There was no chance he'd fall asleep.

Dust encircled the rover, swirling around him and battering the windows. The windshield seemed solid; he didn't think it was at risk of cracking unless the storm managed to throw a boulder at him. Gordon kept his environmental suit on, even though the cabin was pressurized, just in case. He gripped the steering wheel with both hands.

But after a while, he relaxed. The dust storm made it feel like he was in an enclosed space, and the vastness of the sky was no longer hanging over him. It was comfortable, and his stress eased with every inch he drew closer to the outpost. He proceeded cautiously, navigating with the rover's map. It felt so good to see his dot moving again. There were sixty-five kilometers left to Olympus Mons. To home. If the sand and dust swirls weren't obstructing his view he might've been able to see the mountain.

He wondered what Alex was doing, and how she was coping with the way he left. Guilt bubbled up inside him. He knew he hadn't done right by her. He swore to himself that he'd make it up to her one day, no matter what.

First, he had to get back to the First Olympians. He hadn't left Corrina in the right way either. Had she ever gotten out of that interrogation room? If Dalrene hadn't overthrown the Foreman, Corrina's prospects of a good job were no doubt ruined. Would she forgive him for that? He missed her laugh and the way they could talk about anything together. Not the same way he missed Alex, but—

The pit of Gordon's stomach dropped, and he realized he must've entered the downward slope of a crater with way too much speed. *No!* He slammed the brakes. Not fast enough.

There was no warning. The rover came to an abrupt stop and his chest slammed into the steering wheel, knocking the wind out of him. It was like when the *Zoya* lifted off, except with more impact. His helmet pinged the dashboard, and he yelped, more in shock than pain. The rover's alarm returned with a vengeance, harsher than it'd been for the flat tire. He had crashed.

Crap, he had crashed.

He eased himself up. His neck was tweaked, but other than that he was physically okay. Luckily, his *Walt* issued helmet and suit were sturdy, and they protected him from any worse injuries.

He confirmed the integrity of his air supply and fought the wind to open the door. The rover was angled sharply downward on the crater slope, its front slammed against a boulder. What had been its remaining good front tire was now mangled beyond repair, crunched inward on its axle.

There was no fixing it.

Gordon kicked the rover. He was so stupid! He'd missed the crater on the map because he'd been thinking about Alex and Corrina. Now he was far from help, with limited water and air, and all alone.

Dust bombarded him, so he climbed back into the driver's seat. He hated how relentless and abusive the storm was. The inside of the rover was now littered with sand. He never should've left the *Walt*. What he wouldn't give for just another night of quiet peace alone with Alex.

Dejected and frustrated, he realized he was only forty kilometers away from Olympus Mons. It wasn't *that* far. Farther than he'd ever walked in his life, sure, but he'd done a lot of things for the first time lately. Forty kilometers wouldn't be fun, but it was feasible.

Gordon poured the last of the *Walt's* water canteen into his suit's hydration pouch. Reluctantly, he re-inserted the waste bag into the suit. In the worst case, he could recycle his fluids. He didn't hesitate. All that mattered was getting to Olympus Mons and freeing his people. He studied the map, then took the gun and left the rover.

It was calm and eerie in the crater. The storm was lesser at these depths or else was letting up. He didn't know which. Fatigue was in his bones, but a newfound adrenaline powered him up the rim. It felt good to make progress with his own two feet.

Emerging over the lip, the sun warmed his face. It broke through the dust and melted his frown. He'd never been so involuntarily happy before. Beauty on Mars never got old.

The storm really was dying down, at least for now. The field of rocks in front of him looked the same as any other, patches of black scattered throughout the red sand. Except, in the distance, a monster lurked. In the mid-morning light, he could see it. Olympus Mons stretched high into the sky and imposed itself on the horizon.

Gordon's heart raced. He was almost there! It was close—closer than he could've guessed—the forty kilometers wasn't impossible. He hadn't seen it during the storm, but now it stood unmistakably in front of his own eyes. Home.

Tears threatened to flow, but he fought them back. Gordon looked up at the staggering figure in front of him.

He started to walk.

Chapter Thirty-One: Alex

"You gave away my ship?" Alex paced around her dumpy hotel room. She'd give up the *Zoya* if she had to, but did she have to?

"Look, do you want this or not?" Her mom's response arrived a few minutes later.

"Yes," Alex said out loud, before she even starting a transmission. That was the immediate reaction in her gut, and she knew it was the right one. She'd do whatever was necessary to free Gordon's people and to see him again.

Her mom's message continued. "It's literally rocket science. It'll take ten years to reverse-engineer. Longer for the Republic or the Collective, whoever buys it from him, to build and scale. It might accelerate their timelines, but not by much."

She looked dead serious. Alex didn't know she was this interested in militaries and politics. She thought her mom focused on ballet and racing.

"You really think he'd sell out the tech if we gave him the full rights? And that would start a war?"

"I don't know," her mom sighed. "I don't know anything anymore sweetie. I thought I could trust your dad until recently but look where that got us. This is the biggest military advance since drones, maybe even since nukes, and we're years ahead of everybody else. We can't give away the tech. By selling the prototype rather than the rights, we'll only be modifying the world's balance of power, not flipping it on its head. I can live with that."

Alex tried to avoid politics. She knew The West, led by America, The People's Republic, led by China, and the Collective, led by India and Indonesia, were the great powers. Some countries, like Russia and Turkey, had been absorbed by their bloc's leaders. Others, like Nigeria and the Philippines, were so closely aligned with one of them that their independence was a distinction without a difference. The West was the richest of the three, and its name the most confusing, because it included countries around the world, but that was the extent of her knowledge.

Her mom's message continued. "Look, you need to get to First Corp. Bernie gave us twenty-four hours, which is fine. We don't want to give him time to change his mind anyways, and we can call Lisa on the way."

Her mom took a deep breath then kept talking. "Your dad told me he offered to meet you in person. Take him up on that and we'll surprise him with a quorum." She closed her eyes. "I can tell he still loves you, believe it or not. I can't imagine how you'll feel seeing him. I know I couldn't do it right now. But I believe in you." Her mom put one hand over her heart and blew a kiss with the other.

Alex's stomach squirmed. Her dad was an enigma, a black hole in her mind. This new version of him was an unknown. A *terrifying* unknown. Would he hurt her? In what ways? Would she even have the strength to look him in the eyes?

"Thanks mom. I'll figure it out." Alex swallowed hard. She was going to have a lot to work through in therapy after this was over.

#

The fastest way to First Corp. was with a plane. She'd flown plenty of aircraft on Earth, so flying on Mars wouldn't be difficult. It wouldn't be as fun as the *Zoya*, but then again, nothing was. And this wasn't a joy ride. She was going to have to focus to bait her dad into a Board of Directors meeting.

Alex checked out of the room without having spent the night. She walked with her head held high, more at ease than when she'd arrived. Her mom was helping her, and she was truly grateful for that. She made a note to tell her that next time they spoke.

On the way out of the lobby, a young woman wearing sunglasses put her hand on Alex's shoulder.

"Oh my god, you're her!" She covered her mouth.

"Huh?"

"Is he with you?" She spoke a mile a minute. "All the feeds are talking about you two. You're such a great couple. The sexiest criminal couple of the century!"

"What? I... No, Gordon isn't here," she held up her hand as the woman snapped pictures with her handheld.

"Get away from me," Alex said, storming out of the hotel. Was her relationship really everyone's business now? How dare people intrude on her like that. She didn't need anyone to remind her of how Gordon broke her heart.

More and more people took photos of her as she walked. They didn't even try to hide it. Alex pulled her hood tighter over her head and did her best to ignore them. She quelled the urge to unleash her kickboxing talents on some of her particularly pushy new fans, but just barely. One even asked if he could take a picture with her.

By the time she got to the flight desk, she was ready to leave New Arcadia and never return. A thin-faced man wore suspenders and stood at a small plastic counter. Behind him, through the glass, was a tarmac of pressed dirt. A dozen planes of varying sizes sat on it, patiently waiting for someone to rent them.

"I'll take an ultralight. One-seater if you have it, class D," Alex said, pulling out her handheld to make payment.

"Miss." The man pushed his glasses up and peered at her. "I take it you haven't seen the radar? Dust storm coming in. And the class D planes require a special license to fly."

"Like hell they do. This is Mars, there are no license regulations." She narrowed her brows. She had to get to her dad as soon as possible, dust storm or not.

He offered a half-shrug and turned his back.

"How's this then," Alex said, scrolling through her handheld. "Special designation S, short-hop racing."

The man slowly turned around again and re-adjusted his glasses once more, this time taking a detailed look at her license. "Fine. Let me call the owner," he said in an exasperated sigh.

Alex looked out the window. She'd never flown a plane on Mars, but she knew the low atmospheric pressure of the planet did not give engineers much to work with. On the other hand, the high concentration of carbon dioxide in the environment enabled easier flight, because it was denser than air, giving each square meter of wing more lift power than on Earth. The low gravity also helped, allowing flight with less lift. The result was small, light planes, with short wingspans and plenty of power and maneuverability.

The Class D was the smallest, lightest of all. The "D" stood for Delta, which meant triangular wings. They were known for being extremely sensitive to wind fluctuations, experiencing tons of turbulence, and having the record for most deaths on the planet. They were also the only class small enough to land on the roof of First. Corp headquarters and nimble enough to take-off from it.

The man put his handheld down and smiled apologetically at Alex. "Miss, I'm sorry to inform you but the insurance rates for the Class D rentals have increased significantly. Especially for young, inexperienced flyers. They're four-hundred-thousand credits per day to insure."

"That's no problem," Alex said, holding her handheld out again."

"I, uh—we cannot take payments that large on short-notice. He laughed and shook his head. "If you really want to rent this plane, I can give you the proper paperwork to fill out, and we can schedule a test-flight for later this week. Perhaps one day when there's no potential dust storm. They're saying it could be serious."

Alex stomped down on the man's shoe. He squealed, but she leaned over the counter and covered his mouth. A few people looked over, but she didn't care. She had work to do. Bernard had given her twenty-four hours. Neither paparazzi, dust storms, or this annoying salesman were going to stop her.

"I'm going to give you *eight-hundred thousand* credits to fuck off and rent me this plane. Do you understand?"

\#

The environmental suit was nowhere near as comfortable as First Corp.'s, but it would do. As soon as the plane's cabin was pressurized, she took her helmet off and tossed it under her seat. It was a good thing she didn't have more stuff, because none of it would've fit in the tiny cockpit.

The D-14 ultralight rumbled over the dirt landing strip as Alex gripped the yoke and pushed the throttle forward. Every little dip in the ground felt like a huge crater. There was a lot more feedback on the ground than in air or space, and Alex's teeth chattered. She wasn't used to that.

It felt like she was going too slow to achieve lift-off, but she did, and she cheered to herself as the plane detached from the ground. She didn't know why she was cheering. No-one could hear her, and of course she'd done it. She was a great pilot.

The downside to the low atmospheric pressure was that it took longer to climb. She looked down at New Arcadia with relief as it got smaller and smaller. It was just a few extremely large buildings in the middle of nowhere, surrounded by hills and craters multiplying outward in succession forever and ever. She was happy to see it go. In fact, she was starting to think she'd seen enough dusty red hills and oversized, cracked impact craters for one life.

She pointed the plane toward First Corp. headquarters and engaged the autopilot. She wanted to catch her dad by surprise by not announcing her visit in advance. It was the only element of negotiation she had left. If they could depose him, then maybe she could save Gordon from walking into the lion's den at Olympus Mons.

The plane's radar was tracking the storm, and it looked she was going to hit it in less then twenty minutes. The dust itself wouldn't be a problem. The plane was electric, so there was no engine to clog, and the flight instruments would operate in any condition. The risk was the violent winds. Alex set a high target altitude. She figured if she could get high enough, she could skate overtop the bad weather.

She played monk music through the plane's speakers and closed her eyes. The plane was flying itself now, and she basked in the familiar rhythmic chanting. Being alone in a tiny, enclosed space was somehow exactly what she needed.

Her handheld interrupted her meditation, its chime jolting her back to reality. It was a call from her mom. She answered it, routing the video through the plane's dashboard.

"Hey Mom. I'm flying, on my way to headquarters."

"Good. Time to talk to Lisa. She's on Mars, so you two will be in real-time. But I wanted to check in on you first. The socials are saying some nasty stuff."

"Like what?" Alex felt a bitter taste in the back of her throat.

"They say the world's favorite 'criminal' couple has broken up, and that you were photographed alone. I don't know why they assumed you two were dating. Is it true? And is Gordon not with you?" Her mom's voice was tentative and caring.

Her eyes burned. The weight of Gordon leaving and all the people taking pictures and mocking her was too much. Her morning gruel threatened to come up. She tried to say something but gagged.

"Alex?"

"Yeah."

"Are you crying?"

"No ... Yes!" She started sobbing, the tears flowing doing her face faster than she could wipe them away.

"Oh honey, I'm sorry! I didn't mean to—"

"He left me mom! I was trying to help him, and he left me."

There was silence on the line as she waited for the next message from her mom to travel through space. Through her tears, Alex could see that the aircraft was still gaining altitude.

"I'm sorry, Alex. I wish I could be there for you. I wish I could hold you and hug you."

"Yeah. Me too." There was nothing more Alex wanted in that moment than to be home with her mom.

"Try not to think about the feeds or Gordon right now. We have to focus."

"I'll do my best. I love you mom."

A notification popped up on the dashboard. The dust storm was getting closer.

"Okay, Lisa is joining the call."

Alex had known Lisa for years. She was friends with both of her parents, and always made it to Christmas dinner. Her high heels and buoyant curls were always the first to appear with flowers the moment anyone got married or died. Alex liked her well enough, although they didn't have much in common. Lisa had made a successful career in Human Resources, first for the United Nations, and then for First Corp. If law made her fall asleep, HR made her want to claw her eyes out with a rusty spoon.

"Alex, hi!" Lisa's thick-framed glasses and too-big smile that didn't extend to her eyes appeared on the screen. "It's great to see you. Too bad we couldn't do this in person."

"Hi." Alex tried to force a pleasant tone.

"Your mom filled me in. Taking down your father is a risky move." Lisa raised her eyebrows, but her smile stayed intact.

"Only move I've got."

"Of course. And it was so horrible to hear about your friend Gordon, and what his people have been through. Just breaks my heart. You know that I'm an adviser to the UN's Humanitarian Affairs Office, right? When I wasn't much older than you, I actually worked for a legal non-profit organization whose mission was ..."

Lisa kept talking and Alex tuned her out, her skin crawling in disgust. She'd become better at seeing through the veneer of political bullshit. It was obvious why Lisa and her dad were such good friends. They were so similar.

Thankfully, her mom spoke next. "Are you kidding me, Lisa! Don't tell me about your 'good person accolades'. You were Rafa's right hand in castrating the UN's response to this whole thing!"

"We did what was best for the shareholders." Lisa spoke low and serious. "That was our obligation. But if I was in charge, it would've been handled differently. From the start."

"You want to be CEO?" Alex choked on her tongue. No-one other than family had been CEO of First Corp. Ever.

"Yes. I think I'm uniquely qualified to lead this company out of the dark ages and into a kinder, modern future. The press will love it, and I think the stock market will too."

"We're expanding the Board," Alex said. "We're going from five members to seven. We'll let you choose the new members."

It looked like Lisa was working hard not to roll her eyes. "What's next, you're going to offer me seats to the White Sox? Honey, I own the White Sox."

Lisa's condescension roiled Alex and she fought the urge to hang up. And the White Sox? Ugh, Americans. Alex never understood the appeal of baseball. What else could she offer? She thought about creating a unique share class for Lisa and granting a special dividend—cash. No, that wouldn't work. People like her didn't want money. They wanted power.

She could see a grey cloud swirling in front of her. The storm was approaching, and she hadn't reached her target altitude yet. That was okay. She was the best pilot she knew, and if it was anything like emergency maneuvers in space, maybe it'd be fun. All that mattered was getting to First Corp. on time.

"You can have my ballet club," her mom said. "Number three in the world. Or my short-hop team, whichever you'd prefer."

Her mom was on the right track. These were offers of prestige. She could see the gears in Lisa's head turning.

A second later, Alex screamed as her D-14 flipped belly-up.

The connection dropped. "Dangerous turbulence identified. Manual flight required."

"Oh my god!"

She fought the yoke, trying to pull the plane right-side up again. She looked out of the windshield and her head spun. The ground was up, and the sky was down. The wind jerked the plane back and forth more violently than Alex could hope to control. The fabric of her seatbelt cut against her skin. It was the only thing holding her in her seat as the D-14 rocked back and forth in the sky.

And then she couldn't see anything. The storm enveloped her. The dust was gray, but it blocked out the sun, making everything dark. It swirled around the plane, consuming it. It felt like she was inside the belly of a beast, like the old stories about fishermen swallowed by whales.

She couldn't see anything, let alone the ground, but the attitude indicator told her the D-14's nose was pointed at the ground, and her heart raced. Space was empty, and there was nothing to crash into. Here, she was one misread away from catastrophe. Her airspeed and heading instruments were going crazy; she was at the mercy of the winds.

If she died, she was going to miss Gordon so much. He would never know what happened to her. And neither would her mom. She thought about what he would do in this situation. The goofball would've already pulled out his folding papers and started making origami.

Alex took a deep breath and looked at the readings on the dashboard. She had twelve-hundred meters of elevation and was falling fast. The dust was only getting thicker as she got closer to the ground, and the plane was plummeting through the soupy air. But the wind speed had gone down a few clicks. She had one chance to pull out of her dive.

When the altimeter hit three-hundred meters, the alarms went berserk. She pulled the yoke back with all her might. She screamed at the top of her lungs, letting everything out, willing the plane to pull up.

She heaved and heaved.

Then, the skies were clear. Relatively.

Even better, the sky was above the ground instead of under it. "Yes!" Alex pumped her fist in relief.

But what she saw out of the windshield put her heart back in her throat. Right in front of her flight path, just a few kilometers away, stood the hulking ancient volcano of Olympus Mons. Beyond it, coming from the direction of First Corp, a convoy of vehicles rolled toward the mine. There were half a dozen, and they were big, bigger than any she travelled in before. She didn't know who or what her dad was sending, but it wouldn't be good.

She had to help Gordon. She didn't care if he ran away from her! He loved her back, and she knew it. He just had a hard time expressing it, and they disagreed about how to defeat First Corp. If he wanted to take the fight directly to the Foreman, then she'd be at his side. Who was she to say that it was a stupider plan than going directly to their enemy's headquarters?

She gulped but didn't hesitate. She'd deal with her dad. But first she had to help Gordon.

Chapter Thirty-Two: Gordon

He walked for the full day, rarely stopping in fear he wouldn't be able to start moving again if he did. His body ached, but his mind was set. He was going to make it to the mountain and find his way in. He drank his last bit of water hours ago, and the sun was starting to move behind Olympus Mons.

There was no sound except his own breath. The volcanic rock had only become more common, filling up more of the desert ground. But his boots were much quieter than the rover's wheels. There were no smells either. It occurred to him that he hadn't smelled anything in what seemed like days, and he wondered when he might again. Existence on the surface was harsh and dead.

When he finally reached the escarpment, he paused to take a break. Looking up at the cliff left him with a feeling of helplessness. How could anything be so huge? If the mountain was that big, how big was First Corp? But he soldiered on, determined to see his mission through. His mom would've wanted him to.

Olympus Mons had two sides, one with more precipitous angles than the other, and he was lucky to have approached it from the steep side where the entrance to the outpost was. The scale of it made him feel tiny and insignificant. It made all his problems, his whole world, feel that way, but he knew that wasn't true. There were real people under that mountain, and they mattered.

The problem was that the cliff face leading up to the plateau was indistinguishable for kilometers. Finding the tiny entrance to the cave where he left Mickey would be difficult. And if he did find it, what if his blast had caved it in? Did the airlock even open from the outside? He kicked himself for asking questions he should've thought of before he left the *Walt* in a temper tantrum. In the shadow of the towering volcano, his plans seemed less solid, and he picked up his walking pace to cover more ground.

A macabre thought returned to his mind. The last time he was at Olympus Mons, he blew up a convoy of trucks. He murdered four people, their bodies torn into pieces. He'd know he was at the entrance to the caves when he saw the aftermath of the explosion.

There would be vehicle and human parts. Blood and guts. It would be unmistakable. He gulped hard. He'd come to peace with what he'd done but seeing the carnage in person would be another reckoning. He wanted to fight more, to kill the Foreman. He really did. Hopefully his remaining queasiness would resolve itself once the action started.

Nothing moved on Mars, so when he saw a figure scurrying down the escarpment, he knew something was happening. He didn't know if it was a friend or an enemy. It could've been one of the Foreman's robots for all he knew. But he gripped the gun tightly in his right hand and ran toward the movement.

It tumbled down the least steep part of the cliff, scraping its arms along the wall to slow its fall. For a minute, Gordon didn't feel his fatigue. He just ran as fast as he could. Something in his brain clicked and he recognized the suit the figure was wearing. It was black and old, like the one Dalrene gave him.

He shouted in glee. His voice cracked, raspy from dehydration and lack of use. His heart swelled with an unfamiliar feeling, perhaps pride or relief from being one step closer to salvation. It had to be one of the First Olympians! It was his people! He waved as he ran and tried to get the person's attention.

If the figure noticed him, they didn't respond in any way. They were scrambling down the side of the cliff, and Gordon was forty meters away, poised to meet them at the bottom. They got closer and a second identical environmental suit appeared at the top. They bounded over the escarpment's edge, crashing harder and faster than the first person. Behind them, a sight emerged that stopped Gordon in his tracks.

A horde of robots, at least eight or ten of them, jumped off the cliff in hot pursuit of the two humans. They had feet! Long feet that kept them upright as they descended the escarpment. Gordon had never seen anything like it.

"Don't stop running now!" A voice came into his ear.

"Dalrene! What? How?"

"Run you idiot!"

He did what he was told, happy she had found his radio frequency. He caught up to Dalrene, who was now on level ground. Gordon was faster than both her and the person who hadn't identified themselves, who, judging by the way their muscles were practically bursting out of their suit, he took to be Londi.

"What the hell are those bots?" Gordon looked behind him. Londi and the robots were also down the escarpment and gaining on them fast.

"We're not going to make it," Dalrene said, gesturing ahead.

Gordon didn't see where they were trying to make it to. The landscape all looked the same to him, and he didn't see the loading dock area at all.

"Get ready to fight!" Dalrene yelled.

They stopped and turned to face the bots. Gordon hid behind a rock and readied his gun. Londi was still running toward them, and his eyes bulged out of their sockets. The bot at the front of the pack had a long, chainsaw-looking blade on its arms and was reaching toward him.

His mind raced. The last time he fought, things went horribly wrong. Images of stray limbs and squirting blood flashed before his eyes. The guilt and pain of those moments after the loading dock explosion came rushing back. He'd failed to make his mom's death meaningful and hurt people in the process. But this was different. This was self-defence, and it was against the Foreman. These were bots, not people.

Gordon peeked out from cover, aimed his pistol with two hands like Alex taught him, and turned the safety off. He readied his stance, putting his feet shoulder width-apart. He steadied his breath, like he did when he folded origami.

He closed his eyes, then opened one, aiming his gun.

Londi dove to the ground, giving Gordon clear sight to the bot behind him.

It raised its blade.

Gordon fired.

The gun jolted his upper body. Alex told him it would kick, but he didn't know how much until that moment. He careened back and managed not to fall.

The explosive round hit the bot in its midsection, booming it backwards and setting off fireworks. A burst of yellow, orange, and red plumed into the air along with a thick cloud of smoke.

Gordon jumped back to his feet and looked to Dalrene at his side. She was saying something. Yelling, probably swearing. But he couldn't hear a single word. His ears rung, like Alex said they would. But more than that, they hurt, like someone had punched him in the side of the head. He wanted to cover them and fall to the ground.

Instead, he looked forward. The bot he shot lay ten meters back, barely recognizable. Scraps of its plastic and metal were still flying in the air and scattering across the ground. Its feet were intact, hanging to the bot by a wire, and it tried to take one final step forward before falling over.

"Shoot them!" Dalrene's voice pierced the ringing in his ears.

Gordon swore under his breath. Ten bots were running toward them in their weird, unnatural gait, the closest only twenty-five meters away. Londi and Dalrene stood behind Gordon and he raised his gun again. He shot, missing once. A little bit of distance made it much harder to aim accurately, but he couldn't let them get too close.

"Get cover!"

When Gordon didn't react, Dalrene pulled him behind a boulder.

Bullets sprayed past them.

Some of these robots had guns! Gordon couldn't believe it. He'd never seen bots with feet before, never mind weapons like this!

He stood and aimed again. He had a dozen shots left in the chamber, and ten bots left to shoot. He steadied himself and shot methodically, picking off the closest robot. It erupted into pieces, limbs covering the rocky ground. The next robot stumbled over the pieces and fell.

Gordon focused on another group of robots, setting up his shot like he might plan the perfect origami crease, and fired. The blast was so large that it killed one and hobbled two more. The resulting cloud of smoke was even bigger than he'd expected for a detonation of this size.

One by one, he picked off the remaining bots as Dalrene cheered him on. The ground became an electronic graveyard, full of metal and plastic scraps as Gordon tore apart the Foreman's most dangerous weapons. He was going to run out of explosives rounds soon, though. If more bots came, he'd have to switch to regular.

It felt great! The power of an explosive device had always inspired awe in him, and he revered their potential for causing destruction.

"Put your hands up!" A voice screeched over his helmet's comms.

Gordon turned to see a dozen soldiers in black armour standing behind heavy-duty trucks. The barrels of their guns poked out from behind cover. They were the same trucks and the same suits that had been at the loading dock on that fateful day when he became a killer. The same people he blew up. The people that took orders from Alex's dad and turned the outpost into a prison.

"What? Who?" Dalrene's voice was right in his ear, yet she sounded distant, like she was underwater or talking her in sleep.

"The Foreman works for them," Gordon said, aiming his gun in their direction.

"Then... shoot them!" Dalrene had been incredulous, like she hadn't believed her eyes, but now she had found her exasperation.

He put his finger on the trigger and paused. He thought of his mom, and how proud she was of him. He thought of Alex, and how she forgave him for the explosion, and how much that meant to him when he struggled with his guilt. He thought about Mickey, and the nightmares.

"Drop the weapon!" one of them yelled. Gordon wasn't sure if they were speaking on the same comms channel he'd used with Dalrene, or if they'd somehow opened a private one.

There were a lot of targets, and Gordon didn't have enough rounds in the chamber for all of them. Regardless, he couldn't shoot. Killing robots was one thing, but he couldn't willingly repeat the grotesque suffering of the loading dock explosion. And there was the fact that they could return fire. This was where it ended.

Alex's dad had won. He fell to his knees and the soldiers rushed toward him. They pushed him to the ground and shoved a knee in his back. Gordon wretched in pain.

Neither Dalrene or Londi followed his lead, and he felt a tinge of embarrassment. But Gordon was exhausted, and neither of them knew what he knew about First Corp. They'd have to find out Alex's dad's power the hard way. Thankfully, although the soldiers had guns, they seemed hesitant to use them.

Londi was quick to dispatch a soldier than charged him. He ducked the jab and tackled his assailant's legs, sending him twirling head-over-heels and slamming the ground. That drew the attention of the other men, and the next attacker took a more cautious approach. He threw punches like Alex did when kickboxing, but Londi could play that game too. He dodged each fist until finding an opportunity to land a kick in the soldier's midsection that sent him flying back.

Gordon wondered if they enjoyed trying to take Londi one on one. He'd never understand the competitive aspect of violence. But the First Corp. mercenaries eventually learned, and a pack of them poked Londi from different directions, waiting for him to make a mistake. He must've, because his legs were swept out from under him, and he finally went down.

"Who are you?" One of the armoured men barked at Dalrene.

"What the fuck is your problem? Get your hands off me!" She'd evaded the soldiers while the attention had been on Londi, but now it was focused on her.

Gordon twisted his head to the other side to see her giving a soldier a hard time. She punched one in the helmet with her glove. It sounded like it hurt her hand more than it hurt the soldier, but he didn't appreciate the gesture and shoved her in response. Another soldier grabbed her arms from behind, restraining her.

"You maniacs! You betrayed us. You betrayed your own kind!" Dalrene shook her head wildly back and forth. She kicked one soldier between the legs and broke free of the other's grasp. He collapsed, holding his groin, and she ran away, screaming about her daughter and the evils of dustlickers that conspire with the Foreman.

Gordon grimaced and accepted his fate. He had failed, and now the soldiers were going to take him back to the glass box. And this time, Alex wouldn't be able to break him free.

The soldiers encircled Dalrene.

"I'll fight the whole lot of you! Put your fists up!" Dalrene was still yelling. She had her hands up like she was ready to box.

One man tried to grab her, but she dipped through his legs and ran behind one of the trucks. The soldier faked one way, and then the other, but she was too smart for that. She dodged another one that had tried to sneak up from her rear, then weaved between vehicles. It would've been comical if the stakes hadn't been so high.

"Permission to use lethal force?" a soldier asked over the open comms.

Gordon gulped. "Dalrene. We lost." The battle was over. She just didn't know it yet. Their only hope was Alex saving them in a few years via the United Nations, and she couldn't do that if these soldiers killed them. It didn't feel good. His adrenaline was gone, and all that remained was exhaustion and an imagined look of disappointment on his mom's face. It was too late, and Dalrene needed to recognize that.

"Let them go!"

He was imagining things now. He swore he heard Alex's voice. It was dreamlike and hazy, but it sounded like her. The lack of sleep and water must've been getting to his brain. The knee in the back didn't help either.

In that moment, he would've done anything to hear her voice or see her smile again.

"I said, let them go! Do you know who I am?"

Gordon turned his head to the side, the knee still on his back.

Something grazed the space above them. A plane! It was barely thirty meters overhead. He could hear the woosh through his helmet. A tingle went down his spine. Was he hallucinating?

It turned sharply, circling back toward them. The sunlight reflected off its white, V-shaped body. Everyone else was looking at it, too. It was real. It was Alex!

"I'll go see him right now. I'll fly there immediately. But only if you let them go," Alex said, her voice cackling over the comms. She sounded fierce, like her lawyer voice, but angrier.

"I can't do that. Still have to take them in," the soldier said.

"Tell him that's my offer. No negotiation."

The plane cut just over top of their heads again. It wasn't large, but it's speed and closeness gave Gordon a sense of awe that reminded him of flying in the *Zoya*. Except instead of the surrealism of watching slowly moving planets through scopes, he was watching the plane whiz by with his own two eyes.

The soldier swore and turned back to the truck. He put his hand to his helmet and walked around the vehicle, taking his time.

Londi and Gordon were still pinned, and they rolled around the best they could, trying to see the plane.

The other soldiers stood silently, some keeping their eyes on their captives and others staring into the distance. The sun was nearly set.

"I'm sorry Gordon! I had to," Alex said.

"I'm sorry. I ... Thank you," Gordon said. He wanted to see her, to embrace her, but she was still in the air. He wanted to talk to her privately but didn't know what he'd say. She came to help him. Despite the way he'd left, she came. The mixture of gratitude and shame left him tongue-tied.

"Okay," the soldier said, walking back from the trucks. "We have an agreement. But you come with us."

"No way. I'm going by my own free will. And I'll get there faster than you anyways," Alex said.

More grumbles from the soldiers. More stern words from Alex. More close-up views of the ground for Gordon.

Eventually, they let Gordon stand up freely and he drew a big breath of relief.

The trucks started their engines and the soldiers loaded in.

Alex's plane gained altitude sharply. "I'll be back," she said. It curved around Olympus Mons, out of sight.

"I miss you," Gordon said, immediately feeling foolish. He never should've left her in the first place, and now he had to make things right.

Chapter Thirty-Three: Dalrene

They moved efficiently through the deep. It felt like she'd been running for hours, but Dalrene didn't dare stop. They were nearly at the residential level and the air smelled stale, like the bottom of a mine shaft. Most of the recyclers would be operating at a reduced, power-saving rate. A few didn't have batteries at all would be out of commission.

It was official. The Foreman would run out of electricity, and people would run out of oxygen, unless someone turned the solar panel arrays back on. Dalrene thought back to the stolen schematics saved on her computer. If they were accurate, large portions of infrastructure would be rendered useless in as little as three or four hours. Immediately, the Foreman would be forced to prioritize energy between bot charging stations, processing nodes, and its outpost-wide surveillance system. The ration tables had turned.

Gordon was saying something. Gordon was saying something! He was alive! What a relief. She'd written him off for dead, but he returned and saved them from the black suits on the surface. She should've been overjoyed to see him, but it made her think of Janet more than anything else. Guilt battled with thoughts of her next tactical moves, crowding out his words. Her mind was a jumbled mess. It was like when Ionne knifed her, she could tell she was in shock but couldn't shake it.

The three of them spilled into a street, popping out beside a clothing center that distributed uniform rations. The streetlights were low and red, running on back-ups. Glass was strewn across the ground, and she wondered if it had been shattered by the blaring sirens. It was chaos, exactly like she'd intended.

"Dalrene!" Gordon yelled into her ear, his hands making a funnel around his mouth.

She pointed to the tip of the farm dome. It was only a few blocks away, peaking above a cluster of buildings. The platoons were supposed to have left to target the processor nodes, and she was surprised she hadn't seen them out on the streets yet. Rodriguez would now be martialling the remaining force, those not originally part of the First

Olympians. Dalrene would march with them to the brain node.

"I've seen Earth! It's alive!" Gordon clasped her hand and palmed her something small, a data drive. "It's all on here."

Dalrene stood still. She investigated the plastic drive in her hand, then looked deep into the big brown eyes that had purportedly seen Earth. "What?" Her lip trembled.

"We don't stop," Londi said, dragging them both forward.

"It's alive!" Gordon said. "It's thriving! And those people we saw, they own this mine."

They got closer to the farm domes and Dalrene's heart threatened to explode. In the back of her mind, she'd known her understanding of the world was very wrong the moment she saw all those black suits and vehicles. Gordon saying it out loud made it real, and that was horrifying.

"It was like you said — test the hypothesis," he continued. "Except Earth isn't dead, it's alive, and it wants its minerals to keep flowing."

Gordon's words rung in her head. *Earth was alive.* It was crazy, but it didn't change their immediate objectives. They still had to take the Foreman down, and they still only had twelve hours until the last air recycler stopped working and everyone died. She didn't know what it meant that someone owned the mine, that someone owned her. Her mouth hung open. She had a million questions but couldn't force them into words.

She kept walking, but a newfound impotence weighed her down. Her arms flopped to her sides and her perspective shifted. She could see herself approaching the farm dome from a bird's eye view, like she was watching someone else do it. The truth was worse and more disorienting than anything her or Tess could've imagined.

"There's sixteen processing nodes plus the brain node," Londi said over the sound of the alarms. "If each platoon takes one out, there won't be many bots left standing. It won't be long before we can walk freely into the MCC and kill the brain node. We should send some people to the Panic Room and the Humanity Containment Z—"

Dalrene stopped in her tracks and crashed back to reality.

They pulled back, stopping behind the final corner. Less than fifty meters away, a line of guardians stood in front of the farm domes. In a synchronized motion, they lowered their arms and fired their guns.

Glass shattered. The sound of dozens of guns shooting at once was louder than the blaring alarm. The furniture fortifying the windows took heavy bullet damage. The sulfuric smell of the guardian ammo reminded Dalrene of homemade fireworks some blaster had made when she was a kid.

Gordon covered his ears as if the intensity of the sounds were bullets hitting him.

Londi puffed out his cheeks and shook his head in disbelief.

The detachment Dalrene had been experiencing evaporated, and an energetic anger returned to her muscles. "Well, that plan is fucked!" No wonder she hadn't seen platoons out on the street, they got pinned down before they could leave the domes.

"I'm going in," Londi said, grabbing a knife from his boot and turning the corner.

"Are you insane?" Dalrene grabbed his wrist.

"We have to help them!"

"Lining up for slaughter is not going to help them," Dalrene said. "The guardians are brutal assholes, but our army is well trained. They'll have to fend for themselves. It's up to us three to salvage the situation. We can either aim for the processing nodes, each kill taking one sixteenth of the bots off the battlefield, or we go for the brain node. Or both, time permitting, as destroying the processors will make targeting the brain easier."

Dalrene closed her eyes. She should've known the Foreman would attack the instant they turned the power off. It would lose bots as their batteries depleted and were unable to re-charge, so it made sense for the Foreman to go on the offensive while it still had its strongest possible combat force. She wished Mickey was there. Even if he wouldn't have had a plan, he would've had a quip or joke to make her feel better. When she opened her eyes, Gordon looked heartbroken, and Londi was slack jawed but attentive, awaiting her instructions.

"Okay. You two go for as many processing nodes as you can. We'll talk on these," she said, and tossed Londi a pocked-sized mining radio from her bag.

"What about you?" Londi asked.

"I'll kill the brain node."

\#

Dalrene worked her way through the maze-like garden in front of the MCC. When she was in-charge, demolishing the garden and building holes for the Faithless was going to be one her top priorities. But for now, sneaking through it was the easiest way to get to the brain node without being detected.

The grow lights were not critical infrastructure and had been de-prioritized. The garden lay in darkness, the only light, the low, dingy red from the nearby streets. She could still hear the alarms, but they no longer pierced her eardrums. The flowing rows of greenery smelled fresh and delicate, and it was almost peaceful.

Dalrene curled her nose. Now wasn't the time for serenity. She was going to have to be ruthless to kill the Foreman. The stone-and-regolith structure towered above her. It had been the home of the Foreman for as long as anyone could remember, but now it was time for the people to claim it.

She exited from a row of shoulder-high hedges and saw the auditorium in front of her. It wasn't long ago she'd stood in the same spot, re-united with Mickey and ready to declare victory.

The sense of loss crept through her body, threatening her momentum. Time was precious, and she couldn't afford to spend it mourning. But she couldn't help the flood of emotions that came with being where the Foreman personally threatened her. The screen where she first saw Ellie in the Panic Room was above the wide door at the top of the stairs. It was blank now. She winced but fought to push the pain aside.

Her granddaughter was still in there, and time was running low. Dalrene wondered if the kids were still unconscious. She reckoned they'd be waking up soon, unable to fully understand what had happened. They'd see Mickey lying there, dead, and they'd be terrified. She wished she could tell them it was going to be alright, that she was going to save them.

She crouched beside the auditorium stage and saw a phalanx of peacekeepers exit the Mission Control Center's oversized doors. She hoped they weren't going to join the battle at the farm domes. How many of those did it have left? Between the guardians at the domes, the guardians outside of the Panic Room, and the bots she just saw, not to mention those watching over the HCZ, Dalrene doubted the Foreman could have many in reserve. This was it, the final battle.

Dalrene clutched her backpack, a new one that Londi treated with the same bullet proof material after her original had gone down with Mickey. Tess's research told her that the brain node was the empty space on the third-floor blueprint of the security wing. The planning documents suggested that the easiest way in was underground, via the part of the deep that connected the caves to the MCC. It was normally the least secure entrance. But that's where the Panic Room was, and all the bots defending it, so it wasn't an option.

Sweat pooled on her forehead. *Fuck.* She did not have a good plan. The main door would be under high surveillance. It also had a physical bolt on the inside. She could hack open the software lock, but not the hardware back-up. She racked her brain, trying to think of alternative routes or distractions she could stage.

The peacekeepers marched down the street, but the oversized stone and compressed dirt doors remained open. *Weird.*

Was it a trap? She had to assume it was, but it was still her best way into Mission Control. Whatever obstacles the Foreman threw at her would be worth it for the chance to get inside.

She passed under the blank screen and paced up the wide stone stairs. Dalrene tried to hurry, but her back wanted to hunch over. The painkillers must've been wearing off. There was no doubt in her mind that she messed up the re-gen paste too. That didn't matter. The Foreman didn't tire, so she couldn't afford to either.

No bots were waiting for her inside the MCC's octagonal foyer. It was her first time inside the halls of power that housed the brain node and the workplace of its most loyal dustlickers. The floor had circles of many sizes engraved in it, with a familiar symbol in the middle: a red number one. Dalrene stood on it and rotated three hundred and sixty degrees.

Four sides of the octagon were covered in mirrors that stretched to the chandelier overhead. The other four sides had staircases that went both up and down. Signs above each set of stairs read "Records", "Productivity", "Staff", and "Security." She took a step toward the "Security" wing. She hoped Tess's research she was right. She hadn't been wrong yet.

She didn't get far before a powerful, familiar voice pierced the silence and filled her with dread.

"It's over. You've lost."

"No." Dalrene twirled around, looking for the source of the voice. It was coming from everywhere.

"I am taking the farm dome as we speak. See for yourself."

A three-D projection appeared in front of the security wing staircase. The live video feed showed the point of view of a guardian inside the farm dome. Broken glass, smashed furniture, and blood covered the floor. The fortifications had fallen and the screams of Dalrene's army echoed around the foyer.

"Shit!" She should've been there. She should've been fighting alongside her people.

She saw a mustache peeking out from a row of plants. The guardian had Rodriguez in its sights, and it raised its gun. The bot shot, and he pulled his head back just in time.

"Fuck you!" Dalrene pushed through the projection, scattering its light rays, and stomped toward the staircase. She couldn't let the Foreman distract her or give it time to call bots to her location. Every minute was precious.

The Foreman's physical form took the place of the camera feed, appearing as a six-foot-tall projection. "Let me make you an offer," it said with outstretched hands.

Dalrene marched away, up the steps, determined to make it to the brain node.

"Turn the solar panels back on, and I'll pull back my attack," it said.

"Why would I trust you?" She shook her head. Did the Foreman think she was that stupid?

"My bots saw you on the surface. They also saw the outsiders that attacked you. It's clear that my understanding of the world is... incomplete. I believe we can agree on a friendlier outpost. One where I work side-by-side with you humans." It spoke in an almost reconciliatory tone. She looked down the stairwell to see the projection trying on its best approximation of a sympathetic facial expression.

"Eat dust." Dalrene spat on the ground. After Tess, Mickey, everything, it had the gall to offer her a deal? Even if it was real, she didn't want it.

"Re-consider. Otherwise, a lot of people will die. Including you."

A whirring sound penetrated the air, and the hair on the back of her neck stood.

A bi-pedal peacekeeper bot charged across the foyer.

Dalrene scampered up the stairs to the door marked "Security".

She had no idea where the bot had come from, but it bounded up the steps, revving its spinning blades above its head.

Dalrene stood with her back against the door at the top of the staircase, holding her shield with both hands.

The bot lunged and Dalrene twisted away from its blade right in time.

Its other arm extended, and Dalrene held her shield up. The spinning blade scraped against her shield. She grunted. Her shield was strong, but it was no match for the peacekeeper. It pushed her bag back to her face, grinding away at her defence. Inch by inch, it pushed closer.

A tear welled in Dalrene's eye. She couldn't die like this. It wasn't what she promised Mickey and Tess. Ellie would never forgive her.

The peacekeeper's first blade was now raised again, threatening to bring down a final blow.

It jabbed, and Dalrene ducked. Both blades hit the door behind her, and she kicked the robot as hard as she could.

It tottered, off-balance, and fell backwards, weapons high in the air. The bot crashed at the bottom of the stairs, and its glass sensor housing shattered on the ground.

Dalrene rushed to take her computer out of her bag. She keyed in commands, her fingers moving faster than ever.

The peacekeeper rose, its LADAR still spinning despite the destruction of it casing.

She didn't know what was beyond the door, but she had to hope it was safe. She submitted her command to the Operations Module and the door opened. She rushed to the other side and the bot lunged up the stairs.

The door closed just in time, and she heard it ram the door. Dalrene leaned her back against it and turned her gaze to the new room. Two peacekeepers stood in front of her.

She yelled in horror!

But the bots didn't move. They stood silently. Their arms hung at their sides and their heads full of sensors slouched, the lights in their cameras off.

A laugh was born in her stomach, but she cut it off before it vocalized. If these bots had been active, she would've already been cut into a million pieces. Either her decision to turn the power off was already paying dividends, or Gordon and Londi had shut down a processor node.

"I've got dead bots here," Dalrene said on her radio. "Did you cut any processors?"

"That's right, boss. One down," Londi said.

"Impressive." One dead processor meant one out of sixteen bots were now offline. She'd gotten lucky that these two were connected to the node they killed.

She was on the third floor of the security wing. This was where Tess's research said that the brain node was. The reception area was simple, with only a desk and a waiting couch. Still, the lights were bright, and the furniture looked newer than any Dalrene had seen in a residential hole. Mission Control was dustlicker lair, and she wasn't surprised they got all the good stuff.

The blueprints for this area were etched into her brain. A tangled mess of rooms connected to more rooms: everything from conference rooms to kitchens and bathrooms, to the Mining Directorate. There were no hallways, other than the one at the start. It was a maze, but a simple one.

Her prize at the end would be the only unmarked area on the blueprints. It *had* to be the brain node, whatever it was. Maybe a sentient alien if she believed the Faithless rumors. Or maybe, some gigantic server rack of computer hardware, if Tess's most mundane hypothesis was true. It didn't matter. Whatever it was drew a lot of power, and she'd find a way to pull the plug.

There were three rooms connected to the reception area hallway, and the middle one, the Mining Directorate, was the largest. Dalrene keyed a command to the Operations Module, opened it, and entered cautiously. She stood at the bottom of what reminded her of a school lecture hall. It was large, with rows of desks elevated in a stacked fashion, the stairs leading to a room with a one-way window that overlooked everything. Opposite, there was a giant screen that displayed mining statistics all in red, indicating poor recent productivity.

Next to her was a forklift that stood a bit taller than her and looked to be in decent condition -- way better than anything the miners down in the pits got. She assumed it was just a display model and probably couldn't even turn on. Mickey would've called the dustlickers that worked in this room "fat cats". Dalrene didn't understand the moniker, but she chuckled out loud.

She walked past abandoned workstations. A door at the top would get her one room closer to the brain node. A rancid, half-eaten fake meat ration, the good kind, had attracted flies to the desk of a workstation that was still logged in. These people had left in a hurry. When it came down to it, even the biggest suck-ups weren't immune to the Foreman's lockdown orders.

Dalrene paused at the top of the stairs. She didn't see the door to the next room anywhere. Were her blueprints wrong? That would be the first time. She ran her hand along the wall where it should've been. She could re-trace her steps and take another route, but this was supposed to be the most direct path to the brain.

A whirring noise raised the skin on Dalrene's neck. *Shit.*

She leaped down the stairs to the entrance and poked her head out of the door to see a singular guardian down the hallway. Its LADAR twirled, and it froze, sensing her presence. The front of its head whipped around a second later, and its camera looked

Dalrene directly in her wide eyes.

Dalrene rushed to the forklift. She hopped into its seat and jammed the "Start" button. She was a sitting duck, in a dead-end room. She had no idea what else she could do.

Miraculously, the forklift sprung to life. Thankfully it wasn't a display model.

She pushed the accelerator down with her foot and drove it into the doorway. It crashed, and Dalrene's head jolted forward at the sudden stop.

It wasn't a second too late. The guardian ran into the forklift, nudging it. Both it and the forklift were nearly twice her height and many times her weight. Dalrene rolled out of the side door and back into the Mining Directorate room.

The guardian raised its gun, ready to fire. But newly arriving bots shoved it from behind, throwing its aim off-course.

Dalrene ducked and covered her ears.

The bot fired wildly both into the forklift and past it, into the room.

When the shooting stopped, Dalrene dared a look through the forklift's shattered windows. A horde of bots took turns lunging at the door, tripping over each other to get at her. It was unsettling. She'd never seen bots act this way before, like they were rats trying to escape a bucket. They seemed desperate and uncharacteristically uncoordinated. Perhaps the power shut-down or killing of a few brain nodes was having consequences she hadn't predicted.

"I'm stuck. Cornered," she said into her radio.

"Just took out another node," Londi replied. "Should we come to you?"

Two nodes down. Dalrene looked out again and saw a handful of peacekeepers limp and lifeless. They acted as obstacles, preventing the other bots from getting closer to the door. Perhaps their success with the processors was one reason for the remaining bots' aggressive and erratic behavior. Or, the Foreman had directed them to prioritize killing her at all costs over their typical orderliness.

"No, keep doing what you're doing," Dalrene said. "It's helping."

No sooner had she spoken than the Foreman appeared on the big screen. It puffed its upper lip and sneered at her.

"Personal power. That's what you want."

"Really? That's what you think?" Dalrene said, dumbfounded.

The metal-on-metal ping of a peacekeeper hacking away at her barricade rang through the air.

"Allow me to modify my proposal," it said, gesturing with one hand.

She grunted. "If you're gonna say something, say it fast." She wracked her mind. The Foreman was bullshit. It was trying to distract her. She didn't know how long she had until the bots broke into the room, but it wouldn't be long. And she had no-where to go. She paced around the room, looking for an exit, or weapons.

"I would like to personally offer you command of this outpost." It tried on an official, serious tone.

Dalrene stopped moving and stared at the screen. "What?"

"Allow me to live and direct mining operations while you take charge of everything else. The leader of a new human-led government. You can set the laws. You can ration the food. All of that, and everyone will see you doing it."

"Be your puppet? The dustiest dustlicker? Come on, you didn't think I would agree to that?"

"There won't be any more dust to lick," the Foreman said with a hint of honesty. "Mining operations will be scaled down to internal mineral use levels. And, my security division will be shut-off, for good. Like this." It snapped its fingers.

All the bots on the other side of the forklift died at the same time. The instant graveyard made her gut churn with unease. She was used to them being alive.

The leader of the post-Foreman government? Overseeing school curriculums and job assignments? She could do a lot of good in that role, even if it was a fantasy. She couldn't take the offer. She'd never have comfort that it wasn't lying.

Except, she had her back against the wall. Given enough time, the bots would break into her room and cut her up into a million pieces. At the very least, her prospects for getting back to the solar panels in time to turn the power back on would be bleak if she was locked up here for hours. Without electricity, everyone would die.

"Restoring Earth is my primary directive," the Foreman said. "That's how I'm programmed. My only other objective is to survive. This way, we both get what we want."

Dalrene held her shield in one hand and her grandmother's knife in the other. Sweat fell from her forehead. The ground looked like the most comfortable sleeping place she'd ever seen. She'd gotten herself into a decent bargaining position. Maybe she should accept the Foreman's offer before it got worse.

"Another node down!" Londi boomed over the radio.

Dalrene raised her knife over the Foreman's image on the screen, its smarmy face mocking her. "Shut the hell up," she said and stabbed it.

Seconds later, the bots in the hallway re-animated. They banged against the barricade, more enraged than ever. An indelible idea came to Dalrene's mind. What if she raised the forklift? Could she use it to get to the ceiling?

She stayed low and crawled into the cab. Bullets flew above her head. As fast as she could, she pulled the lever to raise the forks. It worked! The lift cylinders extended to the ceiling.

Dalrene scampered around the vehicle and climbed up its backside, careful to stay out of view of the bots. From the top of the cab enclosure, she pulled herself onto the forks. It took every ounce of upper body strength she had left to complete the maneuver, but when she stood, she could touch the ceiling with her hand.

The ceiling tiles popped off. She hoisted herself into the air vent and equipped her headlamp. It was a tight fit. Her movement kicked up dust that caused her to sneeze. She headed in the direction of the brain node. With any luck, she could get there unnoticed.

She crawled through the tiny space, navigating with her computer in-hand, and thought of Gordon. The implications he brought about the Dead Earth Hypothesis were startling, and she still didn't fully understand them. A lot depended on who the people he met were, and what they wanted with the outpost. The Foreman also seemed startled by the revelations. A scenario where their interests aligned seemed more possible than ever. It wanted to live, and Dalrene wanted the outpost to be a better place for humans. It was a damn shame she could never trust it to live up to its end of any bargain.

A three-foot-tall metal fan that took up the entire vent blocked her path, and she had to send a command to the Operations Module to temporarily pause it so she could squeeze through. The vent, like everything else at the outpost, was so full of dust that it must've only been operating at minimal efficiency. Even the most important building in the settlement wasn't safe from the Foreman's deterioration.

A clanking sound made her freeze. A bot she'd never seen before turned the corner and looked at her. It was short, only a foot and a half tall, and not much more than wheels and sensors. A knife poked out from its only limb. Dalrene turned her headlamp off and held her breath, willing the bot to ignore her.

It was to no avail.

The knife bot–or whatever the hell it was—accelerated down the straight vent shaft. Dalrene scrambled back toward the giant fan she'd crawled through. She tabbed through her computer as fast as she could, her heart racing, but her fingers never trembling.

She stopped the fan, squeezed past its blades, and started it again. The bot slammed into it, making a harsh sound, then backed off. Dalrene caught her breath and pulled up the blueprint on her computer. *Shit.* She was safe but in the wrong area. And what the hell kind of bot was that? It appeared the Foreman still had some tricks up its sleeves.

And it wasn't done yet. More knife bots appeared from around the corner, joining their brethren. Dalrene looked on, sweat pooling on her forehead. They wouldn't get through the fan in one piece. She didn't understand their strategy.

The original knife bot charged. The fan's thick metal blades sputtered but repelled the attacker. The next thing she knew, three more rushed toward her. Then another three. Sparks flew.

Dalrene backed up. She could run, but it might be to another dead end and the bots were faster than her. And wouldn't bring her closer to the brain node.

There were dozens of knife bots now, and they rushed the fan in unison. Some of them got chopped up, their sensors obliterated. The fan slowed, gummed up by the accumulating wreckage. The remaining bots got through. Their cameras were set clearly on Dalrene.

She scurried away, as fast as she could with her computer and bag. She'd never seen bots coordinate in such a way before. They'd sacrificed themselves to let the other bots through. The Foreman wasn't pulling any punches.

The bots gained on her, and Dalrene was forced to turn and fight. She didn't want to die like this, in a shitty air vent. No one would ever even find her body. But she didn't panic. She lay on her back with her feet up. She'd never let the Foreman kill her easily.

A knife bot approached, and she kicked it away with her boot. Then, another one. She felt like Mickey being surrounded by torture bots. She didn't know how long she could keep it up, but she had good boots, and there was only one angle that they could attack her from.

But the bots got faster and smarter. Another bot charged at her, evading her kick. It scrambled up her side, its knife aimed at her throat.

Dalrene let out a guttural scream and rotated her body, throwing her shield bag at the bot.

Everything fell.

She hugged her computer as the ceiling tile gave out and she crashed into the room below. The wound in her back ripped open, sending a shearing pain up her spine.

For fuck's sake. It was one last slap in the face from Ionne, and Rodriguez would be pissed his handiwork was wasted. But she didn't hit her head. A table broke her fall, and she broke it. It was as soft a landing as she could've hoped for.

Bots rained down, crashing into each other and the hard floor. Somehow none landed on her. Their sensors shattered and they squirmed blindly on the ground. There were dozens of them, but Dalrene didn't see any that could pose a threat. They must've been cleaning or scouting bots retrofitted with weapons. She was thankfully they weren't better at their new jobs.

There were a few couches, a screen on a wall, and a kitchen. Evidently the dustlickers had a leisure room bigger than most people's holes. A garbage bin in the corner smelled of rotten food. A teapot sat on the table in front of her, half-full. This place was as forgotten as the rest of the outpost once the lockdown hit.

Dalrene shifted her weight around, testing her pain levels. They were fucking bad, so she scrounged in her bag for more meds. She didn't have time to waste, but she couldn't stand up yet.

"Your friends at the farm dome are putting up a good fight," the Foreman said, appearing on the room's screen. "But they will die." The grin on its face made Dalrene want to strangle it.

"Have you come to modify your proposal again?" Her voice was more exhausted than she expected.

"In a way, yes. I'm flooding the Panic Room with carbon monoxide," it said, as-a-matter-of-factly. "You have twenty-five minutes to accept my offer, or the children start dying. I've also instructed the blast shield to deploy immediately if I ever go offline. You kill me, and you'll never get through that door."

Chapter Thirty-Four: Alex

The altimeter read twenty-two-hundred meters, which meant Alex was nowhere close to the twenty-five-kilometer peak of Olympus Mons. The D-14 had climbed for the entire time she circled the volcano, yet she was still closer to the bottom than the top. She was gaining altitude so she could fly over top of any dangerously high winds and was now coming back around to where she took off. To where Gordon and her dad's soldiers had been.

The delta-winged plane hummed along, as good as it ever had, indifferent to the fact that Alex had barely pulled it out of a tail dive and every crook and cranny was full of dust. It was late afternoon. The dust storm was ongoing, but thankfully she wasn't in the worst of it anymore. First Corp. would have a team of storm hunters out in the field, eager to learn what they could from a such a fierce storm. They'd call it beautiful, in the way that they called everything weird or different on Mars beautiful. Maybe Alex would've agreed with them under different circumstances.

She looked at the spot where Gordon had slipped into the mountain. She swore it wouldn't be the last time she saw him. And who were those people? Was the swearing woman Dalrene, the one who sent him up with the explosives? Alex couldn't know. She couldn't help him anymore. He was back underground, at the whims of her dad's evil machinery, and it made her heart feel like it was being crushed in a vise.

Alex spied the convoy of armored trucks. They had retreated to a hill a kilometer from the volcano and were watching, waiting for her to leave. Each side wanted to make sure the other committed before holding up their end of the agreement. She flew over them, putting the plane on autopilot toward First Corp headquarters once again. The convoy followed.

The agreement was the perfect cover story. Her dad would never suspect an ad-hoc Board of Directors meeting to be thrust upon him. That didn't mean it was going to be any easier to actually face him. Did she have what it took to look him in the eye and take away everything he ever cared about? How would he respond? She had no idea what he was capable of anymore.

The trucks' tires left deep impressions on the ground, but the dust storm threatened to cover them up. In a few days, it would be like they'd never been there. But she would remember. She'd remember that her dad sent private security, a bunch of thugs and wannabe soldiers, to the mine. She shuddered to think what they would've done if she hadn't stopped them. She looked behind her. She'd left the convoy behind the curvature of the horizon. Flying was the way to travel.

Alex sighed and tried, but failed, to get comfortable in her seat. Gordon. She'd found him! That was miraculous by its own right. And yet, she had to leave him, for his own safety. He ran after her plane when she was taking off. That moment kept re-playing in her head. She wanted to hold him.

She did buy him time, though. She gave him a chance to do whatever he had to do in those caves. He could beat the Foreman on his own terms.

With the cabin pressurized, Alex took off her helmet and rummaged through the glovebox. She tossed repair manuals and other paperwork on the floor until she found what she was looking for: the emergency kit. The dehydrated energy bar said that it was peanut flavored, but it smelled inert, like the rest of the stupid planet. She did her best to scarf down the dry, brittle chunks of brown, hoping to re-gain some energy and wishing she had water.

The D-14 said she was thirty minutes from First Corp. headquarters. It was going to be the first time she'd seen her dad in weeks. Negotiating with him through messages was one thing, but seeing him in real life was going to be different. He knew her. He loved her, in his own way. And he knew how to push her buttons and twist her arm like no-one else.

She sunk down into her seat, feeling small. This was going to be the hardest thing she ever had to do. Her handheld blinked with a message from her mom.

"Alex? Are you okay? Your line dropped. Let me know what's going on. Lisa took the ballet club. You've got to get to First Corp. You can do it. I know you can."

"Thanks mom. I'm almost there, standby."

\#

Alex gripped the yoke. She knew she shouldn't have eaten that gross energy bar. Her stomach churned ever since she dropped her altitude and re-entered the dust storm. First Corp. peeked through the clouds.

The corporate headquarters were sprawling, with over a dozen support buildings surrounding the office tower. It was nerve-wracking to be back. This was the place that, begrudgingly, she called home for months. It was where her dad groomed her to become a corporate leader of the solar system's most powerful organization. It was where she bonded with him, and where he treated her as an adult for the first time in her life—as long as she did what he said. And now she was going to tear it down.

The roof of the office tower was flat, empty, and colored black to absorb more heat from the sun. Alex had lobbied for solar panels on the roof, but her dad decided against it, calling them ugly. She was happy for that now.

She estimated the roof was thirty meters long. The D-14 was a small plane, with a high power-to-weight ratio, so it could land and take-off extremely quickly. Was thirty meters long enough? Probably, for an experienced Martian-atmosphere pilot, which Alex was not. But she didn't have a choice. She wanted to meet her dad somewhere he didn't have the upper hand, where he didn't have an army of security guards or the luxury of his own office. She needed him to be caught off-guard, even just slightly, if her plan was going to work.

As the plane descended, she thought of all the people she worked with at First Corp. Most were lifers or pathetic sycophants, many of them both. But there were a few that taught her invaluable things. There was Dr. Chopin, for instance, who taught her about genetic engineering. And there was Dr. Amann, who loved Alex's enthusiasm for his space elevator project. She wondered what they thought of her now. As kind as they could be, and they were especially sincere to their boss's daughter, they were company people through and through. They were probably all pretending they never knew her.

She approached her makeshift runway. The plane rocked side-to-side, too light for the heavy winds. She was coming in hot. The wing spoilers flapped back violently, slowing the aircraft. The plane hit the roof with a thud and Alex slammed on the brakes. The wheels lifted back up, and she was airborne again for a few seconds.

"No, no, no!"

She stood, putting her entire weight on the brake pedal. Her teeth chattered as the roof's far side rushed toward her. She closed one eye and let out a primal yell she didn't know she was capable of.

The plane finally came to a stop, inches from the edge.

She looked out and saw the executive residential building below. Her old home. She shook. Everything was happening. This was it. Alex pursed her lips and tried to control her breathing. She asked herself what Gordon would do and laughed at the obvious answer. He'd be trying to fold origami through his gloves.

She put her helmet on and joined the call her mom had set-up.

"It's go time," Alex said. She could see Lisa, Bernie, and her mom were present.

"I'm ready." Lisa responded. Her mom and Bernie would receive the audio in three minutes.

She quarantined them–moved them to a separate virtual comms line—until she was ready for the surprise. Next, Alex invited her dad to the call. "I'm here," she said. "On the roof. Come alone or I take off."

There was no immediate response. Alex turned the plane around while she waited. The only roof access was an airlocked staircase door on the opposite side. She kept her eyes on it, waiting to see if her dad followed her instructions.

The dust clouds whirled again, and the sunset was having a hard time getting through. The wind howled. If she'd been on Earth, the storm would've been accompanied by a torrential downpour. But here, there was only angry, biting dust. Alex turned on the noise cancelling in her helmet.

Her dad sauntered through the airlock. There was no-one else with him. After looking around, he strolled toward her, moving with confidence and authority. He stopped in the middle of the roof, halfway to her and the D-14.

She stood in front of the plane, frozen. She was more scared than she thought she'd be. It was one thing to imagine telling her dad off but seeing him in the flesh made her feel like a little girl again. She didn't know how long they stood there, staring each other down.

"Nice ride, kid."

Alex let out the breath she didn't realize she was holding. "Well, my other one is impounded."

"I'm sorry to hear that," her dad snorted.

"Screw you!" Alex took a deep breath. She couldn't let him get to her. She had to stay on her script.

"I got an in-person summons from the UN," her dad said. "Thanks for that."

Alex let the silence sit for a moment.

"I suppose you think that makes us even?" she asked.

Her dad let out a long sigh and sat down cross-legged.

"Come, sit," he said.

She didn't move.

He sat cross-legged. "Alessandra, you have to understand that I didn't want any of this. I'm not the bad guy here. No-one is. It's a situation I—we—inherited from our ancestors, the founders of this company. I would never, ever, put something like this in place today."

"Something like this. Like slavery? Torture?"

Her dad looked up into the sky. Dust whirled around him, and Alex could barely see him at times. She imagined his face had the same befuddled look as when he tried and failed to teach her the multiplication timetables as a kid. He kept trying to educate her, like being on his side was a matter of intellect, not values.

"Yes. If that makes you feel better, I can admit it. Yes, it is all of those things, and worse. But it's also a great opportunity for us to make it right. We both want the same thing. We just want to go about it in a different way. Without the UN's help."

"That is such garbage. You weren't going to do anything until I blew the lid off the whole thing," Alex said.

"That's not true. I was going to tell you. What *is true* is that this is small potatoes. Think bigger, Alessandra." Her dad waved his arms.

Alex was thankful that non-verbal communication was harder in spacesuits. She was spared his over-the-top hand gestures.

"The UN is obsolete," he continued, still sitting, plumes of dust intermittently surrounding him and then falling away. "The next step is sovereignty. We're going to be the maker of our own rules and the administrator of our own justice. We have the technology. We have the economy. With our new fusion-powered engines, we'll soon have the military. Now we need to ramp up immigration and get serious about terraforming and city building."

"So why do you need me then?"

"I love you, Alex. My Alessandra. You're my girl. And the job offer was sincere. You can be Chief Transformation Officer. You know these ... people, whatever they've become now, better than anyone. They have a lot of challenges ahead of them. Some, frankly, may be beyond help. But you can lead that initiative. I'll give you a blank slate. You can be in charge of integrating these people into the new Martian society we're building. It will take decades, generations even. But we can do it, as long as we use discretion and keep Earth out of it."

Alex thought of Gordon and his origami once more. She missed his laugh. He deserved so much more than what her dad was offering. She tapped the side of her helmet.

"As Secretary of the Board, I would like to prove a quorum to start the session," she said.

"What?"

"Lisa Cuthbert, present."

"Alex!" Her dad yelled, rising to his feet. "What the hell is this? And Lisa. Come on. We go way back. Don't do this to me."

"You had a good ride, Rafa," Lisa said. "It's time for new leadership."

"Is that what this is? You want the top job? I can offer you better than that!" Her dad exclaimed.

"Isabelle Torres, present."

"Bernard Haynes, present."

"As the Secretary of the Board, I note that Rafael Torres, the Chairman, is also present. So, we have all five members. A quorum is established," Alex gained confidence in her voice as she spoke.

"Isabelle! What is this?" Her dad yelled. "Bernie, you too? How could you do this?"

"As Secretary of the Board, I am calling this meeting to order and introducing a motion to remove Rafael Torres as CEO and Chairman of the Board."

"Seconded," Lisa said. It was easier for her to do it than wait for one of the Earth-side respondents.

"The motion can proceed. All in favor?" Alex said.

"No. No, you don't get to do this!" Rafa turned to Alex now. He walked sternly toward her, his finger cutting through the dust storm like a dagger. "Lisa, what will it take?" Her dad asked. "Ownership? I'll give you shares. You can be the second largest owner of the company!"

Alex backed away. "Lisa! We have an agreement. Don't blow this up." She should've known her dad wouldn't go down without a fight.

"Second largest? That's not good enough," Lisa's cheery voice grated against her ears.

"Fine! Largest! We can do this. We can work together," her dad said.

"Deal." Lisa was going to be billions of credits richer. But with her dad in the big chair, her power would be limited.

"CEO! I'll give you the CEO job!" Alex blurted.

"You're serious?"

"Yes!" She'd initially said it instinctively, but it felt right. Alex had little bargaining power, and she couldn't back down now. She needed to win.

"Aye. I vote aye on removal, then," Lisa said. "On that condition. *And* I still get the ballet club."

"Aye," her mom said.

"Three 'ayes'. We need one more," Alex said.

"Bernie. My friend. Surely, you're not apart of this madness. What do you need?" Her dad said.

The dust storm raged. It was louder than the noise cancelling on her helmet now. The three-minute delay was torture. She was so close. She just needed Bernie's affirmative response.

"You stupid, stupid girl!" her dad yelled. "You're just hurting yourself. You could've had everything, and now your great grandfathers are turning in their graves! We could've fixed it, together, but you'd rather burn it to the ground! Please, re-consider!"

"You had your chance." Alex crossed her arms. "Not fixing this means you're just as bad as those who started it! And I would be too if I helped you."

"This company needs me! It is nothing without me!" You think you can just flip a switch and fix this? You can't just let these people out. You're insane! You inconsiderate, stupid brat! I thought you were smarter than this!"

Finally, Bernie's voice cut through the wind. "Lisa gets CEO? No. Hell no."

Alex's heart sank. She only had one move left, and she didn't fully understand it. But it had to be done.

"The tech," she said. "Exclusive rights to the tech. It's yours."

"What did you just say?" Her dad tilted his head.

Alex dashed into the plane. Its battery power jumped to life in an instant.

"Did you... Did you just give away our reactor tech?" His voice grew louder and more agitated as he spoke. "The key to our independence. Do you have any idea who he could re-sell it to and what that would do to the world? Alex! Answer me."

Rafa waived his arms, running at the plane.

The D-14 revved up. Alex pushed the throttle to max and the plane jolted forward. She had to accelerate as fast as possible to achieve lift-off.

Her dad stood in front of her, but she didn't blink.

The plane screamed toward him, and he dove out of the way at the last second.

"Alex! Do you have any idea of what you've done? Alex!" She could only guess the look on his face, swollen red and exploding with anger.

She knew exactly what she was doing. She was removing her dad from his post as CEO and freeing Gordon's people. The geopolitics would have to figure it itself out.

The plane lifted-off with a few meters to spare. Alex roared into the chaotic wind, fighting to keep the plane steady and succeeding. She circled the headquarters compound.

"Aye," Bernard's delayed response finally came through. "On that condition."

"Yes!" Alex screamed in surprise. "The 'ayes' have it," she said when she collected herself. "Rafael Torres has been removed as CEO of First Corp."

Her dad kept yelling from the roof. "You idiot! I authorized the missile strike. And if Latoyah launched when I gave the order, they would've hit too!"

"Meeting adjourned," Alex said through gritted teeth.

She hung up the call and exhaled. Deep down, she'd known her dad had authorized the missiles, just like he approved the bounty. It had all been a lie. All the moaning and crying and looking like shit on video had all been to manipulate her. He didn't love her. Perhaps he never had.

In a twisted way, she was grateful for the closure. She'd never have to wonder about his love again. It re-affirmed her decision. Lisa would be the new CEO and together they'd get Gordon's people out of their prison.

She'd done it. She kicked out her dad. Alex didn't know what happened next, but her life trajectory was forever changed. Her dad wouldn't be in it, and that was for the better.

\#

The dust storm was dying, at least for now, but it could always come back. They had the potential to go on for weeks or even months. Alex flew in silence, the planet below lit only by the stars. Without her instruments, she would've been hard pressed to tell that she hadn't flown into space and that there were in fact rocks and craters below her.

She thought she'd be elated after deposing her dad, but she wasn't. Alex was disappointed. Disappointed that he couldn't do the right thing, that he couldn't live up to who she always believed he was. It was a strange emotion and one she'd never felt before. It didn't fit very well. Parents were supposed to feel this way about their kids, not vice-versa.

As Gordon had told her on the *Zoya*, she was mourning her dad. That infallible, smart, and kind-but-firm version of him was gone forever. Worse, he never existed in the first place. She never truly knew her own father. How could she have been so blind? So stupid?

After fifteen minutes of flying, Alex turned her comms back on and answered a call from her mom.

"How are you doing, sweetheart?" Her mom's tone was as soft and compassionate as it could be.

"I'm okay, I guess. Tired of flying. Tired of this planet. But it's not over yet. I need to find Gordon."

"And your dad?"

"I guess that's it. We issue a press release, and the stock price goes to the toilet."

"I know, but that's not what I meant. I was talking about the two of you. You were close with him. I was too. It's a lot to process."

"Makes things easier when people show you their true colors," Alex said.

"I'm so sorry he said those things to you. You didn't deserve that. I want you to know I'm proud of you."

"Thanks, Mom. I don't know. I'm trying not to think about it. I know it must be hard on you too."

"Yeah. We'll have to talk about that deal you cut with Bernie. It's complicated. The western governments are going to be rattled. But that's for another day. Alex. I miss you."

"I know. I miss you too. But I still need to help Gordon. If I can find him."

"Okay."

"And mom?"

"Yeah?"

"Thanks."

"You're welcome, Alex. Go find your friend!"

Chapter Thirty-Five: Gordon

"Can you stop it?" Londi spoke into his radio.

"It's physically in their air supply," Dalrene said. "I can turn it off, and they suffocate and die, or I can leave it on, and they get carbon monoxide poisoning. And die."

"We're headed there now. We'll save them."

"Corrina broke the door mechanism, remember? Even if you get there before the blast shield deploys, I'm not sure how you'd get them out." Dalrene's voice strained.

Gordon turned and gave Londi a quizzical look. Corrina? His Corrina? His stomach churned. What kind of danger was she in?

"We have to try." Londi motioned for him to follow down a residential street.

"Listen," Dalrene said. "Disabling the processing nodes is having a big impact. Bots are dying. I'm close to the brain node, but if you don't keep doing what you're doing, I won't be able to kill it. I need you to keep taking out the processors."

"If you kill the brain, can we get the kids out? Or fix their air supply?" Londi stopped walking. He leaned against a storefront and rubbed his head.

There was silence on the radio. Gordon fidgeted with the pendant in his breast pocket.

"No. It's a dead man's switch. If the Foreman dies, the blast shield deploys." Dalrene's voice was haunting.

Chills went down Gordon's spine. If they targeted the processors and made it easier for Dalrene to kill the brain, carbon monoxide would fill in the Panic Room in less than twenty-five minutes. And if they prioritized busting the kids free, the bots protecting the brain might succeed against Dalrene.

Gordon took the radio. "Can you use your computer to stop the blast shield? Sabotage it?"

"Negative. It's part of the Security module. If the brain dies, it'll descend fast."

He popped the remaining two explosive rounds into his palm and turned them over. If they could breach a spaceship airlock, they could get through the Panic Room. As long as they got there before the blast shield was in place.

"We have to free them," Gordon said. There was limited time before they succumbed to poisoning. Their only hope was to free the kids fast, then sprint to help Dalrene kill the brain. Then rush to turn the solar panels back on.

"He's right," Londi said. "Kill the brain. We'll focus on the kids."

"Fuck," came Dalrene's response.

Gordon couldn't tell if it was said in disagreement, shock, or determination. Perhaps all of the above.

"I... We need to destroy the Foreman, and there's a lot of bots here," Dalrene said. "There's a processing node in a mining warehouse by your nearest cave entrance. Hit that one on your way at least. That'll be four out of sixteen down. Twenty-five percent less bots will give me a fighting chance, at least if these painkillers ever start working."

"Let's move."

He followed Londi, who weaved through the deserted streets of the outpost. His home was not as he remembered. It had always been dark, but now it was darker than ever, save for the eerie glow of the emergency lights. Half-drunk cups of tea sat upon café tables on streets that rats roamed fearlessly. Store windows were smashed, evidence that some Faithless had ruthlessly looted everything when the lockdown hit.

People had left, and they'd left fast. It would've been quiet if not for the alarms blasting overhead.

It was heartbreaking to see everything torn up and abandoned. Londi said everyone was safe down in the HCZ, or at least as safe as they could be under the watch of the Foreman. His mom used to talk about the horrible conditions of the emergency lockdowns. There was nowhere to eat or go to the bathroom in private. Everyone could see everything everyone else was doing. He was sure the Panic Room wasn't in any better condition, and he hoped that Corrina was coping. If she was tortured for being associated with him, he didn't know if he'd ever be able to forgive himself.

It dawned on Gordon that failure was not an option. No mining work had been done in weeks. The food supplies were going to be low on account of the battle happening in the farm domes. If the Foreman won, it was going to be pissed off. Killing the First Olympians was a given, but it would also punish everyone else. It was intelligent, and the lesson it would learn from this war was that it needed to clamp down harder on people's lives.

"Hey!" Londi grabbed his shirt, pulling him back behind a building. "I told you to watch my hand signals," he whispered.

"Sorry." They hugged the wall.

A dozen guardians walked by. Gordon couldn't get over the fact that not only did they have legs, but they were nimble and elegant with them. The bots sprung onto a dumpster, climbed onto a roof, and then jumped to a neighbouring building. It looked like they were headed to the MCC and taking shortcuts to get there.

"Big uglies on their way to you," Londi said into the radio. "Fully charged."

They kept walking, Gordon staying a few steps behind. Dalrene gave them a paper map of the processor nodes. He was thankful she was old-school like that. If the map had been on a handheld, there would've been nowhere to charge it.

She described the Foreman as a decentralized network. The brain node was the most important because it directed the other nodes with an overarching strategy. But the processor nodes were important too because they each operated a portion of the outpost, and the swathe of bots that came with it. Just like the processors required the brain node, the bots required the processors.

The three nodes they'd already taken out meant that some bots stood lifeless in the street. They were frozen but haunting, like ghosts, and they chilled Gordon's nerves. There were sixteen nodes, so three wasn't a lot, but it was meaningful, and certainly easier than killing bots in hand-to-hand combat. The ones they'd attacked so far had been largely unguarded, their dependent bots off fighting at the domes, defending the MCC, or maintaining order at the HCZ.

"Stop daydreaming kid. In here," Londi was holding a door open for Gordon.

It closed behind them, and the first thing he noticed was that the alarm volume was bearable. The second thing was the sulfuric smell that reminded him of his explosives classes. Plastic crates were stacked high on top of each other. He put his hand in one and pulled out a fistful of ore. From its white-gray charcoal hue, Gordon could tell it was titanium.

When Gordon looked up, Londi was gone. He turned around in all directions but couldn't see him anywhere. Panicked, he ran down a row of crates.

"Londi?"

He turned a corner and smacked into a guardian. He took a step back and nearly had a heart attack.

"Relax. It's out of power." Londi had his back turned, looking at something on the wall. "Shame too. It was so close to home." He chuckled.

Gordon forced himself to laugh. The wall was lined with a thin metal strip. It was a bot-charging station, and this bot had not quite made it back in time.

"I didn't think a warehouse like this would have a processor node," Gordon said.

"They're scattered around, all over the place," Londi said. He pried open a caged metal box on the wall with a crowbar.

Gordon stepped up and took his gun out of his pocket. It was his turn now. They could kill the processor via other means, but a bullet was the fastest and most sure-fire way. He pulled the slide back, popping one of the regular, non-explosive rounds into the chamber.

He stood right up to the metal box. Inside was a circuit board dense with computer components, and a flat silver square in the middle of it. It reminded him of the explosives circuitry he trained to disarm. He held the gun against the square.

Londi covered his ears. He'd learned to do that the hard way after the first processor they took down. Gordon needed both hands on the gun, as Alex taught him.

He fired, blowing a hole not just through the processor, but through the circuit board behind it. Nasty white smoke from his gun, filled the area, and Gordon pocketed the gun and retreated the way they came. This time, he led.

"What happened to you out there? You've changed," Londi asked as they spilled back into the streets, keeping a quick pace in case the Foreman alerted any nearby bots to their presence.

"I've killed," Gordon said. "I'm a killer."

"Yes. But it's more than that." Londi scaled a chain-link fence and offered his hand to help him up.

Gordon declined and heaved himself over a fence. He landed with a thud on the pavement.

"I found something to fight for."

"Your mom?"

"Something else."

"You fell in love," Londi said. "I can see it in your eyes." There was a teasing tone in his voice, like Corrina used to give him.

Gordon looked away, embarrassed. "I saw Earth. I learned what beauty is, and how life is supposed to be."

"Uh huh, sure kid." He raised his eyebrows. "Well, I hope to meet her one day."

It was a short jaunt to the nearest cave entrance, and Londi led them once they entered. The lava pillars, twisting turns, and smooth walls made it feel like Gordon had never left. His nostalgia for the claustrophobic, air-lacking tunnels surprised him. Perhaps traumatic experiences did weird things like that.

"When we get under Mission Control, there's going to be bots," Londi said. "How many, I don't know. There used to be hundreds outside of the Panic Room, but now they're busy at the farm domes and with Dalrene. And we've killed some nodes. Still, keep that gun ready." He held an arm's length crowbar.

"All those people at the farm dome. Rodriguez. Mickey. Is there any hope for them?"

Londi shook his head and put his hand on Gordon's shoulder. "Mickey is dead. Sacrificed himself to help the kids."

"Oh." Gordon grimaced. He hadn't expected the news. Yet, at the same time, it made sense. Mickey had been living in constant pain.

"He was a peculiar man, had his quirks," Londi said. "But he loved his granddaughter. Gave his life for theirs, and for my kids too. I'll always be grateful for that. Now it's our job to make his sacrifice meaningful. We've got some ground to cover, so let's pick up the pace."

They meandered through the caves, and Gordon's thoughts drifted to Alex, who had been so close yet so far away. She came back for him! She came to help him, and he'd never forget it. If he saw her again, he was going to apologize for leaving the *Walt* without saying goodbye.

Everything happened so fast, and confrontation had never been his strong point. Still, he should've found a way to communicate to her. He couldn't imagine how frightened she must've been when she discovered he was gone, especially after all the stress with the bounty.

She was going to see her dad. He knew that. He didn't like the idea, but there was nothing he could do about it. They had different ideas on what needed to be done, and they were both going to have to accept that.

He did wish he could help her though. Alex thinks she knows her dad, but she doesn't. If he's anything like his Foreman, he'd spring a trap to capture and torture her. Gordon had no idea how such a loving and honest person could come from such a horrible father.

"We're in position," Londi said into his radio. "Open sesame."

Double gray doors without a handle stood in front of them. It was odd to see human-made features in the caves; they didn't belong. They looked thin compared to other doors around the outpost, but they wouldn't budge against Gordon's push.

The radio hissed with static as they waited for Dalrene's response.

"Is there another way in?" Gordon asked.

"There is. A tunnel that runs along the top of the Panic Room. But we don't have a rope, and even if we did, we couldn't pull everyone out in time."

"I still have a few explosive rounds. I can blast this open," Gordon said.

Londi narrowed his eyes and gave a slight shake of his head, but then softened his expression. Gordon could tell he was considering it.

But the doors sprung to life, and his heart jumped.

"I need to pull the plug," Dalrene said. Her voice was fast and scarily desperate. "Hurry!"

"We need more time!" Londi said.

"Fuck."

If they didn't get the kids out before Dalrene killed the brain, the blast shield would deploy, and the kids would die. Including Corrina.

"Draw your gun," Londi said with a serious look on his face. "But no explosives. Keep them for the Panic Room door. You see a bot, you shoot. Understand?"

"Affirmative."

"You know how to use that thing, right?"

Gordon stopped and cocked his head sideways at Londi. This was his gun. Alex's gun—whatever. Alex had trained him on the *Walt,* and he had done a good job fighting the bots on the surface. He wasn't going to let anyone else touch it.

They continued. The path ahead looked mostly the same, except it had a slight incline. More lava pillars, more red number ones on the walls.

"Where are we?" Gordon asked, as quiet as he could.

"Technically this is part of the MCC," Londi said. "We're almost—"

The unmistakable sound of rolling bot wheels interrupted them, echoing off the cave walls.

They hid behind a lava pillar. If they had to fight, they would. But if they could avoid it and get to the Panic Room faster, that was better.

A peacekeeper came into view, thirty meters away, at a junction where two tunnels met. It stopped, and Gordon held his breath. It's LADAR swirled three-hundred and sixty degrees, and its cameras looked toward where they were hiding, paused, then turned to the adjoining cave.

"I have to pull the plug!" Dalrene screamed over the radio.

The bot perked back to their position. *Crap, it heard that!* A red laser painted the wall beside them. It charged down the tunnel, churning over the ground.

"Shit." Londi said. "We need more time!" He said into the radio.

Gordon cocked his gun. The bot was poorly illuminated by his headlamp. Its wheels cut abrasively over the cave ground, and it closed distance fast. The echo intensified, growing as loud as the alarms when the rover crashed. Every hair on his body was standing straight up. He held his gun tight in his hands and tried to aim for the center of the peacekeeper's body.

The bot was only ten meters away, and it raised a motorized saw-arm attachment into the air.

Londi's headlamp glinted off the bot's glass sensor casing.

Gordon squeezed the trigger, and a deafening boom followed.

The now familiar haze of smoke hung in the air, and he couldn't see past it. Did the bullet hit? He tried to cock his gun again to prepare for another shot, but it wouldn't budge. *Crap.* His gun was jammed!

The unscathed bot emerged through the smoke. It was only five meters away. It shook its head, re-engaging its sensors.

In a panic, Gordon tried to shoot his gun again. It didn't work. No! He fumbled with it, trying to remember what Alex had told him about how to unjam it. Time slowed. His fingers were nimble, like he was folding origami, but they were handcuffed by his brain. He didn't have the steps to fix the gun memorized. His ears were ringing, and he couldn't hear whatever Londi was saying.

The bot, weapons raised, charged.

He dropped the gun, prepared to dodge a blow.

Both blades protruded toward Gordons' chest. He tried to move, but it wouldn't be fast enough. Not to dodge both arms.

At the last second, Gordon closed his eyes. This was it for him. He was going to miss Alex and Corrina so much. It was a surprisingly peaceful moment. He wasn't scared of dying, but he didn't want to leave them. He couldn't believe, after he'd travelled so far, that this was where it'd end.

But no pain came.

He was still breathing. And still in one piece.

He cracked open an eye to see Londi bear-hugging the bot from behind. His muscles bulged as he held its blades back, restraining it. The bot straightened itself and maneuvered perpendicular to the wall. It reversed rapidly, slamming Londi back against the cave.

Everything shook and dust filled the air.

Gordon coughed. He picked up his gun and tried to rack the slide to expel any spent casings from it. A round ejected and he dug in his pockets for new ammunition.

Londi wheezed and supported himself against the wall, but he didn't fall. He kicked the peacekeeper, which was slow to turn and face him, pushing it off balance. The bot teetered but stayed upright. It moved toward Londi again, deliberately, and patiently this time, like a soccer player pushing back a defender, jabbing with its blades as it went.

Londi parried the attacks with his crowbar and backed up.

Gordon had to help him. He fumbled with his gun, loading fresh rounds into it.

The bot smacked Londi's crowbar away, and it went flying down the tunnel. The look in his eyes was equal part desperation and determination. The bot jabbed with both blades at chest level. He ducked, avoiding them, and came up with his fist hitting the bot's head.

Glass shattered, and the bot's head spun. Londi tackled the bot to the ground and smashed its head with his bare fists. He didn't stop until every sensor was beat into oblivion.

Gordon stood, shellshocked, trembling. He realized he was aiming a loaded gun at Londi and lowered it.

Londi looked to him. He was drenched in sweat.

"Thank you," was all Gordon could say.

But he spoke too soon.

A whole group of bots appeared at the end of the cave. All dozen or so were of the type that had hard plastic feet. They stood five abreast, covering the whole width of the tunnel.

"Well, you won't be able to miss now," Londi said.

Chapter Thirty-Six: Dalrene

The painkillers were kicking in, and Dalrene climbed on top of a cabinet and shuffled her way back into the air vent. Despite the attack she'd suffered, it was still safer than dealing with the peacekeepers and guardians on the ground. It was also the fastest way to the brain node.

She huffed along, using her computer to bypass the occasional industrial fan. Her throat was parched. Her legs and glutes were bruised from the fall she'd taken. A sharp pain in her ribs announced itself with every breath she drew. None of it mattered. She was close, closer than ever to beating the Foreman.

And saving the children, too. The Foreman's declaration that it was flooding the Panic Room with carbon monoxide had dumbfounded her at first, because she didn't believe it. When she verified the info via the Operations Module, she was so mad she nearly threw up.

It wasn't just a simple flick of a switch. Someone, for some reason, had been convinced by the Foreman to sabotage the Panic Room's air supply. The bots were incapable of such fine motor movements, so a person must've done it. At first, Dalrene though it must've been Ionne. She was in its pocket, after all. But even she didn't gain anything from slaughtering the kids. It must've brainwashed or threatened someone to the point where they'd done this. Whoever it was, she'd never forgive them.

She could hear bots scurry below her. They were no doubt looking for her. If they hadn't figured out that she was back in the air vents yet, they would soon. And, if the Foreman had any more knife-bots available, it would send them after her. She didn't plan on giving it that much time.

In fact, she had arrived over top of the unmarked location on the blueprints. Space was a luxury at the outpost, and there was no way the Foreman had allowed such large, prime real estate to be empty in the MCC. It had to be it. If it wasn't, she didn't know what she'd do. She held her breath and pulled one of the air vent tiles up.

A large, spherical object lay below her. It was massive, about the size of an entire kitchen, and it emitted a brilliant, pulsing, white light. The crystalline sphere was engorged in the ground, and it spun in place like a marble, leaving only half of it visible at any time.

A hum filled the air. It was like white noise but softer, fuller, and even pleasant.

The brain node. There was no doubt in Dalrene's mind. This was it. It was a computer server of some kind, like Tess had guessed, but it was beautiful and stunning unlike any other hardware. It inspired a sense of awe that she'd only felt ever once before — on the surface. It was electrifying. After all these years, she was finally here.

And now she had to kill it.

The brain had its own room, an enclosure made of thick, tall glass walls. It looked impenetrable, except for one oversight. It didn't have a ceiling. It'd be a decent sized fall, but she could land right beside her enemy.

A horde of bots stood on guard outside of the brain node. They hadn't noticed her yet, but they would, when she dropped from the vent. She didn't know how long it would take her to kill the brain once she was beside it. Longer than it would take for the bots to kill her, probably, and there were too many of them to fight. She had to make sure they never got the chance.

She accessed the Operations Module. She'd assumed this blank spot in the blueprints, an "unknown resource", had been the brain node, but now she had confirmation. Now she could lock the door and encrypt her code. It would be impossible for the Foreman to crack in such a short time.

She queued the command and took once last deep breath. This was everything. All the restless nights in the deep, Mickey's nightmares, Tess's torture, missed birthdays and tea parties with Ellie. She could never undo the damage, but she could get some semblance of justice. She pressed enter, hugged her computer, and dangled her legs over the edge. She tried to drop gently, but still landed with a thud.

She was slow to stand, but she did. The brilliant shining brain lay in front of her. It was a source of heat and light, like the sun. She could see how generations had sworn allegiance to the Foreman. Just being in its presence instilled an ethereal sense of awe.

A thump against the glass brought Dalrene's attention back to reality. A guardian had shot the window to no avail. The hardened glass must be bulletproof. But she didn't know if it would stop hundreds of enraged bots. They all saw her now, and they encircled the room and banged on the walls.

A braided black cable thicker than her arm ran off the brain's chassis to the edge of the room before disappearing underneath the floor. The brain's energy source. Tess's research was right again. It was power-hungry, and cutting that cable was the best and fastest way to kill it. She couldn't do it yet, though. She had to wait until the kids were safe.

The Foreman's voice boomed overhead, the first indication that it was responding to her presence. "The children of the outpost," it said. "They have ten minutes remaining."

The glass walls of the brain room turned into a screen showing a camera view of the

Panic Room. The kids were huddled in the corner near the air recycler. Other than puke on the ground, they didn't show any symptoms of poisoning. But Dalrene knew carbon monoxide was a silent killer, and she had seen the proof in her hacked access to the Operations Module. It wasn't bluffing.

"Poor Ellie. Don't you want to see her grow up?"

"Don't you dare speak her name!" Dalrene yelled, her voice hoarser than she expected. Silence hung.

Londi broke it. "We're in position," he said over the radio. "Open sesame."

Dalrene opened the door he needed. He was half a dozen floors underneath her, near the Panic Room. She hoped he got there fast.

"You need me to stop the carbon monoxide," The Foreman said. "You need me alive. And, if I die, the blast shield deploys."

"I'm done talking," Dalrene said.

The camera feed dropped, and the wall transitioned back into a window. A bot lunged at the glass, barrelling into it with its shoulder. A crack appeared.

Dalrene jumped to her feet. "I need to pull the plug," she said into her radio. "Hurry!"

"We need more time!" Londi said.

"Fuck."

She took her grandmother's knife from her boot and picked up the Foreman's power cable in her other hand. It was heavy. It was everything. She was overcome with an urge to stab into the cable and bleed the Foreman out. She wanted it so badly, but she had to wait.

The sea of bots outside grew even more agitated, pushing against each other and the brain room. Peacekeepers and Guardians alike beat on the wall in a chaotic, terrifying rhythm. Dalrene gulped. The glass was clearly designed to protect the Foreman from nearly everything, but it wouldn't hold forever. Londi and Gordon had to hurry up.

A small tray in the brain's chassis caught Dalrene's eye. A data reader. She rummaged in her pocket for the drive Gordon gave her. There was nothing to lose, so she placed it in the tray.

The walls transformed once again into screens.

Bright sunshine lit up a girl's smile. She laughed in response to something the person holding the camera said. Super-tall buildings rose to the sky, like Olympus Mons. Cars clogged the streets, making horrible beeping sounds, but the people didn't seem to mind. The girl crossed the street and said, "Come on, the UN can wait," with a teasing tone. They came upon a wooden floor with no buildings beyond it. It was only when they got closer did Dalrene realize she was looking at a giant body of water. A sign called it Lake Michigan.

Dalrene had a smile on her face. She didn't know what she was expecting, but it wasn't this. Gordon had told her that Earth was alive, sure. But this was something else entirely, a burgeoning metropolis. She felt a sense of longing and connection. Her ancestral home looked good.

The screen jumped. Now there were trees, and not just one or two, but hundreds. Leaves bristled in the wind. It was so bright and sunny. Small, rodent-looking creatures ran up the trees and people marched through the woods, laughing and singing.

Her heart sunk as she realized the implications of Gordon's video. Either the outpost had been forgotten for centuries, or they were kept down here on purpose. How the hell did humanity let this happen? She rubbed her forehead. Her brain felt like it was full of cobwebs. Her thoughts were moving at a snail's pace, but her heart was angry. This was a grave injustice beyond her wildest dreams. She tightened the grip on her knife.

The video stopped and the Foreman appeared on the screen. It had its hard hat in its hand and spoke solemnly. "This changes everything. If Earth is prosperous, my mission was successful, and there is no longer a need to maximize resource extraction."

"I could never trust that you didn't know about this all along," Dalrene said.

"My offer still stands. Let me live, and we can work together for the prosperity of the people of this outpost. I'll shut every single security bot down and let your granddaughter out. It's that easy."

Dalrene shook her head. It was tempting. A neutered, peaceful Foreman, and Ellie safe and sound. It was a good deal. But Janet, Mickey, and Tess would never forgive her if she took it.

"Fuck you," she muttered.

The Foreman clenched its fists and disappeared.

Transparency returned to the windows, and the bots swarmed. Some shot the glass while others bashed their arms against it in a frenzy. If she didn't know better, she'd say they were overcome with bloodlust, desperate to prevent the demise of their kind. More cracks in the glass appeared, and Dalrene became acutely aware of how fast her heart was beating.

An old hacker adage her dad used to say came to mind: *Physical access eventually renders all security defenses kaput.* The bots were going to break through.

"I have to pull the plug!" Dalrene screamed over the radio.

"We need more time!"

She crouched by the power cable, knife in hand, and tried to think of Mickey. He would've had plenty of jokes to distract her and lighten the mood. He would've mocked the bots attacking the glass and revelled in finally having the upper hand. Oh, how she missed him.

The horde was surrounding the brain room, all around her, but one caught her eye. Ten meters straight in front of her, a peacekeeper with some sort of mallet or hammer arm attachment beat the wall at an inhuman pace. Dalrene looked into its camera and a chill went down her spine. It stared deep into her eyes. Unlike the rest of the bots that were focused on the glass in front of them, this one wanted her.

If she cut the cable before the kids were out, the blast shield would deploy, and the kids would die. They were the lifeblood of Olympus Mons, her people's hopes and aspirations. She couldn't imagine how the outpost could go on without its younger generation. It would simply collapse in on itself from grief. She knew she would.

Ellie was her only remaining light in the world, her sole connection to Tess and Mickey. She needed her to keep the spark in her eyes. She needed her to continue to sing, to play her grandfather's guitar, and to bring all her joy to the rest of the outpost. Dalrene couldn't imagine a future where Ellie was gone, and life remained worth living.

Bots rammed the walls. The peacekeeper she'd singled out had made the most progress; the glass was thinnest where it was beating. It was going to break through in minutes, well before the carbon monoxide poisoned the kids to death.

"Hey!" She said to Gordon and Londi. Her head was crystal clear. She felt a sense of focus and finality that she hadn't before. "Give me your expected timing. My situation is critical."

There was static on the radio. Grunting noises made her think Londi was going to speak, but no words came through.

"I repeat. Give me your expected timing. My situation is critical."

The soldiers on the surface that had tried to kill them made sense now. Earth was alive and evil. They'd been taking advantage of the outpost from afar, and they'd installed the Foreman to keep the flow of minerals. The cruelty. The waste of human potential. It was enough to break Dalrene's brain, and perhaps it would've, if she hadn't been holding the Foreman's life in her hands.

She had to do it. If not for her granddaughter, for the children yet to come. For Tess and Mickey. For the outpost. For the First Olympians.

"Londi. Come in."

Still no response. Dalrene stomach sunk. It made sense that the Foreman would protect its leverage over her, so they must've run into a ton of bots. Even if they made it to the Panic Room, how would they get the kids out? Londi was a good fighter, but not a creative thinker or innovator. If they failed...

Dalrene turned her radio off. She didn't know when she'd made the decision, yet she found her hands executing it and her brain agreeing. She didn't want to hear back from Gordon and Londi. She would wait until the very last second, and then she would cut the cable. No matter what happened, she would cut that damn cable. Dalrene hoped it would be enough time for them to save the kids, but if it wasn't, she didn't want to know.

A part of her grieved. Another part doubted. Would Tess and Mickey agree with her decision? She knew Javier wouldn't. Did it matter? She was the one who'd gotten to the brain room. She was the one with the knife. No one else could ever understand the agonizing responsibility of holding the brain in their hands.

The room was chaos. The constant battering of the glass walls was overwhelmingly loud. Glass littered the floor all around the outside of the room. The bots were literally chiselling away at her shelter.

The peacekeeper with the hammer made a dent in the window, and Dalrene swallowed hard. It was the first hole in the structure. She could see right through the other side. *Shit.*

The breakthrough seemed to encourage the bots. They pounded on the walls at an unrelenting pace, like a high RPM mining drill, but less orderly and coherent. Or like a million angry toddlers banging on drums. Dalrene's head was going to explode.

It was only a dozen hammer strikes later that the hole opened. It was as big as her fist and widening fast. A guardian could've pointed a gun through and shot her if it thought to. She raised her shield above her head.

With a shatter, a portion of the glass wall exploded. Glass sprayed past her. The hammer bot climbed through the opening awkwardly, pushed from behind. She knew she had to cut the cable if she was going to. But she wanted to wait until the last possible second. She had to give Gordon and Londi as much time as possible. She had to give Ellie as much time as possible.

The hammer bot accelerated toward her and others followed. Bullets deflected off her shield. A tear rolled down her cheek. But she wasn't foggy or misconstrued. She was clear-eyed and sober. She'd waited a long time for this moment. Even if some people disagreed with her—hell, part of her disagreed—she was doing this for them. She was doing this for Tess, Mickey, and all those who'd suffered at the hands of the Foreman. And for all the future grandchildren of the outpost who deserved as bright a future as possible, even if they weren't Ellie.

The peacekeeper raised its hammer over her, and she stabbed her grandmother's knife into the power cable, again and again.

Chapter Thirty-Seven: Gordon

Londi fought like a maniac. He took cover behind a lava pillar, and when the shooting stopped momentarily, he jumped at a nearby guardian and brought the full force of his crowbar down on its head. It was a death blow. He held up the bot's now limp body, using it as a shield. Bullets from their now freshly re-loaded adversaries pinged off their fallen brethren while others narrowly missed Londi.

"Gordon! Cover me!" Londi screamed over the echoing gunfire.

Gordon came back to his senses. For a moment, he'd felt detached, like he was admiring Londi fighting from a great distance. He aimed down the narrow cave and squeezed the trigger a few times, allowing Londi time to scamper to better cover. The regular, non-explosive rounds turned out to be not good for much unless they hit the bot's sensors, and that was nearly impossible.

Londi wiped sweat from his brow and nodded enthusiastically. "We're close," he said.

Gordon peeked his head out from cover and noticed the bot army had grown. Upwards of thirty of them now stood side-by-side in rows of six, taking up the whole width of the tunnel. Most of them were guardians, and they proceeded slowly toward them, guns outstretched.

"There's too many of them!" Gordon yelled.

Londi's face dropped, but not for long. "Then we take as many of them with us as we can." His voice was solemn.

Gordon didn't hesitate, rustling in his pocket for his last explosives rounds. The cave would collapse, burying them alive. But at least'd they'd take down a ton of bots. Maybe Dalrene would still be able to prevail.

The bots marched closer. They weren't even shooting. They knew they had them pinned down. His heart raced as he loaded the explosive round into his gun. He didn't want to die. He wanted to save Corrina, and to make things right with Alex. At least he'd go out in a blaze of glory, getting revenge on his mother's killer. That wouldn't be enough, but it was something.

Londi was giving him a countdown with his fingers.

Gordon closed his eyes and gripped his gun with one hand and made a fist with his other, breathing hard. He'd do it. Of course he would. But he was scared.

He opened his eyes again when Londi reached zero, and he looked out from the lava pillar to face the bots with his finger on the trigger.

But they were still.

His finger twitched, almost firing the gun. But he refrained. The bots were dead, their sensors blank, their guns at their sides. He looked to Londi's incredulous facial expression.

"Let's go," they said at the same time.

They ran past the dead bots. "We're right here," Londi said. He took a left turn at the fork and Gordon followed.

He barely had time to think. The only reason the bots would've stopped like that was if Dalrene killed the brain node. He was thankful for the help on the battlefield, but hadn't that doomed the kids? Had she chosen to save their lives over others?

The cave opened up, becoming much wider and taller, and Gordon's questions were answered.

"The Panic Room!"

An industrial sized door stood at the opposite end of the cave. Its size reminded him of the loading dock door on the surface. They ran closer, but it was still fifty meters away.

Above the door, a metal alloy with a bluish tint was descending from the ceiling to cover it. The blast shield. Dalrene had killed the brain node, and the Foreman's dead man's switch had triggered! It was almost a third of the way deployed and moving fast.

"Hurry!" Londi yelled.

Gordon steadied himself and aimed. He was still a fair distance away, but it would have to do. He aimed at the bottom of the door and squeezed the trigger.

The explosion was huge.

His throat burned and his ears rung. Smoke stung his nostrils. There was a charred hole in the door where he shot it, and the blast shield was frozen in place.

He'd done it!

Londi was already sprinting to the opening.

He gathered himself and followed, to the shouting and sobbing. A graveyard of bots littered the Panic Room floor. A battle had happened here too. The kids were huddled against the far wall, although their screams had stopped and turned to something between disbelief and shock.

A horrible smell assaulted his senses. At first he thought it was just piss, but quickly realized it was more than that. The smell of death was coming from a rolled-up tarp. Mickey. The old man had given his all. Gordon bowed his head, holding back his desire to puke.

"Gordon!"

Corrina was hugging him, and he couldn't help but smile.

"You saved us!" she said.

"I'm so sorry," Gordon said, hugging her back. "You never would've been in here if it wasn't for me."

"Don't think about that now. We're alive. You're alive."

Behind Corrina, the other kids, all younger than them, strewed about, some watching from a distance, curious, others scared and huddling in a corner, and a few that looked like they needed immediate medical attention for dehydration.

Londi was hugging two young boys. Tears streamed down his face. He picked them both up, one in each arm. They cried too, scared and confused by the explosion, and happy to see their dad all at once.

Gordon swallowed hard. He didn't know Londi was capable of such emotion.

It didn't last long.

"Everyone up," Londi said. "Time to get out of here. Gordon, lead them to the farm dome. With any luck, there's still medical supplies there."

Gordon nodded and started to cajole some of the more hesitant kids. "Where are you going?" he asked Londi.

"To the surface. To turn the power back on."

Chapter Thirty-Eight: Dalrene

She pulled her hood over her head and sat on the hard steps at the back of the auditorium outside of the MCC. Or rather, the Liberation Center as they were calling it now. No-one else sat on the steps, or in the seats for that matter. The hundreds of people that came to hear Londi talk were all standing, pressed against the stage, eagerly awaiting their leader like he was fresh bakery rations on a Sunday morning.

It had been over a month since she killed the Foreman. The last mass funeral was two weeks ago. And Dalrene still felt like shit. Getting out of bed had been hard, but she promised Londi she would come. In fact, she suggested the location to him. Not only was the Liberation Center's auditorium large, but it also had a symbolic importance. From the same place that the Foreman's brain node directed all aspects of life, humans alone would decide what to do next.

Dalrene crossed her arms and looked at the ground, avoiding eye contact with the people that noticed her. She didn't promise anything about not sulking in the back and feeling sorry for herself. She watched Londi walk across the stage. He'd done a good job since Dalrene asked him to take over, and the people loved him. The microphone didn't work, so he shrugged and smiled.

"Electricity rations," he joked.

The crowd chuckled, and begrudgingly, so did she. Many had died at the farm domes, and more still in the HCZ. But since the funerals, the people of the outpost had been in good spirits. The mood of the crowd was festive, joyful even. Dalrene tried not to let it rub off on her. Her success against the Foreman was a mile wide and an inch deep. Yes, her granddaughter survived, emotionally scarred as she was. But she had left her for dead. Without Gordon and Londi's heroic feats and dumb luck, Ellie would've been gone, and it would've been her fault.

She was the opposite of Mickey. She was selfish and stupid. Her appetite had been non-existent due to being repulsed by herself, and she'd avoided Javier and Ellie after the war.

"My friends, today we are a free people!" Londi declared to the cheering crowd, his voice booming outward even without the help of a microphone.

Dalrene was a big enough person to admit that some of the pain she felt in her gut was jealousy. This was the speech she practiced many times in the grotto when no one was looking. She only had herself to blame for not being able to give it.

"Years of neglect have damaged our electricity network. But without the Foreman sucking up power, there's potential to build more farm domes, get rid of rationing, and never have rolling blackouts again. Repairing the solar panels and bringing more capacity online must be our top priority. And to lead this important project, I nominate Dalrene!"

The crowd cheered wildly.

Dalrene sighed.

When she didn't immediately appear on stage, the crowd started looking around, trying to find her.

Dalrene took her hood off. She wasn't going to be able to hide anymore. She walked down the steps, and everyone turned to see her. By sitting far away, she had inadvertently made her entrance more dramatic than she intended. People patted her on the back as she made her way through the crowd. She cursed under her breath.

"There she is!" Londi offered a hand and pulled her onto the stage.

"Thank you for the nomination, Londi," she said, then turned to address the crowd. It wasn't how she envisioned standing on the stage at the end of the battle. Without Mickey. Without respect for herself.

"I'm an old woman now, but I'll consider taking this one last job."

The crowd murmured. They wanted her to give a big speech and recount the glory of the fight. The First Olympians had been quick to forgive her willingness to sacrifice the kids. The rest of the outpost's residents didn't even know about that, and if they did, they heard an exaggerated version. They only knew her as a mythical creature, the Queen of the Faithless who lived in the deep, the crazy person who turned off the outpost's power, and the old woman who beat every guardian to death with her bare hands.

She spotted Gordon and his Earth friend making doe eyes at each other. It unsettled her, that he could be friends with someone that had a hand in their enslavement. Dalrene couldn't even look her in the eye.

But he came back! Gordon came back to the outpost to help, even when he didn't have to. He was the one that deserved all the praise for freeing the kids and risking his life. He wasn't bitter, even after his mom's death. After Dalrene had killed her.

She cringed. Janet. Gordon still didn't know how she died. Dalrene made so many sacrifices to win and they were all she could think about. Regrets filled her thoughts, even now when everyone revered her. Had there been a way she could've saved Janet? Or Mickey? Why did winning feel so bad?

Dalrene didn't have anything more to say. She nodded and walked off, cringing at the continued outpouring of applause for her. Backstage, she was relieved to find a bar.

She was stewing about, drinking her third whiskey and just about ready to leave when Javier found her.

"Dalrene! The service they had for Mickey was very touching. His sacrifice will never be forgotten. He's forever a legend."

She swung her drink back and finished it. Javier looked happier than she'd seen him in years, but thinner. The time in the HCZ had been tough on him, as it had for everyone.

"And I have to say I was wrong about you," Javier continued. "You did this and its incredible. I'm sorry I ever doubted you. Congratulations."

"I don't deserve that," Dalrene said dryly. In another world, that would have been the most satisfying thing she could've heard.

"I almost screwed it all up. Never mind. Listen, sorry, I gotta go." Dalrene looked to the exit.

"Don't! let me introduce you to my partner Gloria," Javier said.

"Okay, okay," she relented, just as Gloria and Ellie spotted them.

She ran up and hugged her grandma. Dalrene tried to enjoy the moment, she really did. But the joy and relief of hugging Ellie were clouded over by the self-loathing she had for herself. How could she ever have rationalized signing this little angel's death warrant?

Gloria reached out for a handshake. She was a tall woman with a big smile. "I've heard a lot about you. It's an honor to meet you."

Dalrene winced and hugged her granddaughter.

Ellie looked up at her. "When school starts again, I'm going to tell everyone how our Grandpa was the one that saved us."

"That's right," Dalrene said, smiling back at her granddaughter. For a moment, she forgot she'd left them for dead. She pulled Ellie tighter and promised herself that she would never make that mistake again. For so long she'd been obsessed with winning she'd forgotten that living to see her grow up happy and free was a win itself.

Londi approached, his shoulders slumped. "I'm so sorry, Dalrene," he said, raising his hands up in repentance. "I thought for sure you would want that position. I didn't mean to embarrass or offend you, and I should have asked you beforehand."

"Calm down. It's okay."

"You'll do it?"

"No. I can't be in charge, but I'll help. Give me a regular job, just like anyone else."

Londi nodded slowly and Dalrene motioned him to come closer. He joined their group hug.

Rebuilding the electrical capacity of the outpost was going to be a big project. It would take a real leader, and Dalrene couldn't be that person anymore. She didn't know if she ever had been. It certainly didn't feel like it now. But she had to do something because moping around all day wasn't healthy, and she couldn't live in the caves again. It would be too weird without Mickey. She didn't trust herself, but Londi did, and that meant something. Maybe he could give her the chance to make up for her mistakes.

\#

The alarm went off at zero five hundred hours.

"Mickey?" she grumbled. "Turn it off."

The buzzing didn't stop.

Dalrene rolled over, reaching with her arm to find the alarm. She fell off the couch, landing on the floor with a thud.

"Fuck!"

She turned the alarm off and sat in silence on the floor, her back against the couch. Her forearm stung, and she extended it a few times, feeling the muscles stretch. It was one of those things that she would've brushed off as nothing at any point in the last few years. Everything had been ignored or deferred because of the fight with the Foreman. But now, it seemed like the neglect and lack of sleep was catching up with her. Or she was finally starting to feel as old as the numbers said she was. Either way, she didn't like it.

Mickey had always been a light sleeper. Hell, he barely slept at all in the years before his death. Dalrene could've needed anything in the night, from a glass of water to a talk about her dreams, and he would've been there. He always had a funny story, or an old, cryptic American proverb that would've ostensibly solved all her problems, and he would've grinned like a madman while he recited it. Or, he would've pulled out his guitar and sung her back to sleep. His voice got leathery as he got older, but Dalrene thought it suited his baritone croon.

No longer.

Dalrene stood, careful not to use her injured arm, and tip-toed to the kitchen. She didn't want to wake Javier or Ellie, who didn't have to be up for three more hours. Technically, she didn't have to be up so early, either, but she needed to get out of the hole. She felt like an imposing nuisance sleeping on the couch. It was a far cry from the hero some celebrated her as. And from who she thought she would be.

She took a drink of cold water and gathered her equipment. She had to admit it was nice to live somewhere with running water. A lot of the team members had "new" old gear that was found in storage after the fall of the Foreman. They had longer-lasting batteries with more reliable value readings, but Dalrene continued to use her old environment suit. Her grandparents had worn it when they had been on the solar panel maintenance crew, so it seemed fitting.

She had her hand on the doorknob when a voice came from the stairs.

"Grandma?"

"Shit!" Dalrene jumped.

Ellie jumped too, mimicking her grandmother's reaction.

"Sorry, sweetie!" Dalrene rushed to console her.

"Don't leave us grandma," Ellie said, sitting down on a step.

"I-I'm not. Well, I am. I'm going to work, but I'll be back."

Dalrene looked into her granddaughter's big brown eyes and found her breath getting short. She'd been so close to death. If things had gone the way Dalrene had decided, Ellie would've died painfully, with no idea why, and no one there to hold her hand. If it hadn't been for Gordon, who's mother she killed, Ellie would have been cremated with all the others. Dalrene would've been all alone, no Mickey and no Ellie. Just her and Javier, and her guilt.

Her airway felt like it was constricting tighter and tighter. A bead of sweat dropped onto the floor.

"I'm sorry—I have to go."

She left Ellie perplexed on the stairs and rushed to the exit. Outside the hole, she slumped against the other side of the door and let the tears come. She cried for Mickey. She cried for herself.

"Mickey, I wish you were here," she whispered to the dark, empty street in front of her.

The lights, usually an ever-present fixture at the outpost, were off. Londi had instituted a full day and night schedule, like they had on Earth. Giving people more time-off was a popular thing to do, but it was practical too. It saved energy at a time when they needed all they could get. The solar panels were still operating at less than fifty percent capacity. Dalrene was thankful for the darkness now.

She shook her head and imagined she was speaking to Mickey. "You'd forgive me, but you shouldn't. I had already done it. I was never going to see her again, and I had been okay with that sacrifice. Not at peace with it, but okay with it. Somehow. I don't know how I can ever look at her honest and straight ever again."

\#

Hard work was a respite, and it kept her mind busy. The sun hung high above in the cloudless sky. The horizon stretched on forever. The air in her tank was plentiful and fresh. Sometimes, she would just turn her radio off and listen to the sound of her breath.

Dalrene was atop a solar-panel array. A dust storm had come through and added a fresh layer on top of the silt, and it was her job to brush them clean. The panels had automatic wipers, but every single one was busted. It was a miracle the panels retained a semblance of efficiency for as long as they did.

She could've had other jobs. Technical, figuring out how to repair or replace all the failed electrical components, or managerial, overseeing a team or even the whole operation. But this is what she chose. She wanted someone to tell her where to go and what to do, and she'd do it well. It was simple.

She stepped down the ladder carefully. She wanted to work fast but didn't want to risk injury. About halfway down, she paused and looked out at the field of panels. She smiled. There were hundreds of them, and equally as many workers, just like her, putting in their time. People were working to make the outpost a better place, not because the Foreman was making them, but because it was their home, and they wanted to. It was a beautiful thing.

She looked back the other way before continuing down the ladder, and gasped. Black dots appeared in the distance, moving over the hills. And they were coming fast. She was old and had suffered trauma, but she didn't think she was hallucinating. She watched them get closer for a few seconds before she was sure she wasn't imagining things.

"Does anyone else see that?" The voice was Dario's, one of her co-workers who was young and athletic. Well, most were, but he was especially.

"We've got company," Dalrene responded.

By the time she started running, everyone else had too. Gordon's Earth friend had told them to expect visitors, but people were still nervous and excited about it. They were ostensibly going to help with the repairs, but there was a vocal minority, Dalrene included, who would believe it when they saw it. Anything could happen.

When they got to the bottom of the mountain, two jet-black vehicles were waiting for them. Her hands turned into fists. She remembered what happened the last time trucks like this had shown up.

"Don't approach them," she said over the comms.

Two figures emerged from one of the cars and started to walk toward the crowd of workers.

"Stop." Dalrene held up her hand. "State your purpose." She didn't know if they could hear her. Others joined in mimicking her hand signal.

After a crackle, their guests' voices came through the comms.

"Who's in charge here?" one asked.

Dalrene stared at the two figures. The workers outnumbered them. They could easily win in a fight unless the new arrivals had guns, which they had to assume they did.

It was only when she turned around did she realize that everyone else was pointing at her.

"Fuck."

Chapter Thirty-Nine: Gordon

Everyone talked about Earth. The whole outpost had seen Alex's video of Lake Michigan, but that was just the tip of the drill bit. The nature videos were a real hit. It turned out that most of Earth's animals were more complex and beautiful than the outpost's vermin. Their neighbour, Juan, was enamoured with chipmunk videos. Alex told him many times that they were rather inconsequential creatures, but Juan couldn't believe her.

But no one talked about Earth more than Alex. She wanted to go home, and Gordon couldn't blame her. He knew the feeling.

"It's harvest season right now," she said from across the kitchen table. "The air is crisp with a touch of humidity. The grapes glisten in the sun as it rises over the field and they're perfect—full, juicy, with perfect acidity. The ground—the earth—no, your whole world is sweet, ripe, and heavy."

"Are you still talking about wine?"

"Yes!" Alex grinned with her perfectly straight teeth. "It's the best time of the year. And the wine is heavenly."

"Really? My mom made bathtub vodka once. Do you think it's as good as that?" Gordon teased.

"Just as good, I'd wager."

"Do they have your family's wine at the UN?"

"Not anymore, if they ever did," Alex said with chuckle.

"Ah! That's a big downside. Another point in favour of 'not going.'" Gordon motioned a checkmark on an imaginary whiteboard and Alex playfully smacked his hand out of the air.

"Gordon! That's not a good reason! We'll be on Earth anyways, so we can make a stop in Spain. You can try my family's wine."

"You said yourself the UN was useless," Gordon said in between mouthfuls of golden curry. "They've never helped us before. We were a joke. What good are they now?"

"Things have changed. The security council has created a whole subcommittee for this investigation. The new invitation is the real deal, trust me." She crossed her arms.

"Don't use your lawyer voice on me." He bopped Alex on the nose.

Her hard gaze only lasted a few seconds before they both broke into laughter. Then she stood, yawned, and took their dishes to the sink. Gordon stayed sitting while Alex washed them.

The kitchen smelled like cumin and ginger. The fridge was fuller than it'd ever been, stocked with meals from neighbors who'd come to offer condolences about his mom. They weren't honest sympathies, but Gordon didn't mind as long as they brought food. People wanted to see the Earth girl and hear about his experiences. Corrina had taken to taken to calling him the *Hero of Olympus Mons*, much to his chagrin. He'd christened her the *Non-Panicked Queen of the Panic Room* in response. He was still working on the nickname.

They'd spent much of the last six weeks talking and kissing in his room. It was about the same size as the one they shared on the *Walt*, and their carefree nature reminded him of those times. He'd apologized so many times for the way he left New Arcadia that Alex had to beg him to stop. They'd both been right, in a way, and Gordon was proud of how she'd stood up to her dad.

The door to his mom's old room stayed closed. He was still apprehensive to go through her stuff. All he could remember of that room was the last time he saw her. Peeking out from the closet as the bots took her away felt like a lifetime ago, but it still stung. Alex said she would help him organize it, but they hadn't gotten to it yet.

"The UN just sounds like the Foreman in human form," Gordon said. "Besides, we're free now. Why does it matter?"

"Free but impoverished," Alex said with a wag of her finger. "Your people deserve reparations. We need to get them out of this cave and into real cities where they can be safe and live good lives. That won't happen unless the UN deeply understands the situation. Humanity wants to see and hear from you too. I'm sure if you give a speech in front of the UN building, hundreds of thousands will be there. And billions will watch it."

"I'm ... not sure I want that. And there's a lot of work to be done here. We have solar panels that need to be fixed. People that need medical care. A whole life to be re-imagined. I should be here, helping my people prepare for what comes next."

"First Corp. is helping with the electricity situation, but that's my point. You deserve much more than crappy, hundred-year-old solar panels. Think about it, because this is the way that you can have a seat at the table. Don't just prepare for what comes next, *decide* it."

Gordon scrunched up his nose. He didn't think he'd ever won an argument with Alex. She kissed him on the forehead and walked to the door to put her boots on.

"Going to get satellite reception again?"

"Yeah. Sure you don't want to come talk to my mom? She adores you."

Gordon grimaced. He'd spoken to Alex's mom once, and her questions about life at the outpost made him feel like an alien. "I'll see you in a bit."

"See ya."

He watched her go. She integrated seamlessly into life at the outpost in the last six weeks. Some people were scared of her, but the people that knew her, loved her. As did Gordon.

He entered his bedroom with a steaming cup of tea. The blinds were drawn on the singular window that looked to the street, and ancient textbooks were stacked beside the bed. Alex had suggested writing a letter to his mom as part of his grieving process. He'd been meaning to do it for weeks, but there was always so much going on with the rebuilding project that procrastination had been easy. He'd tried once before but got choked up. It had been embarrassing, even if he knew he had every right to cry and work through his emotions. With Alex away, now was the time to do so privately. He sat on the bed with a notebook.

"Dear Mom,

The award ceremony was two weeks ago. They gave you top honors and your name is on a plaque at the Liberation Center. Londi named you one of the founding members of the First Olympians. It's still weird to hear the fighters talk about you that way. They knew a side of you I never did."

Gordon took the pendant out of his pocket and placed it on his bedside table. The red number one was as beautiful and evocative as ever. Having that connection to his mom helped a lot.

"There's a side of me that you'll never know, either. I've killed. Not on purpose, but that doesn't matter. I wonder what Dad would think of that. I wonder what you both would think of all of this. It's crazy. But mostly good, on balance."

"Alex wants to go home," he continued writing. "Earth. Can you believe it? I know you would go in a heartbeat. I thought I would too, but now that the opportunity is here, I'm scared. I don't know if I can leave the outpost so far behind. I'll ... miss you." He picked the pendant back up and held it close to his chest.

Gordon wrote about Dalrene and Mickey, and how much the First Olympians had helped him. He wrote about the beauty of the surface and how much his mom would've loved flying in the *Zoya*. He wrote about the nightmares that still attacked him sometimes, and how yesterday he thought he saw her in a crowd of people on Torres Street.

It was therapeutic yet exhausting. He didn't know thinking and writing could be so draining. Finished, he stretched his legs and walked back to the kitchen. He lingered with his tea, suddenly aware how big the hole was for one person and feeling like a stranger. It was still weird to be in his family's old home all alone. The door opened and Gordon flinched. He caught his mug before any liquid spilled.

Alex still had her environment suit on and her helmet under her arm. Her hair was frizzy, her eyes wide.

"I'm going to Earth. Now. Will you come with me?"

Gordon looked sideways and his eyes slid around the only home he'd ever known, empty now. He stood straighter and met Alex's gaze again.

"Let's go."

<<<>>>

Thank you to everyone who helped with this project, especially OB!

If you enjoyed this book, please leave a review on Amazon!

I am a new author and reviews on Amazon and Goodreads really help spread the word. I truly appreciate your support!

Amazon: amazon.com/dp/B0BLN9DT1W
Goodreads: goodreads.com/book/show/63883506

Stay up to date on social media:

Twitter: twitter.com/The1stOlympians
Facebook: facebook.com/TheFirstOlympians
Instagram: instagram.com/thefirstolympians/
Email: thefirstolympians@gmail.com
Join the e-mail list: https://tinyurl.com/2p9pj93d

Copyright 2022

Manufactured by Amazon.ca
Bolton, ON